Dreams, Miracles and Jazz:
New Adventures in
African Fiction

Dreams, Miracles and Jazz: New Adventures in African Fiction

Editors: Helon Habila and Kadija Sesay

PICADOR AFRICA

First published by Picador Africa 2008
an imprint of Pan Macmillan South Africa
Private Bag X19, Northlands, 2116
www.picadorafrica.co.za

ISBN-13: 9781770100251

Cover design: Donald Hill of Blue Apple
Cover artwork: Victor Ehikhamenor

Printed and bound in South Africa by
Pinetown Printers

CONTENTS

INTRODUCTION

The turn of the millennium has seen an upsurge in new and young African writers and this has been particularly noticeable in terms of the number of women writers being published.

Helon Habila and I began this project around the time when this 'upsurge' started to happen, after we met at the Kennedy Center in Washington DC in 2002. At that time, he was the second winner of the Caine Prize for African Writing, and his immediate concern was to introduce other young African writers to the world stage. After greeting me he said, 'I have this idea ...' We've been searching, selecting and editing ever since! The result is, *Dreams, Miracles and Jazz: New Adventures in African Writing.*

From the start, our conviction was that we should avoid pigeon-holing the writers into a post-colonial bag or any other stereotype of what certain literary circles regard as 'African literature' and to present writers who had not previously published a full-length book. However, this work has taken quite some time to complete, so that along this journey, our selection of writers have been securing books deals and winning awards. From our point of view, this can only be seen as a confirmation of the strength of our choice.

In this anthology of twenty-five writers, (plus contributions from Helon Habila and myself), four other previous Caine Prize winners are here: Binyavanga Wainaina, Brian Chikwava, Segun Afolabi and the most recent winner, Monica Arac de Nyeko. Two others have been short-listed for that prize – Jackee Batanda and Sefi Atta.

One of our criteria was that writers should be born on the African continent or be of African parentage. Sixteen of the writers included in this selection currently live in Africa, throughout the English-speaking countries of West, East and southern Africa. Of the remainder, there are writers living in the UK/Europe, USA, Australia and Asia. Similarly, the setting of these stories often reflects the place where the writers live (or have once lived), and so, not all of the stories are set in Africa, but in real and imagined places throughout the world.

Aside from this, our intentions were to select stories that covered a range of themes and emotions that conveyed 'African sensibilities' yet were universal in scope. We looked for humour, sadness, tragedy and joy – and we found it. Many of these stories, inevitably, are love stories: gentle as in 'The Month of September,' complex as in 'It will Never be

Yesterday'; love of country as in 'The Promised Land', love of tradition as in 'The End of Skill' and spiritual love as in 'The Miracle Worker' and 'Faith'.

Also included in this selection are stories that stir us with experiences of civil war as in 'Devils at the Door', domestic violence in 'Back Home', family rejection in 'Still Hope Survives', family acceptance in 'Random Check' and the long journey to seek refuge in another country in 'The Legendary Old Crosser'.

Memory provides unforgettable tales encompassing themes of genocide in 'Land of my Bones', African histories in 'Remember, Olduvai', and family in 'An Affair to Dismember'. Politics, too, is a strong theme which is portrayed in various ways, from the favoured son in 'Member of Parliament', the returned son in 'Native Son', the oppressive visa queue of 'A Pocketful of Dreams', serious discussions in 'When Night was Arrested' and the extreme and the ridiculous in every sense in 'The Browns' Safari Honeymoon'. A tender story of old age is found in 'The Wine Guitar', trickery in 'Spokesman' and 'Dancing to the Jazz Goblin and his Rhythm', strength of community in 'In the Clarity of a Third Class Compartment', superstition in 'Superstitions about Rats' and HIV/AIDS in 'On the Last Day'.

Yet, in some ways, this is misleading, as the stories are about all of these and more. Short in length, they encompass layers of meaning and subject matter that provoke strong emotions and discussion, whether on the topic of politics, family or love. But what they all do is to deal skilfully with everyday life or social issues of the day, whether they are set in Africa or the diaspora, using narrative styles that range from poetic prose to satire. They are told here in distinctive voices – voices that we believe show the newness and originality of African writers today.

We wanted to bring you new writers that we believe will become names to be recognised as (African) writers of note in the future – some of them are on the verge of doing so. Some of these writers are new to the craft while others have more experience as journalists and in writing for radio, for example.

More than anything else, we wanted writers who were willing to take risks and break boundaries in terms of style, content or language as, by doing so, in their own ways, they tell you what 'African' literature is.

AN AFFAIR TO DISMEMBER

By Binyavanga Wainaina

There is this game I play, a game that Mrs Green, my former adoptive mother, taught me. She would fold a piece of paper while I watched her hands, watched the piano tendons ripple, the strange blue veins. Then she would ask me to draw the pattern into which the paper folded. I never failed to get it right.

Last night, dizzy with head-fuck after reading Soyinka's play, *The Road*, I lay in bed and closed my eyes, and conjured an enormous piece of paper: I folded it this way and that, folded it in ways I had never attempted. Then, I sprayed it with something to make it brittle. I opened my eyes and put on some music: Moses Mulelekwa on piano, the piece he played at the North Sea Jazz Festival in Amsterdam where he got sucked into a hurricane of his brilliance, then burst out crying after waking to find himself surrounded by a standing ovation.

I closed my eyes again, and breathed in, and let the paper open slowly. The pattern unravelled in my mind's eye: angles and triangles shining and shadowed. I laughed, and let it break in every brittle seam, and let the shards of patterns fly high like the first crescendos of the piano. Then, with ease, I made them fall into place again. I threw them high again, and lost the pattern as they came tumbling down, as Moses crouched over his piano working through something intricate, caught in the most fragile of places, trying to juggle things at the far reaches of his ability. I could almost feel his relief as he passed the threshold and mastered himself. I joined him in his giddiness, throwing the jumble of patterns up again, and marvelling at how my mind so effortlessly put the brittle paper together. Then that crushing, tearing sound of tape getting caught in the cheap tape recorder, and the song whining to a halt. I swear I heard glass break as the shards came tumbling down, tearing into me as I tumbled.

I slept with Mrs Green in my mind.

I was eight years old when she came to my school in Muranga, Kenya. I lived in a tranquil bubble, with hungers, agreed communal rumblings of belly, as normal as the surround of unripe maize plants. Coffee beans bought schoolbooks and fertiliser. I had never worn shoes.

Then she arrived, and asked me to come and live with her. My parents let me go, awed by what she offered; awed by me, now that they

1

discovered I played with numbers and words no primary schoolteacher in the village could understand.

The magic Mrs Green brought was powerful. As we drove off, I saw the maize plants around us take off in a stomach-curling whirl; blending into the porridge I was drowning in. Dust, wind scraping against the Landrover, my first car-ride. Speeding like we did, through the dusty road and onto the tarmac, it seemed like this car was something that defied time and space. How else to explain how, in an hour, I was further from anything I knew than I had ever been? Safe, in a science-built place, with bricks and a microwave.

She smelt like an angel, not the slightest pungency about her, as if the person had been scrubbed away, and only something flowery remained. When she spoke it sounded like her words whistled through her nose before coming out of her mouth. When we Kikuyu people make words, we keep our nasal cavities out of the process.

She noticed my confusion, and smiled, and her mouth opened wide and scared me it was so red inside, like a wound. Against her pale skin, her teeth seemed yellow, but she had television gentleness about her, like the mother in *Little House on the Prairie*, which we used to watch at the headmaster's house every Saturday.

'Do you want supper? Haven't you ever seen a fridge?'

A mouth from heaven: jellies, cakes, doughnuts, preserves, milk and jams, all lit like an altar. I dive into the jaws of the fridge and eat.

'Oh, you'll be my son now,' she said.

She had rented a house in a white suburb in Nairobi called Karen. For the first month she coached me at home, then made an arrangement where I attended a private school in the morning, and special music and mathematics classes in the afternoons.

I learned to read her face: first with some fear, and later with a hidden disdain. I noticed that smiling in this new world is a limited thing. One didn't smile to one's extremities while one spoke of serious things, because just talking to people is supposed to be a happy thing. One used the word 'one' a lot.

Mrs Green was very different from my mother who, when displeased, would think nothing of throwing her slipper past my ear as I made off giggling. Mrs Green's method of punishment was guilt. Her smile would slip, ever so slightly; her voice would shoot up to the maximum shrillness that decorum allowed. Once or twice, the most disciplined tear in the world would swell gently in her eye, and I would wonder what it would take for it to roll down her cheek.

I became alert to everything in that house: to the whisper of her silk slippers on the stairs, allowing me to relax in sleep; to her voice ringing like merry glass when visitors came, rubbing her fingers on my head when I came to say hello, and calling me her 'son' while the visitors looked baffled.

I found her smell after a while, in the mornings before she washed, or when she was upset. It was a peculiar smell, lacking a connection to earthy things, almost the smell of clothes that have soaked for too long. It often bothered my nose in an about-to-sneeze way.

Every two weeks or so, her husband and daughter would phone. I never spoke to them, but she would always pass on my love. Her husband was a vicar: 'Sort of a sleepy priest,' she explained. To my surprise she giggled as she said this. Reverend Kipkemoi, from the local Anglican Church came to visit her sometimes, and she always turned coy when he was around, laughing too loudly, and hugging me, something that she did not normally do.

Her daughter, Jemima, started to write, telling me she wanted to be pen pals. The grant that Mama Green had organised to pay my fees was cut back, and she enrolled me in a government boarding school where my accent was the source of much mirth. My skill with numbers infuriated everybody. My parents came to visit for the first time, after worrying that they hadn't received any letters from me for a while. They assumed I was still under Mama Green's wing, and I did not try to tell them otherwise. I was cold with my mother – I spoke to her in English and kept a distance, terrified I would smell like Mrs Green and suddenly aware that my parents smelt of soil and smoke and sweat. I spent my holidays living in the Anglican mission attached to the school.

The letters from Mrs Green came every month, with photographs and vague promises.

We'll see you soon.

Waiting for the grant.

Things are so busy here.

Three years later, a week before I would be the youngest student ever to sit for the Kenyan Ordinary level exams, Reverend Green wrote me his first letter, telling me that Mrs Green had died in a road accident.

Jemima continued to write, lots of hi-how-are-you saying-nothing letters. I replied, always attempting to mimic her cheer, always failing to be fluent in it. We lost touch after I left school.

* * *

I never wake up in a sweat. Not unless I have a hangover, or malaria.

Generally, when I have one of those Mrs Green dreams, I wake up feeling like a rock has fallen down my gullet and has ripped right through my insides. In the morning, weaverbirds make their way down the chute and flutter about – rebuilding.

The shack is my home and business, in Mwea, on the flatlands not far from Nairobi, Kenya. I sell meat, and carcasses hang above my head when I wake up. There are five minutes of beauty in my shack every morning: light swells slowly through the many gaps in my walls; even the carcasses hanging by the windows acquire a benign gleam, as if a life-light has come to claim them. Between 6:36 and 6:45 the glow dominates every crevice. For these minutes, I feel paradise trying to squeeze itself in and carry me away, a Jesus picture from *Bible Stories*. Then, suddenly, morning is here and I lie on my bed, surrounded by peeled, headless goats. The smell of meat is unyielding, and brings me home with relief. The donkeys start screeching at ten to seven in the morning. It is already 30 degrees outside; I long for water. There is no tap water in Mwea, though there are irrigation canals everywhere for the rice paddies.

Ndirangu brings the water at seven. I am his last delivery. He has a new tank top that says, 'Muscle Beach, California'. He bought it at the second-hand market in Embu Town. They have added to his Nikes to give him a more finished cool. If his donkey survives the month, he will have locked away his vulnerability behind this American arsenal. He tells me he has agents as far as Nairobi looking for, 'Tommy Hirofigaa'.

Ndirangu likes me. Correction: Ndirangu likes my biceps and abs. I get a prod, followed by a full examination whenever he comes round. I don't mind. Those whom he doesn't like get water that has fluffy brown flakes doing languid summersaults just below the surface. I make sure to give him a daily exercise tip – this way I get to drink the better river water. I haven't the guts to tell him that occasional situps do it for me: the muscles I am interested in are in my shoulders and chest.

I linger after coffee. I hate to leave the butchery. Reading *Just William* poses a risk after one of the dreams, and Stephen Fry's *Paperweight* (a delightful series of rants against all things 'twee') is reserved for my lunch break. I settle for the much-thumbed first pages of Mongo Beti's *Mission to Kala*. I stop when Medza, bubbling with superiority, is poised to enter the village like a triumphant conquistador. I am now able to leave home feeling I can paint all the shit around me with good humour.

4

On my way to the post office, I bump into Maina at the bus rank. 'Sasa Einstein! How is the butchery business?'

I grunt in reply.

He wears a double-breasted waistcoat and his polyester tie matches his breast-pocket hankie. Yuppie: 'Made in China.' I was at school with Maina. He was the resident brain 'til I came along and yawned past everybody. His bad suit, his home with an apple-green velvet (deluxe) sofa set, was supposed to be my certificate of success.

I see him in the bar sometimes. He has acquired a pompous guffaw: ho ho! Another round, steward! Hot air ho! My car has sixteen valves! Look at my mobile: hollow ho ho ho ho.

The three hippos are already seated under the tree in the middle of the bus-rank. They are county councillors, waiting for prey. Their grey matter devotes considerable resources to the subject of kickbacks, roast meat and beer.

Mornings for kickbacks. Afternoons for meat. Any time for beer.

This is why we have no tap water. Mwea is a boom town sharing a border with three districts: sometimes mud and sewage; sometimes dust and plastic bags; always the slap of cement on a new, rickety, unregulated building; always talk of cash-money. It is the place to which young, hungry young people who cannot make it in their home districts come to seek their fortunes. They are everywhere, lean and eagle-eyed, standing where they can see newcomers, coiled to chase after any cent. They will make money out of lifting, carrying, ferrying, providing information, and acting as middlemen for anything. If you stop one and say you crave a banana, they will fetch one for you and get a commission for doing so.

The town sits next to the highway to Nairobi. Every evening, cyclists bring boxes and boxes of French beans headed for Europe.

Somebody is calling me.

'Dooolf!'

I hate that nickname, and the action hero that inspired it. I feel like a hulk that thinks with his muscles. Still, it grates less than 'Einstein'. Karanja is calling me. He is 18 years old, and I am sure he will be a millionaire by the time he is 20. I generally avoid him. He talks of nothing but French-bean prices and Aristotle Onassis.

'Hey Dooooolf! Some hot white woman is looking for you!'

I turn. A frail, dark-haired young woman is standing beside Karanja. 'Hello. You're Geoff? Geoff Mwangi? My name is Jemima, Jemima Green.'

I am surprisingly calm. Here she is, the girl who took my adopted mother away, Mama Green's real daughter.

All I can think is: It works! All these years I've used homemade concrete weights that have turned me into a rock, an immovable object. I will not care! I see a brief submission in her eyes, deference. She didn't expect me like this. She would have remembered the stilted boy who wrote letters straight out of *Better English*. I carefully take her hand and look at her the way I was trained to do with white people, straight in the eye. Her eyes are shaped exactly like her mother's, but possess a different energy – not fluttering about to ensure invisible boundaries are never breached. They are curious, with the naive confidence the younger white people seem to have: 'Nothing can possibly happen to me.'

What breaches my objectivity is the smell – that white-girl smell, like cobwebs in the nostrils. That smell is like a mosquito in my nose after last night's dream.

'Hello, Jemima. It's a pleasure to meet you finally. How is your father?'

'Oh, hello! Dad's the same, being a busybody – writing long letters to everybody about the homeless. He's become quite a socialist – absolutely despises Blair.'

I don't know what to say about this. I have never met her father.

'Are you just passing by? Can I offer you a coke, or some tea?'

'No. I came to see you. I'm staying at the hotel – could you walk me back? Now that I've found you, I need to confirm my booking.'

Karanja is just standing there, overwhelmed by a sheepishness I didn't know was possible in him. God! He is actually doodling in the dust with his foot! Standing before me, the reason why Onassis married that Kennedy woman. My eyebrows chase him away, and we head off to Jemima's hotel.

She talks the whole way there, filling up the nervous gaps with questions she answers herself. I am often tempted to leak like this, but can't – even now my impassiveness is pushed to the limit by a brimming of things to say.

She stops. 'I'm talking too much, aren't I? I do this when I am nervous.'

I am angry. My restraint is eternal; I cannot breach it, and it nags like a hard-on that never ends. How could she survive being bubbly, having lived with Mother don't-talk-if-you-have-nothing-to-say Green? Was I so pliable?

Her chatter resumes. 'Oh, my friend Dora – she's from the West Indies – she says that in Trinidad everybody talks like this! From the heart! Oh wow, look at those gorgeous tomatoes! They're never this red in England!'

She dances and dances around the core, never once dipping her toe in to test the heat: 'Oh! Ah! Bugger that! Shit! Bollocks! Really? Wow!'

Shut up!

I tune out. Last month my dad wrote me a letter: he is happy in Muranga, making good money from horticulture. He misses his first-born. His new wife is not like my mother, who died a year after I finished high school. She is flighty, wants to return to school or some such nonsense. He is getting old, and curses the day he allowed that white woman to take me away.

'Come grow carnations,' Dad says. 'Let's make money! Come be with us again!'

Jemima is staying at the White Lion, an old colonial hotel that smells of stale polish and decaying upholstery. There is a group of Nairobi salespeople sitting on one corner, laughing loudly, huddled around their wit as if it is the only thing that will keep them alive in this place. Mr Henderson, the old man who lives here, is in his usual seat at the corner of the bar, the skin on his face cracking as if death is about to burst out of it. Every few years, a member of his family comes to beg him to leave and go back to England, but he refuses. He is still waiting for the Ministry of Lands to return his farm, which was taken by a well-known politician's family twenty years ago.

We sit at the other side of the bar. She disarms me, persuading me to have a beer, then another. Her smell fades by default, and I am able to see her with a friendlier eye. Her face in repose droops downward, with an almost Jewish melancholy. The far ends of her eyes slide down, like a welling tear. Below them, twin lines etch a continuing descent, and below that, her mouth, a thin line, faces downwards like eyes averted.

But her repose is rare. The lines find endless arrangements of expression, giving her face a rubbery mobility and lending a comic element to her melancholy. Her hair is nondescript brown. Yet somehow, her face and her body language are lifted to vitality by a pale, gleaming skin, like porcelain with a dim light behind it.

'It's so bloody hot. I never thought it would be. I really can't picture mother in a place this hot.'

'Karen is milder; that's where we lived mostly.'

She inhales deeply and exhales into someone different, somebody with an eggshell of a voice. 'Look, I came here because we have issues to

7

deal with. I've hated you too long; I can't shake it off. I'm getting married next month, so I need to get clear of this shit.'

I am surprised. When we were pen pals, she was full of sunshine and bubble. I imagined her to be a terribly happy person, glowing behind the rounded script, and prancing around in a country garden like the jolly cartoon animals did on her writing paper.

'Why did you hate me?'

'Because you were the one who made her good. She drove us crazy! Dad and I were relieved when she came to Kee-nya, – sorry, you call it Ke-nya, don't you? Then she became another person, a mother who wrote letters asking me how I felt. How I felt! Then there were the endless letters about you: What a genius you were! Reading at age two! Writing at three! Prizes, awards – and black too, so I couldn't even really hate you! Oh shit – now I'm crying!'

I laugh. I was in such awe of her, it never occurred to me at the time that she could have been jealous.

'Your mother was never a nice person. I was simply the lever on her pedestal: Missionary Adopts Destitute Prodigy! That so-called genius was never mine; she discovered it, owned it, and managed it. Sometimes I think she left with it too. If anything made her a better mother it was the fact that she was an angel from a distance. You should read the letters she wrote from the vicarage!' "Darling" this, "angel" that! I only heard *that* from her when there were guests.'

The barman is staring at me. I realise my accent has changed: it mirrors hers, down to the intonation. This unconscious betrayal irritates me, but I can't seem to find entry to my usual accent.

'Why did she run off?'

'Don't you know? She was having a fling with Reverend Kipkemoi. Then she lost her grant, so the plans to open a school for 'gifted' children fell through.'

'Really? Mother? An affair? Not that old ...'

'I caught them once. He had parked his car in Ngong forest. I used to go there to collect butterflies.'

Jemima bursts out laughing. 'You should have seen dad's face fall when the taxi came through the gate! Did you go back to your family?'

'No.'

'Didn't they want you back?'

'They did, but I didn't want to go back. How could I? I went to boarding school and rented a room in the holidays. I thought she would come back, if only to visit.'

'So do you see your parents?'

'I visit sometimes. I haven't seen my father since my mum died.'

'I'm sorry. You must regret ever tangling with mum.'

My laugh is stones rattling on a corrugated iron roof. 'Education the way I got it doesn't leave much room for that kind of regret. Where I come from, there isn't a single person who doesn't consider me lucky.'

'So why did you become a butcher; why live in this dump?' My voice is surprisingly calm. 'I became a butcher because there is money in it, and because I can't bear to work for anyone. I'm not good with people.'

A mosquito coil ignites in my stomach and begins its slow burn, fuelled by the panic inside me. Conscious of the ambiguous place I am in without my usual accent, I feel queasy, wide open. She is in charge now. She can afford to display herself without fear, and lend me a face full of pity.

'Silly bitch! She lied to me! She said you refused to come with her, that you ... Oh, never mind.'

I am going to fuck her. I will watch those eyes flutter in a drowning panic below me. I will watch them shrink away from the hanging goatskin, wrinkle at the smell of old burnt meat. I will not have her come here, and leave sneer marks like snail trails where I live.

My hand reaches for her cheek, my voice falls to a murmur, and I notice my accent again with surprise. 'I lied, she didn't leave because of the affair. She left because she realised that her life was you, the vicarage and English gooseberries – she never stopped talking about bloody English gooseberries!'

We laugh, and her talk slips into intimacy. My voice simply glides alongside, gravely soft where hers is whisper soft. I say nothing that makes me feel. She opens up completely and starts to give her words to me before testing them out. I can't believe how easy it is.

I am on my third beer when the migraine attacks like a poisonous wart on my temple. I visualise it oozing a toxic green sap into my head. I can't help but be black next to Jemima; I can't just be Geoff Mbiyu, on a Biggles adventure. I can't even be Jean-Marie Medza, a nerdy conquistador.

'Are you okay? You've gone a bit grey.'

'I'm sorry. It's my head. I've got to go to the butchery. I'll catch up with you in the afternoon.'

On my way out, Mr Henderson turns to me and says hello, an expression of distaste on his face.

'One of the Oxfam people, is she?' he asks.

'No, she's my sister.'

I don't wait to see his face change.

The kitten that adopted me is waiting at the door. I call her Karen Blixen, and frequently wish she would get out of Africa. While I gather charcoal and light the stove, she maintains a persistent plea: Feed me! Feed me! I mix tripe and buttermilk in a bowl. The damn thing still can't trust me enough for me to come near her. I head to the bathroom with my bucket of water. I can hear her, her meows charged with question marks: 'Miaw? Miaw? Aw? Raaaouw?' (Are you far enough away? Can I eat now?)

The first touch of hot water on my head multiplies the throb. I lie down on a mat under the flame tree in the courtyard. I want to dry slowly, savour the cool. In the pause between throbs, I set out beacons. I mark a new territory with slow deliberation: Cool, Highland cool ...

No faceless hordes of mindless darkies. 'No Conrad?' said Mrs Green, 'You must read Conrad, he really was on your side.' I let numbers run through me. I am still digesting *A Brief History of Time*, a book I memorised in two sittings. Ideas turn in my brain, until cascades of number-songs calm my mind. I still can't get myself to doubt what Hawking says, or to try and challenge it. I don't have the confidence. I just accept them and dance with the ideas from time to time.

Is this an African thing? To worship understanding? To put our education on the mantelpiece, and spend our lives admiring the fact that we managed to understand, because to challenge these things is to risk failing?

Do Not Deface Your Passport.

Whenever I turn on the mat, the throbbing accelerates. I include them in the waterfall of numbers where they become a potentiality with no mass, no time. Each throb is now a synapse, asking to blow into existence.

I sleep, staccato with the subsiding knock-knocks. Sleep spits and hisses – my selves mixing like hot fat and water.

Jemima comes at dusk and announces herself by rubbing her face feathers on my cheeks.

I wake up abruptly, and pull her down next to me. At first I seek submission, but the pounding nearly splits my head open. She is crying. I slow myself down, and follow her flavours, from crotch to armpit. My senses are closed to all, her breathing seems very loud. I follow the rhythm of her breath, and soon it is as if I am her, white and writhing on a mat under a flame-tree. My headache oozes away, diluting its sap in our pleasures.

We part and lie on our backs, and discover that all this time a whole motion picture is above us. We watch the sun-glowing clouds battle the dark. The clouds seem unreal, moving slowly across the sky, unoiled and effortless. All this was happening while we ground each other to submission.

We open up:

'You know, people keep talking about Green. How beautiful it is to sit in a field of green. I hate green, the strong chlorophyll smell of it. When I was a kid, the hungriest time was when the maize was taller than me and we were surrounded by *that smell*; it would coil into our stomachs, which would churn it like a meal and fill us with the taste of bile. I much prefer the colour of dry stalks tied together, and mounds and mounds of golden maize-cobs heaped by the side. Now *that* is bounty.'

'I feel that if I lived here, I would be strong. England is so tame. Everything has been so done! I can be what I want to be here. I hated it when mother came here – I thought Africa was mine. I loved Karen Blixen! Wasn't she just divine?'

'I've been saving up to travel in the UK. I hope they give me a visa this time. I would love to attend the Edinburgh Arts Festival and buy books and books in London.'

She giggles. 'You could put up a play at the festival, you, a conductor, playing your symphony to an audience of headless goats.'

We trade images, each revealing more, each disappointing more. Night drops like a hot damp towel and clouds block the stars. I hit bottom: my head starts to throb, and I feel raw and bruised. We smell stale, and grit-laden draughts are making their way through the gates.

We start to collect the bits of ourselves hanging loose, then, gathered together, we notice our goose bumps; vulnerable! Yikes! Fortifications are built: our joint gears dislodge, and start to grate on each other.

'So what does your fiancé do?' I ask.

'Wee...ell, since you ask, your sweat is pungent, sharper than Dettol, only sort of muskier,' she says.

'Will you tell your fiancé?'

'Of course I like your smell – it's just different somehow. Oh, don't sulk! On second thoughts, I do like the smell. I feel like you're human now, not just a tight-arsed paragon. Your letters could have been written by R2-D2. By the way, do you say Kee-nya? I thought Kenyans call it Ke-nya?'

My eyebrows rise, then drop like an eagle after prey. 'What

anthropological expertise! Are you ready to write a travel book yet? Or did you read that in *The Rough Guide?* Did they also tell you how to teach me to be a Kenyan? How to pronounce my country? You could start an NGO, you know: use that expertise.'

'Fuck you.'

She wants to leave, and has summoned enough ire to send a rocket to the moon. She is back in a few seconds. I laugh. She heard bullets from the video-show next door: *Universal Soldier.*

I laugh, and tell her this. She gets angry, starts to cry, then gets angrier.

I laugh to myself. There's nothing as scary as being beyond *The Lonely Planet.* I escort her to the hotel. She sulks and sniffles all the way back. I leave her simmering over a warm beer at the bar. As I walk out, I see Mr Henderson making a creaky beeline for her.

As I leave, I see in my mind the old man patting her hand, his enormous hankie floating around her face, held by his Old Africa Hand, with shuddering fingers, and blue veins that will clench to attention when talking about bleeding hearts, and left-wing newspapers, and London perverted. She will tell him about her mother, and he will say sadly, 'She couldn't know.'

Jemima will come to tears when he tells her about his dogs, whose progeny appear in dustbins nearby, bearing bits of the familiar, sometimes just the eyes. They are now wild, wounded and malnourished; sometimes their teats hang, naked and sagging.

In this dark bar, with shadows dancing, he will talk of the dark outside, scrambling to get in, looking for a crack of light to take your last shoe, your last cent, your daughter, your property. You will wake up to hear donkeys screaming, whips slapping. Can't leave clothes on the washing line. In twenty years, this town can't dig a bloody borehole.

She will huff, as he speaks, puff as he speaks; each huff, each puff blowing me darker amongst the shadows.

He shows what was, paint-brushing the air again, this time drawing lions in bathtubs and leopards as pets. Eyes will open wide as she hears of dalliances with the Delamares, and lounging with Lord Errol, hunting with Hemingway, getting bombed with Blixen. By the time he fades into a long monologue about the war, she will be thinking, 'Poor Mum.'

I walk back; mumbling shadows following me everywhere, an embarrassing new respect. I hear Karanja shout out, 'O-He! Van Damme *mwenyewe!*' Van Damme Himself. A new name. I'm sure I will be the first to get clean water in the morning.

No matter, there is a song in my mind:

She says Ke-nya,
and I say Keenya.
Ke-nya, Keenya, Ke-nya, Keenya,
let's call the whole thing off ...

I feel good. I will untangle the Moses Molelekwa tape, go to bed, close my eyes, and let shards of brittle paper fall into place.

There is always a new way to fold the paper, and it always falls into place.

THE END OF SKILL

By Mamle Kabu

The second time Jimmy had a soul exchange with his father was the day they talked about the fate of the *Adweneasa* cloth. It was exactly what Jimmy had hoped to avoid for he knew that if it happened, his father would speak to that part of him over which he had no control. When their eyes locked in that inexpressible way, he heard the word come out of his lips. The one he had promised himself he would not say. His father's reaction shattered his daze.

'He did what?'

There was a painful silence.

'Speak up boy, and let me open my ears well this time because I didn't hear you right.'

Jimmy looked into his father's face again and knew he had heard him very well. He could not stand the burning gaze, full of pain and angry questions. He dropped his eyes.

'I said he put it on the …'

'Silence!'

Obediently, he swallowed the last word. He dared not protest against being ordered to speak and to shut up at the same time. He might be a grown man now – a 'guy' in town, a hero to his younger brothers, a success story – but when his father spoke to him like this, he might as well be five years old again. He kept his eyes on the floor and his hands behind his back.

'Let us not offend the ancestors with this talk.'

His father put down the shuttle he had been gripping tightly throughout their conversation and climbed out of the loom. For an angry man, his movements were gentle, contained, and even graceful.

They walked out into the compound. After the inner sanctuary of the old man's weaving room, the heat and glare of the dry-season March day were like a blow to the senses. They walked past the fragrant cooking fire and the main weaving shed where twelve boys and young men were engrossed in their work, pretending not to notice the troubled pair pass by. As he skirted the line of warp threads stretched out before the looms, Jimmy caught the eye of his younger brother. Kwabena kept his fingers moving so that their father would not catch the look that passed between them. 'You fool,' it said. 'You went and told him, didn't you?'

The sound of clicking shuttles receded as they stepped over the little gutter that circled the compound, stopping finally at a disused weaving shed. Jimmy quickly pulled out the weaver's stool, dusted it off with his hands and set it down for his father. He shooed away a hen and her chicks and perched on a rusty tin trunk.

'Kweku.'

'Yes, Da.'

His father never called him Jimmy. That was the name he had given himself after he had left home. But it had taken over so much now that he only remembered 'Kweku' on his trips back home. His father had never given any indication that he was aware Kweku had any other name.

'What did the white man do with our *Adweneasa* cloth?'

'Father, he treasures the cloth so much. If only you could understand.'

On their short walk between his father's weaving room and the old shed, Jimmy had racked his brains for a way to convey to his father that foreigners simply had different ways of expressing their admiration. Jimmy had never doubted the ambassador's profound appreciation of the cloth. 'Ah, what a masterpiece,' he had said the day Jimmy brought it to him. As he unfolded the great cloth, Jimmy saw the same awe in his eyes that lit them up every time he brought him a piece. 'Ken-tay is so beautiful,' he said, shaking his head with the mystery of it as he stroked the perfect web and traced the colourful geometry with his fingers. 'You really are a master.'

Jimmy did not bother to explain that he had not woven any of it. It made no difference anyway, because he could have done so. But why waste time explaining that it would take one man four months to weave such a cloth on his own, and that all his father's apprentices had worked on it. What mattered to the ambassador was that he had his cloth and it was beautiful. What mattered to Jimmy was that he would be paid. But the ambassador was not ready. He wanted to know more about the cloth. Its name, the meanings of its motifs. Jimmy was impatient for his money but he was no fool. He would not be standing in a cool, plush ambassador's residence in Accra, about to receive several crisp bills of a coveted foreign currency if he had not learned that there was more to a good sale than the exchange of goods and money. That was what set him apart from other young kente weavers. They slaved away in villages under their masters, in crowded city craft markets and in the dusty din of urban roadsides, making a pittance. Jimmy had carved a niche for himself. He had 'made connections' and was now the envy of them all.

15

It all started when he met Cassie at the Golden Sands Hotel. That was three months after he had arrived in Accra to seek his fortune. Jimmy had big dreams and he was smart. He had kept quiet as his father poured libation to invoke the blessings of the weaving forefathers on the loom he would carry to Accra. He had friends who had gone to Accra and found work as waiters, gardeners, and security men. Some of them worked for white people and earned far more than a village weaver could dream about. His friend Boateng had grown dreadlocks and found a white girl at the beach who had taken him to America. Jimmy had heard that he had become a taxi driver there and earned more than a bank manager back home. Someone who could barely speak English when he left Adanwomase! Jimmy knew he could make it too. After all, he had a primary school education, which was more than many of the others had. With his quick brain and flair for languages, he often gave the impression of being more educated than he was. He was also blessed with good looks and natural charisma. He was what people called 'a free man' – good natured, ready to see the humour in everything. This combination of attributes made him popular with people in general, and women in particular.

At first, he had squeezed into the stuffy chamber-and-hall in a suburb of Accra, which was shared by his friend Jonas, his brother and another friend. Jonas worked as a waiter in a fast-food restaurant and he tried, unsuccessfully, to help Jimmy get a job there. Jimmy would walk around town, asking in shops and restaurants and even at some private houses, but everyone seemed to be suspicious of a footloose new arrival. What he needed was a 'connection', but how to get it was a problem. He also started weaving. He had brought his loom to Accra mainly so that he did not have to explain to his father that he had no intention of weaving. However, he soon realised that kente cloth had taken on a new life in the big city. The roadside weavers were not wrestling with the problem of trying to sell twelve-yard pieces of cloth for chiefs and rich men to wear to festivals. They were selling single 'letterstrips' with messages like 'I Miss You' woven into them, which were snapped up by tourists and passers-by.

He went to the central craft market in Accra and saw an astonishing variety of modern fashion items made or trimmed with kente cloth. He bumped into Nana, one of his father's former apprentices. He was making things that Jimmy had never seen, like sets of table place-mats composed of a few strips sewn together and cut into pieces.

'You can sell a set of six like these to a rich tourist for the price of a full cloth back in Adanwomase,' Nana told him. 'And you don't even have to be as careful with the quality as when you are with your master back home.'

Jimmy did not need any further encouragement. He was in debt now and hardly eating properly anymore. He was also excited by the challenge of making something so different. He set up his loom under a tree in the crowded compound. Nana had agreed to sell something for him if he could take a share of the sale. Jimmy's father had given him some yarns to take to Accra, which he had secretly planned to sell. Now he brought them out and began weaving a strip, which he planned to turn into a set of place-mats.

It was good to be weaving again. He had always loved it and had clearly been a born master evident from the time that his father began to teach him at the age of seven. He started creating new patterns as soon as he had mastered the old ones. By the time he was fourteen, his father would boast, 'As for Kweku, my first born, I can sell his work to a chief and tell him I wove it myself. And all he will say is "Egya Kwame Mensah, you've done it again."'

In his loom, Jimmy found an inner peace, which he never found anywhere else. It was another world in which he and his art became one and did not need anyone or anything else. The design flowed out of him and into the cloth. He worked for hours, feeling neither hunger nor thirst. The disappointment of not finding a job and the tension over his uncertain future were lulled to sleep by the rhythm of the loom as the heddles parted the warp threads and the shuttles flew through, trailing their colours behind them.

He had often secretly watched his father at work. Even before he ever wove himself, he knew that otherworldly look on his father's face and understood that stopping work and climbing out of the loom was a transition from one world to another. The closest comparison he could think of was waking from sleep. He knew that not all weavers felt this way. Back home in Adanwomase, weaving was an occupation which all young boys were expected to follow, and many did so simply because it was the family tradition. They learned the technique and produced acceptable pieces of cloth, but they never became masters. True kente masterpieces were made by weavers who entered another world when they climbed into their looms.

It was not a topic one ever heard discussed. He always knew which of his father's apprentices were destined to become masters simply by watching their faces as they wove. He knew his father had seen it in him too, but they never talked about it until the day of his thanksgiving ceremony. It was a great day when Egya Kwame Mensah, bursting with pride, officially declared his first son a competent weaver. After Kweku had presented the customary drinks and a fat white ram to his father, and the requisite libation had been poured for a prosperous weaving career, they sat down to discuss his future. That was when the old man first realised that his son did not want to be a weaver. He could not take it seriously.

'Kweku, I have always been so proud of you. You are my first-born and the best weaver in the family. Yes, one day you will be even better than me. I know it already and I thank God for it. What more could a father ask?'

Kweku was ready. He had rehearsed this scene in his head dozens of times, made a mental catalogue of all his father's possible protestations and prepared answers for each one of them. He was deeply sorry to spoil his father's joy on such a day, but he knew this discussion could not be postponed any further. He was certain it would not end acrimoniously, for the two of them had an understanding beyond the usual filial relationship, which hinged mainly on respect from the son. Although he was not altogether conscious of it, this special understanding was not unrelated to their mutual belonging to that other realm, which they entered through the loom.

It was also due to this special understanding that Kweku knew he could no longer keep up the pretence of wanting to be a weaver. If he was dishonest about it on such a momentous day, it would be even more difficult for his father to forgive him later on. He had never actually misled the old man on this point. However, the assumption that he would become a weaver was so strong that nothing short of a direct refutation would shake it. Kweku's silence on the issue had never been interpreted in any way as ominous. Now, finally, it was time to speak.

'Father, I know that in the olden days weavers rubbed shoulders with royalty, and that our great grandfather wove for the King himself, but how many weavers today can make a living only from weaving?'

If it would not have been disrespectful to his father, Kweku would simply have come out and said that he did not want to be like most weavers today – a poor man. That he did not just want to be a respected village master-weaver. He wanted to live in the city, own a car and a beautiful house, travel abroad … He wanted a completely different life from his father. He was talented and driven and it showed in his weaving, but he knew he could apply that talent to other things and be successful. He could never realise his dreams through weaving, much as he loved it. However, it was precisely this love that complicated things. Even as he argued, as respectfully as he could, against his father's objections, Kweku felt guilty in doing so. He did not intend to admit it, but he fully sympathised with the old man's failure to comprehend that he should want to give up something he clearly loved so much. Still, he was not prepared for what his father said next. What he had prepared for was something like: 'But Kweku, you enjoy weaving so much, how can you talk about giving it up?'

And his response would have been: 'Yes Father, I do enjoy it, but times are just too hard now. If I get a good job and make money, it will benefit all of us.'

Instead, his father said something so simply and quietly that Kweku would not have been sure he had heard him correctly if his meaning had not been unmistakable:

'My son, I have seen the look in your eyes when you weave.'

Kweku looked up to meet his father's direct gaze. They had never exchanged a look like that before. In the interminable few seconds that it lasted, it completed the conversation. For the first time in his life, Kweku realised that he had participated in an exchange between souls that was far more eloquent than the language of spoken words. And he knew that he could discard the rest of his set responses. His eyes had given his father the answer he wanted, and it came directly from his soul. But they had given it involuntarily, startling him in the process. He was uncomfortable with what had happened. It was as if his father had spoken to a part of him that he did not fully know himself and that had betrayed the Kweku with whom he was more familiar. The one whose dreams he was determined to pursue.

Now he tried to rally that person and focus on his ambition. One day, when he was rich and could buy the whole family everything they had ever longed for, cushioning his father in health and wealth for the rest of his life, the old man would forgive him for leaving their secret world. In the meantime, there would be no need for him to know that Kweku was not weaving. After all, he could not check up on him in Accra. It was pointless to cause any further pain now. Kweku wanted to end the conversation but he could not find the words to respond to the look that had just passed between them. As if in recognition of this, his father picked up the spoken part of the conversation.

19

'Kweku, the way you feel when you weave, it is not just an accident. Not all weavers feel that way. Do you know where that feeling comes from?'

Kweku felt his scalp tingle. His father's hushed tones and direct gaze did not frighten him, but they conveyed a sense of something beyond the ordinary, which he had sensed but never consciously investigated.

'Your gift for weaving is God-given and is guided by the ancestral spirits. When you settle in the loom, they invite you into their world, in which you find the peace, inspiration and perfection that make you a great weaver. These things do not belong to the ordinary world. You may not have realised it, but I am telling you now that the spirits of our great weaving ancestors are with you when you work. When you enter the loom and lose yourself in the web, you cross over to their world. It is not all weavers who can go there. Only those with a special gift, like you and I.'

These words echoed in Jimmy's head now as he wove under the tree in the squalid little compound. He had thought about them a great deal since that day. They had made certain things clearer to him. Once when he was a child, his father had caught him 'practising' on the loom in his weaving room. In his confusion at being caught and his haste to vacate his father's seat, he had tripped and fallen. He knew he was in trouble, but had not been prepared for his father's degree of horror and agitation, for which he naturally blamed himself. It was only much later that he learned it was a taboo to fall in a loom and that special rites and sacrifices had to be performed to save the person who had fallen from the curse of the offended spirits. Jimmy also knew that the fixed loom in his father's weaving room was special. Although his father often wove on the mobile looms outside, it was only on the indoor one that he created new designs. Jimmy had watched him pour libation and sacrifice fowls there before. With advancing maturity, he also came to understand that it was their menstrual periods that barred his mother and sisters from that room at certain times, and even barred them from speaking to his father while he sat there. Jimmy knew that not all weavers of his father's generation were so traditional. It was their proud history as descendants of royal weavers that made the old traditions so important to his father.

The day Jimmy met Cassie, his fortunes changed forever. He and Nana were selling their place-mats and table-runners at a craft bazaar at the Golden Sands Hotel. He had brought along his loom. He knew the hotel staff and the other vendors would find it odd, but he had thought about it and decided that it would probably attract people to their stall. He was right.

'Oh look, a kente weaver,' people exclaimed excitedly, hurrying over to watch him at work.

Their goods sold out long before they had anticipated, and they even had difficulty holding back a few to serve as samples. Jimmy continued to weave while Nana took orders. Nana had to admit that it had been a good idea to bring the loom, although he would never have tried such a thing himself. That was the difference between Jimmy and other people. He always thought of that little extra that made the difference between mediocrity and excellence. What really set him apart, though, was that he had the courage to match the boldness of his ideas and translate them into action.

Cassie was the first person who asked if she could have a go on the loom. Nana smiled and was about to explain that it was too complicated for a beginner and that even weavers did not start learning on proper looms. But Jimmy stopped him with a look, that said, 'Of course' and stepped out of the loom and beckoned her into it with an engaging smile. Nana knew that Jimmy's father would never have allowed a woman to sit at a loom or to touch a weaving instrument, but he was beginning to realise that Jimmy, the obedient son and apple of his father's eye, had his own set of rules. Jimmy guided the heddle toeholds between Cassie's toes, placed a shuttle in her hand and showed her what to do. She was extremely eager but, predictably, was confounded by the complexity of it. He placed his hands over hers and guided them as well as he could from behind. It was an agreeable sensation, enveloping her small, beautifully manicured white hands in his. He sensed immediately that he was not alone in enjoying the feeling. Perhaps that was why she was having trouble co-ordinating her hands and feet.

On an impulse, he suggested that she sit on his lap, so that he could help her with the footwork. He knew it was an audacious proposition and did not bother to apprise himself of Nana's reaction. Following bold impulses could be dangerous, but he often felt that it was the only way to pull oneself out of a rut and force new opportunities to open up. The look Cassie gave him affirmed that audacity was not alien to her nature either. They felt this common trait pull them towards each other across the many gulfs of difference that lay between them. It was a tight fit in the loom but Jimmy would not have suggested it if Cassie had not been a slim, small woman. He acted as a full-body puppet-master, not pulling strings, but matching his body to hers and guiding her with his movements. He folded his arms around hers and moved his legs underneath her as a prompt. After a few bumpy beginnings, they found perfect rhythm. She clasped the heddle toeholds tightly between her bare toes and pumped them up and down in tandem with Jimmy, parting the warp threads to create a space for the shuttle, which he guided into place with his fingers – manipulating hers.

They became lovers the next day. Cassie was spending her summer vacation with a friend, Margaret, whose husband worked for a multi-national company in Ghana. Margaret was well connected in the Accra expatriate social scene and soon became Jimmy's most important client and promoter. She had money to spend, time on her hands, and friends with whom to share her new discoveries. Within weeks, Jimmy was receiving a flurry of orders, being invited to coffee mornings where he could display, sell and take new orders; he was frequently receiving foreign currency as payment. He gained a foothold as an exciting young local artisan in many expatriate households and his 'free' character made him so popular that he even started receiving party invitations. By the time Cassie left, he was quite the flavour of the month, and was well on his way to his new, exclusive niche at the top of the kente-trading ladder. Margaret and her friends would ask, 'Oh, is that a "Jimmy"?' every time they saw a beautiful piece of kente, so that his name became synonymous with the textile within the narrow but powerful confines of the expatriate community.

Of course, charisma alone was not enough to sustain this kind of success. Underpinning Jimmy's comet-like rise to artisanal fame and glory, was the outstanding quality of his work. However, it did not take long for the volume of his orders to exceed his capacity. The time had come to enlist help from home. Jimmy made his first trip home nine months after he had left, taking along money, gifts and a stack of weaving orders. It was a sweet return, for he had fulfilled his father's dreams in spite of himself. He rejoiced quietly in the knowledge that his father would never have to find out that he had attempted to be anything but a weaver since he left home. The old man was quite beside himself with joy to see his beloved Kweku again. Although he had expected his son to be successful in the city, he was amazed by the number of orders he brought back home and was speechless when Jimmy showed him the first dollar and euro bills he had ever seen.

For Jimmy's brothers and the other apprentices, his fashionable clothes, new slang expressions and sharp 'American Gigolo' haircut were the clearest signs of success. It had the desired effect when Jimmy asked them to weave letterstrips for him with the messages 'My Sweet Tanja' and 'Vanessa my African Queen'. He told them offhandedly that he did not have the time to do them himself as he had to focus on the main orders, but the truth was that he knew the foreign names and sugary messages would convey the requisite information about his new lifestyle to the boys at home without him having to brag about it. He was right, because when he approached the busy line of looms the following morning, a football match-like chant of 'Ji-mmy! Ji-mmy!' went up. He grinned conspiratorially and told them to shut up.

The message for Vanessa showed his growing awareness of the issue of African-American heritage and its value on the kente market. Vanessa had been his greatest education on this topic so far. Thrilled to meet a kente weaver, she was effusive about what kente meant to her and the sisters and brothers back home. She already owned several kente-patterned items, which she had bought in America, including a backpack, a head tie and a dressing-gown. On the day she took him to the beach and stripped off to reveal a kente-patterned thong bikini, however, the expression, 'Now I have seen everything' came to his mind. Even as he enjoyed the rear view of the tiny kente triangle pointing like an arrow to the shapely cheeks of Vanessa's bottom, he could not shake a niggling feeling of discomfiture.

'How d'you like my kin-tay bikini Jimmy?' she asked.

'It's very sexy,' he said evasively and then added in what he hoped was a casual tone, 'So you like wearing kente like this?'

'Are you kidding me? Man, you know what it means to us. I feel so African when I wear it. I love it, can't you see that? I want it around me all the time. You know Jimmy, I could wear it all day long – day and night.'

Jimmy had perfected the art of keeping his father out of his mind on such occasions, but this time the spectre of the old man rose unbidden before he could stop it. If he could see and hear Vanessa now ... what would he say to the idea of a kente thong bikini making someone feel 'African'? The cloth of kings worn day and night, a kente arrow pointing to the cheeks of a woman's bottom ... Jimmy shuddered. How could love and esteem be expressed in such different ways? He knew his father would never understand that a person who used kente in such ways could genuinely love and esteem the cloth. Vanessa, on the other hand, would never be able to understand that surrounding herself with something and making it a part of her everyday life could show anything but love. She had big plans to help Jimmy break into the American market, and had promised to explore export opportunities for him when she returned home. She assured him that there were many African-American companies that would snap up his cloth for graduation gowns, designer clothes and all sorts of 'heritage' goods. Jimmy showered her with kente gifts. This fulfilled the multiple role of expressing affection, promoting his weaving for future marketing opportunities and compensating for his periodic blunders with regard to her racial sensitivities.

It took an exquisite stole, originally ordered by an ambassador's wife, to appease her the day his friend Nana called her white. Vanessa was one of those African-Americans who had more white blood than black. In Ghana, far darker people were called 'white'. Even Ghanaians of mixed parentage were often called white. Jimmy had actually laughed aloud the first time he had heard her call herself a black woman. He was astonished by the degree of anger and pain this caused her, and was cowed by her scathing attack on him for his failure to recognise his own brothers and sisters from the Diaspora. Jimmy quickly realised that not taking her seriously on this topic would be the quickest way to end their friendship. Although he could not fully comprehend her point of view, he resolved not to make any other careless slips about her colour. He also came to realise that racial sensitivity and an awareness of the issue of heritage gained him incalculable goodwill with his African-American clients, which naturally translated into excellent profits.

However, keeping up his guard with Vanessa was harder than he had imagined, especially as it also meant worrying about his friends' blunders. The day he introduced her to Nana at the craft centre he was nervous. He had warned Nana in advance but was still fearful because he could see that Nana could not take it seriously. Nana gave Vanessa an effusive welcome, which delighted her, and when he teased Jimmy in Twi, 'So this is your black woman' and laughed heartily, Vanessa assumed that they were simply exchanging some guy gossip. Jimmy laughed too but warned him again not to slip up. Nana assured him that there was no need to worry. Everything went extremely well at first, and Vanessa took a liking to the talkative Nana. She admired his kente goods and asked about some of the patterns. Jimmy knew that Nana would be surprised by her knowledge of kente designs. She had read a book about kente and, through her persistent questions and discussions, had even taught Jimmy some new things about the cloth.

'Oh, that's "Fathia is right for Nkrumah",' she exclaimed, pointing at the cloth named for the Egyptian wife of Ghana's first president. 'And this must be "Family is strength".' Nana nodded in open-mouthed admiration and asked if she also knew the names of the newer designs. She had no idea but was eager to learn. He picked out the ones he thought she would find most interesting. 'This one, for your former president – is named "Clinton".'

She was duly intrigued. Jimmy explained to her that it was of the same pattern as the one that had been presented to President Clinton on his visit to Ghana.

'And this one call "Hippic",' continued Nana, thoroughly enjoying himself, 'for people who can't afford.'

Vanessa looked puzzled. Jimmy did not actually know the full term 'Highly Indebted Poor Countries', but he explained as best he could that the cloth had been jokingly named to mark 'Ghana going HIPC'. To their joint relief, Vanessa understood and found it extremely witty. While Nana cast about for another interesting cloth, she glimpsed a heavy rayon piece with a dazzling variety of patterns.

'Is this the Adwi ... Adwen ... I mean, the one that means "the end of designs" or something like that?'

'Adweneasa – My skill is exhausted,' supplied Nana in garbled English, impressed again.

'Oh, is that how you translate it?' Vanessa looked confused. 'So what does it mean, literally?'

Jimmy sighed. Naming kente cloths was a complicated business. His father was one of the few people he knew who could name most cloths with confidence. Young city-based weavers often referred to a popular chart of kente names and meanings when questioned by their clients. That was where Nana's version of Adweneasa had come from. It was a particularly challenging example with a variety of different interpretations.

'Adwen ...' he mused. 'Nana, how do you explain Adwen?' He asked in Twi. They discussed it for a few seconds and Jimmy said:

'Something like "ideas" or "intelligence".'

'Wisdom,' chimed in Nana.

'Art ... creativity, skill,' mused Jimmy.

'I thought it meant "designs" or "motifs",' said Vanessa.

25

'Yes, it does,' said Jimmy, and Nana nodded emphatically.

Jimmy tried to explain that the motifs woven into the cloth represented the inspiration and skill of the weaver, hence the use of the same word for them. 'And "*asa*" means "finished",' he concluded. 'They say that the Asante King for whom this design was first woven admired it so much that he said ... er, how can I put it?'

'That the limits of weaving skill had been reached,' provided Vanessa, who had read about it.

'Yes,' said Jimmy, relieved for this succinct explanation. 'So it means, "the end of skill".'

'But there's another version,' said Vanessa, 'that the weaver who created it used all the designs known at the time in one cloth, so it means "all designs have been used up".'

Although Nana was not able to follow Vanessa's American English with any degree of accuracy, the fact that she was displaying an impressive knowledge of kente nomenclature did not escape him. He could not contain his admiration.

'Ei sister, you have tried! You know kente proper!'

Vanessa was delighted. She liked being called 'sister' and had enough experience with Ghanaian English to know that 'you have tried' actually meant, 'you have excelled'. She thanked him for the compliment.

Shaking his head in wonder, Nana gushed, 'In fact, this is my first time to see a white who knows kente more than me.'

Vanessa's face froze. Jimmy's froze a split second later. It took Nana a few seconds to realise what he had done. With great alarm, he apologised to Jimmy first, making it obvious to Vanessa that they had discussed her sensitivities before. This did not improve things.

She said stiffly, 'I'm not white, OK, I'm black! Just because I come from America doesn't make me white. Man, don't you guys understand anything about our history? How can you say that shit when you're our brothers? I'm an African, like you!'

She stopped there because Nana was losing the battle against laughter. Jimmy was horrified. He knew exactly how Nana felt and fully understood that he had no intention of causing offence. Jimmy was slowly coming to understand that this now familiar scenario was simply a glimpse of the sea of cultural divergence, historical erosion and plain misunderstanding that churned between home Africans and their Diaspora kin. To compound his horror, he was irresistibly infected by Nana's helpless mirth. His face betrayed his own struggle between

Vanessa's anguish and Nana's artless incredulity. Vanessa was beside herself. She rounded on him, but before she could formulate any coherent words, her face crumpled and she dissolved into tears. She ran out, hailed a taxi and was gone before Jimmy could catch up with her.

Although he was able to make amends to some extent with the beautiful 'Gold Dust' stole, things were never quite the same between them again. Their relationship eventually petered out, taking along with it Jimmy's dreams of a lucrative export business and his secret hope of being taken to America one day by Vanessa. Although he was not short of other girls to take her place and gradually to reconstruct his ambitions, he did miss her. The lessons she had taught him about African-American heritage, her struggles with her racial identity and her amazing way of loving kente had somehow touched him, and they earned her more space in his heart and memory than any woman had ever claimed.

The day he saw the *Adweneasa* cloth on the floor of the ambassador's living room, he heard the echo of Vanessa's voice. 'I love it, can't you see that?'

It had been spread out carefully, lovingly, displaying every inch of its twelve-yard length. Few applications could have shown it off so effectively. Exhibited thus in its entirety, it proclaimed the toil, skill and creative ecstasy that had worked miles of plain thread into a spectacular web of colour and art. Its predominant tones of maroon, green and yellow denoted the royal *Oyokoman* warp pattern and its myriad of tiny motifs symbolised a wealth of cultural and historical meaning. In the centre of the cloth stood an exquisitely carved Asante stool upon which had been placed a collection of antique brass-cast gold weights.

'Do you like my arrangement?' asked the ambassador proudly.

Jimmy stammered out a polite response, keeping his back to the ambassador. He could indeed appreciate the beauty of the artistic arrangement, but it took a while to recover from the shock of seeing the magnificent textile, of which his father had been so proud, used in such a manner. The room was so large that the space allocated to the cloth did not impede free movement and Jimmy hoped this meant it would not be trodden upon.

He had become used to seeing kente cloth used in all manner of new ways and had learned to harden himself to it because of the profits involved.

As Nana said, 'Once they have paid, you can't tell them what to do with it. Just take your money and shut up.'

But this time, Jimmy felt a strange, indefinable pain. It was one thing to see a made-in-America nylon triangle, machine stamped with the approximation of a kente pattern, sandwiched between the cheeks of a woman's bottom. It was another thing to see a full piece of *Oyokoman Adweneasa* kente cloth, hand-woven in his father's workshop, on the floor. The ambassador wanted to order an identical piece as a wall hanging to complete his 'Asante kingdom' display. The thought of another generous payment helped Jimmy recover from his shock. However, he knew his father would be curious about an identical order of such magnitude so soon after the first. He knew the old man was already uneasy about the ways in which the foreigners who were buying it were using their kente. He had asked questions before, but after his reaction to the tablecloth and bedspread orders, Jimmy had passed most subsequent orders off as wall-hangings or bodily attire.

As long as the cloth was assigned a decorative rather than utilitarian function, his father could accept it. However, the idea of kente cloth having things placed on top of it was definitely unacceptable. Jimmy did not allow the cutting of strips into small items like place-mats in his father's workshop. That could be done in Accra to save awkward questions. Naturally, the old man suspected that Jimmy was not always telling the whole truth. However, he realised, in the cold light of economic reality, that there was not necessarily much to be gained by questioning his son too closely. That year, Jimmy had paid for him to have a critical operation and for the expensive medication he had been taking ever since. Jimmy knew that his father could turn a blind eye to some things but would never forgive the use of his kente as a floor-rug. He decided that it was not necessary for him to know this particular detail. He would think of a way to handle his questions. Before his trip home, Jimmy mentally prepared himself for their conversation, building up a stock of responses for the various different turns it might take.

The silence in the old shed lasted so long that the hen and her chicks wandered back to see if their rusty tin home had been vacated at last.

'Kweku,' the old man said finally. 'I have only ever heard of one other instance of kente being put on the ground. Do you know when that was?'

Jimmy shook his head.

'In 1931, when our king returned from his long exile in the Seychelles, where he had been sent by the colonial British government, he came here to Adanwomase to see his chief weaver, your great grandfather.

They wove three special cloths in preparation for his visit, and when he arrived, they spread them on the ground like a red carpet for him to walk upon. The people wept for joy. It was a wonderful tribute. You see, only a mighty king could tread upon the king of textiles.'

Jimmy understood what his father was saying, but he felt torn. Conflicting thoughts buzzed around in his head. Several samples from his repertoire of responses should have been of help to him now but they suddenly all seemed inappropriate. His father saw the struggle on his face and said gently, 'I know, my son, we have made a lot of money but we have also paid a price.'

With that, Egya Kwame Mensah rose and walked silently back to his weaving room. Jimmy followed at a respectful distance. His father sat back in his loom. He pulled down a short strip of *Oyokoman Adweneasa* cloth draped on the loom frame. It was a leftover piece from the long strip he himself had woven for that magnificent cloth. He looked at it for a long moment. '*Adweneasa*,' he murmured softly to no one in particular, shaking his head sadly.

Jimmy closed the door and walked away. He had never seen his father cry, and he suspected the old man would rather keep it that way.

MEMBER OF PARLIAMENT

By Ndiwalana Fredrick

The four-wheel-drive cross-country car moved fast up the hill, leaving a big cloud of dust in its wake. As it rolled down the hill, approaching the village, the villagers watched it with little interest. The occupants – the driver, and his boss seated on the back seat with a newspaper spread before him – did not talk. Each was engrossed in his own thoughts. To the driver, this was his duty: to drive his boss to destinations communicated to him at short notice, at any time of the day. The car was good and he enjoyed driving it. He did not need to strike up conversation with his boss, the Member of Parliament. He had nothing to say to him. He only talked when talked to and things had to remain this way. It was for this reason that he never complained when the Member of Parliament sent him to pick up his mistress from the university long after his working hours. It was for the same reason that when the Member of Parliament went to eat lunch and came back to complain about the fibrous steak, the driver just smiled. It never occurred to the boss that his driver was hungrily dozing in the car when he was deciding on whether to have a third course or not. Neither did it bother him that his driver continually chewed on a toothpick, trying to kill the hunger-mill churning inside him.

The Member of Parliament knew this road well. He was born here and was reared here. He could pinpoint the wells where the animals drank, with the precision of the village herd-boy that he once was. He knew the village homesteads and their heads by name. The village pastors knew him and so did the imam. Had they not grown up together and been rivals for the same girls in their youth?

Now, as the car passed a large mango tree, he looked out and recognised the village barber. They had sat on the same bench in the village school years ago. How time had flown! It was ironic that the village barber had turned out to be a barber just like his father before him. In class, the barber had always academically outshone the Member of Parliament. The barber's light had flickered out, though, when his father passed away. The young boy had taken up the father's trade to sustain the family. Perhaps if his father had lived he would have been a doctor, or maybe a lawyer …

The speeding car had now passed the mango tree that was the barber's saloon. The Member of Parliament looked back to see a cloud of dust spreading to where the barber was attending to one of his customers. Perhaps next time he should tell Joseph to drive a bit slower ... But today he was in a hurry. He had forgotten that the road was so dusty. He knew the thinking of the villagers. They always complained about small things, such as a speeding car spewing dust onto their already dirty selves. It had bothered him too, when he was still young and did not know his place. One incident still lingered in his mind. It had happened as he walked to school so many years ago. A speeding car had spluttered water all over his new uniform the day he donned it the first time. It was such a cold morning, the rains having come down heavily the previous night. The stains on his shirt had never come out completely, and the spots were there for him to see two years after the incident. His father could not afford another new shirt, and wearing the stained shirt to school every day took away the little pride he would have had as one of the few kids in the village whose father could afford to pay the school fees.

Today the Member of Parliament was to see the carpenter's son. Word had filtered through to him that the young man, fresh from secondary school, was going to contest his seat in Parliament. Of course, the young man could not win. But he could not take chances. The elections were just around the corner and, despite the fact that he had been elected unopposed to parliament three consecutive times, he wanted to gauge his opposition.

He knew the carpenter's son all right. The Boy had asked him difficult questions during his previous campaigns. He had always known the Boy had political ambitions, but he had never imagined that he would be so foolish as to raise his stakes so high. Now, as he thought of the fact that he was out here to meet the Boy and talk him into abandoning such a foolish idea, he realised that his heart was racing. How could this be? There was no way he could be scared of this boy. The Boy had to drop out of school just last year because he lacked school fees. There were many like him in the village. This one was interesting though, because he was the student with the highest grades in the whole village; it was a pity that his father could not raise the funds to further his education. The Boy had come to the Member of Parliament of course. And, like other instances when people came to his office in the city seeking employment, he had made promises that he never kept.

It was unfair that the villagers wanted him to run all kinds of errands for them. They expected him to get jobs for their uneducated kids, provide transport when a villager was sick and needed to be taken to the city hospital, and even attend all funerals. At first it had proved too much for him. Moving the eighty kilometres between the city and village. Parliament needed him and his own business and social life had suffered. And then, gradually, he had learnt to handle matters the professional way. The same way that the others members of parliament did. He had learnt that the villagers should only be remembered when he needed them and not when they needed him. He would go to them when he needed their votes. This would be their time, their chance to voice their opinions and ask for favours. This happened once in five years, when a new Member of Parliament could be elected into office. It was a convenient way. He knew that in five years he would have accumulated enough resources to buy off the villagers' support. In the space of one month he would spend a fortune, but then he would recover it with profits if he made it to parliament. There would be the abnormal salaries, 'allowances', and more allowances. There would be a pat on the back from industrialists who wanted their grievances heard through him and if he played his cards well … who knows? The president could make him a minister … . And all this came with more pats on the back. It had worked well in past elections and so far, he had always won the seat unopposed. This time he knew that if he made it, there would be a greater reward, as he was one of those that the president had promised to work with in his next government. It excited him to think of himself as a Member of Parliament and a government minister.

It was strange how he had made it up the social ladder. He was no different from all the other boys he had gone to school with but most of them who had remained were now village drunkards. Those who had 'made it up' were, at best, teachers in the village primary school. As he mused over it, he realised that the village had made him. Somehow, unknowingly, the villagers had pushed him up the social ladder. The fact that Ngabo was the biggest of the villages in the constituency he represented had been the most influential factor. It always turned out that whomever the village voted for won the parliamentary seat. He was one of their own and they had kept him there. Three times in a row. Now he was invincible! He was popular beyond Ngabo and it amazed even him how overwhelmingly he had won the last poll.

He felt himself swing to one side of the big car as Joseph turned a sharp corner. Why was he driving so fast? Even as he reached out for the arm support, Joseph braked hard. For a moment he saw them, chickens feeding on something white, probably rice or maize that had spilled in the middle of the road. Too late! As the car veered to avoid them, they scattered, making it impossible to avoid driving over them. He heard the dull sound of a small fleshy mass squashed under a great weight as the hind tyres rolled over a number of chickens. Looking back, he could scarcely make out a few feathers lazily floating in a cloud of dust. What was it with Joseph today? The car could have skidded off the road in his attempt to save chickens. Mere chickens! How long was it going to take these villagers to learn to keep their animals off the road? Only the other day, they had run down a goat and the week before that a dog. He cursed under his breath as he wondered who it was he had to compensate this time. They were nearing the market now and Joseph had slowed down, perhaps recovering from the chicken experience.

They were descending on the market. He could see that there was a huge gathering, although Tuesday was not a market day. Perhaps this was a religious meeting. The crowd was so big that he thought he could use the opportunity to talk to the villagers. He wondered who was in charge and he looked around to see if he could spot someone he knew, someone who could give him a brief of what was happening here.

The market was a large patch of open land where the children played football. The grass grew short on this patch of open land; in the areas that the children trampled most as they kicked a banana-fibre ball in the name of football, the grass had completely dried out, exposing a hard bare ground surface. As the big car rolled almost silently into sight, the villagers turned to look for a moment and then, uninterested, they turned to listen to the Boy.

He was a marvel. Not only was he intelligent, he was a good speaker too. He had a good development plan for the constituency and the village. Could he represent them? He said he could. At first they had believed in 'their son', Keba, but somehow he had let them down. Three times in a row they had supported him into that prestigious chair, yet they had got nothing in return. Their roads were still rough and dusty, there were no basic drugs in the village dispensary and they still drank water from dirty wells. Their children still went to a primary school that was too small. It did not have enough classrooms and so some of the children attended class in the shade of the trees. There was no electricity in the village and folks had to trek to nearby townships to have their maize, which was their staple meal, milled. It puzzled them though how Keba seemed to have enough money during campaign time to meet their basic needs for sugar, soap, and salt. During this time he was always willing to listen, and even volunteered to pay school fees for promising students in the village. Now the Boy was questioning all of his promises and was opening their eyes to the fact that the money Keba used on them during his campaigns was not much compared to the bribes that he got when he was in parliament. For the first time, the villagers wondered about the price of his posh personal car. The price of which, they whispered, was more than enough to build ten new school blocks. They had heard about his hospital in the city, his farm in some far away village, his private international school and, yes, even his bus company. How had he, their own peasant's son, accumulated all this in such a short time? Why did he choose to put his investments so far away where his constituents could not directly benefit from any of them? Did it not pain him to see them piled into an open truck in the rain on the way to a hospital when he had a bus company and a hospital of his own?

Once upon a time the villagers had known hard times. A dictatorial regime that was in power had sown seeds of fear deep inside them. During this time many people were killed if it was suspected that they did not favour the government. One did not have to be outspoken to be labelled anti-government. The villagers vividly remembered, for example, the two young men who had been killed by a firing squad in the very place where they stood. The young men had been paraded through the city, and were interviewed on state television before being brought here to their home village to be shot. The president wanted the villagers to see this, and be discouraged from 'such activity'. The two boys, brothers, had not committed any crime other than that they had the same family name as a famous rebel chief. When security operatives had questioned them about why they used such a name, they could not adequately explain. Their lives had ended because of this. Such were the times that anyone found wearing an offending piece of clothing was ordered to eat it on the spot, at gunpoint. People did not venture out of their houses after seven in the evening, and gunshots could be heard throughout the night. The villagers would wake up to the sight of abandoned bodies in the swamps, the forest, and by the roadside. Bodies they could not recognise; bodies they could not ask anyone about. They had learnt to bury the dead without question. They had learnt to get on quietly with their lives.

Things had changed now. That regime was long gone, but the villagers had not yet awakened to their new freedom – the power they wielded with that single vote each of them cast. Perhaps that was why they had unconsciously bred their own kind of dictator, their own Member of Parliament, who only came to them when it was time to put him back in power. It stirred the anger in them as the Boy took them through a guided tour of the power and freedom that they had had for so long and yet foolishly had not used.

It had never occurred to Ande that he would go this far with his campaign. It had all started as a joke. Having failed to continue with his education, he had pondered about his next move. It had irked him that the Member of Parliament had not been able to assist him with school fees. He had gone to his office many times, using the little money that he had earned from helping with the village carpentry. He had given up when he realised the Member of Parliament was refusing to see him, telling his secretary not to allow in any visitors even when they had an appointment. When elections came around this time, he thought of a better way of catching Keba's eye. He knew that if he declared his candidature, Keba would feel uncomfortable. He would come to him and try to convince him to stand down. Perhaps Keba would let him name his price. That way he would be able to get enough money to keep him in school for the next few years. He had seen it happen in other constituencies; he had decided to try it. Mobilising a group of seven youths, he had started out on a campaign trail that was to take him door to door in Ngabo and beyond. At first, the going was hard. The group had to walk on foot and depend on sympathisers for their meals, but it did not take them long to discover the hidden resentment that the people had for Keba. Within one week, the villagers had volunteered over fifty bicycles, two motorcycles and an old lorry to be used in the Boy's campaign. But he soon realised that it was no longer his campaign. It was a battle, a silent battle between the villagers on one side and their ungrateful son on the other. The Boy was just a weapon. It was therefore no longer in his power to negotiate with Keba. It frightened him, this invisible power that the villagers held. He envisaged himself as a small ship, riding the high waves of a turbulent sea, no longer able to use his sail but praying that the mighty waters would not bash him against the rocks ... .

It did not surprise the Boy that the villagers had turned up in such large numbers. It did not scare him to address these people. He knew them, almost all by name. He could see the same faces that he saw in the village church on Sunday, familiar faces that he saw on the way to the village well, and the children's immunisation clinic. They were his village mates, and talking to them was like the usual discussions he had with his peers when they argued about football or which girl was the fairest in the village. He often stopped to think of how Keba would feel if he found him addressing the villagers, the people Keba called his and his only. Would Keba see what he saw? Would he realise that there was a possibility that he could lose the seat this time?

The Boy's heart skipped a beat as the big car rolled into sight. It moved slowly and then came to a stop a few metres from the crowd. What he had dreaded all along was bound to happen. He halted midway through a sentence; all of a sudden he did not know what to say. At that moment the rear door of the big car opened and the Member of Parliament alighted. He could see him clearly from the podium where he stood, the big man, clad in a clean-cut suit with a matching pair of shoes stood out against the backdrop of ragged villagers. He clutched a bundle of papers tightly in his right hand and a mobile phone in the other. Now in his early forties, his head was beginning to bald at the top, exposing an oily patch of skin that seemed to reflect the rays of the afternoon sun. The Boy felt incompetent; he could never fit into this man's shoes.

Suddenly an idea struck him. With his voice wavering and almost betraying his fear, he announced the arrival of the Member of Parliament and invited him to greet his people. There were murmurs of disapproval from the crowd as the big man made his way to the podium. However, no one would stand up to voice an objection. No one wanted to be singled out as the opposition to the big man. They might find the courage to do it with their vote, but none could muster the courage to tell off the big man to his face. Handing over the papers he held under his arm to the Boy, the Member of Parliament held the microphone and coughed into it to get the attention he wanted.

This was going too far. The Boy had to know when to stop his game, so the Member of Parliament was going to belittle him in front of all the villagers. He was going to show him his place and settle this once and for all. What was the little Boy up to, stirring up the villagers against him? He had seen it on the faces that turned away as he walked up the podium. No one could look him directly in the eye, and he felt like he was intruding. Intruding on them indeed! Did they know how much he had done for this country? Did they know how many motions he had brought to parliament that had been passed? Did they know that he was one of the most highly-rated members of parliament in the country? Did they ever stop to imagine a parliament without him? He did not sleep in parliament like some members did. He had gone there and shone, that is why the president listened to him; that is why fellow Members of Parliament called him a consultant. He did his job in parliament well and everyone could testify to that. It was not his problem that the villagers did not know this. All they cared about was their village and its needs. Why did they not read newspapers? He had to control his voice as he started to speak. The tone of his voice was giving him away but he did not care. He was being betrayed by the people he had fought for, and the anger inside him was overflowing.

'Let us not be deceived by this Boy who we still wash soiled nappies for ...' he started.

'And who are you to abuse our candidate?'

It was Zakayo, the village drunkard. His voice had boomed loud, drowning out Keba's. All along he had been sitting at the base of the podium and no one had dared to shift him from his position. Zakayo was rarely sober and his clothes, like the rest of him, stank of stale local brew. The villagers never took him seriously and now, as he staggered drunkenly towards the Member of Parliament, the Boy made a move to intercept him. Keba was furious. Balancing the microphone between his right and left hands, he could feel his fingers twitch; he wanted to hit someone ... break something ...

Zakayo, despite his drunken stupor, saw the blow coming and staggered to the side; the Boy, facing away from the Member of Parliament, did not see it. It was not meant for him but, missing Zakayo, the open palm caught him on his ear with the fingers extending to the cheek and making visible marks on the Boy's face. There was a temporary silence as the Boy lost his footing, his body momentarily hanging suspended in space before landing on his back in the middle of the crowd. Suddenly the crowd went wild and began throwing tomatoes, walking sticks, sandals and bottles at the Member of Parliament.

From where he lay he could see them. Anxious faces, voices that shot over the din, asking if he was okay. He could hear the sound of small objects hitting the podium like hailstones in a reckless storm. It was the sound of war, a kind of war he could not describe. In a flash he realised it, someone had to protect the Member of Parliament.

Keba had never anticipated such a moment in his life. It had never occurred to him that he could be resented in such a humiliating manner.

He had not intended to strike the Boy down. He had not even intended to hit the village drunkard in the first place; he had acted on impulse and now he was very afraid.

The tempo was rising and they were hurling more objects at him; he had lost the microphone in the scuffle and there was no way he could control them now. A stone landed noisily beside where he crouched on the podium, missing him by inches. It suddenly occurred to him that he could die.

The Boy knew that the villagers would not continue hurling their missiles if he went onto that podium. He could form a human shield for the Member of Parliament, and perhaps he would be able to safely escort him to his car. He could see him trying to shield his head from rotten tomatoes, eggs, dry cow-dung. How had the villagers gotten hold of all these in such a short time? At that moment another stone landed. The situation was getting out of hand. With a single movement, he was up on the podium and moving towards the Member of Parliament.

Throughout all this time, Keba had not dared to look up at the crowd. The sound of the Boy's feet on the wooden podium quickly moving towards him sent him into a spate of fright. He drew his gun, pointing it in the direction of the impending danger.

He knew that the Boy would not harm him, and he wasn't about to pull the trigger, but something hurled from the crowd struck his hand and there was a loud explosion as the small gun went off. In a slow haze, he saw the Boy lurch forward and momentarily raise his hands like a ballerina before collapsing in a heap on the podium. For a moment, time stopped. Nothing seemed to move and the sound of the birds could be heard in the distance. It was the sound of the second bullet that broke the spell. Keba's finger on the trigger twitched, firing a second shot and sending the villagers scampering for cover.

The Boy sat in the four-wheel-drive car, gazing at the road as it sped towards him. Ngabo was a few miles ahead. It was election time again and he needed the villagers' votes. Suddenly, he heard the familiar sound of a small fleshy mass being flattened under the wheels of the big car. Cursing under his breath, he wondered how long it would take the villagers to learn to keep their animals off the road.

THE MIRACLE WORKER
By Sefi Atta

Makinde's only contention with his new wife, Bisi, was that she gave too much in tithes to her church. Ten percent was not enough for Bisi. She had to prove just how born-again she was; each time she visited the Abundant Life Tabernacle, she placed a little extra on the collection tray for the married women's fellowship – a haven for gossips, as far as Makinde was concerned.

Makinde was a panel-beater. He worked on a lot on the corner of a Lagos street. Bisi sold bread and boiled eggs to bus passengers at a nearby depot. When she abandoned her colourful 'up-and-downs' for black dresses, Makinde didn't object. When she stopped speaking to his non-Christian friends because they were sinners, he didn't say a word. When Makinde broke his hand after a motorcycle taxi almost ran over him (he dived into a nearby gutter holding his head for protection; the slime in the gutter masked a bed of rocks), Bisi fasted two weeks for his hand to heal. He ate her share of meals and recovered with his small finger permanently bent at a right angle.

Bisi was prone to zeal, Makinde thought, so on that afternoon when she came to his lot with his usual lunch of bread and boiled egg, and she saw the windscreen of an old car that had been sitting there for years, and she fell on her knees saying it was a vision of the Virgin Mary, Makinde barely raised his head from his sandwich to acknowledge her. He had cleaned the windscreen with an oily rag to get rid of some bird droppings that offended him. The rain had fallen lightly that morning, and Bisi wasn't even a Catholic.

She ran to the bus depot to tell the passengers that she'd seen a vision. About a dozen of them came back to confirm what she had seen. A few, mostly men, walked away joking about Nigerian women and their pious ways. The rest, mostly women, stayed to stare at the dirty windscreen. They trembled and burst into tears. It was a miracle, they said. There was a clear figure all right; one small circle over a bigger mound, and hues of rainbow colours around the small circle. More bus passengers joined the onlookers as word of the vision spread. Soon they were enough to make his work impossible. Makinde drove them away.

All his life he had worked; at least, from the time his mother had stopped handfeeding him. He started off by selling oranges on a tray; he had never attended school. At age ten, he began his apprenticeship with his father, a self-taught mechanic. Makinde pumped tires, and plucked nails from tires and patched them up, before graduating to changing spark-plugs. He was not the best mechanic in Lagos, but he was one of the few that people could leave their vehicles with without fear that spare parts would go missing. He was amazed by some of the clients he encountered: Mercedes owners, who had access to his country's elusive oil money. Yet these wealthy people were frugal when it came to paying for work. They handed Makinde small change with soft plump hands, while Makinde couldn't even remember the colour of his own fingernails. He had black oil under them, and cleaned his hands with petrol dabbed on rags like the one he'd used on the windscreen. He ate 'zero-one-zero' to save money: nothing for breakfast, one big lunch meal, nothing for dinner. This was the real miracle: he was still poor.

'My wife,' he said, after the visitors had left. 'I don't care if you choose to waste your earnings on your church – actually I do, but nothing I say will change your mind. What I won't tolerate is you having a church service here, on my lot, and getting in the way of my work.'

'Why?' Bisi asked.

'Your people will scare my customers away with their wailing and shaking.'

'How?' Bisi asked.

This was her style of arguing. She wouldn't challenge him, but she asked enough questions to drive him to distraction and let her have her way.

'All I'm saying is that it must never happen again,' Makinde answered. He was known as a patient man, because he didn't like talking; talking used up his energy. Bisi called him a stubborn man. He refused to attend church services with her.

The next day, when Makinde arrived at work, a group of about twenty people were waiting in his lot: men, women and children. They wore white robes and were barefooted despite the ground, a black surface of oil and dirt.

'We have come to see the vision,' an old man said.

'In the name of God,' Makinde muttered.

It was about five thirty in the morning. Bisi couldn't have told them. He had not bargained on this – those people from yesterday spreading the news.

'I'm sorry,' he said. 'I can't have you praying on my lot.'

'Unfortunately, that is out of your control,' the old man said. 'Celestial forces have chosen this place. You'd do best to submit yourself to their will, rather than try to stand in their way.'

The old man was smiling, but Makinde was afraid anyway. He believed in a celestial force. He just didn't believe the celestial force considered him special enough to deliver him.

'Over there,' he said.

He pointed at the old car, once a beige Peugeot 405. Now, it resembled a carcass. The seats and steering wheel were gone, removed by robbers. The barefooted group walked towards the windscreen. The old man saw the vision first and fell on his knees. His troupe followed, and then they hummed. Makinde beat a panel loud enough to drown out their noise. At most, he hoped, five groups might visit his lot. Three that day, and maybe two the next. He'd heard about such visions, on dirty glasses in poor districts. He could not read, so he didn't know that, in Lagos, these visions drew what newspaper reporters called Throngs, and these throngs Flocked. 'Throngs Flock to Vision of Mary on Latrine Window.' 'Throngs Flock to Vision of Mary on Popcorn and Groundnut Seller's Glass Cubicle'. Such were past national headlines.

Makinde's prediction of five groups of twenty people was underrated. Two hundred and fifty people visited his lot in the morning. By afternoon, about five hundred had been to his lot. Makinde stopped showing them the windscreen of the Peugeot. A tall thin woman stayed from her morning visit to act as a guide. She told the story to a reporter: Makinde and his wife were newlyweds; Bisi was born-again and Makinde didn't attend church. Nonetheless, this vision had occurred on Makinde's lot, and it was a clear sign that God's mercy could manifest just about anywhere. Bisi came at lunchtime with Makinde's usual lunch of bread and boiled egg. She saw the crowds and immediately denied she was responsible:

'It wasn't me!'

'Don't worry, I believe you,' Makinde said. The situation was out of her control.

The guide approached her. 'God's blessings to you, my sister.'

'To you too,' Bisi said.

'We've been here all morning, without pay, showing the people where to pray for miracles.'

'Yes?'

'Yes, and we are getting quite hungry now, so please can you go back to your stall and get bread and eggs for us to eat?'

The miracle that the guide had prayed for was for others to stop

41

saying she was insane. She knew her calling was to do God's work. Anywhere else in the world, she would be a street preacher. Here, she was sent to a hospital, where the doctors injected her while the nurses held her down and later beat her up.

Makinde told Bisi to get bread and a boiled egg for the guide. Then as both women left to carry out their respective tasks, the thought came to his mind. 'Without pay', the guide had said. The people were standing on his lot, getting in the way of his work. Why not charge them? They paid to attend church. He calculated his lost earnings, net of transportation. He divided that by the number of visitors who came to the lot. He rounded down, taking poverty into consideration, and ended up with a fee of one naira per person.

In front of his lot was the gutter he had dived into to save his life. There was a wide plank over this gutter, tough enough to support vehicles.

He stood on the plank and said: 'Excuse me? I am Makinde. Yes, em, the owner of this lot. I have decided I will not get in the way of your worship today. But ... I ... I am a man of small means, as you can see, and my business is ... em, suffering from the constant traffic in and out. Yes, what I'm suggesting is that ... can you ... can you please ...?'

Talking was exhausting him. Hardly anyone was listening anyway. They were praying, singing, rocking.

Makinde raised his voice. 'My name is Makinde. I'm the owner of this lot, and I'm telling you now, if you wish to continue to see your vision, I suggest you pay me one naira now, each, or else I will take a rag and wipe the vision off.'

A hush fell on his lot. One or two people were asking what he was talking about and why he was getting angry. The guide was explaining this to them when another visitor appeared. Makinde stretched his hand out without looking at her face.

'It's one naira to enter, please,' he said.

'Since when?'

It was Bisi. She had returned with the bread and boiled egg for the guide.

Makinde earned money that month from the visitors to his lot. He was even in the Sunday newspapers: 'Throngs Flock to Miracle at Mechanics'. People came to pray for cures, scholarships, passing marks in school examinations, jobs, promotions, and money. There were visitors in wheelchairs, visitors on crutches, blind visitors; there were insane, evicted, heartbroken, abandoned, bitter, barren visitors. Beggars and gossips too, including the women of his wife's fellowship. Some people complained about the one naira fee. A few refused and walked away. One was a priest.

'H-how can you do this?' he asked Makinde. 'C-capitalise on people's s-sorrows and-and woes?'

Makinde waived his fee, as he secretly did for beggars and sick children. The priest still refused to walk into his lot. 'D-did Jesus charge for miracles? How do you sleep at night k-knowing you do this for a living?'

Quite well, when he wasn't making love to Bisi, who was now talking about having a child and perhaps taking a break from her work. She conceived one night during a thunderstorm. Hearing the rain on his roof, Makinde worried about the fate of his Virgin Mary, although he'd protected the Peugeot's windscreen with a tarpaulin sheet and secured its edges with rocks. Had he known the wind was strong enough to shift one of the rocks, and that the rock would roll off the roof of the Peugeot, freeing an edge of the tarpaulin, and that the tarpaulin would flop over the bonnet of the Peugeot, and that the raindrops would fall on the windscreen and wipe the vision away, he would have worried more.

He arrived at work the next morning; there were only two people in his lot. One was a vagrant who usually came to look for scraps of food; the second was the guide woman.

'Our vision is no more,' she said.

The ground in his lot had turned to mud, and the gutter in front was overflowing with slime. Makinde could see only the clean windscreen of the Peugeot. He was thinking about how to get back to panel-beating.

The guide continued. 'It appears the storm last night is the cause. Our work here is done, then. We don't expect you'll have visitors anymore, and as you know, the Lord giveth and the ...'

'Quiet!' Makinde shouted, so loudly that she ran out of his lot. What kind of Lord gaveth, and then taketh and taketh and taketh? He kicked the Peugeot, which appeared to be grinning, with enough force to dent it. Then he boxed it with just as much force, and the impact straightened his bent little finger.

He did have one visitor that day. A tax assessor, who seemed to be studying the sweat on his own nose.

'Mr Makinde,' he began. 'Eh, I read about you in the papers. You've been getting a lot of attention here recently, eh? Since you can't call this a church, nor yourself a priest, it means that you are liable for taxes.'

Makinde had not paid taxes before. Tax was for people who wore shirts and ties, people who received cheques regularly. He thought the tax assessor was a con man.

'From where are you?' he asked.

'I represent the government.'

'Couldn't they give you a clean shirt?'

'You're practically in tatters yourself. What have you done with your money?'

Makinde stroked his bandaged finger, feeling exhausted. Perhaps the man really was a tax assessor. If so, why didn't he go back to the people he represented, those who had access to his country's oil money, and assess them?

'This is my lot,' he said.

'Where is your title?' the tax assessor asked.

'What?'

'Your title deed. To show that the lot belongs to you.'

Makinde trembled with anger. How dare the tax assessor question his ownership of the lot.

'My father left me this lot,' he said. 'My father found this lot. He cleared this lot. He worked on this lot long before this part of Lagos became a slum.'

'So it's yours,' the tax assessor said. 'Then you must show me evidence, at least, that you've paid ground-rent on the property from the time you inherited it. Don't look so vexed. That is another department's business, but I will make sure I alert them after I have finished my assessment of your taxable earnings, eh?'

Makinde removed his shirt. His earnings were hidden under his mattress at home. He slept on them.

He wasn't about to let this messenger of wealthy men have access to them.

'What is this?' the tax assessor asked, expecting a blow.

'Here I am,' Makinde said, unzipping his trousers. 'Tax my head, my arms, my broken finger. Tax my legs. See: my foot is sprained, tax that. Here: tax my balls, and when you finish with them ...' He turned his backside to the tax assessor. 'Tax my ass.'

The tax assessor promised that he would return with henchmen.

'You will pay,' he said. 'Or they will help themselves to your wife.'

A wife who wouldn't even allow Makinde access to her. She was nauseous and eating dirt now that she was pregnant. Dirt.

'I can't help it,' she said. 'The sight of it makes me want to touch it. The feel makes me want to sniff it. The smell makes me want to eat it.'

Makinde watched as she scooped up soil and licked it. He tried to stop her by reminding her of worm eggs. He couldn't afford to take her to a doctor. He couldn't go to work for fear that the tax assessor would return with henchmen. They argued. She eventually packed a portmanteau and said she was going to her mother in the village for a week.

Makinde decided to seek counsel from Rasaki, a local man who was known as the Duke of Downtown. Rasaki's work included playing the pools and brokering assault contracts. People said he was personable with thugs and armed robbers in Lagos, that he smoked marijuana, and drank *ogogoro*, and called out to Lagos chicks, 'Baby, I've got a big one.'

And they replied, 'Bet it's the size of a Bic biro.'

But the Duke was also known as a person who helped those who were in trouble with the authorities – the police, the mobile squad known as Kill-and-Go, customs and excise, and taxmen. He knew exactly who to bribe.

Rasaki was smoking a Bicycle cigarette as Makinde talked. His fingers were as black as his lips, and his teeth were the colour of curry. 'My friend,' he rasped. 'What is wrong with your head? You don't insult a tax assessor.'

Makinde mumbled, 'It's too late for that advice.'

Rasaki scratched his armpit. He had just woken up. On his wall was a calendar. The girl of the month, Miss February, had one breast pointing east, the other pointing west. Her teeth had a centre parting. Her name was Dolly.

'You should have kept your mouth shut,' Rasaki said. 'Or else you want to offer your wife?'

'My wife,' Makinde said. 'She smells of boiled egg most days. Right now she eats dirt. I love her. I would not offer my wife to the president if he wanted her.'

Rasaki coughed and smacked his chest. 'I thought not, and I'm telling you, these tax men are not normal human beings. They have a lot of hatred in their hearts, and they are vengeful. It is how they get their jobs in the first place. I suggest – and you don't have to take my advice, I'm only suggesting – that you pay him the money he asked for.'

'Pay?'

'Yes, because right now he's offended, humiliated. He's a small man psychologically, and nothing you do will pacify him. From my experience, he will probably ask you to pay enough to buy the whole lot.'

'How will I ever do that?'

'How much money do you have now?'

'It's here in my pocket.'

'Place it on my table, my friend.'

Makinde did. Rasaki studied the naira notes. He tilted his head to one side and then he smiled. 'You got this by duping believers?'

Rasaki was a Moslem by birth. The last time he visited a mosque was to marry his only wife, who later divorced him.

'I didn't dupe anyone,' Makinde answered. 'It was an admission fee.'

'Call it whatever you want. You were in the game of chances, and you were master of it. People trusted you and you spat on their faith. I'm not blaming you. They were fucking fanatics and they deserved it. Who knows what Mary looked like? Do you?'

Makinde was getting impatient. Rasaki seemed to have a lot of knowledge, except about how to help him out of paying the taxman.

'What can you do for me?' he asked.

'My friend,' Rasaki said. 'Do you play the pools?'

Rasaki was an expert. How else would he have survived without a job for years? Playing the pools was not a risk, he said, and only those who played the pools long enough knew this. They studied odds and they beat odds. Those who lost were outsiders, like believers looking for miracles in lots.

'Give me your money and I will return it tenfold,' he said.

'How?' Makinde asked.

'Ah-ah? Will I tell you what has taken me decades to learn?'

'Why should I give you what has taken me a month to earn?'

'It's up to you.'

'My choices are limited.'

'The possibilities are endless.'

'You know a lot. How come you're not a rich man, yourself?'

'I choose not to be.'

'Why?'

'Where else will I be a Duke?'

Makinde had to concede; he did not know one person like Rasaki, who, despite his appearance (he was skinny, and had a rash on his neck), walked around downtown as if he were royalty. He wore trousers that were long and flared. 'Keep-Lagos-Clean' that fashion was called. His grey hair was cut high on his crown. 'Girls-Follow-Me' that hairstyle was called. His girlfriends were prostitutes, he lived in one room, and people knew his wife had divorced him because he was incapable of fathering children; yet he was extremely sure of himself.

'I came to you because you're a man with connections,' Makinde said. 'I was hoping for something not so out-of-the-ordinary. A name to slip a bribe perhaps? Let me think about this.'

At home, Makinde considered his options: On the one hand was his lot, and in his hand with the broken finger was the money he hadn't earned from working. Free money. It seemed to him that Rasaki was right. He had become master of the game, unwittingly. Who from his lot left with a miracle? Who walked out with more money in their pockets, except him? Those who came on crutches hobbled away, those who came blind shuffled off without seeing. He had not heard from the guide, but he was certain she had found another place to preach. Not one of the visitors to his lot was a Mercedes owner – the big masters in his country, so masterful they were actually called 'master' and 'madam'. They were as huge as gods. No matter how long he worked, circumstances remained according to their design. Never his. Never his.

He sweated and salivated. He drifted into that most powerful of mental states: total dissatisfaction. He went back to Rasaki with the money. Rasaki promised a return within a week.

How did Makinde hear about his money? He kept going to Rasaki's place and Rasaki was not to be found. He asked about Rasaki's whereabouts. People said Rasaki had travelled up north. He hovered around the row of collapsing bungalows in which the Duke had a room. No Rasaki. The Duke had completely disappeared downtown.

It wasn't until Bisi returned, full of her mother's vegetable stews and no longer craving dirt, that he heard from her. She heard from her friend at her married women's fellowship, who'd heard from her husband, who'd heard from his colleague, that Rasaki had taken money from someone to play the pools. He had lost the money, and the person from whom he'd taken it was unlikely to ask for his money back, because this person was in big trouble with the tax men, and Rasaki knew exactly who to approach to make sure this person ended up ruined, and this person was Makinde.

'Is it true?' Bisi asked him.

'Apparently,' Makinde said.

'In the short time I've been away?'

'Yes.'

'How could you?'

'I had little choice.'

'Well, I am disgusted.'

'Why?' he asked, as she would. After all, it was not his fault. She saw the vision on the dirty windscreen. She told people and they came, and stopped him from doing his work, got his name mentioned in the papers and attracted the tax men's attention.

'This would never have happened,' he said, 'but for your vision.'

'On the contrary,' she said. 'It is you who went wrong, being tempted by a man like Rasaki. We were blessed with that money. You lost it the moment you thought you could multiply it by other means.'

'How else could it have been multiplied?'

'You should have taken it to church.'

'For what?'

'To give as tithes. Your fruit would have been abundant.'

'My dear wife, when has my fruit ever been abundant?'

Bisi had to think. Becoming a father was one blessing, even though Makinde might not want to hear that. She couldn't think of another.

'I give tithes,' she said. 'My prayers are answered.'

'The miracle you prayed for on my lot, was that answered?'

'No.'

'Ah, well.'

'It will be! I know it will!'

'Tell me when that happens. Me, I feel as if I've been fighting a will stronger than mine. A mischievous will. It wreaks havoc and I'm done fighting it.'

Bisi had a solution to their problem: She was entitled to support from the Married Women's Crisis Fund – 'On condition you join my church family.'

Makinde was truly exhausted. 'For God's sake …'

'It's stipulated. You want this help or not?'

'It's not as though I have several options.'

The following Sunday he attended Abundant Life Tabernacle with Bisi. There Bisi told him that his presence in her church was the miracle she prayed for.

'I'm so glad you found your way,' she said.

THE PROMISED LAND

By Mialy Andriamananjara

Mrs Ratrimo inclined her tiny round head to the right and chose a package of bright red strawberries from the rainbow-coloured fruit stand. With a flourish of her chubby hand, she placed it in her treasure chest – one of these red grocery carts from Giant food store – at the same time humming a merry song. She did not know the lyrics; she was quite light-headed when it came to remembering songs, and had been overheard unabashedly transferring lyrics from one song to another. No embarrassed offspring was present to keep her from humming her fill. Her 23-year-old daughter, Maeva, was coming home tonight after a ten-month stay in Madagascar, her very first trip to the island of her ancestors. This made Mrs Ratrimo so joyous that the wrinkles on her face smiled.

Maeva had announced on the telephone that she had a pleasant surprise for her mother and had reiterated this promise several times by email. Mrs Ratrimo could not imagine what the surprise might be. Perhaps a portrait painted by the celebrated master, Ramanankamonjy? Maeva had long known her desire to own one. Or did she have some unexpected news that might precipitate her parents' long planned retirement in Madagascar? Photographs of the 150-year-old ancestral home maybe? Or had she met someone special during her stay? Would he be a handsome Andriana, a noble fellow from the Highlands? Refined and educated? Light-skinned, with straight hair to match her daughter's Afro-Asian features? Mrs Ratrimo stopped short of imagining grandchildren, but still felt entitled to some kind of celebration. She executed two hip-swaying dance steps before pirouetting towards the amused Somali cashier girl. This was Saturday night and Mrs Ratrimo was among the numerous Virginian suburbanites who rushed through cashier lines before heading home to collapse on their oversized couches. But she was certainly one of the few whose indelible smiles would not surrender even to the grumpiest cashier, whom, by some trick of her magic arsenal, she always managed to evade.

Mrs Ratrimo had been carefully thinking and planning for tomorrow's event, Maeva's homecoming, for at least three weeks now. She had been mentally admitting dishes to her menu according to the strictest criteria. Only the very best dishes would do for her precious only child.

How delighted and surprised she would be tonight at the sight of the delicately spiced, stewed sea bass, the crunchy pork samosas and the fragrant rice with greens. She let the cashier girl scan her carefully selected purchases; then, with her cart fully loaded again, her minuscule hand tended over a Bank of America debit card and her lilliputian finger punched the required digits into the machine. Off she walked to her car, having completed her errands, a cheerful, delicate woman, with coppery skin and almond-shaped eyes and silver-white curls rushing all over her head like a saintly halo.

Mrs Ratrimo lived in a fairly old neighbourhood with her husband. Their imposing colonial-style house, with red bricks and white shutters, sat in the middle of a sea of velvety green grass and purple azaleas.

The house was flanked on the southern side by a detached two-car garage. Mrs Ratrimo's black four-by-four monster vehicle abruptly stopped in the garage path. The conductor's door opened and loud melancholic music escaped from the car, preceding its owner:

Six routes
partènt du pied de l'arbe-yoyageur:
la prèmiere conduit au village-de-l'oubli,
la seconde est un cul-de-sac,
la troisième n'est pas la bonne,
la quatrieme a vu passer la chère-aimèe
mais n'a pas garde la trace de ses pas,
la cinquième
est pour celui-mord-le-regret,
et la dernière ...
je ne sais si praticable.'

Mrs Ratrimo was so small that she had to make a small jump from her seat to land on the gravel, making it screech underneath her Italian black pumps.

In a practiced *tour de main*, both hands carrying grocery bags and fumbling just a bit to introduce her key into the keyhole, she hurled all her bags in the kitchen. Her surprisingly strong and resounding 'I'm home!' was greeted by complete silence. Undeterred, Mrs Ratrimo haphazardly shoved her buyings into the fridge, while still loudly longing for her far-away home.

The little Swiss bird that nested near the wooden sculpture of a Betsileo woman's head was chased away from its wooden nest, and whistled shakily eight times. Mrs Ratrimo stopped singing and made a quick mental calculation. She had exactly two hours to herself before Maeva showed up, accompanied by her father who had gone to pick her up at Dulles International Airport. Maeva had fulfilled her dream: she had spent the last ten months experiencing and living her parents' previous life, before the American dream had lured them away from their beloved red island and its poverty, which begets a peaceful but destructive revolution every ten years.

They had arrived in America, as Mr Ratrimo liked to say, with nothing but hope for a better life, 72 pounds of luggage, their high-school-level English, and the determination to head back to Madagascar as soon as possible. Their grandparents had blessed them by spitting water on their foreheads. Mr and Mrs Ratrimo had taken handfuls of red soil from their ancestral tomb and had sewn it tightly into a silk pouch. The pouch had been tucked into Mrs Ratrimo's brassiere cups, safely hidden from unsuspecting US Customs officers. At Maeva's birth, a piece of the umbilical cord had been mixed with the precious content of Mrs Ratrimo's red soil – an important gesture that symbolically tied her to the ancestral land, and one that would ensure her safe journey to the tomb one day. Or so her parents hoped.

Over the years, tapes of songs were mailed from Madagascar in brownish crumpled boxes. The songs unfailingly lamented the misery of exiles, who missed their beloved Iarivo, as they liked to call their home town, and the land of their ancestors. The songs found a perfect audience in the Ratrimo family. They decorated the walls of the living room. The forlorn family had spent 30 years yearning for a never-to-be realised return. And so, Maeva, the American-born daughter, fluent in Malagasy language and customs, had grown up learning to miss a land she had never known. Or never been given a chance to know, until this year. Mr and Mrs Ratrimo had kept delaying their return under various pretexts. First, it had been the lack of money:

'Who would go home without at least a couple hundred thousand dollars?' they said. 'What shame! We will go home when we save up enough to live without ever having to work again for some nepotistic ignoramus in Madagascar.'

Then they had bought a house, panicked a bit at the permanence that this implied, and consoled themselves with the thought that it could always be sold. Real estate investments had never been this good. Then the delay had been for Maeva's sake.

'We will go home after she graduates from high school. From college.'

And here they were, 36 years later, with the mortgage paid off, their bank accounts boasting substantial savings and Maeva having graduated one year ago.

But what could Maeva's surprise be? Images of well-behaved, good-looking grandchildren kept shaping up in front of Mrs Ratrimo's eyes, despite her best efforts not to get over excited. They were soon distorted by the aromatic bouquet of ginger, garlic, onions and pepper that came sashaying out of her enchanted pans.

Mrs Ratrimo's approving glance swept across the mahogany dining table and took in the culinary miracles she had accomplished in two hours: heaped snow-white jasmine rice; vivid green barely-boiled spinach and Chinese bok-choy; red-green-white *rougaille*, the Malagasy version of tomato salsa; a bed of carrots, onions and grape tomatoes; ginger beef slowly cooked to the consistency of soft butter. And Maeva's favourite dessert, a strawberry cheesecake decorated with fresh strawberries and fresh mint leaves. Mrs Ratrimo's wrinkles smiled with her. She had also chosen good Californian wines to accompany the feast. Her silverware, crystal glasses and delicate china sparkled under subdued lighting. Even her great-great-great-great-grandfather, Prince Andrianantompokoindrindra seemed appreciative, as he looked down from his portrait. Conforming to Malagasy custom, the portrait hung on a north-east oriented wall, the corner traditionally reserved for the eldest and the ancestors. Oh, Jesus! An engine snored loudly outside, announcing Maeva and Mr Ratrimo. Plus the announced surprise, whatever it was. Mrs Ratrimo rushed to the door to welcome them.

'*Tonga soa!* Welcome home,' she said excitedly.

Maeva ran into her arms like a four-year-old child. They hugged, crying and laughing at the same time, talking without listening to each other. Mr Ratrimo 'tsk-tsked' to hide his emotions, then glanced nervously at the car. Mrs Ratrimo did not see the glance, engrossed as she was with her daughter. She passed her hands around her daughter's waist, marvelling at her presence and at the same time appraising her, making sure she had come back whole and unscathed. Her greedy nostrils quivered, trying to sample Maeva's scents, hoping to absorb places and experiences. Maeva had lost weight, she had let her hair grow, and her skin had darkened to a rich brown colour.

A towering presence intruded on them. Mrs Ratrimo looked up.

'Mama, I want you to meet Fanilo.'

Mrs Ratrimo let go of her daughter. Wide-eyed, she looked at the young man. So this was the surprise. She could not really see him in the dark. He was tall, big, and had an incontestably virile demeanour with his large shoulders and solid neck. She managed to mutter words of welcome. Her daughter laughed, proud of her surprise.

'Let's go inside,' interrupted Mr Ratrimo. 'We are not going to grow roots here. Fanilo, help me with the luggage, while Maeva gets a chance to talk to her mother.'

'So, who is he? Where did you find him? What is he doing here?'

'Oh Mama, he is wonderful. You are going to love him. He is so smart! And I did not find him, as you say. I met him at a concert – he was hanging out there with a bunch of Peace Corps Volunteers.'

'Oh you mean, he is American?' Relief was audible in Mrs Ratrimo's voice.

'Mother! Why would I go to Madagascar to meet an American? No, he is Malagasy, like you and me!'

'But he is not from the Highlands, is he?'

'No, he is Antandroy, from Tulear. Is that a problem?' A slight edge in the question.

'I haven't had a good look at him yet. '

A giggling Maeva called out: 'Fanilo! Fanilo! Come here. Mama wants to have a good look at you.'

Fanilo was carrying three large suitcases while Mr Ratrimo happily waved one brightly-coloured raffia handbag as Maeva beckoned to him. Maeva complimented her mother on the food and set-up, excused herself and disappeared in her room upstairs. They were left alone in the living room with Fanilo. He was not the refined Andriana fellow she had imagined for her artistic daughter. Why, he was not even of her tribe, Merina! He certainly was good-looking, she grudgingly admitted, if one did not mind a charcoal-dark complexion and features that were much more African than Asian. He had honest eyes that looked straight at her and a wide smiling mouth. He had folded his large hands in his lap and was quietly waiting for her to finish her circumspection. Who was he and what did he want with her daughter?

Meanwhile, Mr Ratrimo was serving whiskies. He always served whiskies when he had guests. He usually reserved the first capful of newly-opened bottles for the ancestors. He poured three drops under

Andriantompokoindrindra's portrait. The illustrious prince would have to content himself with that. He poured two fingers of whisky for himself. The young man asked for Perrier water instead. A good point for him, thought Mrs Ratrimo, whose rigid Protestant upbringing did not approve of alcohol. Mr Ratrimo winked at her. She pretended to smile. So, Fanilo, where are you from? What do your parents do? What are you doing with my daughter? An avalanche of questions tumbled through her mind.

'May God and the ancestors bless you.' Fanilo raised his Perrier-filled glass to them.

'To our lands and those in power!' answered Mr Ratrimo.

Maeva had come back from her room and was now sitting next to Fanilo. They exchanged a lust-loaded look that made Mr and Mrs Ratrimo shudder down to their horrified toes. Mr Ratrimo stood up and walked to the dining table, not forgetting his glass of whisky. The others followed. Dinner was silent, but for Maeva and Fanilo's flirty repartee and laughter. They told stories about people her parents had never heard of, about places they had never dreamed of going to, in a Malagasy dialect in which they had never spoken. Antandroy it was called. It was vastly different from the only dialect they knew: the Merina dialect and the official Malagasy language. They did not understand Antandroy and from the sight of their tight faces, they did not care to understand it either. It was a dialect from a tribe they had been taught to disdain. Indeed, the only Antandroy person Mrs Ratrimo had ever met was the gatekeeper from her childhood home and in all, she had not exchanged more than ten words with him. Pictures she had seen of Antandroy people had been of starving children with ballooning stomachs. Look at how this one seemed at home, at her table, sitting in her chair, his feet firmly planted on her expensive Persian carpet. And look at how carelessly he crunched her samosas! How he swallowed one spoonful of rice after the other, how he helped himself to her fish, not even bothering to offer Mr Ratrimo first! Look at how he monopolised Maeva's attention. She watched as long fingers lovingly enveloped her daughter's slender hand, making it look very pale in comparison. This would definitely not give her the grandchildren of whom she had dared to dream this afternoon. How dare Maeva do this to her! Did she have to go to Madagascar to come back with a dark-skinned, kinky-haired, bad-mannered man? Mr Ratrimo laughed at something the young man said, and she mentally shot daggers at him. It seemed she was the only one ill at ease. Her husband of many years sensed this and invited Fanilo into the kitchen on the pretext of getting wine to accompany their meal. He knew that his wife had a sharp tongue when she could not have her way.

She resolutely turned towards her daughter and asked: 'What about your plans to study archaeology?'

'Oh that! I really want to go back to Madagascar, Mama, and do something for the people there. There's so much poverty, so many resources, so many things to do! I do not want to study archaeology and then rot in a museum admiring things plundered from the past. You know how useful I'd be in Madagascar – even going to grad school may not be the best idea – and I should go work there immediately.'

'But you've been dreaming of studying archaeology for so long, after we insisted on you majoring in International Relations. And really, renouncing grad school?'

'Mama, you haven't been to Madagascar in thirty years, and even if you went now, you would go to your cocoon Andriana family, and you'd look at the outside world from behind the smoked glass of your rented SUV.' Maeva rolled her eyes and sighed, 'You do not know what poverty is like.'

'And you know what poverty is like, Miss Suburbia America?' said Mrs Ratrimo exasperated.

'After seeing what I have seen, I feel guilty not doing anything.'

'And this Fanilo fellow has nothing to do with this 360-degree change of plan?'

Again, that exasperating dreamy look spread over her daughter's face. 'You know, I think, it's complementary. I mean, you have shown me all the glamorous sides of Madagascar: culture, painting, history and all that. Look at your living room – even a museum in Madagascar does not have that many valuable artefacts. Fanilo has shown me other aspects of what it is like to be a Malagasy. He's shown me what home is and what my future may be.'

Mrs Ratrimo suddenly felt very tired. 'Your father and I have saved all these years so that you could go to grad school without any debts. And you are telling me you want to go to some godforsaken region in that godforsaken country – you are not telling me where but I am guessing it is probably in the Androy, right? To live in the dust and dirt, eating cacti with half-naked people?'

'Mama, do you hear what you are saying?'

'Why can't you choose something like saving lemurs, or protecting the environment, or rescuing under-age prostitutes? At least that will give you a nice tidy job in some NGO in Antananarivo and our relatives could take care of you. And didn't we agree that after your stay you would attend grad school and we would give you a nice stipend until you finish your PhD? It certainly did not include bringing back some fellow we do not know from Adam and Eve! A nice surprise, indeed.'

'Don't be such a snob, mama. And a tribalist, too. And do not speak so loudly, he will hear you.'

'This is my house and I will speak as I please. I mean, this fellow is not even capable of appreciating beauty. Did you hear his comment about my painting downstairs? 'Oh, such a large painting. It must be expensive.' I bet he will just use my rare first-edition books as plates to eat his cassava off – or whatever they eat from where he is. And don't you dare lecture me about poverty. I have lived it. Why, we were so poor we ate yam for Christmas and pretended it was one of those fancy chocolate yule-log cakes! And I had only two shirts and one pair of sandals when I grew up. My father repaired their soles with rubber from tires.'

'You've always told me I should be proud of my heritage. He is from Madagascar too, and he is like the majority of people there.'

'Not the Madagascar I know.'

What did she know about the Antandroy? She had never thought of them at all. In fact, she had never considered them and herself as having anything in common, such as being from the same country. She had seen pictures and heard stories about them, but these had remained distant and impersonal, as distant as the African coast of Mozambique. She felt they did not share the same history; at least the Betsileo, the Sakalava and the Betsimisaraka at some point, even though violently, had interacted with her ancestors. She remembered reading stories of how Antandroys massacred herds of zebus for funeral feasts to show off the deceased's wealth. Enamoured pretendants had to steal herds to prove valour and virility to their intended. She tried to imagine Fanilo symbolically stealing a packaged frozen steak from the Giant store to prove his worthiness to Maeva, and laughed hysterically. She wiped an eye and tried to lend an ear to what her daughter was saying.

'... because you're stuck in time, Mama. Things have changed there since 1964. Tana is an example of an urban-planning catastrophe. Your vast ancestral lands? Your siblings have leased it for 99 years to a Mauritian company that manufactures those silk sweaters you marvel over at Petite Sophisticate's when you see the Made in Madagascar tags. Mauritians are taking over Madagascar. Your ancestral home? You know you have been sending money for repairs all these years? Well, your siblings have sold the ancestral home, Mama. They sold it ten years ago to a wealthy Karana, an Indian. They have been taking your money without ever telling you there was nothing to repair anymore. In its place now, there stands a hideous two-story hotel where expatriates take their prostitutes for, shall we say, quick interludes. Those promenades under the arcades of the Avenue of the Independence you keep dreaming about? You'd be too bothered by the beggars to enjoy them. Your beloved stone stairs still overlook the Zoma, but they have become open-air toilets. You cannot make two steps without encountering the smell of human faeces.

'I grew up with your stories about how you used to pay visits to your cousins without ever announcing yourself and how you were always fêted and welcomed, and how your mother always cooked extra rice just in case someone showed up. Well, I learned that impromptu visits to relatives are considered impolite and even inconvenient. People hold at least two jobs to make ends meet; they lead stressful lives, more stressful than here. You know how many men die in their sixties, or even fifties, from heart attacks? And, by the way, most people I have met only dreamed of getting out of there. It's too tough living there, mama. It's not the paradise you made it out to be.

'I know that Papa and you have been thinking of retiring to Iarivo, but the Iarivo you knew is no more. If you were to retire there now, it would be like emigrating to a different country, and you'd be living among strangers once again. Plus, what if your health failed you? Hospitals there will fall way short of your expectations ...'

What did she know about Madagascar? Maeva put her arms around her mother and cradled her.

'Is he Protestant at the very least?'

Maeva giggled. 'No, his family is Lutheran, but he says it's a white man's religion and he follows his ancestors' god, Zanahary.'

Pause. Before Mrs Ratrimo had a chance to recover from the shock of getting a potential non-believer son-in-law, Maeva went on.

'Mama, I paid a visit to all the cousins whose addresses you gave me. I do not know if it was a coincidence, but each time there was a young man opening the door when I showed up. Luckily for me, they were always five feet tall and skinny – not at all my type.'

'You'd rather go for brutish?'

They laughed.

'Yes, I do not like inbreeding.'

'Maeva!'

'Well, that gives this family its second racist member. '

Mr Ratrimo came back into the dining room with glasses and an open bottle. He smiled. 'My two women!'

'You're about to lose one. She's talking of following that fellow down south.'

'You mean to Alabama?' Mr Ratrimo's voice reeked of irony.

'No, to Androy. I hope your daughter knows Antandroys have a polygamist tradition.'

'Yes, I know. I'm to be the third wife. Don't make such a face! I'm kidding, alright? That was a stupid remark and you know it. Where's Fanilo?'

'I did not know we were talking marriage already. Fanilo's coming. He wanted to brew us some tea.'

Well, that's the one civilised thing he's done since he arrived, Mrs Ratrimo thought, but dared not formulate aloud. Maybe there was hope after all.

'Mama, Papa, you have not asked anything about Fanilo. Don't you even want to know what he does?' Her daughter's voice contained a hurt reproach. Mrs Ratrimo simply shrugged her shoulders in a helpless gesture.

The kitchen door opened and a smiling Fanilo came back in, pushing a tray, on which he had arranged teacups, Mrs Ratrimo's beloved Japanese cast-iron teapot, sugar cubes and fresh lemon verbena sprigs. He had also managed to tuck what looked like the *ébauche* of a guitar under his right underarm. Mrs Ratrimo stood up to help him, but he shook his head.

'Fanilo composes songs,' said Maeva, ever the proud girlfriend.

He smiled to her, lifted the hat of the teapot, sniffed inside and said, 'It needs to brew some more. What about I sing for you as we wait?' Mrs Ratrimo recognised the instrument. It was what was called a *kabosa*, an artisanal and traditional guitar-like instrument. It produced rough, sorrowful, rhythmic tones that somehow always sounded nostalgic. Pictures of idle young men from her childhood neighbourhood flashed through her mind. They would sit on brick *tamboho*, singing in groups, while the sun died its glorious death and bathed the city's twelve sacred hills in purple and orange rays. The young men would whistle their admiration when the young Mrs Ratrimo haughtily passed by.

That is how she had met Haga, her first love. He had been sitting on a wall and had whistled his lungs out as she passed by. They had been inseparable like water and rice, as the proverb says: united in the fields, inseparable in the pot. Then her noble Protestant family had decreed his Catholic ancestry unsuitable. It did not matter that they were desperately poor and his family was immensely wealthy. Her parents still branded Haga a *mpisavy saranga* – an unworthy caste snatcher. She was hurriedly married off to a poor but princely cousin, Mr Ratrimo. They were a good match and she had come to truly love him. She later heard through the family grapevine that Haga had married a rich *Hova* girl like himself who bore him four children. What would her family think of the 'heathen' Fanilo? Their ancestry radar would promptly declare him a nobody – even more so than Haga. Was he at least a prince in his own tribe?

Fanilo's throbbing fingers extricated burning, excruciating notes from the *kabosa*. Then he started singing. Mrs Ratrimo could not understand the lyrics, yet goose bumps ran down her spine. This had nothing to do with Haga's singing. Fanilo's rough and deep voice sobbed amorously, full of reproach, like a jilted lover. Was he singing about a barefooted little boy, taking home his zebu herd, in a march cursed upon him by his forefathers, accompanied by the sunset? Or about muscular fishermen forever dragging their hollow canoes, their multicoloured voiles saluting the pure blue of the sky, on the white sand of Morondava, the never-ending coast? Or about the rice labourer's perpetual bet against nature? She balances a full basket of freshly harvested rice grains on her head, shiny gems of perspiration weighing down her neck, while her sleeping baby clasps her back like a baby lemur hangs onto its mother's tail. Or might it be about a little girl that strongly resembles Mrs Ratrimo? Contemptuous waiters chase her away from the windows of the French pastry shop, on the Avenue of the Independence, after her too hungry stares disturbed its patrons. Her tears are as abundant and as loud as the red-stained Betsiboka Falls that crush, protesting, into the Mozambique Canal Sea. She walks away. She is only ten years old but her illustrious ancestors have already lent her tears the mantle of their past dignity.

A long wail escaped Fanilo's throat and his fingers blurred on the *kabosa*, striking it faster and faster, echoing her heartbeat perfectly. Suddenly she could not bear the wondering anymore. She wanted to be part of this magic. A look at her daughter's face told her she was equally entranced.

Maeva's lips were feebly mumbling the lyrics, and her shining eyes were holding Fanilo captive. For her, this young man embodied the key to all mysteries of the red island. What did Maeva understand that left her mother alienated, forever banned from her daughter's and ancestors' land? Mrs Ratrimo went to the kitchen, under the pretence of looking for powdered milk, to hide her tears.

A 'For Sale by Owner' sign waved to passers-by. It was still early in the morning and early birds had responded to the garage sale signs that had been posted by Mr Ratrimo. They looked at Mrs Ratrimo's formerly immaculate grass. Dozens of crates were now covering it. Some were obviously new and gleamed under the morning sun, while dust thickly covered others. All wore labels detailing contents and date. They were opened at the request of the customers. One contained glass bottles, in various sizes and different shades, from dark and thick-waisted vinegar bottles to pale-green elongated ones that, on some distant day, had contained pristine mineral water. In another crate, minuscule baby clothes lay undisturbed. Thirty years of lingering had turned them yellow. Unopened boxes with unused obsolete kitchen appliances were scattered on large sheets on the lawn.

'Look, I did not know this was what coffee-grinders used to look like,' said a thirty-something woman in white leggings, pointing at a bulky brownish thing.

'One dollar,' said an imperturbable Mrs Ratrimo.

'What? I am sure you could get at least ten dollars for this at the Reston Antiques Centre. Why, you could open a whole shop with all you've got here.'

'Oh, that's all right. I just want to get rid of them. Too much trouble.'

Too much hope, really, she thought looking at the countless items that she still had to sell. Or throw away. How useful they would be to someone back home. How useful she once thought they would be. She had lost half of her soul believing in their usefulness. Mentally shaking her head, she rendered the change to the beaming woman. It had taken her a mere thirty-two years to collect these items. And they would be no good in the still undetermined direction in which she and her husband of thirty-five years were heading. But wherever they would go, her kitchen would no longer contain appliances. She was done with the collecting and the waiting. This was a vow she intended to keep.

Meanwhile, the ancestor, Prince Andriantompokoindrindra, was carefully enveloped in bubble-wrap, and the still-exiled singers of the tapes waited in the garage, in the excellent company of Fanilo's *kabosa* since its arrival one month ago. Maeva had accompanied Fanilo to New York, with their dream of irrigating the cacti-populated, dry Malagasy South neatly printed on a thick booklet that was packed in their luggage. They were to meet people from various foundations. Hopefully these people would be the kind that believed in water dreamily streaming through thorny wildernesses.

Mrs Ratrimo had been doing some research of her own. She glanced at one of the glossy brochures that the United States Postal Service had just dropped in her mailbox. It promised her infrastructure, permitting golfing, swimming, shopping, as well as in-house medical care. It portrayed attractive black, white and brown older people with blinding grins, inviting her to join them at their 'active-adult' community, under the ruthless sun of Florida, USA. It was time for what remained of her Malagasy soul to let go of the Promised Land.

REMEMBER, OLDUVAI

By Biram Mboob

Kanja was to palaver with the elders today. Everyone in the Rift palavered with the elders when they were the right age. He had an hour to wait, so he sat on the northern bluff, his legs hanging free. He watched two rhinos trotting briskly for the Engoro hills, until they were no more than indiscernible black specks. Arusha lay scattered beneath him. The silvery roofs of the *enkang* buildings reflected the sun's glare, something like pearls huddling in a placid sea of mustard dust and grey-green thorny bramble. He could see right into the nearby stockyard. Men and women were working on the rusty *maquinas*. The *maquinas* were magical things that could plough food and water from the air. His father had told him that the *maquinas* could also do terrible things if they were asked to.

The day was clear, and he could just see the peaks of Oldoinyo Oibor, the White Mountain. In ancient *livres*, this mountain was marked with the word 'Kilimanjaro' and the ancient symbols: '3°07' S, 37°35' E'. He watched the lonely wisps of white cloud swirling around its summit, celestial dancers on the endless sky.

Kanja walked through the door of the town *nyumba*, his footfall clattering loudly against the hollow wooden floor. He looked around. Old man Zhan was standing in a doorway. He grinned widely as Kanja approached.

'*Habari* young *mwana*! I've been waiting for you.'

Zhan grasped him lightly by the shoulders in traditional Rift greeting. Kanja grasped him back, pleased to see him. Zhan was wearing a dark-blue kaftan that hung loosely on his lean body and flowed gently down to his easy brown slippers. Zhan had always been somewhat of a novelty in the Rift. In all his life, Kanja had seen no more than three others like him – people of a discernible olden race. His eyes were thin upwardly curving slits, like everyone else's, but his skin was an odd yellow hue and his hair fell about his head in thinly textured strands, which were beginning to show signs of grey. His genealogy was a straggler of long centuries during which the Chinamen had barricaded their dwindling empire from the world. Most of the peoples of the Rift had black skin tinged with red copper, a consequence of millennia of acrimonious solar glare.

'Sit down, *mwana*, I am going to fetch something,' Zhan said, before disappearing into a back *chambre*.

Kanja poured a cup of warm lemon-grass tea and reclined in a worn *silla* near the window. He stared out at the White Mountain and had nearly begun to dream when he felt something heavy fall into his lap. Zhan had come back and had placed something there with a stealth that was surprising for such an old man. Kanja picked up the object. It was a *livre*, thick, but small enough to be grasped in one hand. Its cover was leather buckskin, smooth and unmarked.

'We will have to present that thing in an official manner when the elders arrive,' he said grinning, 'but it is just us boys now, and we have no need to wait on ceremonia, yes?'

Kanja nodded, but was thoroughly uncertain of what Zhan was talking about. The old man always seemed to be speaking in riddles.

'What is it?' he asked.

'It is a copy of a *livre* that is dear to us all. Now that you are a man, it will be of some importance to you as well,' he said.

Kanja nodded again, fingering the smooth skin of the *livre*.

'When they arrive, tell them I am outside in the *jardain*,' Zhan said. He began to make his way out towards the back door, then turned again. 'Take care of that *livre* young man. Keep it safe. We will talk more about it when our palaver begins.'

When Zhan had gone, Kanja opened the *livre*. The handwritten script was large and scrawling, almost archaic. It was a copy of some ancient text.

I do not know if anyone will ever read my journal, or indeed if I will ever permit anyone to see it. I have decided to commit the truth to these blank pages. Maybe I hope that someday, someone will read it and understand it better than I, or maybe I just do not wish to take my story to the grave with me.

I was *immigrè*, but I was one of the lucky few. As a young man, I was allowed inside the city of New Londres to take work as a teacher's assistant. It paid well and provided a bed. I had an aptitude for the work, which was why they gave me the job, and subservience to a machine was something I could live with, or so I thought at the time. The *maquina* taught rudimentary Maths and extensive English. It never taught Geography but it taught plenty of false History.

Over time, the *maquina's* lessons began to pain me deeply. Increasingly, I found myself modifying the *maquina's* scripts during quiet afternoons.

I had never been trained as a subversive, but the sabotage was easy. I scripted the *maquina* to teach the truth, the truth about the Great War and its real purpose. The truth about the *immigrè* problem. I still do not know why I did it. It served little real purpose. Or to be honest, no purpose at all. I put myself in jeopardy more than I knew, and my employment came to a rather abrupt end when the *maquina* was scheduled for unexpected maintenance. I came perilously close to being shot or gaoled, but again I was lucky. I was given a militant imprint and simply removed from the city. It may be hard for you, my reader, if you ever do exist, to understand. In those days, being removed from a city was a lingering death sentence. And once you were out, you stayed out.

With nowhere to go, I spent the next forty years in a nameless *favela* ten kilometres outside the walls of New Londres. Strange, such long years, and I can write of them in so few lines. They did not give the *favela* a name, I think because that would have acknowledged that it was there. We called it Londonderry. There was a starvation about it, of every kind. Market economics was as unyielding as ever. The *favela* had nothing to sell but brute labour, a much-unneeded commodity. When desperate, we worked in the sprawling stockyards that were too dangerous to be kept inside the city walls. They were foul places where we laboured with insane *maquinas* and built weapons.

The blight came and the world fell.

I am not sure what else I can say about that. I will say, that in the last days, they still took the time to lock down the *favela*. They set battle *maquinas* on the perimeter to make sure that no one would escape. They blamed the blight on the militants, but even they must have known this to be untrue. It was a last act of hardness and nothing more. We all knew that the game was up. Even the *maquinas* were dying.

Kanja closed the book and exhaled deeply. He had been holding his breath almost without realising it. From the first sentence, it had begun to occur to him just what it was that he was holding. This was Isa's *Diaro*. He had heard of it in snatches of conversation, and in lessons. But he had never known that copies of it actually existed, here in the Rift. Here, in his hands.

He recalled now, a night when he had woken and found his father reading a *livre* in the front chambre. A *livre* with a leather buckskin cover. He had thought nothing of it at the time. He turned it over in his hands now, examining every inch of it with fired interest. This was Isa's *Diaro*.

The front door began to creak open. The other elders were arriving. There were greetings. Zhan appeared, his face smudged with *jardain* dirt. They took their places on the wooden floor and palavered until the sun fell out and the stars fell in.

That night there was a *festa* in the *ville* square for his name and for the names of several others that had come of age in recent days. All of Arusha came. The grown-ups smiled at the guests of honour and gently gripped their shoulders. The Arab was playing his kora, its rich acoustic a myriad of echoes that gently drowned the square. They called him the Arab because he had come from beyond the desert, from a place he called Jericho. Many years ago, he had walked across the wastelands to come to Arusha. He had been dying of poisoned air and raving about monsters when he was found. When the elders finished with him, he had been sane again. Now the Arab worked in the stockyard mostly and taught *musique* lessons sometimes. Kanja liked him. He was droll, funny in a dry and tired sort of way.

Sheep were slaughtered for their names. The air was filled with smells of roasting meat dripping with thick, sweet honey. There were platters of steaming fish and green legumes. Bowls of thick *ugali* and spicy pimento sauces. The Arab played his kora and the Arushans feasted like olden kings in the moonlight.

As meals were finished, a single grape was pulled in on a rollered toboggan. The width of thirty men, it had been specially grown in the stockyard that afternoon. Its soft jelly was scooped into hundreds of clay bowls. Pots of warm frothy milk and small mountains of rich *fromage* were followed by gourds of sweet, heady palm wine. They drank, and the Arab sang a throaty ballad as he played, his sombre voice reverberating through the square and rendering all silent.

After food and drink, they danced in circles; some revellers leapt in the air to the furious beat of wooden drums. The *festa* continued until the gleaming amber fingers of dawn had begun to wrap themselves around the White Mountain. When the night was finally over, Kanja went home and read.

In the days after the blight, everyone I knew in the *favela* was dead, so I stayed in my hut and watched holovision, wondering when I too would die. I used to get four hundred channels from a hacked sat-signal. Now there was only one obscure channel left online, and it continuously looped the same holofilm over and over. It was a bloody movie with

British soldiers fighting Zulu warriors. The Zulus were losing the battle. It must have been a few hundred years old, for no one had made a film since the Great War. In the city, the genteel went to the theatre. Holovision was the stuff of *immigrés*.

I stayed indoors and watched the film again and again, until the power died. With the last of the holochannels gone, there was just me in the world. I left my shanty hut and began the long walk to Curson's place on the other end of the *favela*. I knew that in the false ceiling of his douche, Curson had many bags of fine white powders. He dared to keep the stuff in his hut as the narc drones never bothered to search for drugs in the *favela*. The drugs killed us, and this was no bad thing to them.

I tried to ignore the bodies in the road, the bodies in makeshift front *jardains*. Dead faces that were leaning against the broken windows of lifeless huts. There were many bodies in the street that were riddled with holes and were badly burned. The battle *maquinas* had been doing their work well, before they too had succumbed to the blight. I saw all these things, and unsaw them.

Then I came across the foxes. Foxes were not uncommon in the *favela*. These ones were in a group of ten, maybe more. They were silently loping down the broken street on their padded feet. I tried to ignore the obvious signs of drying blood on their solemn faces. The one that may have been their leader was gripping a dismembered infant in its wet feminine jaws. It stopped in the middle of the road, its bushy tail swishing.

Our eyes locked. It was daring me to me to stop them. But I had no right, and somehow we both knew it. I remember how the blood on one of its whiskers coalesced into a drop and fell to the ground. Foxes in the *favela* usually slinked away. This fox strode away, dead baby bouncing in its jaws, its dreadful procession in tow. It knew that it had won some terrible victory over me.

I walked to Curson's house and tore down his false ceiling. I took his powders. The world fell to a dream as I walked back to my hut. Days passed, and time stopped flowing in sequence. I took powders and I drank water, but I do not remember eating. There was commotion in the foggy background. I could hear cannons firing on the African plain. Beyond their din, Zulus were shouting; they were dying. These were the killing fields, and I could hear them. This was the crushing. Some disconnected part of me knew that all this was impossible, because the holochannels had shut down, and the power that fed into the *favela* via hacked taps was gone.

A time came when the cannons stopped firing. The battle cries ceased, and a single voice came through. I can remember exactly what it said to me. The drugs were strange that way – sometimes you remembered nothing, but sometimes you remembered everything in unnatural detail.

The voice was deep. It spoke in the hesitant English of a foreigner.

'Mwenzi,' it said, 'open your eyes.'

'Who are you?' I remember saying (or thinking?). 'The world is dead.'

The voice spoke to me quickly, impatiently. 'You not dead, Mwenzi. I fight the *umlungu* many days and I am not dead. Outside, Mwenzi, follow me.'

I remember being compelled to follow the voice blindly into the night. 'Look in the sky, Mwenzi.'

'Which sky?' A fog descended upon me, a sweet oblivion.

Then I remember my cheek stinging furiously. I had been slapped, hard. As I began to protest and wave my arms in front of my face, my head began to clear. In moments, the fog had lifted and I felt myself again. I remember being confused about being outside in the middle of the night.

Then I saw him, standing right next to me. He was pale and translucent. He was the Zulu from the holovision. He had come out and grown life size. His skin was as black as coal. His face was young, but his eyes were old. In one hand he held a large shield of animal hide. In the other hand, he was gripping a short stabbing-spear. Its tip was caked with drying blood. He had come from the battle. Then I thought, I knew, that I had finally gone insane. At the time, it was not an unpleasant realisation.

'You not … crazy and time is … is finishing,' he said through gritted white teeth. He was struggling with the language. His eyes blazed. He was angry. I remember shielding myself from him, wary of another slap, or worse. He dropped his shield and pointed into the sky in one quick movement.

'Look in the sky. *Nyota*! Look at star!' he said impatiently.

I followed his finger into the night sky. I saw what the nameless Zulu was pointing at, and it was no star.

It was the space station.

'The *nyota* will fall?' he asked me, a sudden waver of uncertainty in his voice.

The space station looked wrong. It was normally a long glimmering cylinder in space. Now it was slanted and not half as bright as it was supposed to be.

'It is going to fall,' I said, strangely certain of it.

'It will … it will break the world?' the Zulu asked, his English suffering.

Although the space station was nearly two centuries old, it dwarfed every other object in Earth's orbit. It had been useful when we still had dreams of travelling to Alpha Centauri and the stars, before our Great War had preoccupied us. Now it was just another relic of a time gone by, an extremely large relic. If it fell ...

I nodded dumbly. Yes, it would break the world.

'Then you must come with me, Mwenzi,' the Zulu said quietly. He did not seem angry anymore but the authority in his voice had somehow grown. Like a man who had just had a terrible foreboding confirmed and was all the more at peace for it. But unlike him, I was not at peace. I feared him. I feared the space station in the sky. I remember shutting my eyes tightly.

When I looked at him, I saw that his expression had softened. There was even a trace of a smile on his lips. He gripped me by the shoulders, the soft light pixels of his illusory hands rippling through me.

'Do not be afraid, Mwenzi,' he said. 'It is ... written long time.'

He was lying down on his *lit*, his copy of Isa's *Diaro* safe under his pillow. The sun was riding high in the sky and Kanja had slept fitfully. The elders had told him not to read too much at any one time, but he could not wait any longer.

Outside, an eagle screamed.

He tore off his sheets and pulled the *livre* from under his pillow.

It is a very strange thing but this morning it seemed as if the sun rose in the west. I do not understand it. The light has grown poor and it deceives the eyes.

All the world seems changed.

For several weeks now, we have been walking across the wasteland of North Africa. We have generally been staying away from the dead cities unless we badly need supplies. Who knows where *maquinas* may still lie in wait?

I have still not been able to bring myself to write about the attack. But reminiscence of it is consuming me. I have written that we left our faithful ship berthed on the Suez coast, its purpose served. I had not mentioned that its hull was nearly torn in half. We were attacked by an amphibious battle *maquina* on the open sea. It was like a giant fish with gleaming red eyes. At one point, I thought it was simply going to swallow us. We were saved only by the sturdiness of our ship, and the ferocity with which we fired its defence turrets.

The water *maquina* did not fall to the blight. I vaguely remember reading once that the newest models were capable of rebuilding their own subquantum power cells. That means that ... that thing ... may hunt in Atlantic deeps until the very end of time. I do not know why, but the thought overwhelmed me at the time and made me weep. Maybe it was then that I realised that the world could never be safe. It was changed forever. I could not bring myself to eat for days. Eventually Jungbaeur brought me some soup and insisted that I have it in his presence. He grates me at times, but he is a good man.

'You know the way, we're all counting on you,' he said to me.

The people are weary but they have faith in me. I no longer see the nameless Zulu, but I am sure now that I know the way. We are going to the Great Rift of Africa and travelling south along it to Olduvai. I know that we must get there soon, before the station falls and scorches the polar dams and drowns all the world.

Olduvai.

I don't know why, but it feels like we are on the road home.

SPOKESMAN

By J Tsitsi Mutiti

There were certain people, of whom my grandmother was wont to say, 'He is nothing but an empty sack, floating in the wind, blown here and there. A man of no worth at all.' Spokesman was such a man. This was not his real name, but he had been called 'Spokesman' for so long now that we could hardly remember his real name. Every Saturday afternoon one would see him staggering home from the beer hall. He was a big man and I used to watch him carefully to see how he'd float in the wind. It was only when he was drunk that he came close to doing so. This really puzzled me for I would have expected the drink to give him a little bit of the weight that my grandmother valued so much. The beer hall was his life and it was there that he earned his nickname. Only when he was about to drink, was drinking, and when he had drunk, did he really live. Most of his energies were expended in obtaining the means to do so. He kept a careful record in his mind of every favour done, so as to be able to make a claim on it later – should the need arise.

Spokesman did not own property and this no doubt added to his lightness of being. How can anyone respect a man without property? Most people I knew made disparaging remarks about him, particularly when he was not there. He was a *rombe* through and through, and on many occasions Gogo held him up to us as an example of how not to develop.

'See what comes of not listening to your elders, my grandchildren. To see that man strutting about with his hands in his pockets, you'd think he was someone. Tsk. It's a shame. To think he is somebody's child. Are there any people where he comes from? You'd think he grew from a hole in the ground!'

Indeed, all sorts of things were said about the strangeness of his upbringing and place of birth, most of it fabricated no doubt, but there is nothing quite like a fertile imagination on a long wet afternoon when no one can go to the fields. Spokesman was every gossip's bait.

If he had been cleaner, perhaps people might have been a bit more charitable towards him. As it was, his skin and water were strangers and, unquestionably, his clothes never had contact with that liquid. The only use he had for it was drinking it. It was said that his *mangoromera* fetish that he brought with him from Mozambique came with a taboo on

70

bathing. Some people even claimed to be able to smell him through closed doors when he passed their houses. His lugubrious expression rarely varied and one would often see him ambling glumly in the streets, lost in his thoughts. He didn't even seem to notice when people passing him in the street carefully gave him a wide berth.

A great fighter, he remained undefeated until the day he became known as Spokesman. His *mangoromera* talisman enabled him to trounce anyone who dared fight him. Few men dared to do so, as every previous bout invariably ended in ignominious defeat for the foolish opponent. It was said that his *mangoromera* would turn one's blood to water and sap one's strength. Didn't Phiri have to live on liquids for two months after Spokesman broke his jaw? As for Moyo, he spent a month in hospital after a beating. And Mountain, and Major and … the list went on and on, as it did not take a lot to provoke Spokesman into a fight. The victims would never say how they had been injured when questioned by medical staff. The only man to beat Spokesman in a fight had managed it duplicitously and even so, he had not lived too much longer to enjoy his victory.

This is the story as told to me by our gardener: Spokesman had been somehow cheated by the foreman and his attempts at getting justice were abruptly ended when the foreman started to insult the morals of Spokesman's mother as well as question the identity of his real father. As if that were not enough, the foreman also spat in Spokesman's face! The entire field was swiftly filled with silence, so that you could hear the wind brush past the birds soaring in the air. What would happen next? Spokesman disappointed all those expecting him to thrash the foreman. He did nothing. Aloud he simply said, 'You are a *shura*!', almost to himself and shook his head uneasily, expecting such astounding behaviour towards him by the foreman to be a harbinger of the death of a loved one.

As it happened, no word of death came to Spokesman that day. After mulling the incident over, he decided to quell the rising tide of his rage in the soothing taste of opaque beer. As he sat there brooding, who should strut by but the devil himself in the form of the foreman? He bought his pint of beer, swaggered past Spokesman and winked lewdly.

Spokesman restrained himself and took a long deliberate draft of his beer. A little while later, the foreman passed Spokesman again on his way to buy himself another drink. Spokesman resolutely looked the other way as he passed. The foreman continued to taunt him through all manner of looks and leers. Our gardener said that the foreman's ancestors were bent on causing grief and kept pushing him further. Finally, as the foreman swayed past Spokesman on his way to his umpteenth beer, his drunken grin seeming to suggest victory, Spokesman leapt up and threw a punch at the foreman's jaw. The latter ducked and swung at Spokesman's back with a closed fist. The big man fell to the floor with a loud yell of pain, while the foreman took the opportunity to make a quick getaway. People quickly went to help Spokesman up, and discovered a bicycle spoke protruding from his back. Some joker who witnessed this incident immediately named him Spokesman. Thus he was known ever after, except no one dared use the sobriquet to his face. Meanwhile, the foreman didn't get very far. In a bizarre accident, he ran straight into a cyclist speeding past the beer hall and was knocked unconscious, dying a few days later without having enjoyed his seeming victory.

When sober, Spokesman had a shambling walk as if his legs had a life of their own, independent of the rest of him. I believed this was merely further evidence of his lightness of being. I heard Gogo talk about levity and Spokesman in the same sentence so often that he seemed to be the embodiment of it. Although nature is said to abhor a vacuum, Spokesman could create one by his mere presence. Totally sufficient in himself, he never seemed to care about what anyone might think of him. Mostly, he drank alone in the beer hall, not caring for company except for that of women, unless he wanted money for beer. More often than not, others preferred to stand rather than sit near him, especially those who might owe some debt. One never knew when Spokesman would start hassling one for the money. This was because he often made money on the side as a debt collector. Any vendor who wanted to recover a hopeless debt would hire Spokesman to do it for him. Even the loan sharks used him. One had only to receive a visit from Spokesman and the money would appear as if by a miracle. He was truly a man who could squeeze blood from a rock. Sometimes the mere threat of his name was enough to make someone cough up what he owed. It could be dangerous to employ him in this manner as one seemed to incur endless and onerous debt after receiving Spokesman's services. Bigmore was one of those who discovered this to his cost.

Bigmore sold clothes in his spare time, on the usual 'buy now pay later' basis. Occasionally he found it necessary to use Spokesman's services on stubborn debtors. He had always paid Spokesman's commission and thought no more of it, though it irked him to have to pay it, miser that he was. Spokesman carefully added these favours to his record. Then one day, months later, as Bigmore sat with his friends in the beer hall, Spokesman came up and sat next to him casually announcing, 'Today I'm drinking pints.'

'Really?' Bigmore replied with pointed coolness, and carried on talking to his friends. Spokesman remained obstinately sitting there, watching him expectantly. Bigmore noticed his continued presence and looked at him warily.

'I'm drinking pints today, I said,' he repeated, with a note of impatience.

'I see,' Bigmore responded with some trepidation, starting to realise what was about to happen.

'Well, what are you waiting for? I'm thirsty!' This with a meaningful look, the kind known as 'a talking eye' – it said, 'Watch it! Remember you owe me!'

Well, what else could Bigmore do, if he was not to fall victim to the same terror he had employed upon others? Ruefully, the reluctant Bigmore watched his whole week's drinking allowance, and some more, disappear down Spokesman's throat.

This happened as often as Spokesman liked. What about Paraffin, a loan shark, who heard that his daughter had been seen several times in the company of Spokesman? Didn't he rush, seething with anger, to object, only to be met with the contemptuous response:

'Do you think I work for nothing? So I'm good when it's money you want but when it comes to your daughter, I'm not good enough. Leave me alone or else it will be your wife next time.'

There was nothing for him to do but keep quiet, knowing Spokesman could make good his threat if he persisted.

Many others fell victim to different forms of extortion. Life was certainly good for Spokesman before the advent of Suspenzi.

Gogo was full of opinions about people and expressed them freely. There were other men of whom she would say, 'That one is weighty. See how respectable and dignified he is. He walks down the street and anyone can see that where he comes from are real people. He has character, that one. He is wise from listening to the words of his elders.'

We considered Suspenzi to be one of those, when he first came to the estate. He came as a clerk, a highly coveted job. It was unheard of to find one so young holding this post. When his property arrived in a pick-up truck, mothers and their children gathered round and marvelled to see so much property owned by one man. Why, he owned so much he could even compare with some of the *chefs* on the hill – and a single man too! He even owned a small black and white television and a radio. Someone heard from somewhere that he had once lived in the city, and Suspenzi climbed higher in everyone's estimation.

It was not long before he became the most popular man on the estate. Though small, Suspenzi had a calm confidence that lent him the illusion of size. It must have been the weight of his dignity. I thought a lot about how, replete with the wise words of his elders, he would probably tip the scales at a greater weight than Spokesman. And how he could dance! At the beer hall, during the weekend, he could drink and drink and still retain his respectable deportment. How the girls loved him! The local *n'anga* made a lot of money selling love potions and many a sleepless night was spent hatching plots to catch his eye, but Suspenzi remained unsnared.

When Suspenzi came up with some scheme (I forget exactly what) for everyone to make lots of money, not surprisingly, it met with a wildly enthusiastic response. Everyone, it seems, wanted to be a part of it, including Spokesman. Everyone that is, except for Gogo. She criticised the scheme in her usual cynical way.

'No good will come of this, mark my words. Money has to be earned, my grandchild. I always said this boy was too good to be true, just you wait and see. He's like one of those *tsotsis* that we hear of in the city.'

Every member of the scheme contributed fifty dollars. Though the scheme sounded horribly complicated, the people placed ample faith in Suspenzi. Why, he could read better than everyone else in the compound, including the foremen. And he obviously knew about making money, considering his assets. In the beer hall the only talk was how so-and-so was going to buy a TV or an electric stove or a radio with his money when it came.

A month went by, and then another, and no money came. People started to get restive. After all, fifty dollars was a lot of money then. Suspenzi explained that patience was required for this type of venture.

'This is not the sort of thing where the money comes just like that, as if we are selling sweets. You people must know that these English things are very complicated. Surely you don't think that I would cheat you!'

He could be very persuasive when he chose and they were reluctantly convinced.

Two more months went by, and still they waited. Spokesman decided that he did not have this sort of patience. Fifty dollars could have kept him in drink for a whole month. He went to Suspenzi's house to demand his money.

'But I don't have it here! I have invested it in town. I can't return it to you yet,' Suspenzi stated confidently, knowing how easy it was to convince this sort of man. 'You see, this ...'

'I DON'T WANT TO HEAR ANY OF YOUR STORIES!!!' Spokesman roared.

'Look, I am not here to fight with anyone. We've got to talk like two reasonable men. Let's ...'

'I SAID I WANT NO STORIES! GIVE ME MY MONEY NOW!!' Spokesman was starting to hyperventilate and his chest heaved as he panted, 'If you don't produce it right now, I'm taking your radio with me.'

He made as if to grab the radio, but Suspenzi quickly lunged between him and it. This enraged Spokesman, who swiped at him. Suspenzi ducked and, quickly recovering his balance, let loose an uppercut that caught Spokesman on the jaw; Spokesman did not even budge.

'Today I'm going to show you what everyone else here knows. You dare strike me? You son of a she-goat!'

He spat into his hands and went into action. The blows rained thick and fast upon the doomed Suspenzi: a fist in the teeth, a kick to the kidneys, another in the stomach. I don't know if any part of him was lucky enough to escape a blow. Suspenzi only gained consciousness in the hospital.

A week later on a Sunday, Suspenzi returned from hospital in a Golf driven by a very smart-looking gentleman in a suit. The car headed straight for Spokesman's house and parked in his yard. The gentleman in the suit got out and gravely helped Suspenzi out. The sinister air about him was exacerbated by the dark glasses and harsh expression he wore. Briefcase in hand, he strode up to the front door, a limping Suspenzi in tow, and knocked energetically on the door. It took a while before the door was opened; Spokesman stood leaning insolently against the door.

'I am Mr Suspenzi Brain's lawyer,' he said briskly in a formal tone. 'Mr Brain alleges that it was you who assaulted him and also that you stole his radio. Now these are serious offences and I can put you in jail for ten years for this.'

The gentleman paused, eyeing Spokesman as if he were some nasty creature that had just turned up in his food. The sight of the man's suit, his bearing and the mention of jail, all served to unman Spokesman. For the first time he was heard to speak humbly.

'Yes, chef, it is all true. I have the radio still and will return it if he gives me back my money.'

'Do you know how much he paid in the hospital for the injuries that you inflicted on him? It is you who owes him money, according to Section 3 of the Miscellaneous Offences Act.'

He pulled out some very official looking documents from his brief case and handed them to Spokesman.

'Sign here. This says that you admit it was you who injured Mr Brain, and that if you do it again to him or anyone else you will be in serious trouble. Sign this. This shows that you owe Mr Brain one hundred dollars for hospital expenses.'

In a daze, Spokesman carefully marked X in the spaces indicated. Since he, like most of his fellow estate workers, could not read, he had a fear of official documents and always felt helpless when confronted by things with strange English names. Everyone knew that Acts could put one into jail. No one was sure what they were exactly, but they knew enough to know that the miscellaneous one was serious. It could get you on any grounds at all. The tales he heard about the unnatural practices performed in jail were enough to turn his blood cold. No, he did not want to end up there.

To all the others on the estate, this was sensational. No one had ever challenged Spokesman and gotten away with it before. Why, the only man ever to defeat him before had been buried before the week was out. Everyone waited with eager anticipation to see what would happen next. The whole estate was divided into different camps, some supporting Suspenzi's action and others laughing at Spokesman's defeat. Gogo pointed out that it was the fools who had invested money in Suspenzi's hare-brained scheme who now supported Spokesman.

'I suppose they now expect him to be a real spokesman and recover their money.'

There were mixed feelings, as they had begun to suspect that Suspenzi might not be quite the model they had made him out to be. For the first time in his life, someone seemed to be on the same side as Spokesman.

Some warned him, 'Look, you just don't mess around with educated people. You can't compete with them. He will get you into trouble. Now you have lost more money. Just leave him alone now. We are also worrying about our investments. We don't know whether we will ever see our money again. This man is sharp. He knows all kinds of *chefs* from town and if you don't watch out you'll end up in jail.'

Others laughed vindictively.

'Yeah, good for him! It's about time he was brought down a step or two. He thought he could get everything just by owning *mangoromera*! He got a good dose of his own medicine. Against the police, nothing, not even juju, is effective. These learned men rule the land. That Suspenzi wiped him out totally. Did you see the foolish look on his face as he signed?'

This, followed by spiteful titters.

As for Spokesman, for a while he acquiesced to a power greater than him and held his tongue. The taste of defeat lingered bitter in his soul. At first, he tried to forget about the unprecedented defeat that he had suffered and get on with his life, but found himself losing the battle against the relentless wrath growing in his heart. Clearly, he had been cheated and, for the first time in his life, something would not give in to the power of his fist. In his solitude, he nursed his anguish, going over the scene again and again. Like cancer it grew, filling his mind until it was all he could think about night and day – and how one day he would get his revenge. Meanwhile, the thought of pen and paper terrified him; his inability to write and read was more frightening than any duel with a man, and it stopped him from doing anything rash. To many who were waiting for Spokesman to exact a bloody revenge, it came as a total surprise when, instead, he enrolled for Grade One at the mine's evening school.

IN THE CLARITY OF A THIRD CLASS COMPARTMENT

By Pumla Dineo Gqola

We make the walk from my front door to the subway in record time because we are running late and need to hurry if we are to catch our train. From the top of the road we can see the empty platform, signalling to us that we have missed the train we intended to catch and therefore have ten more minutes before the next one. Realising that it is now safe to do so, we slow down just before we reach the tunnel. We do not talk much as we descend the five steps, giving ourselves time to catch our breath and enjoy the coolness of the below-ground-level channel. At the same time my nose flinches at the sharp smell of urine inside. It is not yet sunset and the evening will be warm, perfect for a Friday evening *braai*.

The train pulls into the station as soon as we step onto the platform. Third class is always crowded at this time of day, but that is where we get in nonetheless. Being university students and broke, we take the chance and board the train without tickets because rush hour-trains rarely get ticket spot-checks. The conductors know that many people ride third class for free and they have, of late, been coming up with increasingly cunning ways to catch out the likes of us. I know that there are people for whom the difference between buying a monthly ticket and a weekly ticket so that they can buy some other necessity is a real one. For others, the defiance of riding for free in the non-European section of the train has been too long a part of their lives. They are too set in their ways to notice that it is 1996 and everything has changed in the country. My brother thinks this kind of behaviour is scandalous. He can go on about how counterproductive it is to use the same tactic for apartheid enemy and friend in government alike. He is right, of course: there is no longer a need to refuse to pay for the state's poor services. Nonetheless, here am I, ticketless, making my way from Observatory to Wynberg.

We are lucky because many people change trains at the next stop, Mowbray station, so we do not have to stand the rest of the way: there are a few vacant seats as the people ebb out of the carriage. Ignoring the prominently displayed 'no smoking' signs, several people light up and there is cigarette smoke all around us. The woman next to me is one of them. Just when you imagine that the carriage cannot get any smokier, that eyes could not possibly sting more, another person lights up. And the cycle begins again. I am only half listening to my companion as I continue observing this action all around me. Some faces bear the distinct mark of fatigue, others are clearly relieved that the weekend has come and that, for two days, they need not be up at the crack of dawn to work.

Other odours in the carriage are quite persistent in competing with the smoke. There are the fresh apples, whose fragrance escapes from the bag of the woman standing in front of me; the fiery mince-curry pie from the woman who has just stubbed out her *stompie* on the floor; the obligatory sweat and perfume smells. With so much commotion I am amazed at the young woman at the top of the bench who has managed to keep her face buried in her Danielle Steele novel. She seems unaffected by it all, does not smoke, and moves only to turn the pages between colourful covers. Her face is buried so deep inside the book it is as though she seeks to merge with its pages.

I am surprised that there is such a large crowd ready to alight at the usually quiet Newlands station. Maybe there was a cricket match at the stadium today. My companion interrupts himself to comment on how there really is no more space for any more people to get into this carriage. I grunt my agreement but none of it will make any difference. Those waiting to come in will do just that and space will be found. It is so hot that all the windows have to be opened just so we can breathe inside. I notice that the crowd is only coming in through one door and, as soon as I turn my head, I realise why.

Five young men enter the carriage and their presence immediately alters the atmosphere. One leaps in dramatically, while the others simply saunter in casually as though they own the space. Mister Theatrics has the stereotypical appearance that accompanies the images of those responsible for train violence a few years ago. He has a scar on his left cheek and the bright reddish-purplish lips that people associate with many years of excessive consumption of strong alcohol, or with sniffing methylated spirits. His pals are variations on the same theme. Some are wearing the multicoloured baggy jeans that were in vogue a few years ago as an obscure commentary on race harmony. They all wear blood-shot eyes.

My fellow travellers simply glance at the newcomers and continue with their business. Although they caused a stir, and wore deliberately defiant looks upon entry, they cause no immediate trouble. The other passengers observe the new arrivants without directly looking at them. Nobody wants to invite confrontation. Soon they loudly begin to converse among themselves.

My companion is still talking about his day whilst playing with my hand. He is smiling; I smile back, and he misses the dishonesty in my eyes, as I am paying more attention to the young men's chatter than I am to his story.

'It's the best cure for *babbelas*. That and a fat *dagga* joint. First thing when you get up, you mus' get yourself some,' the first one announces to great applause.

A second one half sings, 'Ja, to chase all your hang-over blues a-w-a-y!' before breaking into raucous laughter.

'Ja, but what if you're a *shoemaker* like somebody here? You *mos* can't just go *gryp* any *cherrie*,' another says, teasing.

Their loud uproarious laughter is punctuated by simultaneous shouts of 'Why not?' from the others. What follows leaves me so cold I forget that this is the end of a very hot January day.

Mister Theatrics who has not taken part in the conversation so far decides that his input is necessary after all.

'You jus' take what you want ... from where you want ... and if you need to deal with the husband or the boyfriend before ...'

He is interrupted by, 'Or the father.'

'Ja, or anybody, then you deal with them. But you grab the *cherrie*!'

Most of the carriage is quiet now. Apart from the Danielle Steel reader, there is a man speaking on his cellular phone and a couple in the corner who seem oblivious to the rest of the world. And my partner continues to talk to me. The young men fail to notice the dearth of other conversation. Nor do they care about the vicious looks thrown in their direction.

'And if it's the mother or the sister or the granny?' one chants in a mock little-girl voice.

'Well, then you *sommer* get two for the price of one!'

I want to throw up. But I continue looking straight ahead of me, out of the window, at nothing in particular. My partner continues, oblivious to the war of emotions going on inside me. He speaks none of the languages used by these men to spew hatred of me. He does not understand these constant threats of rape. He does not know that, while he chatters happily, I am frightened because these youths will not permit me even the false safety that comes with being in a man's company. The young men seem to find the last part of the conversation about two *poese*, two vaginas, for the price of one particularly amusing. Their laughter at this 'joke' is kept up through two stations; when they do stop it is due to distraction rather than because they no longer find themselves so entertaining.

A teenage girl walks into our carriage at Claremont station. She has on the short navy-blue skirt of her school uniform and her shirt remains crispy white even at this hour of the day. She is also wearing the uncool kind of black shoes with a buckle across the foot that teenage girls only wear because they are forced to, along with the obligatory bulky black school socks. Her school blazer, green with gold stripes, is hanging over her school bag on her left shoulder. She has freed her long braids from the school-required ponytail. Watching her, I am reminded of myself ten years ago. I recognise that skirt – so short that only a fifteen-year-old can feel unselfconscious in it. I remember too, the lure of the lipgloss and how much more attractive it was than the usual lip balm or tried and tested lip-ice. She walks like one who has recently discovered that she is a young lady, that her body has no more surprises by way of new bulges in the wait. I must be smiling because my companion asks me if I know her. I tell him that I used to be her.

As the train pulls out of the station, the rowdy men decide that she is to be the object of their attention. One of them moves closer to her and, leaning into her face, begins to say something at her. The expression on her face betrays her irritation at this unwelcome attention. I want to jump up and tell him to leave her alone but I don't. He continues like this while one of the others delivers a running commentary on her legs, all the while calling her 'girlie'. When she turns around to ignore the one who has been breathing on her face all this time, the others take it upon themselves to join in, taunting her.

'What's the matter, girl, you too good for us?'

'No, don't be like that ... we jus' want to talk.'

'What's your name?'

I choose to glance over at my talking partner and in that brief moment, I miss seeing one of the rowdy men grab the schoolgirl. I turn back to face them when I hear the girl let out a scream. She turns around and pushes the one immediately behind her, shouting, 'Who told you you can touch my bum?'

'*Hei*! She's hot *nè*?' the offender laughs.

The girl says something, which I cannot make out because the entire group is now insulting her all at once. They start with their typical running commentary about how she is a *sfebe*, thinks she is better than they, and must not come and 'front' like she does not come from the township.

Out of nowhere, a woman's voice shouts, 'Come and sit here, my girl.'

The young woman obeys. One of the bullies follows, imitating her walk with the exaggerated hip-sway that men sometimes use to mimic women. A man in his mid-twenties stands up and prevents the bully from going any further.

'What's the matter, *my broer*? You going somewhere?'

'*Ek is nie jou broer*. Get back to your *skollie* friends and leave this girl alone,' the older man orders.

Knowing he has the backing of his friends, the young man continues, 'Listen, *my broer*, you mustn't get yourself in things that don't involve you. You could get hurt, *ek sê*.'

He says this with a self-congratulatory smirk accompanied by a bopping of the head backwards. He must think he is a play-gangster in a music video or something, and not the low-life that the real gangsters in Hannover Park would break into two with just a stare. His friends cheer. But this time they have overestimated their own power. The male passenger, still standing, now has the vocal support of the rest of the carriage. In no time there are voices of older women chirping in, scolding, and anger in the carriage is building.

'Hey! hey! hey! *Mamelani apha! Asizokuphathwa nini!*'

'Don't mind them, my girl, they are *skollies*, hooligans!' adds another.

Soon there are many voices. Some scold the group, and others still console the young woman.

'You have been spewing your nonsense since you came in here, *sies!*'

'I pity your mothers! Whose sons are you? Such rubbish! Shaming your mothers in public like this! What are your names? ... Huh? Answer me!'

'It's bad enough that you come here with your nonsense about rape and drugs! *Nx!*'

'You don't even see us! Grabbing the girl's body like *'at!*'

'Don't mind them, lady, don't mind them, my girl. You are not a slut, my dear. You are a lady, hear?'

Even after a few rounds of scolding one of the young men misreads the situation and remarks, 'Oe! But the *aunties is kwaad, nè*?'

From somewhere comes the suggestion that these boys need to be taught a lesson, that they need a good *klap*. But who is going to do this now? This is now another matter. Nobody really wants to start beating up anybody and get involved in something ugly at the beginning of their weekend. It has been a long week and everyone just wants to go home to their families.

You can tell by their faces that the older women are already dreaming about the Epsom-salted water in which they are going to soak their weary feet before they ask their elder daughters to make them a nice cup of rooibos tea. The last thing they need is to be standing in a police station arguing about some stupid boys who got themselves beaten up for 'being rubbish'. They have been on their feet all day. And besides, do you know how few seats there are at police stations? And the whole thing would take all night with so many people. No, they'd just rather go home.

Those who are slightly younger want to get home and have a beer or a brandy and coke with lots of ice, while they dance around the place getting ready for that braai at a friend's place. They have already decided what they are wearing, which earrings to put on, and what salad to make and take. They can almost smell the grilled meat, chicken and fish. Why spoil a perfectly good Friday evening, especially when it is so warm too, by spending all night in the police station? No, they'd spent enough time at police stations arguing with the police when they were students in the struggle during the early eighties. No, really, what is the point of all this democracy and freedom if one still has to spend all that precious time at a police station?

Young women in their late teens and early twenties still have to get home and do whatever their parents ask of them before they can start getting ready to go out with friends to a nightclub. They must still wash the dishes, call a few friends and spend a few hours making up their minds about what to wear. Make more phone calls about who is picking up whom, where and when. 'Parking' at the police station is the last thing on their minds. Where would they find the time? And they don't feel like dealing with the police now, especially since they only just left school and all that constantly-getting-arrested business a few years ago.

So, nobody takes the man up on his offer. Instead, a few voices coming from a different part of the carriage summarise my suspicions about what everybody else has been thinking.

'Where are the police when you need them in Cape Town?' somebody asks out loud.

'... As soon as you beat these boys up,' another ventures ...

'... Or throw them out the window like they deserve ...'

'... while the train is still in motion ...'

The three women start laughing at the craziness of their thoughts.

'Then the whole lot of us will be in jail for the murder of scoundrels who deserve worse than jail time!'

'Ja, look at what happened to that man who shot the gang member who raped his daughter!'

It is as though this has become one long meeting in which everybody adds their opinions. As the temperature inside the compartment keeps rising, the bullies realise that it is best for them to keep quiet. They do not cower, but maintain their devious physical posture as though trying quite hard to feign indifference. I suspect that this is a performance to mask the surprise they must be feeling; hooligans usually get away with anything on the train. They know that although it is possible for a handful of men to terrorise an entire community, there is never any telling when people will decide they have had enough and explode. They also know that these days all sorts of things are happening to serious gangsters, thugs bigger and more notorious than them. If everybody in this carriage simply kept quiet about what some might decide to do to them, who would ever know? And it's no use hoping somebody would tell the truth – it is one thing to be a religious person, it is another to send justifiably angry people to jail in order to satisfy your Christian or Muslim conscience. Who knows what people in Cape Town will do when they really get fed up?

The young men decide to hold their tongues, all the while pretending that they have dismissed the entire population of the compartment as unworthy of their attention. There is no point in getting yourself killed by a group of crazy people on the train. Perhaps they can simply go and pick another train and go joyriding all the way to Simonstown and back again to the central station.

The people in the train are still scolding but I am no longer listening; I just feel grateful that so many people are braver than I could ever have been. I am glad people in the third-class compartment did not look away and mind their own business. I begin to wonder if this would have happened in first class, where people sit in their corners with their newspapers and more space, in privacy.

The taunted girl has put her bag on her lap and for a few seconds I imagine that she has tears in her eyes and wonder whether they are tears of anger, fear or relief. But then, perhaps she did not cry at all. The woman next to her is still talking to her, and before I disembark I see her smile at the older woman beside her.

The Danielle Steele reader at the top of the bench opposite me eventually decides to take her head out of her novel, which she now stuffs hurriedly into her purse. Did she miss all the action? I reach into my bag for my cigarettes before I remember that I stopped smoking months ago. Why do people who ride third class bother to stop smoking? But it prompts me to remember something else: the Danielle Steele reader's face is one I used to see regularly without make up, when it belonged to a boy. Her eyes pass over me as she readies herself to leave the train ahead of us. I wonder if she noticed me sitting across from her all along, and I wonder whether I should run after her and say hello. I decide not to; passengers in third class deserve their privacy too.

I am not bothered by the much stronger stench from this tunnel. So much has happened that I am less irritated at how people use station tunnels as toilets when there are public toilets nearby. The bits of broken glass and the *stompies* lying around in the tunnel make no difference to me this evening. They will be gone in the morning after the council cleaners have been here, and the tunnel will smell overpoweringly of Jeyes fluid detergent. I even pay a little more attention to what the graffiti, freshly illuminated by the lights, says – gang names and rap lyrics competing for wall space. And then I sigh because things are really not as bad as they sometimes seem.

The streets of Wynberg are alive this evening; everybody is in the mood for a party. 'There is music in the air', as the Margaret Mcingana song I loved as a child, goes. I am smiling again to myself and humming a little, remembering the tune.

My lover is at the end of his narrative and, turning to me, he comments on how quiet I have been. He makes a joke about how unusual this is. I know he has realised that something happened in the train, but some form of gangster commotion happens in train compartments every day. He is not focused on understanding the specific ways in which things played out today. I am envious of the protection that language offers him, as I will tell him later. I will also share with him my relief for the young woman in the school uniform. I wonder what he would think of the lady whose face used to belong to my friend as a child. In a few moments, with the lights coming on, and the pulsating life on this street, I decide against discussing my friend. Maybe I did not see my friend's face after all. And if I did, and the recognition was mutual, then walking away was a plea for privacy. I am saddened by this until I recall that I had not seen this person I now want to claim as my friend for many years. Had my mind played momentary tricks on me? I know I can never be sure.

I realise that my lover is looking straight into my eyes with a deliberate frown on his face. He has been talking to me and again, I have not been listening. After deciding that there is nothing wrong, he wants to know how my day has been. Not knowing where to begin, I squeeze his hand, smile brightly and answer, 'Okay.'

WHEN NIGHT WAS ARRESTED

By Nhamo Mhiripiri

In the candlelight, her face flickered and slowly flapped. Her usually deep blue eyes turned a hypnotic crimson in the night under the thatched balcony where they sat. Still, Ngoni wanted to embrace and kiss her. He felt like licking her bright trembling lips, yet at the same time there was an unexplainable revulsion and horror in him. His was a lust and fear that he could almost see and touch in the shivery shadows that tumbled and turned, yet the same shadows constantly stayed under a mysterious control.

The candle was burning down and the two glasses, one of wine and one of brandy needed refilling now and again. Fresh cigarettes were lit and puffed out. They did not feel like retiring to bed as the rest had done. Instead, they sat there, talking, going through bouts of charged silence, at times sizing up and taunting each other quietly, daring each other to make a move. Past, present and future were sealed in an envelope and laid forgotten on the balcony's cigarette-butt-littered wooden floor.

'My supervisor says my language is rather journalistic for a dissertation; that it's too descriptive,' Katrina sighed, not the least from resignation. 'He acknowledges that it's good. My past contacts, including my mother, are an excellent source for the compilation of data on women's roles in the southern African armed liberation movements. He then insists that I can't quote my mother because it's unethical and outside acceptable research methodology.'

She puffed at her Camel Light cigarette and blew out the smoke in a straight whistling barrel that disintegrated into grey feathery strips like a mind scattering into the night. In the magical dissolution, smoke became one with the environment; and somehow she was an integral part of it all.

'You see, my mother worked for an NGO in Dar es Salaam. My mother's boyfriend was an MK fighter and he used to tell her about life in the training camps. Many of her friends were MK fighters too. They used to visit our home and that's where I met them.'

Ngoni gazed at Katrina's ankle – her leg was folded on the cushioned armchair into which she had curled herself – and in the candlelight, the tattooed icon, a flying eagle, stilled and pulsed as if about to break free from the confinement of her skin. He wanted to caress the dainty ankle, but restrained himself when he saw the predator's sharp beak make an ugly snap. His hand shifted to rest over his fly where an involuntary stirring and bulge was growing. It was a silly embarrassment that he didn't want her to notice, so he quickly talked to fill in the silent spell that had followed her talk.

'Petty academics,' Ngoni growled in support. 'They use elitism as a false rite of passage into a haven of self-importance.'

He said he didn't believe the social sciences could attain the same objective status as the natural and physical sciences, and that art, for instance, had its own laws and rigour but if the tools from physics were used to try and test and appreciate these laws they would be ridiculed. Bias was as natural to history and literature as were different people's interpretation of the same painting. Art creators and educators therefore shouldn't pretend that they had no effect on their subjects since none of their finished products was free from bias. Perhaps the only way to avoid pretence was to build the bias in, and reveal it.

She remained silent and he didn't know whether he had made sense. In her company, everything was unpredictable and disquieting. Perhaps it was because they had never been alone together. The first time that conversation almost came about – two days ago – she had kept her distance and had behaved as if his presence brought her discomfiture. They had gone shopping downtown with Jack and his fiancée, Carmaine, a pretty but docile kind of girl, who talked very little and always held Jack's hand as if for support and security. Jack had decided to watch rugby live on TV as the Aussies played the Springboks, and Carmaine went with him. Wolfgang, the German student, excused himself to make a phone call and so Ngoni was left alone with Katrina. He wanted to buy brandy and cigarettes and she wanted some wine and cigarettes. She didn't talk to him. When they got into the liquor store, there were two women there – one Indian and the other white. He spent time choosing the brandy; from the wine shelves across the store, Katrina gave no hint that she was with him – not even a minute sign of recognition.

The Indian saleswoman left the till and approached him cautiously.

'Can I help?' She looked him over with a concealed sneer on her face.

'No thanks, I'm okay.' Ngoni gave her a cursory glance and no more.

Standing there, watching him calmly taking time to read the contents on the bottle labels as if to spite her, smacked the sneer off her plump face. She felt foolish, but couldn't just leave. A calculated nod from the other woman who was monitoring the scene from behind the counter seemed to free her from the spot, and she waddled away.

Ngoni picked a château and a packet of Peter Stuyvesant cigarettes and turned to pay at the counter. That was when he noticed that Katrina was no longer in the shop. At the till, the white woman served him with civility and a smile that anybody would have interpreted as most welcoming.

Katrina was leaning against a pillar in the mall. She hadn't bought anything from the liquor store. Ngoni walked towards her, but stopped a few paces away, leaving her some space. He felt that she disliked him. The way she had abruptly disappeared from the liquor store made him feel unsure, uncomfortable.

'I want to go home – let's call Jack to drive us back,' she suddenly said, nervously twiddling her fingers. Home was Jack's house. Jack was South African and he rented out rooms to international students at the local university. Ngoni had come to exhibit his work and was staying in the country for two weeks. The organisers of his exhibition thought it would be ideal for Ngoni to stay in a home of sorts that would give him a family atmosphere.

In the city valley below, the Durban lights sparkled all colours, trying to tame the sprawling expanse of night. On the hill across the phallic university tower was a pinnacle of bright luminosity challenging a surrounding darkness.

'I hate those pigs for treating you like that in that shop,' Katrina burst out. 'That's why I didn't buy a thing from there. Their quiet bigotry shrieked out loud in all that silence. They had no right to do that to you. The sassy bitches!'

Her outburst took him unawares and he didn't know what to make of it.

'And I hated you for buying from such lousy idiots.'

There was an intensity in her voice; a kind of fervour, even in the most ordinary thing she did or said, that at times left Ngoni overawed and speechless. Ngoni had come to know Katrina over the past few days while they stayed in Jack's house, and he was intrigued by the way the young woman seemed to do everything with passion. The mere dragging on a cigarette – meant to be an act of relaxation – could make an altogether different impression and expose her inner tensions and agitation. At times, she could talk as if not really caring whether she was listened to or not; talking in order to vent that tension that would have constricted her soul, baring it all. Like the way she casually said all her front teeth were false and were now in bad shape. They needed changing, but she didn't have the money since she was living on government loan. She had lost her teeth and had broken her nose in one of those many gruesome street fights against skinheads in Oslo streets. The skins were on one of their xenophobic streaks in the neighbourhood and her group decided to 'speak' to them in the only 'language' that they seemed to understand.

'That day you wouldn't have had the guts to look at me twice,' she said. 'But we beat up the morons and they stayed out of our neighbourhood for a while. When I was recuperating, this old lady in a wheelchair, a compatriot of my grandpa's, visited us. Just to see me. She clasped my hand in her shaky, gnarled ones, and said, "Young lady I hear you're doing good works. Don't let the dogs get away with murder – kick them out of our midst. We too played our part during our times, and I still have the resolve to stand up and do it again if nobody else commits themselves. We stood up, even during Hitler's time."'

'She certainly meant what she said and I felt proud and humbled in spite of the painful stitches on my face. It was a spectacle, with my grandpa standing next to us and hissing quietly in his tremulous voice, "Don't just beat them, kill the bastards. Crash the damn vermin. They don't deserve to be on this earth. Kill the dogs! Don't just hurt them!"

'You see, grandpa has never forgiven the Nazis for invading our country. He was part of the internal resistance and lost several close friends. He has no respect for any type of chauvinism. Yet the local liberal press painted my group with the same brush as the skins, rapping us for degenerating into the same savagery as the dogs and bringing violence into the streets. We argued that we weren't bringing violence but returning it to its originators, and it would only cease if they stopped race attacks and treated others as humans. They should learn to take what they are fond of giving. One lousy paper had the audacity to expose its own narrow-mindedness by stating that our clashes had nothing to do with xenophobia or racism, since the fighting parties both largely consisted of white youths. For them it was a skirmish between spoilt anarchist skins on one side, and my group on the other side were labelled as punks with nothing better to do. The paper then started preaching about proper socialisation of youths so that they don't become misfits. What crap!'

Ngoni stared at the tower and back at Katrina. Her face was flushed and she had smoked three cigarettes without a break. Her hand was continuously smoothing her long blonde braided hair. Cherry lips and high cheekbones made her look like a cherub in the candlelight.

'You're very beautiful in the night. I feel like touching your face,' he said suddenly.

She didn't answer; nor did she give an inkling of encouragement. He didn't touch her.

The French door to the balcony creaked and Wolfgang, the German student studying architecture on an exchange programme in South Africa, walked in. He had a wide grin and a mischievous glint in his eye that said, I know you guys have taken a liking to each other and you are certainly up to something steamy.

'You want to fuck the night up screwing the booze?' he said in what was supposed to be a singsong voice.

Some people think that to get along with others, or to lighten up the atmosphere and appear carefree and easy-going, they ought to make silly sexual innuendos now and then, and Wolfgang was one such person. On this instant, his stupid grin was just too painful for Ngoni and Katrina to bear, and they wished he would spare them the ordeal of putting up with him. It was the wrong timing for banal, unsavoury remarks. They barely managed to be civil enough to hide their unease and annoyance.

'You heard that the US and the Israelis walked out of the World Anti-racism Conference today?' Ngoni asked, looking straight at Katrina. 'And there is talk that some Scandinavian countries are also supporting the action for Israel to be removed from the agenda.'

'It's pathetic,' she said wringing her hands. 'I wonder what dullard can't see that Zionism is apartheid. The Israelis mustn't have the cheek to accuse anti-Zionists of anti-Semitism. These are two different issues. There is a marked difference between where Jewish identity and Judaist faith ends, and where narrow political nationalism starts.'

'It's like confusing religion and an ethnic community,' Ngoni agreed. 'Not every Jew is a Zionist and vice versa.'

'Sick politics has wrongfully used the Bible to justify some of the worst moral crimes in history. Quite often, they use the myth of the white man's burden of civilising the dark primitive other. It's all a sham. Zionists babble and rave about being people of the book and the light of nations, yet they trample on other people's rights. They are nothing but bloody jackals snatching food from the mouths of babes. It would be shameful if my country took the villain's side to please Uncle Sam.' She was wringing her fingers.

'This is about land and birthright and someone is just being greedy,' said Ngoni. He shifted to look at Wolfgang who was moodily puffing at a cigarette, feeling snubbed and ignored. 'Wolfgang what's your country's position at the Race Conference?'

The outburst was just stunning: 'I don't want to talk politics, no, no. I just don't want!'

Wolfgang hastily stamped out his cigarette and stormed back into the house, leaving the two with wry smiles on their faces. Wolfgang had experienced that strange but direct sense of intrusion never expressed but somehow implicit – and when Ngoni finally decided to acknowledge his presence he felt embarrassed at being exposed.

Ngoni realised at once the frature he had created with his seemingly innocent question. Earlier that afternoon, he too had nearly stormed out of his own art exhibition because of some secret frustration that took root and grew inside him with the occasional careless remark passed by the art viewers.

'Where are you from?' one viewer asked.

He told her.

'Oh, Rhodesia!'

'Zimbabwe,' he repeated with equal haughtiness.

His piece, 'A Visit to Great Grandpa's Grave' at Mr Dupont's Farm, was on display. It showed through an extremely sensitive use of dense oily colours, the entangled unkempt foliage surrounding a small mound of stones on an anthill and a silhouette of a man; it wasn't clear whether he was arriving or leaving the scene.

'Brilliant, just exquisite,' another exclaimed. 'What intuitive insight into the dark and mysterious.'

'Just look at the visitor's torn shirt blowing off his thin body like an angel's wings!'

'It has a surrealistic aura. The gloomy ambience is palpable.'

'True, you can actually feel the mood.'

'Eerie but spiritual, visiting a grave at night.'

'It's creepy, you know.'

'You said the artist is from where?'

The gallery attendant told them once again.

'Oh, a nice country gone to rot. My nephew once lived in Salisbury, you know. He had the good sense to leave for Australia a couple of years ago. Nothing good ever comes out of African countries. Thank God our rainbow nation will never come to that – we won't allow it. We South Africans have good sense.' The old lady finished, already walking away.

Others presumed he had come to stay, or even to set up fort here, like many that were escaping the hunger, bickering and despair that plagued his country. A typical three-way conversation:

'You're now based here?'

'No. I'm only here for two weeks.'

'The press here says the bastards are gagging free expression?'

'Yes, there have been excesses by both government and journalists.'

'The press should have no restrictions whatsoever.'

'The bastard doesn't want the world to know he is a racist grabbing land from good farmers.'

'Honestly, it's rather difficult. But the land problem is real.'

That was not juicy enough. They wanted something spectacular and newsy.

'You can actually work from there?'

'The bastard Mugabe is a gay-basher. Hasn't your "gay lovers" painting brought you trouble?'

'No. I paint what I want. I'm not restricted.'

Not sensational enough again.

'You can make it here. The market is quite understanding and receptive.'

'You should set up camp here.'

'It's better that I visit occasionally.'

'Oh! I thought standards were better here. And the troubles back there in Zim ... ' There was genuine consternation in the tone, as if it were simply crazy for Ngoni to prefer it any other way.

Ngoni felt his belly turn and he went out to walk the city streets, away from the high culture where his works were obviously misplaced. The way they tried to patronise and pamper him was so infuriating, especially when he was aware that truckloads of his countrymen were forcibly repatriated every day from South Africa because they were mainly illegal unskilled immigrants competing with locals for menial jobs. Again, being a recipient of alms and uncalled-for pity was just too demeaning and he would never feel apologetic about what was happening back home. Facts and secrets were obscured depending from which vantage point a person decided to look. They didn't just one day wake up and say, 'Bye-bye Ian Smith!' and then start killing each other and plundering. They went through a process of change, admittedly one full of blunders, erring, greed and a shirking of responsibility; but all *that* was nothing that couldn't be gotten over. Indeed, what was transpiring could entail a new beginning, a new realisation that nothing can be taken for granted in the same way that promises need fulfilment. What he couldn't take was people drilling it into him at every turn how worthless and doomed everything was, nullifying a certain vital essence in the whole purpose of life. He rejected the narrow images of either being an accomplice or a victim in the unfolding process. What he hated most was strangers talking patronisingly and fervently about Zimbabwe – strangers who often were not genuinely interested in listening to him speak his own mind about the conditions in his own country. They had pre-established opinions and positions, and they only wanted a confirmation of those ideas.

At the gallery, the two-week exhibition was not much fun, because he disliked attending to the viewers. He painted more for his own pleasure and merely shrugged if other people seemed to be impressed by them. Some paintings he made to satisfy some idiosyncrasy within him, others he made to relate to his surroundings, and yet others were for sheer fun or just to pull the stiff, sniffing nose of the overly serious critic. The starting point was purely himself, and everything else followed after.

Amongst his collection was 'The Pit Latrine' – a painting of a shadowy reddish form of a man from the waist downwards, standing pissing with legs wide apart. On the ground between the legs, lies a torso facing upward with eyes closed as if in sleep. The mouth is exaggeratedly big and wide, overshadowing all other features of the face; an irregular yawning hole, something like the teapot-shaped map of his country, with jagged edges into which piss is falling. 'Tom Kissing Paul in Uncle Bob's Village' has two gay lovers in denims and T-shirts embracing and kissing in a crowded city mall. The faces of passers-by and by lookers-on in the painting show different attitudes and feelings toward the spectacle, ranging from total oblivion, offhand dismissal, surprise, scorn, matter-of-fact acceptance, 'shame-on-you keep-it-to-yourselves' irritation, 'whom-do-you-want-to-show' rebuke, 'pth-it's-just-nauseous-and-vile' disgust, and 'cool-it-fellows-welcome-into-the-open' approval.

As he thought of the paintings and the exhibition, he was glad that Katrina had not yet seen any of his works and had not referred to them in any way; she took him for what he was without the self-consciousness of hosting an artist.

She was silent again, rapt in thought. His eyes followed hers to the luminous varsity tower.

After a long spell of silence she stirred and spoke: 'I wish I could see Dumi again. You see, he was like a father to me back in Dar es Salaam after mum and dad divorced. I just want to see him for old times' sake, you know.'

Ngoni knew whom Katrina meant: Dumi, her mother's lover, and a temporary surrogate 'stepfather' who she had spoken fondly of the previous evening. The man only returned home from exile five years after majority rule because he was ostensibly afraid of being re-united with his wife. When he finally came down he promised to return to her mother. He wanted to settle a few things with his family, he said; but he never returned.

'Mother followed to see what was up. She made contact with his mates in the new government. The friends came back to her and said that his wife was really mad and wouldn't let go of him. "If she hears you're here she'll kill you," they told her. And against everybody's advice she went to the location and found him at a shebeen. He was down and out and hitting the bottle quite hard. There was a scene at the shebeen when this stranger walked in, looked at mum, and swore, "Rotten fucking white trash!" Dumi jumped up but the man swiftly pulled out a gun. Dumi stood there shaking with rage, and mum had to pull him back to the sofa. The gunman guffawed something much more vulgar and walked out. The place certainly wasn't doing Dumi any good but he refused to return to Dar es Salaam. Mum couldn't understand why,' Katrina said, and she took a swig from her glass.

Dumi was partly the reason why she had chosen to do her studies here. She wanted to see him, at least for old times' sake, but she lacked the resolve to go and look for him. Perhaps she was hesitant to go and look for him because she didn't want to be disillusioned by seeing the wreck that he had become after failing to secure a meaningful role to carve out a purposeful future in the new dispensation. Sitting there and watching him waste himself on drink was just unbearable, as the last time she had seen him he was strong and confident of himself and his role in his country's future.

'You know, even back in Dar es Salaam he used to drink – but not that aimlessly,' Katrina said, with something akin to an appeal in her eyes. 'I remember asking about the scars on his arms and chest. He wouldn't tell but would reach for the beer and gulp it all down. I stopped asking.'

'Freedom can be dissatisfying,' Ngoni said, sipping at his brandy.

Yes freedom – that bittersweet, paltry residue of the euphoria of majority rule, international debts to repay, rising prices and falling wages, food shortages, concomitant floods and droughts that caused misery and hunger. One had to munch and savour it with caution, lest you choked over the grit of it. Even here, the signs of the times were already present: street kids begging at city crossroads, indigents dragging pushcarts uphill, prostitutes murdering diplomats in seedy Durban hotels.

'Yeah, freedom without profit,' Katrina sighed from the depth of her heart. 'The kind of freedom I saw in Mozambique, where there is more poverty now than there was in wartime. The only difference is that Castle Lager and small useless gadgets from South Africa are easily available from street vendors. And sure, there are also the latest car models and hi-fi's as signs of progress.'

Ngoni expected her to go into another tirade against the IMF and how its policies were a new form of colonialism in poor countries, or how her country would never be hoodwinked into using the Euro and getting drowned into a dubious union where bigotry had not yet died away. He expected her to say something more, but she kept quiet. Her face was tilted at a haughty angle and he thought she looked sexy and beautiful, with her pouting mouth slowly softening, her skin exuding a fresh hue in the candlelight. She looked like she was yielding to the spirit of the night; she was the candle melting and flowing down, only to coagulate anew in unexpected new vistas on the candlestand. And the passion and intensity of it all was what drew him to her – it was also what scared and repelled him. She was so transparent, as if she had nothing to conceal, and all her acts were a perpetual exposure of all the secrets and intimacies of her life – yet after every revelation, she became even more intriguing. Hers was as openness that was possible only for those people who are capable of giving all without reservation in whatever they did. It was a generosity of self and soul that spurned all half measures; for her, it was either all or none at all. Her outpouring of words and emotions could be as soothing as cool spring waters in a desert, yet the same waters had the potential to scald with the wrath and fury of hellfire. She could devour one with her passion – and it scared Ngoni. He wanted a communion of souls that would leave him with a face and an identity; he did not want to be drowned in the abyss of her kind of love. But he desired her still.

'You're beautiful,' he said, softly caressing her face.

96

Her full lips parted a little as if yielding, inviting. Ngoni stood up and went to sit on the armrest of her chair. He started stroking her hair.

As his hand slid down her neck, she started giggling in smooth soft jerks like a reed in water. He stopped and stared at her, unsure.

'Sorry,' she said, through titters. 'I'm just thinking of this guy who tried to jump me in Oslo. I pulled his dick off his scrotum and bashed his head in.'

Ngoni froze like that for some time, and then he stood up from the chair's armrest.

'Maybe we should go and rest,' he said. A new vague fear was flowing in him, and he simply wouldn't take a risk.

She waited a moment to see what his next move was. When he picked up his packet of cigarettes, she said something that sounded like an apology and walked after him into the main house.

He saw her next in the kitchen, sometime the following afternoon, preparing a cup of coffee.

'When did you wake up?' he asked.

'I didn't sleep,' she replied.

'What's the plan today?'

'Nothing.'

She was in a sulky mood, and her tone and mien weren't welcoming; he felt she didn't want to talk to him. She shuffled past and left him standing by the doorway.

DEVILS AT THE DOOR

By Brian James

The chain on the front gate rattled, shattering the early-morning stillness. Even before my younger sister, Olayinka, started to rouse me I knew it was them.

'Ayo, wake up! The rebels are here.'

Her voice was low, strained in a way that I had never heard before. I opened my eyes and sat up in the darkness of the small guest room of our two-storey home. My family and I had taken refuge there since the rebels had stormed into Freetown, announcing their arrival in the capital city with tremendous gunfire.

We had been in that little room for almost a week, trying to be as inconspicuous as possible, using almost no light and moving from the room only when it was absolutely necessary. It had taken only a few days for the inevitable to happen. The rebels, whose mind-numbing brutality I had only read and heard about, had turned their attention to the large house on the hill.

Intermittent flashes of torchlight penetrated the room's only window and danced on the wall.

My father was peering out of the window and trying to hide behind the curtain at the same time. My mother stood on tiptoe behind him, in an effort to see over his shoulder. My sister sat on her mattress with her arms around her knees, her eyes shining brightly.

I had to see this for myself. Creeping over to join my parents at the window, I caught a glimpse of several shadowy figures pacing outside our front gate with two or three torches. It must have been about six o' clock in the morning, but it was still so dark it may as well have been midnight. At the best of times electricity was scarce. Since the infiltration of the rebel forces, Freetown had been plunged into permanent darkness.

The chain rattled more impatiently. '*Una opin dis gate! If una allow wi for opin am wisef una all de die!*' one of them screamed. (Open this gate at once! If you allow us to open it ourselves, all of you in there will die!)

To say that my breath froze in my throat with fear or that I felt my insides shrivel up with terror would be, quite simply, untrue. Oddly, I felt nothing but calm curiosity as they shook the padlocked chain again and again. I couldn't have been less scared if it had been the bread-man making his daily rounds.

'Wait, gentlemen, I'm coming to open it,' my father suddenly shouted to them. Still in his pyjama trousers and without stopping to put on his slippers, he went into the guest sitting room, unlocked the front door and disappeared into the early-morning darkness. The rebels' torch beams glided over my father's bare torso as he walked quickly toward them and unlocked the chain.

The gate creaked open. One by one they strolled casually into our front yard. I moved to the front door to get a better look. I counted about nine of them. They were armed with rifles, knives and hand-grenades. One of them carried a battered paint can that gave off a strong smell of petrol. Three of them were in combat fatigues. The rest were in dirty worn clothes. Wild-haired and filthy, their eyes stood out from their dark faces, shiny and glazed. Almost all of them had plasters on the sides of their heads. I had heard from somewhere that rebels cut themselves, applied cocaine to the wounds and covered them up with plasters. It was supposed to turn them into sadistic killing machines.

From the onset it was easy for even a non-military person like myself to see that the group lacked any military order whatsoever. With their bedraggled appearances and languid gaits, they reminded me of a sorry pack of hyenas. My father came with them up the porch steps.

My mother, who had come to join me at the front door, tried to be brave.

'I greet you all in the name of Jesus.' Each word was less audible than the last as they filed past us into the sitting-room.

My father continued to babble to them in English. I wondered why my father was not speaking krio, our lingua franca, to them. As I expected, it aroused their suspicions. One of them, a man with a slight build and a mean glare suddenly rounded on him.

'*Una na Ghanaman dem*?' he asked threateningly.

If we had been Ghanaians, I would probably not be alive to tell this story. The ECOMOG peacekeeping troops that aided the government forces in stopping the rebels from reducing the country to a smoking pile of debris consisted mainly of Nigerian and Ghanaian soldiers. The rebels therefore looked on their civilian compatriots living in Sierra Leone as enemies. Some Sierra Leoneans in other parts of the country were killed because the rebels thought that they were Nigerians or Ghanaians.

'No, I'm a Sierra Leonean like you,' my father replied quickly. I began to find his English-speaking maddening. How would they believe we were Sierra Leoneans when he wasn't speaking our language?

The rebel's forefinger hovered over the trigger of his weapon. That seemed to make my father realise that he was not dealing with an intellectual like himself but with a thug from the bush. He started to speak rapidly in Krio and I released my breath, which I hadn't realised I was holding. It was not a good idea to be misunderstood by rebels.

'How many of you are here?' asked the rebel, whom I decided must be the Commando.

'Four of us,' my father told him. 'My wife, my two children and myself.'

'Four of you? I only see three.'

My sister, who until that moment had been hiding in the guest room and obviously listening to what was going on, came out and stood in the doorway. At that point, I must confess, it did not occur to me how much danger a young girl was in with nine rebels staring at her in her nightie. It is only now that the thought makes me shudder.

The Commando turned back to my father. 'Who lives upstairs?'

'It's the same house,' my father replied. 'There's no one up there.'

My parents had decided that with all the bullets and rocket-propelled grenades whizzing through the air, upstairs was not safe. We had moved downstairs to the guest apartment in case stray bullets pierced through the zinc roof or smashed through windows. There were three rooms down there. The four of us had occupied one of them. The adjacent room was used for cooking and keeping things we frequently used. The sitting-room was empty.

'Search everywhere,' the Commando barked sharply to his men.

For those not acquainted with rebel-speak, what he actually meant was: 'Strip this house of anything that may be useful or valuable to us.'

The men eagerly moved forward, peering first into the bedroom and then the cooking room. We knew better than to ask exactly what they were 'searching' for. My parents went with them, while my sister and I stayed in the sitting-room. I heard the Commando threatening to kill my father if he did not give them all the dollars and pounds sterling in the house. There were muffled negotiations. Whatever my father gave him he must have found satisfactory because it was not long before they all trooped out of the room. Some of them were pocketing things that they had picked up from the bedroom, and others carried several black plastic bags in which we had stuffed clothes, food and personal effects the night before in case we had had to flee.

The Commando left two of the rebels downstairs to watch us while he and the others forced my father to lead them upstairs. I followed one of the rebels, a tall muscular fellow, into the cooking room. There was nothing valuable in there. He shined his torch first on one thing, then another. Then he turned around and saw me standing in the doorway. He trained his light on me and peered closely.

'This one looks like a *kamajor*,' he said loudly.

The other rebel, who was in the sitting room, either did not hear or was too busy going through our possessions to care.

The *kamajors* were the local paramilitary forces, originally village hunters, who had joined forces with the government and ECOMOG troops to fight the rebels. It was said that they were much feared by the rebels because of their feral nature, their astounding knowledge of bush warfare, and their sheer numbers. They dressed in animal skins, underwent frightful initiation rites and rituals and generally looked like people you did not want to have a disagreement with. They were a real asset to the pro-government forces, and were a thorn in the flesh of the rebels who killed them on sight.

I look nothing like a feral village hunter now, and I looked even less like one when I was in my mid-teens. So hearing that was like a punch in the stomach. I could only stare at my accuser in disbelief.

My mother, having heard, came running. It took more than a little convincing to make the fellow believe that I was nothing of the sort. In an act of desperation she moved her face close to mine so that he could see the resemblance that everyone who saw the two of us together never failed to remark on.

'You see, he's my son,' she said.

The rebel pointed his torch in our faces, staring first at mine, then at my mother's.

'Oh, yes,' he said. Rearranging his weapon on his shoulder, he moved past.

The other one who had stayed downstairs – a thin haggard looking shadow of a person in dirty combat fatigues – was sitting on a couch in the sitting room, busily poking bony feet into my favourite pair of trainers, which I had left in a corner. His own scuffed, moth-eaten boots lay on the floor beside him. He gave up when he saw me watching him.

'These are not my size; they're too big,' he said regretfully, pushing them aside.

The ones who'd been upstairs to 'search' the house were coming back downstairs from the main living quarters, and were talking loudly. One of them was carrying two half-empty crates of drinks, one in each hand.

Another was wearing an expensive T-shirt of mine that I had bought only a couple of weeks earlier. I took it all in, not saying anything. There was nothing to say. A voice growled suddenly in my ear, startling me.

'If the Commando tells you to do anything, don't do it.'

I turned to see a short stocky rebel, who looked vaguely like a teacher at my secondary school, staring intently up at me.

'What?' I said even though I had heard him quite clearly.

He gestured with the barrel of his rifle at the Commando, who was trying to decide which of the ornaments on the bookcase to pocket. He decided on all of them.

'Look at him,' the short rebel continued. 'He is just a common thief … not even our real Commando. He just joined us after our Commando was killed. Don't do anything he tells you to do,' he repeated and marched away.

The Commando saw me and approached me. I wondered how much he had heard of what had just been said.

'Don't you have any shoes that could fit me?' he asked. Apparently he had heard nothing at all.

I stared at the shoes he had on, if they could be called shoes at all. They were more like bits of cloth, leather and cardboard held together by bits of string.

'I've got another pair upstairs,' I told him. 'Maybe those will fit you'

I did not actually want him to have my boots but I did want to go upstairs and find out what was going on with my parents. I had not seen them come back down with the rebels.

'Go and show them to me,' he said.

I led him up the stairs, hoping he would not notice that the boots I wanted to give him had gone out of style and were not in the best of shape. My bedroom was strangely tidy. The rebels must have passed over it. The Commando followed me, looking more out of place than a vulture in a chicken's nest. As soon as he saw the boots, he grabbed them, plonked himself on the bed and began to undo the bits and pieces on his feet.

I heard my parents' voices out in the corridor as they made their way down the stairs and I wished I had not brought the rebel upstairs with me. At that moment he stood up and began to walk around. The boots were several sizes too big for him, but he seemed satisfied. He began to take stock of the room. I groaned inwardly as he snatched my pair of sunglasses from the headboard of my bed. He put them on and had the audacity to ask me how he looked! I just nodded, thinking that he was the most ridiculous spectacle I had ever seen. He found my baseball cap and put it on backwards. If he had been on one of our local comedy shows I would have laughed. But he was an armed rebel, at liberty to do whatever popped up into his sick, drugged mind – so I did not laugh. He walked to my wardrobe and opened it.

'You must understand why I'm doing this,' he said, flipping through my Tupac and Reebok T-shirts. 'I've been in the bush for seven years, and in all that time I've not had much to wear. Look at what I'm wearing. I've had these for a really long time.'

I did not care that his clothes were filthy, tattered and smelly. I did care that he was taking them off and tossing them onto my bed so that he could put on my clothes. I heard footsteps running up the stairs. Two more rebels walked into the room. Their Commando was trying to find a way to keep my jeans from slipping down his waist. As I expected, they too went to the open wardrobe and began to grab things. In no time at all, my room looked like sales time at a department store. The frenzied rush lasted only a few minutes; once they were satisfied (the Commando had found a piece of string to keep the jeans on) they all trooped out, leaving me to stare at the debris of filthy rags they left strewn over my bed and the floor.

I went back downstairs and found them taking stock of all the things they had collected. Two of them almost got into a fight about how much money my father had given them. Their Commando snapped at them to be quiet and ordered them to start carrying the loot outside.

The rebel who had come down earlier carrying two crates of drinks saw me and shoved one of the crates into my arms.

'Carry this for us,' he said, motioning me outside.

The sun was beginning to rise and I saw in the compound a small group of three woebegone women and about five frightened little children who were sitting on the ground under the guard of a dark, fierce-looking rebel whom I had not seen before. He must have arrived with them while we were inside with the other rebels.

'Go and stand over there and wait for us,' he told me, pointing to the women and children. 'When we are going, you go with us.'

I did as he said and put the crate down next to the silent, waiting group. One of the stories went that one of the rebels' favourite methods of abduction was to get people to carry things for them. Once they were many miles away from their home, they forced hard drugs into them, shoved guns into their hands and ordered them to join in the fighting as rebels.

I still had on only the shorts I slept in. The chilly morning wind swept over my naked torso. I shivered. I grew tense as the group that had been in the house trooped outside with my parents and my sister. A feeling of numbness came over me. There I was, looking at my family, probably for the last time, but I still felt no fear. It was all so surreal. It was as if I was standing outside my body like a stunned onlooker, watching events unfold.

I heard the Commando warn my father: 'As soon as we leave, you should all get white pieces of cloth to tie around your heads and go outside to demonstrate for peace. I shall kill anyone I find in the house when I return.' My parents and sister went back inside to get the cloths.

The Commando turned to his men. 'Let's go round to the back.'

They all stomped off after him to the back of our house to see what we had there. I imagined they would be disappointed. All they would find was our houseboy, huddled in the boy's quarters with his wife, and our gardener, also keeping a low profile in his little hut with his wife and young daughter.

I shifted from one foot to the other. I shivered again. This time it wasn't so much the cold as the fact that our 'keeper' was now staring intently at me. I stared back. He must have been in his early twenties, handsome, dark-skinned with a strong, chiselled face.

'Do you know,' he began conversationally, 'I have been in the bush for almost ten years? Since the war started, I've killed, raped, cut off hands and feet, torn out ears and noses. I do these things with no hesitation. I've also drunk blood and eaten human flesh. Veeeeery tasty. Mortal man's beef contains oil, you know. It's better than chicken. When you roast it, the oil drips from your hands. You should try it one day.'

My eyes went to a large pink plaster sticking to the side of his face. Ten years of hard drugs applied into raw flesh had had their effect. The man was a complete nutcase.

'Do you go to school?' he asked me.

I nodded.

'I don't believe you.'

I found that so ridiculous that I smiled. 'I'm not lying.'

Silence. Then: 'I've never been to school but my knowledge is far greater than anything you will ever know.'

I wasn't going to argue with that, so I kept my mouth shut. He began pacing in front of our little group, and then stopped as suddenly as he had begun.

'I say,' he said to me, 'aren't you feeling cold? Why don't you ask your mama to bring you a shirt?'

'I'm okay,' I told him.

'No, no,' he insisted, 'you'll catch cold if you don't put on a shirt.'

He turned to the porch. My mother had come out with an old white bed sheet.

'Mama,' he called out, 'why don't you go and bring him a shirt so he won't catch cold?'

My mother must have been surprised at the rebel's thoughtfulness, but she hurried inside. Minutes later she came out again with a striped shirt that belonged to my father.

'Go and get it,' he told me.

I didn't know what to do. The rebel saw my hesitation and grinned.

'Go on, I won't hurt you. Go and take it.'

I walked across the yard, took the shirt from my mother and put it on. I went back to my place by the group. The rebel nodded and began to pace again. My mind must have drifted at that moment because the next thing I knew, I was being brought to sudden reality by a shout from the rebel.

My father was standing on the porch facing the rebel. My mother was nowhere to be seen. I did not know where my sister was.

'Pa, I'm going to kill you for your family,' the rebel informed my father matter-of-factly. He slid his weapon from off his shoulder and held it in both hands. My father stood immobile, as if etched in cold stone. The rebel began to raise the rifle and then stopped in mid-air, turned and looked at me.

'Is that your father?' he asked, gesturing at him with his head. I nodded. He continued staring at me. I stared back.

'Because of you, I won't kill him,' he said calmly.

He hung the gun back on his shoulder and began his pacing once more. That was when I began to realise that we were not alone in our troubles. The self-confessed cannibal had been in a position to kill my father but he had not. God was with us. I must have known it in my spirit from the beginning. It was why I felt no fear.

The rebels who had gone round the back returned. Our houseboy, Mara, was with them. Head and shoulders taller than all but one of the rebels, he was laughing and chatting with them. I wondered whether I was the only one who noticed the strain in his voice.

'Mummy,' he addressed my mother who had come to join my father on the porch.

'These are my friends. This one,' he said, indicating to the one who was as tall as him, 'was at the barracks.'

'Mara, please ask them not to take Ayo away,' my mother pleaded.

'Ah, mummy, don't worry,' he said expansively, like he was in charge. 'Ayo is not going anywhere. Ayo, you go inside,' he said to me, 'I'll take the crate for them.'

I did not need a second bidding. I left the crate and went to join my family on the porch. The pacing rebel did not appear to notice.

As if to once more assert his authority, the Commando reminded us of his earlier warning about the strips of white cloth and the demonstration for peace, before leading his men and their group of abductees, which now included Mara, out of the compound. The four of us went back in; no one said anything. My father closed the door, but did not bother to turn the key. Strangely, it seemed that now we had seen the rebels face-to-face there was nothing left to dread. We had weathered our worst imaginings.

Back in our little room, we discovered that the rebels had taken not only my father's reading glasses, his small radio and my mother's wedding and engagement rings, which had been on the table by their bedside, they had also taken all the black plastic bags that were filled with our possessions I realised then that almost all my things were gone. However, it did not make any difference to me. If something like that had happened a few days earlier, I would have been really angry. But after what I had just gone through, they mattered nothing to me. Being alive and being with my family were worth more than anything.

Realising that the danger was not yet over, my father went upstairs and collected all our passports and other important documents, which he put into an envelope. It was a good thing no one had decided to put them in the black plastic bags, otherwise the thieves would have gone off with them as well. My father also had some naira notes left over from his last visit to Nigeria. He set fire to these in case the rebels came back, saw, and concluded that we were really Nigerians.

Sometime later, my mother was tidying our bedroom when she gave a cry of joy and disbelief. She had lifted the mattress on the floor that I slept on when she saw an envelope. Inside was forty pounds sterling, which she had put in one of the black bags the night before. It must have fallen out and been kicked under the mattress during the rebels' raid.

The odds of that happening were almost non-existent. All I can say is that God came to our rescue once again. My father gave thanks for the miracle, put the money with the other documents, and hid them.

'What do we do if the rebels come back?' I asked, thinking of the Commando's parting threat.

My mother tore the old white bed sheet she had found into strips and gave one to each of us.

'We won't go out yet, but keep them near you,' she told us. 'If they come back, we'll pretend we were just getting ready to leave.'

There was nothing else to do after that, except to occupy ourselves with anything that would stop us from thinking of what might happen next. My mother put some eggs to boil on the fire in the cooking room and told my sister and I to continue tidying up the room in which we slept. While that went on, I discovered the pair of jeans I had put on the night before when we had thought we would have to flee. There they were, hanging conspicuously on the only chair in the room. They were Levi's, and I just could not understand how the rebels had missed them. To add to my delight, I found ten thousand leones in one of the pockets. I gave the money to my mother to add to everything else.

Just then, we heard the sound of the gate opening. I rushed to the window. It was Mara. He came bounding up the steps as my father threw the front door open.

'What happened? How did you escape?' we asked, crowding around him.

He laughed heartily. There was relief in his voice.

'Ah, these rebels,' he began, still laughing. 'They are all cowards. As we were going down the road the ECOMOG Alpha jet passed over us. You should have seen them. They started running in different directions. So I just flung the carton into the bush along the side of the road and came back.'

We sat together in the small room listening to the sounds of incessant gunfire outside. For some reason they had increased twofold over the past half hour, turning into a cyclone of thunderous noise. Realising that it was no longer safe for Mara and the gardener to remain in their flimsy quarters at the back of the house, my father told them and their wives to join us in the house. They pushed the furniture in the sitting-room aside, and spread sleeping-mats on the floor. As time went on, a security guard from next door, a Lebanese man from down the road with his family, and a woman whose house had been burnt down the night before, came to seek refuge in our house.

By the end of the day, our little hide-out, in which there had been only four of us, held fourteen people. That night, the floor of the sitting-room was littered with sleeping people, many of whom I had seen before but had never spoken to.

The night passed uneventfully, as did the rest of the next day. We expected a group of rebels to wander in at any moment, but none came. We kept our strips of white cloth near us in case we were required to use them. Whenever we heard shooting, especially close by, we kept as far from the windows as possible.

The four of us remained in our little room. My sister and I found an old set of seven books, *Chronicles of Narnia*, written by C Lewis. They were books that we had read many times over but never tired of. *The Last Battle* was my favourite. We spent the hours reading. In the sitting-room, someone had found a Ludo board. There was a sound of rattling dice and hushed voices as games went on.

Everyone was settled and comfortable – except Mara. Used to being out and about, the houseboy wandered around the house despite warnings to stay put. Everywhere he went, he moved with his little radio. He spent a lot of time upstairs. Every so often, he would come downstairs and relay snippets of news to us that he had heard on the radio. He would also give us a rundown of the level of damage to the city from the view he had up there.

It must have been a little before six o'clock when we heard him bounding down the stairs from my bedroom, where he had been peeping out as usual, while listening to the BBC programme,' Focus on Africa'.

'ECOMOG *don kam*!' He was jumping up and down, shouting hysterically.

Everybody leapt to their feet. Those who had been sleeping woke up from their troubled dreams. We were all talking at once. 'Where are they? How do you know? When did they come? Who told you?'

'They've just come,' he told us. He was almost incoherent with relief. He was, after all, a man with a death threat hanging over his head and the arrival of ECOMOG fighting forces was a reprieve he could not have imagined.

'They've come in an armoured tank,' he informed us. 'You can see them from Ayo's bedroom window.'

I rushed up to my bedroom and looked out. Sure enough, there was an enormous dark-green tank stationed imposingly in the middle of the street. I rushed downstairs again to inform everyone that Mara's eyes had not deceived him. My mother, my father, Olayinka and a few others went up to see as well. Just then a disembodied voice came through a hand-held loudspeaker:

'All civilians out! All civilians out!'

We were suddenly plunged into confusion. This could very easily be a trap. Even though I had actually seen the tank with my own eyes and I knew that the rebels did not possess anything as sophisticated as that, I could not bring myself to obey the voice. Where were the rebels, anyway?

'What do we do?' my mother asked fearfully, looking to my father for direction.

'All civilians come out here! You are advised to come out for your own safety!' the voice insisted.

'Let's go outside,' my father said decisively. 'Where are the strips of cloth?'

Olayinka and I rushed into the bedroom for them, whilst my mother tore more off the strips she had already made and began to pass them round. As soon as she gave me mine I tied it around my head and, as if propelled by some uncontrollable force, I was out of the house like a shot. From a distance, I think I heard my father calling to me to come back, but there was no stopping me. In a flash, I was out of the gate and racing down the rocky slope that ended in the street in which the armoured tank stood.

There was a small group of ECOMOG soldiers and *kamajors* standing a little distance from the tank whose massive barrel seemed to be aimed directly at our house. I ran across the road to meet the men. Immediately, one of the *kamajors* reached forward and whipped the white bandana off my head.

'This is for rebel supporters,' he said, throwing the piece of cloth away. 'You are not one of them, are you?'

He flashed me a sudden grin.

'Lie down flat on the ground behind us,' he told me.

I liked him at once. He was wearing the traditional *kamajor* attire, which in itself was quite scary, but he looked so composed that I could not help admiring him. Later, I learnt that his name was Paul, a very strange name for a *kamajor*. I did as he told me and went to join some men, women and children who were already lying flat on the red earth behind them.

When the others arrived, they all had their white bands whipped off, and were told to lie as flat as they could. Curious and not wanting to miss any of the action, I raised my head. My eyes met with those of a small child. She looked at me with large frightened eyes, from where she lay in her mother's arms. I smiled to reassure her that it was going to be all right.

The long barrel of the tank swivelled slowly and pointed up the hill in the direction of our house. Then there was an ear-splitting explosion. A huge flaming projectile streamed out of the cannon and exploded in the hill, way beyond our house. Another one followed it shortly and exploded elsewhere. There were two huge cavities where the missiles had bitten into the earth. I watched in silent fascination. The barrel swivelled again, as the unarmed ECOMOG commander barked orders into a black walkie-talkie. The tank aimed down the street and began to blast repeatedly. The blasts were deafening and, because I was not very far, I got the full impact of them. I thought that my hearing would be impaired for life. The well-trained soldiers, with a handful of *kamajors* thrown in, advanced in style. I watched, enthralled, as one crawled past us smoothly on his belly, gun pointing towards the unseen enemy as he fired. Others were up in the trees, while some ducked into the gutter across the street from us. Even in that tense and dangerous atmosphere they were a beauty to watch. Paul seemed to be having a great time as he leaned against the trunk of a tree yelling out commands to his *kamajors*, and roaring with laughter every time a particularly heavy weapon was launched by one of his men. Sometimes he did the launching himself.

Suddenly the barrel of the armoured tank swung into our direction so that I could see right down its great dark smoking throat. People cried out in panic.

'It won't launch on you. Keep quiet,' Paul said, sounding irritated.

Then he fired a round of ammunition down the street at a target I could not see at all. To my disappointment, the tank began to roll forward, leaving us behind.

Before he ran off to join his men, Paul advised us to leave the area.

'Don't go back to your houses; some of the rebels might still be around and if they find you they will not spare you. Find somewhere else to sleep tonight.'

Mara immediately took charge of our group – that is, all those who had come from our house. He suggested that we head for Tengbeh Town, the nearest settlement area to where we lived. We took off at a brisk trot, using short cuts that only Mara knew. We ran through people's compounds and through rugged little paths. The stench of rotting dead bodies hit our nostrils even before we came across them. We averted our eyes to avoid seeing the stinking, fly-infested, bloated horrors as we ran past. Once I almost fell over one and had to take a flying leap over it.

As we drew farther away from the deafening gunfire, I prayed that we would find somewhere to stay before the curfew hour, when we would then have to worry about suspicious, patrolling ECOMOG troops. Impatient to get away, one of our neighbours, Simeon, and I left the rest of the group behind. His elbow was dripping blood from a wound he had gotten when a piece of shrapnel had flown off one the soldier's guns and hit him. He removed his shirt and bound it but the blood continued to flow. We ran on in silence.

We had been running for some time before I realised that I could no longer hear the sounds of the others behind us. We stopped and listened. There was no one around and we did not know where we were. Without realising it, we must have taken a different route from the one our group had taken, and we were lost. It was getting late and my companion was beginning to fade from blood loss. He needed a doctor – fast. Rather than go back to look for them, we decided to continue. With the curfew closing in on us we were far from safe. The devils were still knocking.

IT WILL NEVER BE YESTERDAY

By Wonder Guchu

It's hot on the balcony. Hot and dusty and noisy. But there is no better place than a balcony in October when the sun mercilessly scalds Africa. And there is no better time to stand on the balcony than 9 a.m. on a Sunday, dressed only in boxer shorts and a vest, waiting for breakfast and watching the cars zoom past along Samora Machel Avenue, going towards Eastlea to Mtoko or Mutare or possibly to Beira in Mozambique.

Somewhere beyond there in the villages were huts painted white and black, and lines of roads and rivers and mountain ranges. Somewhere there, I once herded cattle and goats in green valleys and climbed mountains looking for lost cattle or goats. Somewhere there, old people with nothing to do laze around hunting for beer in villages across the rivers. Somewhere there, young rural girls bathe in rivers while young boys, free from herding cattle and goats, hunt for mice and small game. Somewhere there, lovers lie in the silence and the comfort of being together in the dusty bushes.

That is a part of Africa.

Let them lie in the bushes or riverbanks, or wherever they want and with whomever they want. Let them, because I have Eva. My big-bosomed Eva. An on and off thing. Something like the weak flame of a homemade lamp struggling to shrug off a heavy darkness. First it was Mutare, then Masvingo and now Harare. There is never an end to the feeling. Like a seasonal flower that dies at the end of one season, it always sprouts and blossoms at the onset of another season – a friendly season.

Thirsty.

'Darling, another Holstein please!'

'But can't you wait?'

'Wait for what? It's hot here, can't you see?'

'How many have you had so far? Six?'

'I do not count what I drink. Can you count the grains of water in the river? Or the drops of the falling rain?'

'Wait for the food. I am almost finished.'

Lingering on the hot balcony, crushing the empty cans between my fingers, I look below and then beyond me. The trees are browning. There is dust on the few remaining leaves that cling to them.

The city is weary this morning. A few cars whiz past, the sounds of their engines dying down immediately.

Beyond the horizon, the hazy blue sky gives the morning a lazy feeling, which gets to the bones and weakens them. A slow headache works its way from somewhere deep in the head. It throbs, feebly in the beginning, getting harder and stronger every minute. A *babalaas*-induced headache that triggers thirst.

'Please darling, another beer. I'm dying of thirst.'

'Just hold on, darling. You will not die.'

That's her problem: Stopping things. Well she knows what happens afterwards. Walk, walk out. And the return later. Some kind of a seasonal blooming. But Masvingo was something else. Two long years away from each other, and then one morning the calling came and I rushed to the bus terminus where I got a bus back to her. It was late at night when I arrived at the school. I was not sure whether she was still there. But I still remembered that her house was the only big one, stashed away in one corner of the school field. As I approached the house I smelt her perfume and felt the softness of her skin. I remembered the many times I had gone and returned – mostly during the night – and she had opened the door for me, welcomed me without question, as if we had been together that morning.

Such was her character. It reminded me of one of our sheep. Molly, we called her. She was warm like a puma blanket. The one mother brought back from Botswana the only time she went to shop there. Molly was kind, considerate and understanding. Little children played with her. Some even kicked and spat at her, but she just stared, blinking, as if saying: 'Stop it now, child. It's alright.'

Eva was something like that. A mother whose heart was big and whose spirit was strong, like Geisha soap (big enough for a hundred years). I could not count the many times I had done her wrong, but every time I returned she would welcome me without reproach. I could not count the times I had slapped her, called her names and told her I would go away and never come back to her. But each time I returned, she would be there waiting for me, like the Biblical rich man whose son asked for his share then went away to a far-away land where he squandered the money with friends and women, and who then returned home to his father and was forgiven.

The prodigal lover – that was what Eva made of me.

I remembered the golden sun-rays in the mornings from when I was here last time. And when they fell on Eva, as she combed her hair whilst standing before the life-size wardrobe mirror, a pattern of intriguing colours formed. That morning breeze – free of sewage smell and the heavy, damp smog and traffic noise – refreshed me before I woke up.

On Thursdays, I would lie in bed listening to the whistles of the herdsmen as they drove their cud-chewing cattle to the dip-tank below the school. Often a stray calf would gallop past the houses to catch up with the rest of the herd, and often dogs would bark as they ran after it. And I would always run to the window to watch the calf kicking and sniffing at the dogs. Freedom, unfettered, unbridled, on the run.

Sometimes the voice of the village caller would wake me up as it announced that day's beerfest in one of the villages.

'Ngome! Ngome! Ngome!'

Or it would announce a meeting at the headman's homestead, where villagers would seek counsel, or reprimand or chastise one of their own for doing wrong.

Lying alone in bed, savouring Eva's scent, listening to all those voices, I was touched in a way nothing has ever touched me since then. I felt that I belonged to the whole village community. The love that abounds in the village was also given to me. Somehow, the whole atmosphere was like the coming together of a family, a mother calling her children to supper.

So with my heart pounding hard that day, I stood before the dark window realising that I had been away for two long years. This had been the longest time I had been away. The last time that I went away, it was for seven months. The other time it was for less than three months. But two years would surely raise questions that I was not able to answer. Even our sheep, Molly, would weep and curse and question. What would I say? Sorry, perhaps? But that was the one and the only difficult thing.

'Sorry. Sorry, Eva, I deserted you. Sorry, Eva. Please forgive me. Sorry, Eva.' Or just, 'Sorry, Eva.'

Ugh. It's a mouthful. Maybe I had to practice.

Cautiously, I made a step towards the dark window, which seemed to stare at me reproachfully, asking me what I had come back for. The window ceased to be just a window and became a one-eyed judge who wanted to know why I was troubling Eva.

'But what if she is no longer here? What if she no longer wants you? What if there is another man with her?' the window asked me.

I almost turned back, but anger held me. My feet remained dug deep into the dust, and I challenged the window to dare to ask more, telling it that no one was supposed to be with Eva.

Anger rose in me. It was anger directed not at Eva but at myself, yet I would not forgive her if I found another man in her arms. Another man! Oh God, I had not thought about that as I travelled all the way from Harare. What the hell, I had come for her and she was mine alone! No other man had a right to her body.

My head throbbed with dark anger as I made another step towards the window with my right hand raised high, ready to smash the window-pane. But I stopped and my hand fell back, limply.

For a long time, I stood before the window, unsure of what to do now that I had arrived. What was she going to say?

My head thundered and its echoes rumbled endlessly. I thought of going back to Harare. It was unfair for me to come like this and disturb her – again. She needed freedom and the choice to be with whomever she wanted.

I was about to turn when I heard sounds of contented sleep from within. The familiar, contented sounds of Eva's soft snores, which were almost like a gentle fall of water over a cliff. A rustling of a slow wind on soft leaves and grass in the morning.

Eva was a great sleeper. I used to watch her sleeping. Her face was always calm, contented. She never changed sides. And if I was sleeping in her arms, I could never break free.

My mouth dropped open. Warmth coursed through my body and I mechanically tapped on the windowpane, which rattled and stopped the sounds of sleep within.

I waited. Tapped again. Then waited. The dark window stared at me, still inviting, tantalising and mocking. I rapped harder.

There were groans inside. The bed springs creaked. And then there was silence.

After a few moments, I rapped again. The bed springs creaked sharply and a sleepy voice asked: 'Who is it?'

Eva! I almost shouted. At last, I was home with Eva. Home to love, respect, warmth and laughter. Eva, yea, Eva! This time, I told myself, I shall not leave her. I shan't go away!

'Who is it?' the voice asked again.

Tailoring my voice to suggest a happy mood, I said, 'It's me.'

There was silence within. And in those few seconds of heavy silence, I asked myself again whether I had done the right thing in coming; whether she was alone and still willing to accommodate me, and whether we could strike that happy chord again – bath together, splash water at each other and walk holding hands in the bushes or along the stream near the cattle dip-tank where some of her rude schoolboys had written our names on the walls; or go to the nearest township where we would sit and sip warm Coca-Cola and munch dry buns while watching kids playing in the dust along the road.

All the way here, I had not thought about exactly what I would do once I arrived. I had not prepared a speech to say exactly why I had come back after two years. My mind had simply been set on coming.

'Who is it?'

I remained silent.

Something inaudible was said and then silence fell.

I tapped again. This time, my traditional four quick, short raps.

'Who are you?'

'I'm home!' I said, unexpectedly sounding happy.

Those groans again and then sounds of feet across the floor. I stood, waiting, sweat-beads breaking out on my back. Then the curtain was parted and a head appeared.

'It's you. Come to the door.'

I found myself standing before the door, like a Grade One pupil eagerly waiting to receive his first set of books.

The door was opened and light from the bedroom filtered through into the kitchen, casting Eva's huge figure against the wall.

'Can I come in?' I asked, as if I had never been to this house before.

She moved out of the way as I stepped in, brushing against her breast. Something in me stirred. The old times were back.

She moved again, this time stepping behind me and outside into the dark night. Next I heard the splashing sounds of urine hitting the hard ground. The last time I was here, we would go out together and urinate side by side; her squatting and me standing. If I finished before her, she would ask me to wait and I would.

This was home. A home of good memories. Then I heard her long sighs. The door was bolted shut and her *pata-patas* slosh-sloshed on the floor. She almost walked into me in the dark kitchen, which was illuminated only by a candle in the bedroom.

She stopped, and said in her motherly voice, 'Why are you standing there? Get into the bedroom. You must be cold. You have been out in the night for long.'

She walked past me and like a child who had done something wrong, I followed her into the bedroom. I noticed that she had grown bigger, and felt that she had nothing underneath her nightdress. That was characteristic of Eva. I remembered asking her why she slept pantless; she told me that there was no need. The night was time for freedom.

In the bedroom, she opened the wardrobe doors and took out a gown to put over her nightdress. It was then that she turned to me and smiled, revealing her even white teeth, some of which I almost knocked out in one of our fights in years gone by.

I was still standing close to the door, staring wide-eyed at her.

'Why are you standing there? Sit on the bed. Why do you act as if you are a visitor here?'

I chuckled and said, 'I was about to.'

'Sit down and let me prepare something for you. You must be hungry,' she said, moving away from the wardrobe towards the door.

I reached out for her and drew her close to me. She did not make any effort to break free.

'You are hungry, aren't you? Let me make you something to eat first,' and she pushed me away gently.

'Don't worry, Eva,' I said sitting down carefully. 'I'm not hungry.'

'Have you eaten anything?'

I shook my head.

'So you must be hungry,' she insisted.

I was not hungry. It was like this every time I came back. I wanted nothing but Eva.

'I haven't eaten anything but I'm not hungry,' I insisted.

'Then, I will make you a cup of tea,' she said moving away from my reach.

Left alone, my eyes searched the room for any signs of another man's presence. I went over to the wardrobe and checked the clothes. There was nothing except her old dresses. I saw the red dress I had bought her on St Valentine's day years ago. It was a bribe to stop her from leaving after a heated argument.

I searched the drawers. There were lots of envelopes. One contained photographs. With shaking hands, I took them out one by one. I recognised her young brothers – Jefta, Simbarashe, Terence and Blessed.

Then there were Eva's photos of herself as a young girl: sitting on her father's lap at home, at school with friends and at college. I had seen some of these.

Then I heard her footsteps coming to the bedroom. I quickly shoved the photos back in the envelope and rushed to sit on the bed.

'Do you want your tea here or in the kitchen?'

'Just bring it here,' I said, shifting my position uncomfortably, taking off my shoes. She went back into the kitchen and returned, carrying the small teapot with a cracked spout.

'The small teapot,' I said nostalgically.

'You cracked it,' she accused lightheartedly.

'It was your fault.'

'Our fault,' she corrected.

'Those were the times,' I said. 'We were deeply in love.'

'Just let it pass,' she told me sternly. 'How many sugars do you take now?'

'The same.'

'So you haven't changed?'

'Have you changed yourself?'

Sitting down beside me, she sighed and said, 'I don't know what to believe any more.'

We looked into each other's eyes and she held my gaze only to drop it later.

'Is there anything wrong?' I asked.

'Yes,' she groaned, eyes cast down.

'What's wrong? My coming here after two long years?'

She stared at me briefly and I saw a shadow cross her face.

'Not just that,' she said. 'Everything is wrong.'

'Is there another man in your life?'

Again she stared at me and then at the opposite wall. I saw tears welling in her eyes.

'Is there another man in your life now? Tell me. Just let me know. I would not want to interfere,' I told her, sweat breaking out all over my body. The mere thought of another man with her made me weak.

'I wish there was,' she retorted.

I felt my strength coming back into my bones. I took advantage of the moment and said, 'Now listen.' I took her hands in mine. 'There is no need for you to think of another man. I have come back to love you and make you the woman you want to be. I will make up for the time I have wasted. I have grown up now ...'

I stopped when I realised that she was staring at me the way Jesus' portrait stares at people in the church. Those eyes of a higher force that see and know human beings' hearts and minds. The stare rendered the words I had just said hollow and meaningless. I had, of course, said them many times before.

118

Slowly she shook her head and said, 'You will go away one day. Sooner or later.'

I stood up and paced up and down the room. I wanted her to see that I was serious, that I meant what I was saying.

'Not this time, Eva. Please believe me.'

'You are like wind,' she told me. 'You come and go. Sometimes you remind me of *Mashuramurove*. They too come during the rainy season and go away when the season ends.'

I reached out for her then and she fell into my arms, sobbing softly. It was forever.

I pace up and down the balcony.

'Another beer, darling.'

And then she comes through the door carrying food.

'Help me put them down,' she pleads.

I hold some of the plates and, before placing them down, I drink the soup and say: 'Reminds me of Masvingo.'

She laughs and kisses me on the forehead and says, '*Shuramurove*.'

'*Shuramurove*,' I laugh heartily.

A POCKETFUL OF DREAMS

By Jackee Budesta Batanda

Four o'clock in the morning and it's starting to rain. It starts as a slight drizzle, a drop here and another there. Each drop harder than the last. It hits the soil, making depressions that will turn into miniature valleys. Soon there will be no trace of the once-tarmac-now-murram-dirt-road-now-muddy-road. It will just be a flow of chocolate-coloured water rushing forward.

The special taxi driver hoots outside. He has kept his word and has made it on time. I grab a jacket and pull it over my head as I make a dash for the car. The strong wind and rain hits my exposed face. I suck in my breath as a chill goes down my bones.

UAE 194D.

I take note of the number plate. It's too early in the morning to take risks. The raindrops have gained confidence and are hitting me harder. I open the passenger door and slump in the seat.

'Morning,' I say, 'you made it.' Like I do not see he has made it.

'Morning,' he grunts and starts the engine.

He has to warm it first, he says, before driving off. I nod understanding. Our breath has clouded the windscreen. He rubs it off with the back of his hand. He turns on Radio One: Great Songs Great Memories where our car radio stops. And we hit the road.

The streets are flooded. We drive with our windows up, as the UAE 194D slices through the water, separating it right and left. Our poor drainage system is the least of my worries. My heart pounds heavily against my chest, above the lyrics of Shaggy's 'Strength of a Woman'. There is a hollow feeling in my stomach. I'm anxious about getting the visa and about the visit I'm to make to the UK to see my mother for the first time in fifteen years.

The driver travels at breakneck speed, making a U-turn here, entering the road at the wrong spot there. But the Ugandan traffic police officers do not work at four o'clock in the morning. And I don't stop him driving 'express' probably because I think it will help me get my visa quickly, or perhaps the feeling of driving swiftly through the neon-lit streets of the city centre is thrilling. You know, like trying to test God. And perhaps it puts my mind off things ahead. I can't say. We get to Parliament Avenue in half the time it usually takes, and I'm surprised that we arrive in one piece. He squeezes through the other cars, lets me out and drives off before I can breathe again.

So here I am on Parliament Avenue. A huge, dull, brown building stands along the avenue. This is where parliamentarians meet and discuss important state matters – like when our vice president, a Member of Parliament, voiced her concerns about male parliamentarians wearing smelly socks. The British High Commission is located along this street. What greets me first are the waist-high half-yellow painted concrete barricades that grace the place, occupying half the pavement.

I notice them before the long crowd of people lining up forms clearly before my eyes. Some are sitting on round portable stools that they have carried from home while others stand. Still others sit in their Japanese reconditioned Toyotas with blaring music. Apparently four o'clock in the morning was not early enough. Under the cover of my jacket, I run and join the line behind the barricades. The line crawls with people like a parade of safari ants. We're all waiting for 8:30 in the morning when the consulate offices will open to the public and the privileged few for the day are let in.

The previously distant cold bites through my jacket. My teeth chatter. I rub my fingers together to generate some warmth. The rain is now falling slowly in little drops. In the line we make friends, whereas in normal circumstances we would pass each other on Kampala Road. I greet the man in front of me when he turns to acknowledge the slight wave of warmth that my presence behind him has created.

'Morning.'

'Morning.'

'Your first time?'

He nods.

'Mine too.'

'When did you come?'

'4:13.'

'Oh! Just before me.'

He turns forward.

'It's a long line,' I start again.

'Yes. Some people spent the night here.'

At this point we sit on the pavement and restart our chit-chat.

'What? All in the name of a stamp?'

'Look behind us, the line is now longer. Pity those guys coming now.'

'Yeah, they will not make it into the barricades.'

'By the way I'm Taaka.'

'Kugonza.'

'Nice to meet you.'

'Same.'

'What are you going for?'

'I'm going to study. And you?'

'Holiday. So where are you going to study?'

'Manchester. Where are you going on holiday?'

'London. To see my mother.'

As we talk, the mist from our mouths forms a film before our faces.

And in other sections, in the line, I imagine similar conversations are taking place. It's a way to pass time as the minutes lazily tick away. The discussions are interrupted only temporarily by the arrival of other visa applicants. The waiting does not mean that we will get through the barricade. I'm not sure I can handle a refusal. My fervent prayer after all this standing is that I be granted a visa. Anything less will shatter me, I'm positive. I've told everyone who cares to listen, as I've done for the past three years, that I'm travelling this time. I don't think I'll be able to face them if anything went differently from my plan.

Seven o'clock in the morning. One and a half hours to go. The rain has ceased and the consulate security guards make an appearance and usher us through the barricades. We walk in a single file as we wearily lift our immobilised feet. They stand watch to sieve out anyone trying to cheat through the line. And now we are on UK soil. During this time, the operatives strut their stuff. They patrol around us as if we are prisoners of war or terrorist suspects awaiting extradition. Each time they talk through their walkie-talkies, it makes me nervous. My stomach threatens to revolt. I reach into my bag for my bottle of vinegar and take a sip. Miraculously it clears my stomach. Don't ask me where I got the prescription.

'It's good for the stomach,' I explain to my new friend of two hours and forty-five minutes. He nods in understanding and smiles down at me. His sparkling white teeth, like a Close-up toothpaste advert, brighten his dark complexion, and the dimples that appear on his cheeks are unbelievably deep. He smiles with his eyes.

Now that my stomach has been disciplined, I take out my A5 brown envelope, which contains my credentials and look through it, just in case ... Passport, one passport photocopy, completed visa application form, three months' valid bank statement, letter of invitation from my mother, letter from employer, land title, marriage certificate, British Airways flight itinerary. I chose British Airways rather than Emirates because it might better my chances of being granted a visa. The envelope has all the stuff I need, but looking through it is a way to deal with my apprehension. Another way to convince myself that this time I will get a visa.

I smile to myself. This is my fourth passport. Not to say that I've travelled anywhere before. No! This will be my first trip out of Africa. My first trip out of the country. I've been through this four o'clock in the morning stuff and had 'Entry Denied' three times before. The reason I'm on my fourth passport is because I want … no, I need to have a clean passport.

My eyes scan the line in front. Dear, dear me. I lay my hand on my chest. I see a Member of Parliament in the line ahead of me, tugging at his tie. I also see Elly Wamala, a respected local musician. He is probably humming tunes to himself. A minister's wife talking endlessly on her mobile … I count the personalities on my fingers and there are quite a number. This year the XVII Commonwealth Games are taking place in Manchester, so the Ugandan sports team is in the line. There's a party of Scouts and Girl Guides probably travelling to camp in the English countryside and a delegation of gospel singers travelling to Europe to spread the word of God too. And we all have one thing in common. I raise my eyebrows.

I see a girl ahead of me and in my mind I create reasons for her being in the line. She is travelling as a spectator to the Commonwealth Games. She probably has a supporting letter from the Ministry of Education and Sports to support her claim. And when she gets to the UK, she'll disappear. She will not go as far as Manchester. Perhaps she will get a babysitting job and work for six months, and then come back. If denied the visa, she will go back to the ministry for another letter and if she fails again, she will pay the guys who deal in forged passports and visas and will sail through immigration as easily as luggage on a conveyer belt. It's a risk she's willing to take.

We all talk to forget that we might be denied a visa. The fear can be heard in our voices.

'You know, summer is a bad time to travel.' A conversation is started further down the line.

'Why?' I chip in. The speaker does not look at me as an intruder but rather as an addition to his already growing audience.

'Because everyone is travelling to Europe. In fact most of the officials have already taken their summer holiday and the ones left are anxious to do their work too and go on holiday. So they're quick to deny you the visa.' He stops to see whether he still holds his audience captive and continues when satisfied.

'I tell you, winter is the best time to travel. They give out visas to anyone who applies.'

'Who would want to go in that cold?'

'Yes, that is how it works. They know that the cold works wonders on Africans – few opt to travel in winter.'

And I'm wondering what he is doing in the line, since he seems to be an authority on the visa procedures.

'Last year I came here in December and when the woman asked me why I wanted to go to the UK, do you know what I told her?'

The eager ears wait for his reason.

'I told her that I had heard about winter and the cold, so I wanted to experience the snow. She laughed and told me to come back in the afternoon for my visa.'

The crowd bursts out laughing. The laughter sounds like cracking wood. Our visa expert laughs loudest, and then suddenly stops.

When he has our undivided attention again, he says, 'Pray the official behind the counter is a man. The men are easy. Woe unto you if you get a woman. Some may take one look at you and decide they don't like you. No visa. They ask too many questions, waiting for you to slip. And cram your address of stay in the UK so that you know it as soon as they ask you. At least they'll know that you're serious. The last time I was denied a visa because I had forgotten one letter in the address. The phone number too.'

In his endless speech, I find something I can keep to help me answer the questions in the consulate.

Eight-thirty in the morning: the consulate gates are opened. The progress in the line is slow. I can tell the depth of anxiety when I see people making the sign of the cross and calling upon Jesus, Mary and Joseph to please help them get the visa. Amen. I see some reciting the Moslem rosary and hear others hum the 'All Things Are Possible' hymn while I pray for a man to be behind the counter. And when a tall, dark, unsmiling Consulate official comes and counts a number of people, I'm on the border. I am nearly skipped, but one look at me and he includes me among the chosen. I sigh, take a deep breath and reach for my bottle of vinegar. It was narrow. Kugonza looks at me and throws me a relieved

124

smile. Four o'clock in the morning was early enough. I reciprocate the smile as I wipe my mouth and add,

'It's ... '

'... good for the stomach,' he completes my sentence and smiles his deep dimpled smile.

There is commotion behind me. Among the unchosen that have been told to come back next week, a boy has fainted. He can't be more than nineteen. One minute he is standing in the line and the next he's down. No warning. A man runs to the scene. He's a doctor. The doctor is among the unchosen. He kneels over the boy. A crowd has formed a ring around them. Consulate officials run to the scene. The doctor feels for his pulse as he screams at the crowd to back off and let the boy have some air. He talks on his mobile phone, shouting and gesticulating. The crowd pushes back, stepping on each other. Only the unchosen have run to witness the unfolding drama. We, the chosen, can't wander from our posts lest someone takes our place. So we steal glances behind us and count our blessings. All this time the doctor hovers over the boy. Suddenly he stands up. He looks up to the sky and shakes his fist at the heavens. He grabs his jacket, slings it over his shoulder as he punches his phone again. The news seeps through the crowd. Dead. The boy is dead.

The spectators walk off shaking their heads. The doctor walks past me and our eyes meet. I look down and tighten my hold round my A5 brown envelope. My security. An ambulance comes and takes away the boy. The crowd slowly disperses. And what goes through our minds is the question – what has he died of? It has been a long morning.

I try not to think about the death. I try to convince myself that this was the day designed for the boy to die. He could have died anywhere at that exact time. I don't believe myself. So I focus my attention on the visa applicants coming out. I can tell who has been denied a visa. The smile they wore when entering the consulate offices has been wiped off their faces. They walk in a hurry and almost break into a run to hide from the stares of the crowd. The dramatic ones come out crying, sobbing and wailing as they walk away.

I'm not prepared for the man who walks out shouting abuse at the consulate officials. None of the security men moves to throw him off the premises. He is off UK soil. He stands in the middle of the road and reaches for his face, pulling off his fake moustache, sideburns and beard, and throws them on the ground. And all this time, he shouts, 'Fuck the UK! This is bullshit! Fuck you!'

He tears his passport in half and throws it to the ground to join the fake moustache, sideburns and beard. He spits on the miserable heap and walks off. Oh! I know he'll not give up. He'll get another passport, another name, and another look. Then he will come back to the consulate and try his luck again. I just know.

I can tell the ones who have gotten their visa. They walk out with a new bounce to their steps. They toss me irresistible smiles; I'm moved to smile with them. I suck out some of their luck and add it to what I have already collected from the others before them. My heart jumps in joy with theirs. Some lose their balance and land in heaps on the ground, but they jump up and skip away. It is a happy-sad thing.

Twelve o'clock in the afternoon: I'm ushered through to the waiting room. I'm at ease because I've been here before. I see the applicants that go no further than the counter and pay their visa fees, the ones sent back for more information and the ones told to sit and wait for the interview. We are all seated in this air-conditioned room on blue plastic and metal ultra-modern seats. Waiting. My feet tap the marble floor, following the rhythm of the song, 'Knocking on Heaven's door', which I'm singing in my mind.

Kugonza gets up. 'Good luck,' I whisper to him.

He smiles uneasily. 'Thanks. I need it.'

As he walks to Counter 1, I move up one and into his seat.

Counter 3 is free and I'm next. I take a deep breath and manage to cover the distance from my seat to the counter without falling. 'Good afternoon,' I brightly greet the man behind the counter as I pass over my documents through the opening in the glass partition that separates us. Thank God it is a man!

'Afternoon,' he replies in a bored voice. 'Where are you going?'

'London.'

'For how long?'

'Two weeks.'

'What is the purpose of your visit?'

'I'm going on holiday.'

'Have you been to the UK before?'

'No.'

'Have you travelled out of the country before?'

'No.'

He asks me all the questions, except for the address of my stay. All this time he writes on the section on the application form that is reserved for official use only.

'Pay at the last counter, and come back at four pm for your visa.'

'Thank you,' I say, with a smile bigger than my face.

He nods.

Three days later I board Emirates Air with a pocketful of dreams. I close my eyes and I'm in London donning a purple wig, crooning *911* and traipsing like I just got off the catwalk. At this time I can say life is good to me. And I will not mind the multi stops – Entebbe-Nairobi-Dubai-London – of Emirates Air. The ticket was cheap. Being in the air is an exhilarating feeling. My head feels light. I don't throw up or have a nose bleed like I had been assured I would.

Terminal 4 in England is many times bigger than our Entebbe International Airport, and many times busier. The size of Terminal 4 is equal to three Entebbe International Airports.

Instruction 1: Be careful because the airport is so big it can swallow you up.

I walk directly in the footsteps of the people in front of me all the way to the immigration desk. I hand over my papers and smile at the man. He wears a straight face. He asks me the same questions that the man at the British High Commission asked. He looks at my picture then at me three times. I hold my breath and only let it out when he returns my papers.

No one meets me at the airport. Mother can't leave work and neither can her husband. I have to find my way to Wood Green Station, in North London, where her friend has offered to meet me. Armed with directions, I go in search of the ticket office.

Instruction 2: Buy a Travelcard, board the northbound Piccadilly Line and get off at Wood Green Station. Follow the exit signs out.

A man materialises and asks me, 'A Travelcard to Zone 3? Six pounds fifty.'

The money and card change hands. As I wait for the Piccadilly Line I read through my Travelcard. 'Not for resale,' it says.

Instruction 3: Stand as far away as you can from the yellow line on the platform. There could be racists hanging around there who will not hesitate to push you over the platform.

I lean against the wall, covering the poster of *The Guru*: Coming Soon. My voice is ready to scream if I'm attacked. I come from a clan of ululating women, so the sound of my voice would surely be heard above the approaching train.

A guy comes and joins me. He wears a chequered, brown-red scarf round his neck. His black jeans hug his hips tightly, and his black hair is gelled into place. He sports an earring on his left ear. I'm not prepared for this. Where I come from, the president ordered the arrest and prosecution of a gay couple who got married in Kampala. We even have a Ministry of Ethics and Integrity! I move away and in the process knock over my suitcase, which lands at his feet. He picks it up and reads the airline tags stuck to it. He smiles at me as I thank him profusely.

'This your first time?' he asks.

I nod, 'Yes.'

'Where you from?'

'Uganda.'

The name of the country does not register. And he's too young to have heard about Idi Amin, otherwise I would have tried to jog his memory a bit.

'In Africa,' I offer.

'Oh, South Africa,' he smiles in recognition.

'Not South Africa.'

'Southern Nigeria?'

'I'm from East Africa, you know, where Kenya and Tanzania are located. You know, Mount Kilimanjaro?'

'Oh! Like in *The Lion King*,' he says excitedly as though he has discovered a new toy.

All this time he talks with his hands going east, west, south, north and in the end, cupping his cheek. He talks like a girl acting shy in front of her boyfriend.

'I'm also a visitor. I'm from Paris,' he offers. 'Excuse me,' he adds, and then takes out a pocket mirror and lip sheen, which he applies to his lips. An equally small comb finds its way out of his pocket and goes through his gelled hair. Satisfied with the effort, he packs away his beauty accessories. He looks back at me and I notice that his eyebrows are finely shaped. 'So what you here for?'

'Holiday.'

'Really? You'll like it then. I'm a student.' He draws closer and cups a hand over my ear. 'You know the British are not friendly,' he whispers.

But he is one of their kind, so she is pleased by his statement.

'They are just not friendly people. I can't wait to go back home.'

I'm glad when the Piccadilly Line arrives. It's been a long journey.

My new friend and I sit in the same compartment. I stare around me, trying to understand the unfriendly British. My friend is at it again, applying more gloss to his lips. He gets off at Piccadilly Circus and blows me a kiss as the doors close him out. Then the tube moves on. The girl opposite me has a great bunch of hair. I feel like reaching out to touch it, feel it, but I manage to keep my hands to myself. She feels my eyes piercing through her bunch of hair, looks up and asks, 'Whatchulookin' at?'

No answer.

'Ah asked, whatchulookin' at?'

'Sorry,' is all I manage as I hastily look away, trying to find a focus point for my eyes to rest on. They land on the London Underground map. She lets the gum she is chewing burst in her mouth, but I will not stare at her again. Mother forgot Instruction 4: Do not stare.

Wood Green Station: I'm nearer mother than ever before. I'll be seeing her face-to-face and not in the smiling party pictures she sends at Christmas, New Year and Easter. As the tube slows to a stop, I wait for the doors to open so that I can run away from the 'whatchulookin' at?' girl. I follow the exit signs and discover that I have to get onto escalators. From what I have been told about escalators, you have to be careful when getting onto them. Not one step at a time but two feet at a time, otherwise you are torn apart. I take a deep breath and stumble on with my case bumping into the person ahead of me. I hastily mumble my apologies, but not before the person asks, 'What's wrong witcha?'

I hold onto the side for support as I move up. Some people go running up or down them as if they are normal steps. The walls are covered with framed posters of the latest movies premiering in London. I get to the exit and insert my card into the machine so that I can pass through. My card jams and I start to get frantic. I'll get caught and be charged ten pounds. I look at the security official. And when I'm about to open my mouth and confess my sins about the resold card, it comes through and the doors open. I walk out and my eyes try to pick out mother's friend in the sea of faces. As the crowd around me thins out, my eyes settle on a lady who keeps looking at a picture in her hands and then back to me. Our eyes lock.

'Taaka?' she calls questioningly.

Ah! This is mother's friend.

'Yes,' I answer, and she comes running towards me and pulls me into a hug as if we have been best friends all our lives. Well, this is better than the 'whatchulookin' at?' and 'what's wrong witcha?' welcome I have gotten so far.

'I'm Anika, your mama's friend.'

'It's nice finally meeting you,' I tell her.

'You look far cuter in person dan in dem pics you been sending your mama.'

'Thank you.'

'We goin' to ma home; den your mama will come pick you up, okay?'

She takes my suitcase and leads the way to her car. She talks all the while and I only get half of what she says. She speaks too fast for my ears to follow. To avoid saying, 'Pardon? Pardon? Pardon?' I say, 'Okay, okay, okay' and a little 'yeah', here and there. Anika is a huge woman with generous lips who applies lots of makeup. She wears her hair, in a wig I'm sure, because it doesn't look as good as the 'whatchulookin' at?' girl's hair.

After driving through grey cobbled streets that all look the same, we park at No. 44 Nightingale Road. Anika gets out of the car, opens the boot, and carries out my luggage.

'Welcome to London,' she says. 'How does it feel to finally be in London?'

'Thank you,' I say and shrug my shoulders. I cannot say what I feel because I feel no excitement and I'm exhausted.

Anika does not let me rest.

'Gal,' she says after offering me a glass of apple juice, 'dere's tings we gotta sort out afore your mama comes to collect you.'

I nod.

'Listen an' listen clearly.'

Another nod.

'Now don' go around callin' her "mama" afore her husband. You her lil' sis, an' dat de way it gonna be. Okay?'

Silence.

'Do I make ma self clear?'

'Yes, Anika.'

And I feel my pocketful of dreams flattening in my chest. What is another lie added to it? If this is the price of seeing my mother, there is no harm in stringing along. I mean look, I had lied at the consulate in Uganda about my age, my marital status, assets, and had even bought a bank statement for a small fee. So what's another lie added to the list? What's 10p to Mohammed Al Fayed?

Ten o'clock at night, Mother comes straight from work to pick me up.

'Taaka, my darling,' she shouts and pulls me into her embrace.

After our goodbyes to Anika, we walk the short distance to No. 42 Nightingale Road.

'Has Anika told you about the rules?'

'Yes, she did quite a wonderful job – and don't worry, I'll not be spoiling your cover.'

'Thank you. I knew I could count on you. And I hope you understand.'

She grabs my hand and squeezes it. I do not pull it away but let it hang in hers.

She introduces me to her husband as her little sister. He pulls me into his huge embrace and smiles; he seems extremely happy to meet someone from her side of the family. And I wonder why mother lies to her husband and then risks having me live with her. It does not make sense. My life is being woven with lie after lie and it is getting too deep.

Later in my room, mother comes and sits on my bed. She tells me about her job in a blanket factory, where she arranges blankets for packaging. On good days, she says, she does the counting. Her shifts vary. Sometimes she leaves for work at six o'clock in the morning and sometimes at three o'clock in the afternoon. She does not explain to me why she does these manual jobs when she has a master's degree in Organisational Psychology. And I do not ask.

She's happy, she says, that we're finally together. After our talk, she plants a kiss on my forehead and switches off the lights.

As I sleep that night, I don't dream about the wonders of being in London but rather about the boy who fainted and died in the line at the Consulate. Then I feel like my body is falling into a bottomless pit. My heart is fluttering around and I can't save myself.

DANCING TO THE JAZZ GOBLIN AND HIS RHYTHM

By Brian Chikwava

Independence Day, Wednesday, 18 April 2001. I still remember the morning clearly enough. Save for my suitcase and sax, the bulk of my grubby belongings were still scattered in the open courtyard. Over the city of Harare, a dirty grey sky sagged like a vagrant's winter rag, but I couldn't care less. I had just moved into my new bedsit flat. One I didn't have to share with anyone. Not with pimping goblins again. Never!

The bedsit was in a state, with paint peeling off the walls, a quarter of the parquet floor tiling coming off, and a broken geyser. Still, I did not mind. The squalid loneliness of my new home was a welcome relief. Whilst I felt I now understood Harare and its people, I also felt that there was something that I had completely misunderstood about the city. Perhaps nine months is not long enough to fully understand a city. Before he died, my grandfather always said you can never really know a place until you have:

1 fallen in love with its music,

2 fallen in love with its women, and

3 tried the *mbanje* that grows out of its soil.

I had done all but fall in love with Harare women, and my faith in my grandfather had deserted me.

I thrust my hand into my junk-filled pocket and excavated a sachet of *mbanje*. I rolled it with care. Malawi gold. The best that you could get in Harare at the time. With hindsight, I think this may be where I went wrong, because Malawi gold was smuggled in from Malawi. I avoided Harare-grown *mbanje* because I imagined there was not much difference between smoking it and smoking my grandfather's white beard.

'See where you got it wrong? You didn't smoke *mbanje* from Harare,' I can imagine him croaking.

As I puffed away, I could hear the wailing of sirens from a distance. Being Independence Day, I knew it could only be Uncle Bob's motorcade on its way to the National Sports Stadium, where he would be addressing the nation – reminding it again why it should never forget the liberation struggle. I admire Bob though, but for reasons that are completely different to those held by his ministers, who dread plopping out of his rear. I just like confidence tricksters.

Sitting on the dusty floor, I lit my Malawi gold and started to reflect. It had been nine months since I left Bulawayo for Harare. My mother had thrown me out of the family home.

She had said, 'I'm not disowning you my, child, but it brings bad luck for a woman to keep on looking after a child who has grown a beard.'

I didn't have much of a beard, but I didn't want to start another quarrel. When I got off the bus in Harare, I flung my bag over my shoulder and headed straight to The Terreskane Beer Garden. I didn't want to go to my cousin's house straightaway because I wanted to defer expending her hospitality as long as I could; also I wasn't quite ready to immerse myself in her heroic domesticity. She had a couple of toddlers and had just had twins who cried all the time and stuck to her breasts like ticks. It made conversation with her a bit like shovelling coal onto a truck with a teaspoon. And the arrival of her husband from work did not change much either. After walking into the house, he would come to stand in the kitchen doorway in his grey suit. Looking startled, either by my presence or by what had become of his life, he would remove his heavy-rimmed glasses and rub his eyes, before saying, 'Hullo Jabu.' Then he would disappear to change clothes. After that, I would only see him pottering around in flip-flops like a caged animal, never saying much, never listening to much, just waiting for an opportunity to give my cousin another baby.

I remember stopping to buy a cigarette from a street vendor at the corner of Herbert Chitepo Avenue and Second Street, not far from The Terreskane or, 'TK' as everyone called it. I put my bag down, stretched my shoulders and yawned. My bag was fat with a pumpkin that my mother had asked me to take to my cousin, two pairs of jeans, a couple of T-shirts and an African shirt that was Made in Malaysia.

'*Une* Madson?' I asked.

The vendor nodded, opened a box of Madison Red and shoved it into my face. I took one cigarette and lit it.

'I've got a pumpkin, you can have it for a good price,' I said to him after my first puff.

He smiled knowingly, shook his head politely and stared straight ahead as if I wasn't there at all. I picked up my bag and left him alone.

I contemplated first dropping the constipated bag at my cousin's, but I knew it would be an involved process, requiring excuses, a bunch of lies and a host of other forms of deceit that would leave me carrying a skipload of guilt. Where would I dump such a load? I had been to Harare several times, but not enough to know where its emotional garbage dump sites were. In the end I just went to The TK and got drunk.

The TK is a place that writhes with sleep-starved civil servants, labourers, prostitutes, musicians, thieves and daring tourists – all after foul sex and disease. That's what I think anyway. Still I had not counted on coming across Tafi, The Jazz Goblin. I met him at The TK two weeks after my arrival. People called him The Jazz Goblin because his band was called The Jazz Goblin & His Rhythm. He was their frontman, ripping it out on vocals and guitar, accompanied by two absent-minded musicians: Zuze, on pennywhistle, and Costa, on percussion. This meant that Tafi had to be the goblin, propping up the performance with mad showmanship.

'You drop and die on the dance floor, you on your own. You wan stop us having fun?' he would bark into his mic every so often. Predictably, he had a colourful following: hard-drinking clerks; *mbanje* vendors; Figo, a football-crazy security guard who also sold *mbanje*; and nearly always, a troupe of girls that lived by a motto they never uttered: 'Wherever I lay my *punani* that's my home.' I liked the set-up. I also had a desire to join The Jazz Goblin & His Rhythm even though I knew they were rubbish. I thought of it as an interesting entry into Harare's live music scene.

Joining the trio was easier than I expected. Tafi seemed pleased by my desire to join his band. I thought he was a useful idiot – the kind of creature who feels compelled to befriend people he feels intimidated by. Tafi thought I was cool, I could tell, but didn't know why. Maybe it was because I had approached him with a fist-on-fist greeting and he had fumbled with an open hand before folding it and reciprocating my salutation. Then, I knew I had the upper hand. I was more streetwise; I had dictated the way someone ten years older greeted me. I felt cool.

The downside of this is always that coolness comes with a grossly magnified awareness of self-invention in other people. Because you are all too aware of your own self-invention, you see it in other people and lose your nerve when you see someone being cool with satanic deftness. That happened to me when I asked Tafi what days the band rehearsed. He threw his head back on his chair, lit a cigarette, blew smoke up into the air and shrugged his shoulders with a dab of detached swagger.

'Just bring your sax when we have a gig. You can play what you want, no problem.'

My heart leapt. He looked cool. Really cool. For a moment I worried that I would be rumbled in that psychological hide-and-seek. That was the first time I remember being overawed by his presence.

Over the coming weeks new things about Tafi began to emerge, but they did little to diminish the effect he had on me. For instance, he carried his guitar everywhere. I learnt that this had nothing to do with his dedication to his craft and everything to do with his housing issue. I had also heard that he spent his afternoons with a gang of touts and pickpockets at Market Square who were hired to unleash violence on intransigent members of the public. But by the time all this came to my realisation it was too late. I was already caught up in the affairs of The Jazz Goblin & His Rhythm.

I had just gotten a job as a motor-mechanic apprentice and was moving out of my cousin's place into a two-bed flat some ten minutes walk from The TK. I was looking for someone to take the other room. That's when The Jazz Goblin came to me to say:

'I can take the other room and can look after the flat during the day when you are at work.'

I sensed an implicit threat of malicious burglary, yet I wasn't ready to live with Tafi so that he could guard the flat against himself. After an awkward silence I answered, 'As long as you're happy with the rent. It's Z$10,000 a month.'

He was quiet. He threw his half-finished cigarette onto the floor, and took his time to put it out by grinding it with the sole of his shoe. I knew him well enough to know that he could not afford to throw away half a cigarette, but I did not want to let it bother me even though I sensed something lurking beneath his calm exterior.

A couple of days later, after a gig, he asked me if he could spend a night at my flat.

'Just tonight. I won't bring the girls,' he said.

'Yea, no problem,' I said, trying not to sound thrown off. You don't want someone thinking that you are sensing their threats: it gives them an upper hand. Inside, I was praying that it would be just one night.

When I came from work the following day, I found him still in the flat. I didn't say anything because I didn't want it to look like I was kicking him out. That would ruin the dynamics within the band, I reasoned. But he had eaten all my bread. I locked myself up in the bathroom for an hour while he strummed his guitar and smoked *mbanje* in the lounge. For the first time I hated the smell of *mbanje*. Tafi looked too comfortable in the flat. I consoled myself with the fact that he could not possibly hijack the other room, because a colleague from work was going to be moving in over the weekend. Half an hour later I was back in the bathroom kicking myself for having just told Tafi he could stay until Saturday. He had just gazed at me vacantly and continued strumming his guitar when I expected gratitude. My insignificance weighed down on me.

I know it may look as if I didn't like Tafi, was scared of him or something like that. That may be true but I also had other plans for the flat. After thinking about it for the previous month, I had decided that, this being the first time I had lived independently, I would turn the flat into an environment with which I would be able to make an emotional connection. I had read from an interior decoration magazine that 'emotional connection' was the 'in thing'. But I doubted I would be able to create such a place while living with a jazz goblin. I figured out that for me, 'emotional connection' meant sticking photos of my family all over the flat – a kind of shrine to my family: my mother, sister, my grandfather, my disappeared father, and my late younger brother who was run over by a truck at the age of nine. Looking at his photos, I remembered him for his grasp of the concept of 'intention'. One day he bawled after I threw a lemon at him because he kept following me around in the house, stopping me from stealing my mother's condensed milk. When my mother asked him what was wrong, my brother had said I had narrowly missed hitting him with a lemon. My mother thought it was ridiculous. So did I. But that was because I failed to appreciate that what he was querying was my intention to hurt him. This may explain my unwillingness to appreciate Tafi's intentions when he asked to spend just one night at my flat.

When, on Saturday, my work mate, Andrew, moved in, Tafi simply dragged the reed mat I had lent him to the lounge. Save for a Tonga stool, the lounge was raving empty anyway, so I didn't say anything. I wanted to preserve my street cred. A month later Tafi had successfully drilled himself to eat Andrew's food during the day and remained impervious to any protests. Andrew promptly moved out of the flat, sneezing distress. Unlike him, I was not affected by Tafi's eating habits as I had quickly stopped buying any food and only ate out. With Andrew gone, Tafi quickly hauled a horse-sized prostitute into the vacant room. He called her Bhiza Ramambo – the Emperor's Horse.

Another month down the line, my 'emotional connection' project looked like a preposterous endeavour and if I had died pursuing it, my epitaph would probably have read 'Died of misadventure.' Tafi owned both the flat and myself; the band rehearsed at the flat and Tafi told me when to come in on a song. He even told me who to buy *mbanje* from, which meant *mbanje* vendors he had not yet fallen out with for abusing the credit they gave him. He bought fish on credit from a fishmonger who regularly came to our block of flats and expected me to pay.

'The fish was for the family,' he would remind me and I would nod sheepishly, knowing that 'family' meant Tafi since I never even once tasted the fish. But there were times when my resentments congealed and I felt pushed to challenge the inequity of our silent agreement. Then I would try to bring up the rent issue, and Tafi would simply slither into his unfathomable persona.

'You know why I sometimes write poetry, Jabu?' he would ask.

'Why?'

'It's a better substitute for things that I sometimes feel like doing,' he would say, rolling some *mbanje*. Not knowing if this was meant to be a threat or performance poetry, I asked, 'What do you sometimes feel like doing?'

But he would not answer. Instead he would start strumming his guitar, his guttural voice softly singing:

I found it
A snake under my blankets
Cold and clammy
Tonight I will kill a snake
Tonight I will kill a snake.

I ignored him, and we left it there.

By the beginning of April 2001, Tafi was demanding that I make him tea and bring it into his room because he was the band leader. By then, the Emperor's Horse had bolted out of the stable with The Goblin's guitar. It turned out she had been servicing The Goblin on credit, and in the end had told him that if he was not paying up, next time he should buy himself a rubber *punani*.

'There are plenty available for sale now!' She had screamed from the front door.

I kept well out of it because I didn't want what Tafi owed her to end up as another family expense. That was not so hard, given that I had paid every time I delivered myself into her legs. In return, though, she had been generous with genital lice, which I began to suspect originated from Tafi; I anticipated nightmares in which armies of lice were marching into my room, instructed by Tafi to seize control of my body.

Meanwhile I owed workmates nearly Z$120,000. That's six months' wages. From a wall in the lounge, my grandfather stared with ever increasing incredulity, my brother chuckled, my father disconnected, while my mother glared.

Then one Friday evening, I came back from work to find that Tafi had moved a pair of prostitutes into the flat. One, Maria, had lost her front teeth but said that it made it easier for her to suck it, and the other, Ranga, said for Z$3,000 she could make me cry. '$5,000 for both of us?' Maria offered. Sitting on my reed mat, his eyes mere slits, Tafi was puffing *mbanje* from the corner of his mouth and likely calculating his cut. Without a word, I scurried into my room and found myself taking stock: a pimp in his vice shack with his vice girls? That was it for me. I spent the following week quietly plotting a stealthy exit. On 18 April, when Tafi, Maria and Ranga left the flat for free food and a free football match at the independence celebrations, I made my move.

I'm not going to go into the boring details of it except that, for a loaf of bread each, I hired a ragtag platoon of street kids to carry my belongings. In just under an hour and a half, my independence had been won. That's why I still remember the morning clearly. From the cold floor of my new flat, the rhythm of The Jazz Goblin was distant. All I could hear coming in through the broken window was the wailing sound of sirens; a creature of folklore was strutting its stuff, on its way to address the nation about independence. I had just won mine, so I took another drag of my Malawi gold, and opened my lips to let out a lariat of smoke that caught my bolting thoughts by the neck and brought them crashing down. They accumulated and multiplied in the far corner of the cold floor, like my mother's beads. For the first time, my thoughts were collected. It felt like home.

SUPERSTITIONS ABOUT RATS

By Lesley Emanuel

Geometry was always just before break, at the hottest, stickiest part of the day. It was hard to concentrate and Aniline was thinking about what it would be like to water-ski. She preferred the 'what-ifs?' in algebra to geometry. If *x* could equal *y* and *a* could equal *b*, what if all the letters just fused into each other? What would happen to words? If 'what if's?' equalled real things, what would happen to her? Aniline closed her exercise book and doodled on the cover, over the school emblem with its curly capital letters 'TRUTH IS THE KEY'. H over T over U over R over T. 'TRUTH' looked a mess. It really needed the little key below it to unlock it.

At break Aniline walked towards Neo and Lindi. Her inclusion in their friendship was recent and her stride since was different, more assured. Before she became their friend, she had had to go off to the library every break-time to avoid the shame of being alone. Neo and Lindi took a few moments before breaking their conversation to squint up at Aniline.

'It's so hot. Are you going to stand there and block the sun?' said Neo, but Lindi shuffled backwards and opened their space for Aniline.

The grass was brown and prickly; Aniline tucked her dress carefully beneath her bottom before she sat down.

'Do you still want to do The Test?' she asked.

'Oh my God, what now?' Neo rolled her eyes. 'I feel a stomach-ache coming on.'

'I mean lunch. Ready?'

Aniline placed her plastic lunch-box purposefully in the middle of their group. She braced herself for their response, expecting her new friends to scoff at her idea, but then Lindi said, 'I haven't opened mine yet,' and put her lunchbox next to Aniline's.

Neo reached behind her for a plastic bag and dumped it unceremoniously in the middle. Aniline breathed in deeply – it was relief that made her do this, but it had dramatic effect.

'OK. Before we look, let's go over the rules. Brown bread means you haven't got a chance. Right?' She checked for support.

The two girls nodded solemnly.

'White bread with spread means you're on the list, but they're not sure yet. White bread and meat or cheese means you're in – you're definitely a prefect.'

As they gazed at each other before the deciding moment, none of them thought about the pin, labelled 'prefect', which you could buy at the stationers opposite Pick 'n Pay. They each saw instead the red brick building of the private girls' high school outside town, the cobbled paving polished by foot traffic, the wrought-iron gates and freshly painted shutters. They heard the trees that lined the entrance catch the wind and sigh elegantly. The prefect pin was perhaps the most important criterion for the annual scholarship there. The scholarship was a chance to get away from the shabby prefab classrooms, the scorched quad, the handed-down uniforms, to all sorts of carefree opportunities beyond the litter-trapping chicken-wire fence of their school. The scholarship equalled a future – no 'ifs' in that equation.

'So let's do it,' Neo mumbled.

'First we have to swap, two times to the left.'

Neo and Lindi seemed disoriented at Aniline's order.

'Else it won't work if you made your lunch yourself. OK? We have to do it together. On the count of three ...'

Lindi opened the plastic bag. There were three drumsticks, leftovers from Kentucky Fried Chicken. Grease had saturated the breadcrumbs. Aniline had Lindi's box: an apple and a white bun. Neo opened Aniline's. There were two slices of white, cut into triangles and glued together with cheese spread. They surveyed the food silently. The siren started.

Neo said, 'It doesn't matter. C'mon, we've got five minutes. So can we keep the food we swapped?'

'No way, uggh.' Lindi swung the bag over to Neo.

Aniline prodded the bun furtively before she handed Lindi's box back to her. It was dry. Nothing sandwiched in it at all.

* * *

Aniline's mother's car was old, really old. You could tell this from afar, even if the car was clean, which it never was. The bonnet was speckled with rust and there was a particular grind whenever you changed from first to second. Fortunately her mother only had to change gears once, when she turned into the school gates.

Aniline had finished her homework on the concrete bench beneath the bluegum tree, where she always waited for her mother. She wished her mother would allow her to be a weekly boarder. She wished they didn't live so far, then she could travel home on the bus like the other girls. She wished the car would be reliable, just often enough so that she didn't have to go to old Mrs du Plessis' house opposite the school and ask to spend the night when her mother didn't arrive at all. She swung her legs and considered the road leading up to the school. If the next car was her mother's blue Datsun, it would mean she'd get the scholarship. No. A furniture truck. Well, all right then, if the car after the next was her mother's, it would mean that Ma would write to her father to ask for money for the private school. The first car to pass was a red station-wagon filled with small children sitting behind the driver. The back window was filled with their various limbs flapping as they played. Then a concrete mixer. Aniline straightened. A concrete-mixer doesn't qualify as a car! And neither did the van that was next. It slowed and turned into the school. Aniline slumped. Her mother had sent Theo. She stood and picked up her bag. There was tree gum on the back of her dress. He kept the engine running while she opened the door with 'Theo's Garden Maintinence' painted on it.

'Hello, lovey, climb in, climb in, one big happy family, all my girls, shift, up Debbie.' Theo breathed out cigarette smoke as he spoke. Aniline's aunt had been sitting close up to Theo on the van seat, but she hoisted one leg over the gear lever and bounced herself even closer to him. Her jeans cut thick denim wrinkles into her thighs.

'I'm teaching your aunty to drive,' Theo said. 'Here, Debs, put your hand on my gear stick so I can show you. Nice and slowly now. There's it.'

Aniline scanned the parking lot to be absolutely sure she was the last to leave.

'Annie, you pay attention, I'm gonna be teaching you next. We just gonna stop at Solly's – you can run in and get me a six-pack, then you can have a turn, hey?' Theo laughed and threw his cigarette butt out the window.

'They won't sell me beer; I'm underage.' Aniline hoped the tree gum would stick on Theo's van's seat. 'And I'm too young to drive.'

'Reall-y, Miss High-and-mighty?'

'Ag, Theo, leave her alone man.' Debbie slapped him playfully on his shoulder. 'Get your own beer, your boep needs the exercise.'

Theo's stomach was so big that it brushed against the steering wheel.

'So, love, how was your day?' Without waiting for an answer, Debbie continued, 'Your ma said we must fetch you; she's busy in the *mielies*. She's got her stick and her mission and she says today's the day she's gonna find water.'

'Jesus,' Theo mumbled. 'Why doesn't she just sell the bloody farm and be done with it. Nothing's going to grow on that dump.'

'Oh, she even tried Jesus, believe you me,' Debbie said. 'That was before your time. Then the squatters moved in next door. Now not even God could sell the place for my sister. Here, lemme light that ciggie for you.'

Aniline rested her forehead against the window. Theo turned the van onto the highway, and soon there were fewer buildings and greater stretches of coarse brown veld. After the tile factory, Aniline sat up. The gear-lever knob was still covered with Theo's fat fingers over Debbie's hand. Aniline rolled down the window to just below her nose. There it was, phosphorescent, brilliant green: the kikuyu farm where they grew grass for suburban lawns and golf courses. Then, just after, the rich, wet smell of onions growing. Great robotic arms sprayed water in sweeping gestures. Aniline wound up the window and pretended to sleep.

Debbie's Maltese poodle yapped at the van when they arrived home. Aniline shoved the door against it as she got out and it flipped onto it's back with a yelp.

Debbie scuttled out to it, 'Fritzie, Fritzie. Ag, shame man.'

Aniline dropped her bag in the kitchen and turned on the kettle. Her mother came in, wiping her hands on her pants. There was a coffee-coloured stain on her T-shirt that matched the liver-spots on her face. Lindi's mother said you should put sunscreen on your face every day. Aniline passed on the advice, but Ma just laughed and said that her skin would drink it up too quickly and then be as thirsty as a drunk forever. Now she picked up Aniline's bag and put it on a chair.

'Told you before, Annie, don't put your bag on the floor. You don't need to become a poor woman like your ma.' She came up behind Aniline and pulled the rubber band out of her hair. 'So? Is my girl a prefect?'

'They haven't told us yet, Ma.' Aniline spilled the teaspoon of sugar.

'Well, if the ants still come after you've cleaned up that sugar, it'll mean you're getting it, OK?' She gently gathered the hair again and wound the band back into a ponytail. 'When you've fed the chickens, you can peel potatoes. Theo's got his mates coming around later for a braai. I'm making potato salad for him.'

When Debbie came to live with them, Aniline had to move to the room off the porch. Aniline didn't mind as it had large windows up to the ceiling and at night she could see the yard beyond the shapes of the furniture on the porch. She changed into shorts and a T-shirt and went out to the chickens. Watching them while she sat on the tractor tyre with her knees pulled up to her chin, she tried to track patterns in their behaviour: If they scratched in one direction – say Route A – would they know to go a different path – say Route B – the next time? But most of the hens were lying in the dirt and the rooster was still, just cocking his head from side to side. Quiet chickens meant no rain.

Once, at school, Mrs Coetzee said they should bring in some information about eggs that they thought nobody would know about. She said it was 'collaborative learning'. That was before Aniline became friends with Neo and Lindi, so she had had no one at school to talk to about the project. Quite a few of the girls said something in class about eggs proving that chickens weren't mammals. That was really lame, but Mrs Coetzee nodded at them. Lindi said that the chicken was related to Tyrannosaurus Rex, and she even held up a dirt-encrusted figurine of the monster that she must have taken from her little brother. Mrs Coetzee asked what that had to do with eggs, and said that she doubted it was true anyway. For her turn, Neo unfolded a piece of tin foil and carefully drew out an opaque piece of membrane from a boiled egg.

Aniline heard Valerie say, 'Neo brought her snot!' The girls around her snickered.

Neo was trying to stretch the skin between her fingers and tap it at the same time to make a sound like a little drum, but then it tore and Mrs Coetzee said they had to move on. 'Aniline?'

Aniline, began but Mrs Coetzee interrupted her and told her to speak up.

'If you rub egg-white on a baby's legs, the baby will walk early,' she said.

'And how exactly will that work, Aniline?' asked Mrs Coetzee.

Aniline didn't pick up Mrs Coetzee's sarcasm quickly enough. She was too busy remembering exactly what her ma had told her, trying to get it right: 'Oh, it has to be on the back of the baby's legs,' Aniline explained.

'Aniline! Engage your brain!' That was one of Mrs Coetzee's favourites. Everyone turned on their stools to look at Aniline.

'This is a science class! All you've proven is that the human brain has a great deal in common with the chicken's brain, and you are evidence of it!'

Aniline turned away from watching the chickens to a sound above and behind her. It was a speckled mousebird, clambering chaotically in the dead branches of a bush. The branches were only thin arches and the bird couldn't get a footing. It dipped its tail and thrust its head forward as it tried to balance. Fritzie's piercing bark started as an old Landrover came along the sand road to the yard. The mousebird lifted away.

'Ani-leen!' her ma called between Fritzie's noise. 'Come say hello! Annie?'

They could all see her from the yard. Aniline pushed herself up, pulled her T-shirt down as far as it could go and walked towards them.

After the hellos, Aniline's ma said, 'So come, let's go sit on the porch. It's too hot here.'

The shorter man went back to the vehicle for beer. He walked with his legs apart and his arms stuck out on the sides, as if his appendages would stick to the little bulges of muscle under his clothes if he let them get close. The other one, Ray, had blue cycling glasses on. He looked like a close-up picture of a fly that Aniline had seen in a *National Geographic* in the library. Aniline went inside to start the potatoes. The house, at least, was dark and cool. She listened to the rats cavorting in the ceiling as she peeled. Theo had said they came from the squatters, that they'd brought with them the sewage that oozed between every piece of litter and tin sheet of that hellhole. He brought home rat poison – a bank bag of tiny colourless beads.

'Purest stuff. Supplier did me a favour. No buggering around with pellets,' he told Ma.

Then he made Aniline climb up his work ladder, into the ceiling. It was completely black inside there, and quiet. Aniline knew the rats were watching her, lined up like an audience on the furtherest side, waiting for her move. What if they could smell her sweat? Aniline's mother said rats could predict death. What if they knew she had come to kill them, and they suddenly swarmed to her, diving and somersaulting over one another to attack? Aniline emptied the poison into the pocket of her shorts very slowly and inched back to the sunlight. When she got to the bottom of the ladder, she showed Theo the empty packet.

After they got their drinks, and talked about the squatters, and had more drinks, Theo got the grill going. He waved the braai fork vaguely to the left of the dirt road.

'Shade cloth for the saplings over there,' he told Ray, who was standing next to him. Then he pointed with his beer bottle in the other hand, 'and the big trees on that side.'

When they'd first started dating, Theo had said they could start a business together – that, what with all the building that was going on, people needed trees right away. Ma had said it would be beautiful to watch trees grow, and Theo had bought her a dream-catcher. Aniline looked up to where Theo had nailed it onto the porch ceiling. There was a fine layer of dust on it now, and the strips of leather hanging down looked like dried biltong. Smoke from the chops drifted up to its web.

'Only problem, Theo, is trees need time. And money for extra water, because the first water we're getting is for my mealies. Aniline, don't you want to empty that ashtray for us?' Ma sounded tired.

Aniline looked over at Debbie. She was on the rusted steel bench that was supposed to have a canopy over it, that you were supposed to be able to swing backwards and forwards on, with a glass of lemonade in your hand and people pocking tennis balls in the background. Fritzie was asleep on her lap; Debbie's eyes were half-closed and she rocked her body slightly as she stroked his fur. Aniline picked up the empty bottle at Debbie's feet, then she put the ashtray on top of it. She'd see if she could balance it all the way to the kitchen ... but the rooster crowed. Of all the strange times to assert himself the rooster chose this, to stretch his scrawny neck and yell to the smudged, dust-covered sunset. Fritzie leapt off Debbie's lap and scrambled over Aniline's feet. Aniline jerked back and the bottle smashed on the concrete floor. The other guy, the muscley-one, was looking down at his shirt covered in ash. He got up from where he'd been settled next to Debbie.

'*Eina*, shit!' he called out.

First Aniline thought a cigarette butt had burned him, but then she looked down. He'd stood on a piece of the glass. His shoes were under where Debbie was still sitting and his blood was spreading all the way to them.

'For Chrissake! Look what you've done, you little bitch!' Theo yelled and slammed his own beer bottle onto the floor.

A second smashing. And then a third, his slap across the side of her head. It wasn't strong enough to knock her down – Aniline was pleased about that. It was numb at first but then her ear started to pound, thwacking faster and faster as if the tennis players were into a volley. She swayed a bit. Ma said clearly and calmly, 'Don't you take a step, Annie. Don't you move, you're also barefoot.'

Aniline went straight to her room after that. She didn't even change into her pyjamas; she just got into bed and pulled the sheet over herself.

She put the sore side of her face against the pillow and listened to the adults on the porch. Theo was telling Ma how to bandage the foot. Every now and then she could hear Debbie say, 'Uggh, gross!'

Ma said, 'He needs stitches; it won't stop bleeding.'

'Rubbish, man!' said Theo. 'He's an *oke*, my main man, hey boss? You're OK, hey?' and then to Ma, an order, 'Get him some ice, that's all he needs. And some extra – he needs another drink!'

'Only one I'm getting ice for is my daughter,' Ma said decisively.

Then it was only Theo speaking, 'Bloody knows everything, that one. You got a problem, she can sort it – anything. She's even gonna find water. You gotto see it – big arse out like a mama, like this ...'

Aniline raised herself on her elbows to look outside. He'd made the *braai* prongs open like giant scissors, so they looked like Ma's divining stick. He held onto the handles and took a few steps, narrowing his eyes and rocking to complete the picture of her ma.

'Move up for me, love?' Aniline's mother whispered.

Aniline hadn't heard her come in. She shifted over and her ma lay next to her.

'Which side? Here? I'm just going to hold this against it. Lie here in my arm, Annie.'

Aniline put her good side against her ma's shoulder. The cold felt good, but she knew the ice would start melting soon and she hated it when it dripped.

'Look, love, look up,' ma said. Aniline moved her head and followed the shape of her mother's pointed finger to the moon in the top corner of the window.

'If there's a ring around the moon, it's going to rain in as many days as there are stars in that ring. Count them for me, Annie?'

Aniline tried. She even squinted her eyes to blur the outline, but the moon was waning and dull. When she closed her eyes the orb repeated its own shape in a line against her eyelids. It was better that way, reduced to a mass of molecules arranged in a neat and orderly fashion, like the pictures of polymer crystals Mrs Coetzee had shown them. Aniline had liked the way the chains lined up, tops of new pencils in a box. Most of the girls brought sugar to class, for their examples of crystals. They had to stir their crystals into beakers of water. Aniline's wouldn't dissolve.

'What is that, Aniline?' Mrs Coetzee asked, and the other girls leaned closer.

'It's rat poison, ma'am.'

Outside, Theo said, 'Hell it's a bloody circus here. We should charge people to come see … . You OK now, mate? You not going to leave now, c'mon man.'

But they were leaving. It was too early, Theo would smoke and drink and swear to himself for hours still. Aniline considered getting up, going to apologise. Maybe that would make them stay.

'They haven't had the potato salad yet, Ma,' she whispered, but her mother was asleep.

Aniline waited until her breathing was deep and regular, then she opened her mother's hand and lifted the towel out of it. She sat up, put her feet on the floor, and listened. Theo was quiet, but she'd have to make sure the coast was clear before she went to the kitchen. She stood and listened again. This time, the sound of the old bench's steel springs straining; then, whispering and a smothered giggle. Aniline scanned the darkness outside. They were both on the bench. Theo had one knee next to Debbie, the other foot on the floor for balance as he sprawled over her. Fritzie lay near them, inert and unsurprised. Theo shifted enough for Aniline to see his fingers clutch at Debbie's naked breast, as pale in the darkness as Fritzie's fur. A sliver of ice cube slipped out of the towel. It slid over Aniline's fingers and dropped onto the bed.

'Ah, no,' groaned Aniline's mother, as she turned and brushed at it in her sleep.

* * *

On Monday morning Aniline's cheek still looked like it had had an iron held against it. Debbie was up, smoking and drinking coffee.

'I'll fix it,' she said, and as she left the room. 'You get on with making your lunch. And make Theo's too.'

There was only one leftover chop and the potato salad. Aniline started putting the food into a container for Theo. It was new, this making lunch for him. Her ma had never asked her to do it before. Aniline pictured him in his van at lunchtime, peeling open the container lid and biting down into a chop. She hoped he'd be in a hurry, she hoped a shard would work loose from the chop bone and stick itself sideways. But then Aniline imagined coming home, Theo seething at the kitchen table, waiting for her. Debbie would be behind him, saying, 'But it was Annie, she made the lunch, it was Annie …'

Aniline took the chop out again. She searched for her stash of crystals in the junk cupboard beneath the stove and used a teaspoon to sprinkle on the meaty part.

'Fritzie? Fritzie!' she called.

The dog wasn't used to her voice. She tried again, just as Debbie came back from Aniline's old bedroom with her make-up bag. Fritzie scampered in after Debbie and went straight to guzzle the chop on the floor. Aniline watched him silently while Debbie dabbed at her face. When she'd finished, Aniline looked in the bathroom mirror. The bad side was beige, the good side shiny and tanned. She'd say she went water-skiing, that she fell hard against the water. She'd say they'd spent the whole weekend at the dam with friends. She put the lid on Theo's lunchbox.

Nobody asked Aniline about her face at school. On the way into assembly, Valerie opened her arms behind Neo, Lindi and Aniline and clucked, 'Come, come, chickies.'

They lined up in their class rows. Aniline was at the end and there was no more room, so she moved into the line in front of Neo and Lindi. After 'All Things Bright and Beautiful', the principal announced that the prefect list for the year would be finalised at the end of the day. The prefects would maintain the honour of the school, serve its reputation, and uphold its rules. Now was a good time, the principal said, for a reminder of those rules: courtesy, litter, hemline. Swearing, gum, jewellery. Make-up. Aniline shifted her weight from one foot to the other. She glanced at Neo and Lindi behind her. They were singing the school anthem:

'We believe, we believe, truth and vigour are the keys ...'

As the '-eys' note wavered, Aniline saw Mrs Coetzee at the back of the hall, studying her closely. She caught her breath, ducked her chin and turned back.

At the end of assembly the girls filed out and started collecting their bags, which were strewn around the quad. Aniline had put hers on a chair that had been discarded because the backrest had fallen out.

'Aniline? May I speak to you for a moment?' It was Mrs Coetzee.

Aniline looked around. She was one of the last left, Neo and Lindi were probably in class already.

'I thought I should speak to you personally. I always think it's good to be prepared.' Mrs Coetzee was scanning her in the same way she inspected the lab benches after the girls had scrubbed them. The thumping rough-housing of the rats in the ceiling started in her head.

'I know you were hoping to be elected a prefect. I just don't think you're ready for such a responsibility, Aniline.' Mrs Coetzee's hand lifted as if she was going to touch Aniline, but she dropped it back to her side. 'You're too … fanciful, Aniline. You need to get a better take on reality, that's what it is. You need to think things through logically.' Mrs Coetzee sighed. 'Sometimes I think you avoid logical explanations on purpose. That's not a good influence to have on people, Aniline.' She looked at her wristwatch. Then, more brusquely, 'So I recommended that you shouldn't be on the prefect body. I hope you take this in the spirit it's intended. I hope you'll work on it. You can, you know.'

Aniline looked at her questioningly.

'Work at it, I mean. Improve things for yourself. You know, things will work in your world only if you have been correct and precise,' she said.

Aniline nodded her head. Nodding would help to get it over with.

'All this voodoo you're inclined towards – it doesn't give you control, it takes it away from you. I read my horoscope, but I don't go on about "the dog's eating grass, so it's going to rain".' She sighed.

'I know ma'am. You told us they might eat grass because of an intestinal obstruction,' Aniline tried, but it didn't seem as if Mrs Coetzee heard her.

'Well, then, at least you won't be upset when they announce the names later. OK?'

Aniline did some more nodding.

'Oh, for heaven's sake, Aniline, look at you standing there … . Say something girl, do something, start living in the real world! … Just get to class!'

Mrs Coetzee turned away from her and set off for the staff room. Aniline watched her go, then she looked up at the brilliant blue sky. Some clouds were gathering.

With any luck, Aniline thought, it might rain later.

THE LEGENDARY OLD CROSSER

By Osita Obi

Billy stood in the shade arguing with the old man about something none of us understood.

The moon was bright overhead. It was not a full moon, but it was bright enough to cast dark and scary shadows everywhere and to make us feel exposed. We could see the stars bright and cool in the infinite expanse of the cloudless sky. The dark and hideous hills were etched inartistically against the greyish horizon alongside the silhouettes of hunched, wind-bent trees and craggy rocks. The surrounding scenery was of waste and wild – of rock boulders, towering trees and high-rising cliffs that made us feel so thoroughly inferior, insignificant and powerless. The damp and cool night breeze moaned from behind the adjacent hill, starting off blunt echoes from the ravines, valleys, caves, twists, bends and from the branches of trees and blades of grass. Now and then, a nightbird flapped noiselessly across the silvery face of the moon. A cricket shrieked behind or around our feet. We heard a slimy motion, indistinct amongst the dark and stony undergrowth like some reptile slicing through clumps of grass. But we stood, chilled to the bones, not knowing any safer spot to put our feet on. Our eyes rolled and searched the dark and the damp undergrowth. Our ears were strained and painfully set. Our nostrils were dilated as the nauseating perfume of dust and crushed herbs played around the tips of our noses. We dared not sneeze or cough. We were warned strictly against any such mistakes. We could only scratch our noses to hold the tickling sensation in check.

The eight of us were huddled up at the foot of a small hill, near the crevice of a large boulder of rock. We were silent and trembling, more out of apprehension than out of the cold that later came with the breeze. The old model Mercedes car that brought us here, its headlamps like the eyes of a grasshopper, was parked deftly beside a cluster of grass so that you saw only a little of its back fenders. The driver was still inside waiting to take Billy back when the old man must have started taking us into the hills to Ceuta. That driver, I dare say, was a daredevil. He had given us not only the most frightening, but also the roughest, ride of our lives. And how he managed to cram us all into that car confounded us. The eight of us – Sandra, Tonia, Dolly, Chibuzo, Suzzie, Jerry, Osaro and myself. Jerry and Osaro were in the boot of the car, but that didn't leave any more space, considering that Suzzie was pregnant and that only the driver, his friend, and Billy sat in the front seat. Well, that wasn't the most confounding thing ...

Why was Billy taking too much time arguing with the old man? We were getting more restless. From where we stood we could see the old man pointing at the moon and pointing at his wrist, indicating probably that he worked with time or that we had delayed. The tension in the atmosphere there was easily felt by every one of us. It seemed the old crosser wasn't going to be persuaded. We could even hear his voice, tight and angry, from the distance. And we could see Billy, too, gesticulating feverishly and matching the old man's antics in every respect. Was Billy withholding some money, or what? Why didn't he pay the old man outright and get us out of here? None of us could afford a situation where the old man would accept this crossing half-heartedly only to bring us to disaster. After all, we had paid heavily for this man's services. Six hundred dollars per head couldn't be called chicken-feed in any country. I heard that Jerry and Chibuzo paid only five hundred each, but Osaro and Suzzie paid almost seven hundred each (perhaps for the extra risk Suzzie's pregnancy portended). My case was different from the beginning, although Billy tried to resist it. But I gave him only three hundred – after all, he had been my lover and had always had it free with me since I met him in Tangier. Silly. Why did men prefer it when you made them pay for sex?

Now Billy started in our direction, while the crosser followed him closely. The crosser was short and bent at the shoulders and didn't at all fit into what I had expected of such a legend. The moment I came to Algiers I had heard about a certain old man, called Ediomwan, who, knowing the shortest and the safest route, 'crossed' people through the heavily patrolled borders of Morocco and the Spanish enclave of Ceuta into the Calamocarro asylum camp. Others had said they heard about Ediomwan even while still beyond the desert town of Asamaka. It was said that all who had him as guide eventually found their way to Europe. So it wasn't with little delight that we had looked forward to meeting him. Earlier in the day the prospect of meeting him had made us lightheaded, breathless and fulfilled. You couldn't quantify the chaotic flux of emotions that raged through us as Billy approached with the seasoned crosser behind him. It wasn't surprising either that, despite the cold and the gathering mist, I was sweating on my forehead and in my armpits. Was the man behind Billy the famed legendary fox of the North African hills?

Was this he who was said to be responsible for the crossing of over seventy per cent of the asylum seekers into Calamocarro? Was he truly the man called the Messiah of the Foggy Mountains? Was this the legend of the Moroccan waste? Or had he sent someone else on his behalf?

A streak of disbelief ripped through my mind. Why had I expected to see a man who was tall and huge, with powerful biceps and tints of white on a coarse, medium beard? Perhaps I had subconsciously battled with my gender weakness and the fear of the interminable ranges of rocky mountains on our way, and had thought of a Superman or a St Christopher who carried one across obstacles. A man with thunder in his voice, whose powerful vocals alone lifted one across rifts and ravines. A man who could take up one's defence at the threat of bandits and the border guards.

But Ediomwan the crosser was not a man like that. He fell far short of all my expectations. When he and Billy reached the spot where we were huddled up, restless like slaves awaiting a slave-driver's orders, we instantly gathered round them. I stood close to the old crosser, but shuddered too much to peer into his dark and aged face. And as I began to remember that he was even rumoured to possess metaphysical powers with which he bewitched the border guards, I withdrew slightly and altogether avoided any eye contact with him.

Anyway, it was difficult to see his eyes. Below the bundle of Arab headgear he wound round his head, it was only his long and crooked nose, on which the moon fell, that you saw. But above his nose, the gap left for the convenience of his sight – a gap that was dark and puzzling, like a mouse-hole – gave you the uneasy feeling that something toothy and creepy lurked and waited to snap at you. His lips his beard, (he must have some beard), and his neck were all wrapped up inside the dark headgear. He had a small shepherd's bag hanging on his shoulder. Despite tying his bogus kaftan at the waist with a piece of cloth and folding its sleeves up to the upper arm, he wasn't dressed as if he bothered about his chances of escape in the event of a chase. This was strange because even pregnant Suzzie, like everyone else, wore jeans and a tight-fitting blouse. Rather, he wore only a pair of canvas shoes, which were easily seen in the moonlight alongside his wooden staff.

Then Billy began to address us.

'Now,' he said, 'you must be made aware of these vital points so that you don't bungle up your trip. First, you must bear in mind that the moment our man delivers you at the entrance to the camp, my commitment to you ceases. Right?'

This was too businesslike, I thought. Was this really Billy, suddenly talking like a lawyer too eager to protect his legal fees from an unsatisfied client? His tone this night was really worrisome to me.

'Especially to the girls,' he continued. 'You must be strong by yourselves. And always, promptly do as the old man directs you. The responsibility for your success is directly on your shoulders now. Don't count on the boys, because as soon as you are in these hills and mountains it is everyone for himself or herself. And at all times stay close to one another and be sure not to break the link, because you could be lost in the dark where you can't call for help. Of course, the border guards will be too glad to rescue you, but you know what that means – not only to you but to others as well. And at all times your mouth must be shut, no blah-blah-blah along the way.'

The old crosser touched Billy's arm and droned fiercely in Arabic, like a masked ancestral spirit.

And quickly Billy turned to us and continued, 'The emphasis is that you must do whatever he tells you, even if the border guards are close by and are looking on. This is important. Then another vital issue: to avoid the stupidity of that girl whose photo was found by the Guardia Civil the morning they entered into the camp, you must tear photos and documents now if you still have them. Chew them up and swallow them 'cos you won't need them for anything afterwards.'

Silence.

Billy then took a deep breath, looked us up and down one after the other – his eyes did not even settle on me for even a second longer – and said, 'Finally, phone me as soon as you wake up in Calamocarro in the morning. Safe journey.'

He turned and walked toward the old Mercedes car, while we looked on, speechless. The driver rolled the car noiselessly out of the grass, and Billy entered and closed the door quietly. And, without switching on its headlamps, the driver started the car and drove off. Soon, the noise of the engine dropped into a drone, and then into a buzz that quickly fizzled into the solemn night.

Instantly, tears rushed to my eyes and my heart began to pound. Billy had not said an extra word of encouragement to me – not even a glance in my direction to show that I had slept with him for months. How callous and brutal were the ways of men. A feeling of abandonment creased my joints and ran like cracks all over my head. You must be careful, I warned myself, or others would notice what had happened.

True. And the beast had told us to phone him. Who? Me? Not unless I got there first! He'd never hear from me ever again! Callous man.

The tears rolled down, nevertheless. But I didn't want to be caught crying. I wiped my eyes dry.What with what lay ahead, wouldn't it be stupid of me to let in further corrosive emotions to melt this final resolve? I had come a long way without Billy and I'd go a long way without him. A journey that had lasted for over eight months was bound to be peopled by characters like Billy. Hadn't I seen worse in Abidjan and Tamaraset? Ah, wipe your eyes, I told myself. And that was what I did.

'… *cuatro, cinco y tu, aqui, aqui.*' The old crosser was counting us with his wooden staff. He cleared his throat and continued, '… *seis, eh, siete y ocho … . Que? Por que? Dios mio! Embarazada? Embarazada?*'

He was muttering and examining Suzzie. He was clearly alarmed, and what he meant by those words we couldn't tell. They were either Spanish or Arabic. Even Osaro, who claimed a little understanding of both languages, was at a loss. Yet everyone knew the cause of his outrage. Why hadn't Billy the beast told him, or given him the extra money that Osaro and Suzzie had paid? What if this man were to leave us here and walk away? Sure enough, he hadn't expected a pregnant woman as a passenger. And, as if he had read my thoughts, the old crosser turned away and railed in the dark, stomping his feet hard on the ground and swishing his staff through the air. When he was through, he came to us, shuddering and letting steam gush out of his nose. But we were relieved that he came to himself quickly enough.

'*Quien es tu hombre?*' he asked Suzzie, as calmly as he could.

Suzzie pointed at Osaro. How did she understand that?

'*C'est moi,*' Osaro said in French and stood out.

'*Tu? Con ésta?*' The old crosser pointed at Suzzie's stomach.

'*Qui, si,*' Osaro nodded.

'*Vale.*' The old crosser nodded too, seemingly pacified that someone was at least going to take charge of that. And saying something else to Osaro which neither we nor Osaro understood, he motioned us to follow him, muttering, '*Avance. Desde ahora es caliese y silencio. Caliese, silencio.*'

We shuffled after him, apprehension in our breaths and in our steps. The fear of the dark crept into my heart once again. This wooded side of the hill toward which he led us was so dark that it looked like an entrance into an evil forest, as if the paling moon did not shine on it.

154

Walking blindly in a crooked line behind the old crosser and making frantic attempts not to break it, we soon disappeared into a hideous grove. The brightness we had enjoyed earlier was snuffed out by the absence of the moon and by the thick, matted foliage overhead. I felt a chill in my heart but kept on, reassured by the presence behind and in front of me.

And so we groped along until we came out on a short stretch of open field that was shut in on all sides by dark and clumsy hills. We could see in the hazy distance ahead the old man leading the trail, but couldn't in the world imagine on which side an outlet lay.

Then suddenly, the old crosser stopped and bade us lie down on the ground. He walked some distance ahead, crawled in short bursts and stopped. He waited, stood up and pointed his staff in the air, brought it down, pointed it to the left, then to the right and stabbed it on the ground before him. Then, he motioned us to advance. When we got to him he raised his staff and bade us walk beneath it, all the time keeping the staff pointed to the sky. As I passed beneath that staff, the fear I felt earlier melted away in his protective presence. But walking past him my heart went cold again at what I saw on the side toward which the old man faced.

There, two patrol jeeps were parked a few metres away, behind a great mass of rocks. A man was leaning on one of these jeeps while another, with his back toward us, stood looking into the dull sky, exactly in the direction in which that old crosser's staff pointed. Up in the sky I saw a shooting star swish through the air and vanish in a thin, colourful streak. And soon we were crawling on our hands and knees far away, toward the foot of an adjacent hill, my heart still beating wildly in my chest. Was this, I wondered, how the old crosser bewitched the border guards?

Right around the rocky track at the foot of this hill the old crosser led us, until we came to a clearing beside a dense mass of what looked like elephant grass. He counted us again and made signs that we should calm ourselves and wait for him. And quickly, he disappeared behind the misty haze of the grass beside us.

A blanket of darkness came over us soon afterwards, and I saw on looking up that an enormous mass of dark cloud sailed slowly, as if with difficulty, across the hill tops, obscuring what was left of the hidden moon. And from the side whence we came, a wide stretch of grey fog came unfurling and spreading toward us. I heard the sound of the breeze, whistling through the blades in the grass and rustling the dry leaves and twigs on the ground. The insects became festive and noisy, shrieking and chirping raucously as if tonight were the last hours of a mating season. This made the night more intimidating; we stood huddled up close to the clumps of grass murmuring amongst ourselves in voices one could scarcely hear if one were a foot away. Our breaths were hot and steamy and if one listened hard enough, one heard his neighbour's heart hammering at the cage of his chest. Suzzie sat down on the undergrowth and breathed noisily through her mouth.

'I can't make it,' Suzzie muttered. 'I can't.'

Osaro knelt beside her, solemn and exhausted.

'Easy,' he said. 'Don't go on talking; try to catch your breath first, right? It will be alright. I'm sure we aren't far from Ceuta now. We aren't.'

'I know I can't. I can't continue. Go with them Osas, you can come and take me later,' persisted Suzzie.

The remoteness in her voice and the finality of its tone really made us panic.

'No, Suzzie, you can't say that,' Sandra chided her. 'How can we leave you here and go? And in such conditions?'

Everyone else was silent, not knowing what to say. We had felt earlier that she was completely Osaro's responsibility. But that attitude had suddenly changed and I was fuming inside. How could any girl have allowed herself to be pregnant in these circumstances? Some girls are certainly nuts, I swore. I felt like letting a slap fly across her face. The bitch. Even before we left Tangier, the prospect of her imperilling this crossing was a constant concern. But now we could only cluster round her as if she were a queen bee and try to persuade her.

We were so preoccupied with persuading her that we did not know when the old crosser crept upon us.

'*Qué pasa?*' he asked, circling us swiftly. And without waiting for an answer, he counted us again and motioned us to follow him.

As we rushed after him, leaving Osaro and Suzzie behind, Sandra or whoever it was, stumbled on a stone and made some noise. The old crosser flew back from the front and gave her a knock on the head. And not a word of sympathy was uttered in the preceding silence. Then I turned and saw that Osaro and Suzzie had caught up with us. Osaro was carrying Suzzie in his arms in front of him. How else was one to carry a pregnant woman? Osaro was the strong wiry type, but we hadn't climbed any real hills yet and I wondered how he would manage a steep one.

Nonetheless our tense procession continued along the side of another hill. We weren't taking the rocky cliffs straight on, but went around and around at the sides so that it felt as though we were going up a spiral staircase. This old crosser certainly knew the terrain. And just at the point when we were in a sheet of stagnant fog and our legs were beginning to ache, we began a slow and trying descent to the bottom of the hill once more. Here the grasses were tall and thick and the earth was soft – and in some places marshy as well. Then we heard the sound of running water and the solitary croaking of a frog. The smell of dung and goats' urine wafted pungently through the air, quickly erasing the freshness from the cool air we had enjoyed earlier at the hilltop.

Unperturbed, the old crosser swiftly walked to the end of our trail and, in the dark, began to count us again. Then he took us through a path that was covered by tall reeds that rubbed against our faces. Out again on a clearing, beside a low-running fence of reeds, we began to hear a thunderous splashing of water against the rocks. I was convinced now that we were very close to the sea and my heart leapt up and began to beat.

But then we continued through a patch of small bush, jumped down a boulder beside another gurgling brook and burst out onto a dirt road that, on both sides, ended in darkness. We crossed this road after the old crosser had surveyed it, and went towards another hill in front of us. At the foot of this hill he stopped and pointed out a path.

'Arriba aqui, moreno, muchos morenos,' he said.

We did not understand him.

'Vamos,' he said. 'Aqui, Calamacarro, arriba.'

We looked up the path he had pointed out right to the top where it disappeared into a dense grove. From the way we stared at one another in the dark, I knew that I wasn't the only one who panicked. It was unthinkable that anyone could be living on top of that hill. Besides, we were expecting to be brought into a city, not into a forest. We were stone-footed and lost in wondering. But perhaps, if we got to the top we could walk into the city on our own. Maybe that was what the old man meant.

'Vamos,' we heard the old man mutter behind us once more.

And we began to climb the hill. When we were midway up dogs began to bark. This put a fresh fear in us and we halted and searched around us for signs of life. From the height we had already gained we saw balls of light through the swaying foliage. On the ground were plastic bags, cartons, cans, and bottles of all shapes and sizes littering the hillside. There was a sharp and choking odour of decay curling around us, sometimes taking on the pungency of stale urine. And there were sneaky movements on the ground that frightened us, until we saw that they were made by dozens and dozens of rats. Yet, all the while, the barking of dogs intensified and we looked back to seek courage from our guide.

But he was gone. Vanished.

Left with no option, we began to trudge up the hill with both hands on the ground. In the lowering darkness, worsened by the matted foliage overhead, we felt relieved that the winding path to the top was still visible. We followed it in a single file, totally disregarding the hysterical barking of dogs around us.

When at last we got to the top, we examined the scene that awaited us. It was a dark and gloomy campsite with a few lampposts strenuously pushing the darkness away. This was no doubt the refugee camp that we sought to enter. It was like a clearing carved out of the heart of a forest with its thick canopy untouched. There were no brick or cement houses, but rather clusters of loathsome tents lumped together like a herd of resting camels chewing the cud and contemplating a tedious trek at sunrise.

Mysteriously, the dogs stopped barking and a deafening silence ensued. There was not a movement in sight, other than the patter of rodents through the litter. We chose the nearest tin-shack contraption on the left and tiptoed toward it, two at a time. And nothing – no sound still– but the same staccato patter of rats led us through the many tree trunks that were standing like guards here and there. I followed closely behind Jerry who led the way, my eyes darting about. Near the shack, past a couple of tables that leaned on broken legs, we saw a man bent over and engaged with his zippers. He started and stared at us on hearing our footfalls. I stopped while Jerry approached him.

'You're just coming?' he spoke to Jerry first.

'Yes. Please is the ... ?' Jerry's voice was shaking with distrust.

'This way,' the man said and left what he was doing. 'How many of you?'

'About eight.'

'This way, and make it fast,' he said, and took us to the tin-shack contraption. 'Sit anywhere in here, but don't stand. The camp guards walk around sometimes. Where are the others?'

'They are behind those trees, over there.'

'Go inside and sit down. I'll fetch them myself. You are now in Europe.'

At the mention of Europe, a swirl of haziness came over my head and made me stagger. When it cleared I walked behind Jerry into the enclosure in which the man had told us to make ourselves comfortable, picking my way through the human bodies wrapped up in blankets on the floor. There was a warm, offensive odour in the air, which I ignored. I sought out a small space in the corner and sat down. Resting my head on a water can, I began to revisit, in all its vividness, the eight-month journey that had brought me here. I did not know that I had dropped into a bottomless sleep until ...

'Call the guardia!' I heard a voice shout. 'No, no, call the secretary first. He will call the ambulance. Quick!'

The Guardia Civil? The name terrified me and I jumped up wide awake. As I grew accustomed to the daylight that pricked my eyes, I heard a lot of fuss at the other end of the room. Near the door somebody was on the floor tossing and twisting, heaving, groaning and sighing and stretching like a worm dipped in salt.

'Hold her hand and don't let her roll over,' somebody said.

'Gentle, easy, easy. It'll be over soon. I hope this isn't trouble for her?' You could feel the panic in that voice. And it was Osaro's.

I got up and saw Suzzie lying on the floor. Two girls and Sandra held her legs together while an elderly woman talked soothingly to her. In one moment she subsided, in the next she raved and ranted, groaned and twisted. I had never seen anything like this. And so the commotion continued, attracting other people who passed by.

Minutes later, the thin wail of a siren was heard. In seconds, it blossomed into a full-blown clamour and an ambulance appeared behind us. Its passengers were white men in white and red clothes, with bold Red Cross emblems on them. Working like ants, they hurriedly whisked Suzzie away into the ambulance. As Osaro stepped up to the rear of the ambulance, an invisible hand and voice pushed him back out. He walked around and around, confused and shaken. And none of us slept after that.

ON THE LAST DAY

By Patrick Mangeni wa'Ndeda

Ouma had just completed his final year examinations. This was his last day at the university. From his room in the Northcote Hall of residence, the din of the Hall drums filled the air. A barrage of verbal missiles, as the students commonly referred to the trading of inter-hall insults, was being launched towards the neighbouring Nkrumah Hall. Despite belonging to a most militant student hall of residence whose conduct was as violent as it was infectious, this aspect of hall culture had never been to his fancy. He resented the often immature and violent conduct of university students in the so-called culture of protecting and advancing 'hall sovereignty'. He had strongly despised the inter-hall violence that was a likely aftermath of a football match between his hall and their arch-rivals, Lumumba Hall. He couldn't forget the time during his first year when Mukiibi, his roommate, ended up in hospital after a fight in which stones were hurled. On this particular day, a student had molested the Vice-Chancellor of the university. This kind of behaviour could not be excused in the name of 'Hall culture' and from then on he always walked away when he heard the sound of drums.

Ouma sighed. The noise outside was approaching like a storm. He fingered his keys uneasily, picked them up, pushed them into his jacket pocket and moved to his window. His final paper gave him a feeling of having crossed the line. He did not feel part of the school anymore. He was waiting for the next day to go back home and help his parents on the farm. He also planned to do some part-time teaching at Lumino High, the secondary school near his home, as he waited for the results to be announced. It would be good practice for him before starting his teaching career, Ouma thought, smiling to himself.

Ouma had consistently received A's in the first two years of university where he was studying Literature in English and Music. The Vice-Chancellor had officially acknowledged him as the best-performing student. With a grade point average of 4.8, Ouma was heading for a first-class degree. He had been earmarked for staff recruitment, and the Dean of the faculty had encouraged him to work harder.

'You have a very bright future ahead, Ouma Joseph. If you keep up this performance, we are going to sponsor you for your Masters. Do not lose your focus.'

The examinations had been easy and he knew where he was headed.

'Books first, everything else later,' he would intone, before humming to himself.

So as he stood in the now empty yard, he could hear the din from the drums go up the Main Hall towards the football pitch. He felt like taking a walk. To where? He did not know. But he just wanted to walk.

Although the evening haunted him with a desire to free himself of the now boring routine of student life, he was undecided where to stroll. All he felt was a growing urge to be free.

As he trudged towards the Main Hall, the air was calmer. The sun was just setting and the Main Hall tower stood prominently like Kim Ll Sung's monument – 'Juche' – on Mansu Hill. A calm easterly breeze whistled through the giant jacarandas of the Library Park and as he turned, a sweet fragrance from the freshly-mown grass brought the freshness of the country air.

His walk led him to the slighly ajar doors of the St Francis Chapel, where the sound of the Kampala Singers' performance of Handel's 'Messiah' was irresistible. Ouma tiptoed in and slid unnoticed into the back row. The melody was that of seraphs and cherubs at a celestial dinner. There were about five people in the audience. Two of them were stooping professors of Mathematics; the other three were the Vice Chancellor, who held his head high as if he was posing for press cameras, the Archbishop, whose mind was in 'minor key', and a middle-aged lady, who listened with a plastic smile. But no sooner had Ouma listened to one movement than he started feeling congested; the soles of his feet were itching. He turned uncomfortably on the pew like a laying hen. What did he want? Where did he want to go? He knew no answer. But at least he knew what he felt. He felt out of place. Rather than force himself to stay, he got up and followed his feet.

The urge, somehow, took him to the gates of Complex Hall, fondly called 'crocodile land' because its residents were referred to as crocodiles. Now he could call on one of his friends and chat about the exams and their prospects in their field of study. As he was contemplating which of his friends he should visit, he heard a female voice:

'Hallo, mature!'

It sounded familiar.

'Hallo, pre-mature!' he sighed back inquisitively, trying to locate in his mind whom it was.

'What crocodile has stolen your heart?' She approached. It was Jane.

A third-year student of Statistics.

'It's her skin I seek,' he quipped, turning to her.

They faced each other awkwardly.

'It's been a long time, Jane!' He smiled back, instinctively saying what crossed his lips. 'I heard you changed rooms'.

'Since when?' She dared him with a theatrical frown on her face.

'Since Jesus was at school,' he answered and they laughed as he played it off safe and light.

At 22, Jane was a mortal harvest. Ouma looked at her admiringly and thought the creator had spent his time well. She had the eyes of a calf. She was tall, she was black and she walked like a deer. She knew she had great eyes and she used those eyes well. Ouma often said that nature had been lavish with her.

His heart thumped. Realising she had noticed his discomfort, he scratched his chin and tried to look as though he was lost in Socratic thought. Her feminine sensibilities stepped in immediately to restore him.

'Eh, why not join me in seeing off this cake?' She smiled, pointing to the cake she was carrying. 'I just bought it in the canteen.'

Visiting Jane would not be a bad way to pass the evening, he thought, licking the fringes of his sprouting moustache.

Jane was a very gifted student; she loved her books – just as much as she loved kissing, he remembered. He smiled a sigh of surrender, and followed her up the stairs. Ouma looked at her legs as she went ahead of him. They looked more beautiful with each step she made. He liked their shape, he liked their elegance, he liked their fullness and he liked the baby-soft skin. She said something to him but he did not hear as he was fixated on her legs as they climbed. Climbing with them. Climbing into them. There was a feeling that was beginning to tempt him downward, to dip his tongue into the dimples of those legs. Then he bumped into something; it was her back. He looked up and noticed that she had stopped. She turned to smile at him, stepped aside and pointed ahead for him to lead the way.

Ouma had first met Jane in their first year at university when they had both attended an instrumental of Bach's 'Jesu, Joy of Man's Desiring' performed by the department of Music, Dance and Drama of Makerere University. On that day, the hall had been packed to capacity like a church on Christmas Day, not out of any classical taste on the part of the predominantly student audience but because of the break-dancing show that would begin soon after. Ouma, who amidst the pushing and squeezing had secured himself a seat, was awakened to a voice asking to share it with him. He had ignored it, but when it persisted, he looked up into a woman's eyes and what he saw broke something inside him. To this day, all he remembered of the performance was the glow in her eyes and the warm feeling of her hip on his side. From that time on they became friends and saw each other often.

And just when they were beginning not to care about what the world around them was saying, after one of Jane's visits to his room, Mukiibi, Ouma's roommate, had fallen in love with her. He had spent a week describing two things: her eyes and her legs and how they had condemned his heart to a sentence he must serve. He said he would just die and die again and again if Ouma did not honourably step down in solidarity.

'I will give you anything for that girl,' he moaned.

Ouma knew there would be no peace if he did not relent. Besides, his growing involvement with Jane in the past few weeks had cost him higher grades on two assignments. So Ouma, to Jane's puzzlement, had given this relationship a second thought and then retreated to the library.

Mukiibi made his move and he and Jane were soon to be seen side by side at the Guild canteen and beyond the gates of Makerere.

'A man can now die!' Mukiibi had said one afternoon, after having woken beside her that morning.

Ouma hadn't known what was to happen – how could he? But now he couldn't think of those words without a chill running through him. He missed Mukiibi. He wondered if Jane did too.

Staring into his half-empty cup of coffee, Ouma remembered that conversation with Mukiibi vividly. He turned the last leaf of Jane's photo album, which he had seen more than once before and only took from her out of politeness. He noticed that something was missing: Mukiibi's photographs. There had always been one on the first and last leaves of the album. Turning towards her pillow, he noticed that the photo of him that had always been by her bedside was also missing.

Their eyes met and Jane looked away with a mixture of pain and something like guilt. He sighed, fumbling with the cup of coffee in his hands.

Remorsefully, Ouma recalled the scene of Mukiibi's premature death in that accident: a pudding of bone, flesh and blood smeared on the tarmac by a trailer that had not veered from its course.

For a long time after this grotesque spectacle, Ouma could not imagine that he would ever eat meat or touch liver again. A policeman who had extracted Mukiibi's identity card from the mass of flesh and bone had called the university, and soon the hall warden had picked up Ouma and their hall chairman to accompany him to the scene to help with the identification.

Ouma grimaced thoughtfully as he put aside the album and sipped the now cold coffee absentmindedly. Jane sighed. A silence whose hollowness defied filling descended between them. Ouma's mind got bogged down on the subject of this silence. He turned as if he had heard something ominous. He could hear in the corridors, heavy shoes approaching at a measured pace. They sounded distant but familiar. Ouma could not remember whose they were, but they sounded familiar. The footsteps became more cautious and softer as they approached. The silence was magnified by the ghostly sensation that surrounded their haunting grotesqueness. Ouma felt taut. The feet came close to the door and stopped. Jane, who had been watching Ouma closely, now looked confused. He looked up and their eyes met. Ouma looked to the latch of the door. Jane too looked at the latch, wondering. It did not turn.

'Ouma, what is the matter?' she asked.

But he did not hear. He was staring at the door. Then, he heard the footsteps again. They were going away, back towards where they had come from. Back downstairs.

'Who was that?' he asked quietly. 'Who?'

His hand reached for his coffee. It was now cold, really cold. He lifted it to his lips, paused and put it back slowly, without drinking from it. He swallowed with a dry throat and looked at her. She was still staring at him with a blankness that seeped into him, through him, beyond him, to that infinity that had come in the silence and claimed it. She sighed and got up. There were tears that shone like beads of silver in her eyes. She turned towards the wardrobe, opened it quietly, her back taut with unease. She reached inside and brought a towel towards her face.

She turned around with a slight smile. That put some life back into the room that had suddenly chilled and haunted them. She signalled for him to shift his chair away from the window to allow her to clear the cups. Although he knew that it was not necessary for him to shift to enable her to remove a cup and a teapot, he got the message in her aching stare: he was in the same place and seat that Mukiibi used to occupy.

A female voice screaming outside demanding an explanation as to why someone had again used her meal-card to claim her food. She was threatening to call a press conference if the offender did not give a public apology. Jane and Ouma burst into laughter, easing the tension. She giggled some more, throwing her neck back, and he liked the cascades that rippled its length. But Ouma, still had no words, and they fell quiet again.

He could not bear this any longer. He sprang to his feet. He was leaving.

'What is the matter?' she asked curtly.

'Just stretching my lousy feet,' he answered, and immediately wondered why he had said such a thing.

Why in the first place had he not just stated his mind? The feelings he had for Jane when they first met were beginning to stir in him again. They were beginning to cloud his mind. Deep inside him there was something he was sensing; something like fear of the truth began to cloud his mind. He was in no mood to cope with disappointment. He feared losing her. Then, sheepishly smiling, he heard himself inviting her for a beer at the Guild Canteen. He bit his lower lip, berating himself. Wanting to escape from the room too, she promptly accepted. With a deep sigh, they walked to the door.

One year on, Mukiibi's death still haunted Ouma. Could Mukiibi have dived into the trailer's path to avoid a certain, slow and painful death? Ouma wondered, popping the second bottle of Nile Special. Mukiibi had suffered from recurrent fevers for a protracted period of time. And he had lost a lot of weight. His eyes had stuck out of his head like demonstration ball-bearings and the skin on his torso had hung like a shirt on a hanger. Sores had filled his mouth and his bowels moved when he was not aware. As his roommate, Ouma had seen the close-up deterioration of his friend's health, and waited for Mukiibi to confide in him. But it never happened. The trailer had claimed his friend and confidant first.

'When did your affair with Mukiibi stop?'

'Why?' Jane jolted a bit, pushing her beer back.

'Ah ... I was simply asking.'

They looked away from each other in the semi-darkness

'About one ... I mean, two years ago. Why?' She looked him in the

165

eyes.

'No reason.' He shrugged his shoulders. Ouma smiled an insecure and shallow smile into this darkness between them.

'Ouma, are you fearing me because you think that he could have committed suicide?'

'No ... I was just wondering.'

'You do not have to worry yourself if you do not feel comfortable with me.' She paused. 'We had broken up and I do not want to go into that now.'

Jane remembered the day she argued with another woman over Mukiibi. They were entering a restaurant in Wandegeya when a lanky woman barely plastered with a swimsuit, grabbed Mukiibi by the fly of his trousers and demanded her money. When a blinking Mukiibi denied any knowledge of her, the woman yelled so loudly that she quickly attracted a sizeable crowd. She accused him of having slept with her on credit and then defaulting on payment. At first Jane, like many around, did not believe it – until the woman mentioned his name, hall of residence and room number and described the four fingernail scars across his buttocks. Jane burst into tears, pulled out a five hundred shilling note and cast it at the woman.

That night she had wept. Her chest got so wet that she had to spread her nightdress on the drying line. She was heavy with embarrassment. She was hurting. She had always suspected him to be reckless but not to this extent. That is why she had insisted on condoms from the start, except for one day when she had woken up to find herself in his bed, naked and damp. Mukiibi was not there. When he returned to find her in tears and confused, he explained that they had returned from the hall reunion party and that she was drunk and would not hear of keeping their clothes on. He had borrowed condoms from a student in the neighbouring room, he said, and had disposed of the used condoms that morning while she was asleep. She did not know whether to believe him or not.

But after the incident, Jane did not want to hear about him. His death had worried her and made her sad. Once, a friend for whom she was to act as bridesmaid, asked Jane to accompany her to an AIDS information centre. She tried to persuade Jane to have a test as well. But Jane had declined explaining that she, unlike the friend who was doing it as a premarital requirement, was under no such obligation. She was not prepared for it. She said she would concentrate on her books, make new friends and live her life. So Jane had put the past behind her. She was happy with it that way. She did not want the ghost of Mukiibi to haunt her. She wanted just to enjoy her life.

She sipped her beer and smiled at Ouma meekly.

Ouma smiled blankly back. He was lost in thought. He recollected seeing Jane and Mukiibi engaged in an intimate act three months before Mukiibi's death, at night against the back wall of St Augustine's Chapel. Mukiibi's white cap was unmistakable. Curiosity had denied Ouma breakfast and led him to the spot, the following morning, where he counted a cluster of used condoms. That week, he thought the Chaplain was right in sending out a circular asking the university community and its visitors to show fear of God and respect the sanctity of holy grounds.

'Is she being honest? Could she be censoring truth in self-interest? Maybe she knows she has IT. Although she doesn't look like she has it ... But could Jane lie to me ... when it involves my life ...? Can such beauty be so void of heart as to risk another's life ...?' He gulped another mouthful. Some of it went the wrong way and he fought hard against choking. He fought it and cleared his voice. His eyes watered slightly ... Is she meddling with the truth as a shield against stigmatisation? Questions and questions ploughed his mind. He looked at her searchingly as she rolled her eyes. Desire surged through him. The temptation to have her was growing by the minute. Jane was too beautiful. Jane was too beautiful to be false, he swore. He swallowed nearly half a bottle of beer and stared ahead as if to conjure up courage, feeling the yeast warming up his skull, causing lightness in his head as if he was spinning around in the game of *dedededede kalira munamwenge*.

'Is anything the matter? You look distant!' she asked, straining to focus on his face in the low light.

'I was thinking what beautiful eyes you have!' he whispered.

Resignation lined his voice.

She returned his compliment with a look through her eyelashes. He was literally feeling her in his loins, his underside churning with a lemonish tingling sensation. It had been brewing over time. The desire to have her increased another level. 'The only way of getting rid of a temptation is by yielding to it.' The adage crossed his heart and loosened his fancies.

She popped her fifth beer. The sound pronounced another period of stalemate. The proverb of a boat that capsizes as it is about to anchor crossed his mind and he sighed.

Was Jane worth the risk? Had he not spent his three years of study usefully, faithfully and safely? Why the hurry? What for? Yes, he could wait for his day, his girl ... But is there any difference between these girls anyway? Right now, the so-called Miss Right could be giving some rascal a lift.

He opened his third bottle.

'If I am asking myself all these questions am I not trying to be wiser than fate?'

He recalled that he had nearly lost his life three times: He had once shared a blanket with a black mamba; when still a boy and in the mango season, he had fallen off a branch and slumped between chiselled tree stumps; and he'd unknowingly eaten poisoned fish that his grandmother had set to trap house mice.

'I could not have survived this by sheer chance,' he thought. 'God must have been protecting me for a purpose; he must have some wonderful plan for me. Can a real God have the heart to watch the only son of a widowed mother eaten by a beauty of death? Can He, when He commands the power for all to cease, turn and progress at His will? A true parent like God can have no hand in that ... . He Himself must have led me to Jane this evening ... the Lord always works in strange ways.' Such positive thoughts progressively crowded his mind.

She gave him an inviting smile and he felt its warmth stir his heart. 'She cannot have it ...'

He gulped another mouthful of beer.

'Well, even if she did, where is the guarantee that I would contract it? Yes, I would go about it the slow and smooth way – that way I would avoid bruising myself, maximise pleasure and avoid being infected with AIDS ...' He swallowed and paused in his thought. 'But even if I got it, would I be the first or last? ... Well, if my time has come then it has come ... I could even live with it for ten or more years ... Hasn't it been said that some people have been HIV positive for over ten years without getting sick? And in ten years time, a cure should have been found. Or I could even eventually get used to it and join those who are living positively with AIDS. Everything has its positive side.'

He felt more encouraged.

A ray of light licked her chest, revealing her nipples. He was gnawed by the urge to squeeze them, to suck them ... His lips twitched, leaking out the finer bits of his emotion. He slipped his right hand under the table and found her bare thigh, and she lowered her head and paused as if she was listening to him. He snaked the hand up her thigh. She held his hand, gently.

'Ouma, it's not safe,' she mumbled with alluring resistance. He started getting strong. Charging in cascades of desire.

'Like most women, she does not want to take the initiative,' he thought, his breath rising in crescendo, a relentless ghost stalking the night of his fate. He groped under the table, held her hand and pressed it with the tender urgency of lovers taking advantage of a sudden blackout.

'It is not safe, Ouma!' she said, lowering her other hand under the table and stroking his hairy arms. He felt her fingers tremble, and saw her eyelids grow heavy.

'Jane, I need you like I will never need again.'

'Ouma, please, let's not lose control,' she whispered helplessly.

'I am in full control,' he whispered back, as their feet fell towards Northcote Hall.

'Ouma, do you have protection to wear?' she mumbled, leaning on his torso.

'Relax. I will take care of us,' he cooed, his spirits buoyant, her warmth lining his side.

Surely, if Jane had it, she would have symptoms ... at least a cough ... a pimple, even, just on the nose ...?

He hooked his fingers into the warmth of her fleshy hips.

Could death be so warm? Besides, Mukiibi never had sex without condoms ... so Jane cannot have gotten it.

He hesitated ... What if there was an exception? ... but most times Mukiibi took women back to their room when he was drunk, too drunk for abrasive sex. This should have eliminated the risk of infection for Jane.

He swallowed warm saliva.

But what if there was an exception? There must be a day for things to go wrong ... that could have been the day when Mukiibi did not wear a condom. Ouma's spirits fell.

'Jane, when ... when ... could I ask something?'

'Mh?'

'Have you always ... I mean, used condoms ... before?'

'Are you asking if ... if I mind them?'

He nodded.

'They are safer.'

He looked into her face and their eyes locked. Save for the heavy breathing, a silence covered them as they felt their way past the statue of Kwame Nkrumah in the quadrangle of Nkrumah Hall.

But what could be worrying her? Why is she so quiet? he wondered. The problem with some of us Africans is that we are either busy being suspicious or superstitious. Let the departed nurse their own spirits!

In the corridors of the hall, a lone voice saluted him, declaring him a 'Field Marshal' for daring the uncertainties of combat in this dangerous era.

He banged back the door with his foot, kicked off the shoes in splitting directions as his hands reached for the drawer of his reading table. He fished out his room-mate's spectacles case and flipped out two condoms. The mathematics was simple: the more condoms applied, the lower the risk of infection.

Even if a bomb had gone off behind him, Ouma would not have flinched. Even if the world had ended, Ouma would have witnessed it second hand. He was sailing on rejuvenated waves of pleasure, pleasure in arrears.

How have I been living without this? Sex in a condom had always been equated to sucking a sweet with the wrappings on. But with Jane the sweet was covering the wrapping.

***

Uncoiling, he rolled over and pulled the pillow to his head. He inhaled the air. The smell of sex reminded him of fresh fish. He turned his head and winked at Jane, and with a mellow smile he looked down his naked body as if to thank a part of himself. He stopped and sat up suddenly.

'O mama ... mama ...!' he screamed, like a man with a soldier termite on the tip of his manhood.

'What is it Ouma?' Jane leapt off the ruffled sheets, exposing her naked body.

A crumpled condom fell onto the floor. Jane shook the sheets desperately as if she had lost something. Then she turned to Ouma, who was on his knees perched on the pillow sobbing, 'But I put on two! But I put on ... .'

A broken condom hopelessly hung on his manhood, like a T-shirt.

RANDOM CHECK

By Ken N Kamoche

Maina was jolted out of his sleep by the shrill ringing of the phone. He grabbed it before it woke Polly.

'*Wei,*' he said, with a mixture of irritation and apprehension.

There was no answer.

'*Wei!*' He repeated the Cantonese greeting.

Still no answer. But he could hear heavy breathing and the sound of traffic at the other end. The call was being made from a busy street. He peered at the caller display, and in the dim light could only make out 'Private'. The number was blocked, just as he expected. Struggling to contain his anger, he replaced the receiver and then took it off the hook.

Polly was fast asleep. She hadn't stirred. Maina left the bedroom and walked to the kitchen. Without turning the light on, he poured himself a glass of cold water, lit a cigarette and lay down on the sofa in the small living-room. A few minutes later, he went back to the kitchen and fetched a beer. After this incident, he figured it would be ages before he could get to sleep again. This was the latest in a series of late-night nuisance calls during the month. Trying to run a business in Hong Kong was turning out to be a difficult and dangerous preoccupation.

'So now you're really turning the screw!' he lamented to himself as he sipped the ice-cold Heineken and contemplated the burning end of his cigarette in the semi-darkness.

Polly found him slumped on the sofa in the morning.

'I thought you leave for office already, *lougong.*'

He rubbed the sleep from his eyes and tried to sit up.

'Why you come to sleep here, *la?*'

'To think, Polly. I hope you didn't hear the phone last night?'

'No,' she replied, puzzled. 'Again? Is that why you leave it off the hook? I just place it back, I hope you don't mind, *la.*'

'You're so lucky! You sleep like a log.' He laughed, in spite of himself. 'They've been at it again. I can't stand this anymore!' He got up, and paced around the living room, breathing heavily and shaking his head.

'Maina, calm down, *lougong.* Please sit down, *la.* It will be okay.'

Earlier that year, a large shipment of electronic goods and machine tools destined for Mombasa went missing, and neither the insurance company nor the shipping agent seemed to be doing anything to help.

Maina had been fighting with them for months, while they tossed him around from one office to another. This was supposed to be his biggest break. He was finally going to break free of the grip of unsympathetic financiers and be his own man. Containers did not just disappear into thin air, and he hadn't heard of any ships sinking to the bottom of the sea.

Meanwhile, the creditors who had put up more than half the finance were fast losing patience. So was his bank. This one event had damaged his creditworthiness so much that it was proving impossible to raise funds for another consignment. The house and office rent had not been paid for two months.

Then there was the ongoing saga with Polly's parents. Her parents had been opposed to her seeing Maina, a black man, and were at a loss as to what to do now that she was pregnant. And they weren't even married. When he first met Polly, Maina had a lot of misgivings about the relationship because of things he had heard about Hong Kong people.

In his six years in China, he had dated local girls but had never imagined tying the knot with any of them. His family would never have approved. And he expected serious opposition from the Chinese side too. He had seen it all too often, amongst his friends. Many were happily married, but for Maina the cultural differences were not worth the trouble.

'It would never work,' he argued with Mberi, his Tanzanian friend. 'Can you imagine a Chinese girl cooking *ugali*, and rolling up *chapatis*? Or you think I want to eat rice for the rest of my life? No way, *ndugu*.'

'All you think about is food, my brother,' protested Mberi. 'Look on the bright side.'

'What bright side?'

'Well, it will enrich your culture, for a start.'

'Don't make me laugh!'

'So what are you going to do, then, follow Ouma's example and import?'

Maina thought for a while. His friends in Kenya had tried to fix him up with girls for years. But he was never there long enough to get to know any of them that well. He had attempted a few long-distance relationships, but eventually got weary of the effort. Some of the girls he met couldn't get over the idea that he chose to live in China, of all places. Why couldn't he try America, or even Europe, like everyone else? One girl openly told him she simply couldn't see herself living in that kind of place – Asia! Her feelings were somewhat coloured by a cousin's painful experiences in India, where he struggled to acquire a degree amidst race discrimination and financial problems, and eventually abandoned it, but not before undergoing a nervous breakdown.

'I would rather starve in Africa,' she had declared. 'And I'd do what there, anyway, eh? They have jobs there? I would have to learn Chinese? Give me a break.'

Another girl said she didn't want to live under communism: 'Give me democracy and freedom in the West any time.' She spent a fortune trying to get a US visa.

This was a recurring problem for Maina. Nobody in Kenya understood why he chose to live in China, and later Hong Kong, when he could so easily move to America, or at least London. London was the Kenyan generic name for the whole of Europe.

'How's London nowadays?'

A puzzled look. 'Actually I live in Milan.'

Edinburgh. Lyons. Never mind. It was all London.

'My son,' coaxed his mother, 'your cousin is in New York. Are you saying that he cannot arrange an invitation for you to join him? That Asia of yours, ai! We just don't know what came over you. We hear they eat dogs and rats. What madness! You've got your degree now; you can move on.'

Maina had been to the US once. The company he worked for in China sent him to Chicago for a month of training. He liked the lifestyle, but he saw very little in the way of business opportunities for what he wanted to do. Trading was what fascinated him. In America, he would have had to get a job, something that didn't appeal to him.

'In the States,' he told Mberi as they sipped Tsingtao beers in their favourite bar in the Pudong area of Shanghai, 'you can drive fancy cars and live in a nice apartment, but for me there's too high a price to pay.'

'Like what? You have a good career: you don't have to flip burgers at MacDonalds.'

'As a black man you'll always be a third-class citizen, especially if you're from Africa.'

'So how is it different here?'

'Here people kind of leave you alone,' said Maina, with unease. 'Anyway, here at least I can smell out the business opportunities. And you don't get mugged.'

Maina knew at the time he was being naïve. When he moved to Hong Kong and had to travel in and out of town frequently, he felt as though a force beyond him was prising his eyes open, making him realise he 'wasn't going to be left alone', as he had once put it. He became increasingly aware of just how frequently he was stopped at the border as he crossed back from the Chinese city of Shenzhen. Once, he was asked to open a newspaper, the only item he was carrying, while hundreds of locals were waved on, dragging heavy suitcases and bulging bags of shopping. The customs officer searched through the newspaper, laying it out, page by page, while Maina looked on, a bemused expression on his face.

'What do you want? What are you looking for?'

'Random check.'

'All these people with these huge bags, you don't think they could be carrying something illegal? What do you expect to find in my newspaper?'

'Random check. Official policy.' Standard answer.

Maina walked away exasperated, wondering what section of the Immigration Act the officer was quoting from. At the award-winning Hong Kong International Airport, whenever he asked the customs officers why they always stopped the black man, that was the standard answer: random check. One day, after a tiring flight, he was so angry, he demanded to know why he was always targeted.

'This is racism!' he cried, as the officer calmly shook his head and said:

'Is just your thinking.'

A few officers had begun to gather around their embattled colleague. Maina glared at them, oblivious of the stares and frowns from Chinese people weighed down by heavy suitcases that seemed immune to 'random check'.

'Look around you! Look at that other black man they've stopped. Why is it that all black people are stopped? Is that random?'

'Is random check.'

'Do you know the meaning of "random"?'

'You can write letter. Complain letter. Up to you.' The officer shut the suitcase and waved him away. Case shut. Dismissed.

The matter of marriage had become like a mantra that everyone in his family repeated every time they spoke or met. He often wondered whether he should follow Ouma's example. Ouma met a girl on one of his trips back to Kenya. They corresponded for a year. Then he arranged for her to visit for a few weeks. It cost a fortune but, as he explained to his friends, it was an investment that was worth every penny. The imported lady liked Hong Kong, even though she had trouble getting work.

Maina started dating Polly to 'buy time', as he put it. He did not expect much from the relationship. He still entertained the hope of meeting a Kenyan on his next trip.

His worst fears about their cultural differences being irreconcilable were confirmed when Polly insisted on eating *ugali* with chopsticks. He had never seen anything so ludicrous. He couldn't stop laughing. Polly dug daintily into the maize meal, a Kenyan staple, with the chopsticks and carved out a small piece which she then dipped in soya sauce and proceeded to bite into, a morsel at a time.

'What's the matter?' she demanded.

'Can you follow what I'm doing? You eat this with your hands,' he explained.

'Yeeh!' That was how Polly expressed disgust. 'Not so nice.'

'Just try it,' he urged, as he taught her how to wrap the *ugali* around a piece of meat and soak it in the succulent beef sauce before placing it with exaggerated zeal into his mouth.

'Oh, looks disgusting. Like primitive village people. Use chopsticks, *la*.'

They had been dating for almost two years when Maina realised 'buying time' was not quite what the relationship was about. Polly had become an indelible part of his life. He had not imagined it possible that he would fall in love with her. In his mind, he still dwelt on cultural differences – real and imagined – which he believed would come back to haunt them.

What finally won him over was the love she showered on him. She seemed to have refashioned her whole life around his, and to make changes to her life to accommodate him more than he was prepared to accommodate her. She took to calling him by the endearing term *'lougong'*, old man, which is the way a loving wife addresses her husband in Cantonese. She behaved as though she were born to care for him. To him it was like a throw-back to his grandmother's generation. He recalled with amusement how his grandmother was often described as her husband's 'walking stick'.

When he informed his family about her, all the resistance they had always expressed came flooding at him. But this time, rather than rethink his options, he found himself defending her. A few years earlier, this would have been unthinkable.

His father told him he was in God's hands, which sounded more than a little ominous at the time.

It took a long time for him to gather the courage to meet Polly's parents.

'You've brought shame to us!' cried Fong-tai. 'What do you mean you're dating a *hak gwei*?' A black ghost.

Fong-tai did not speak to her daughter for a month. She refused to take her phone calls and totally ignored her when she visited them. Maina was shocked when he found out. Polly tried to reason with her mother, but Fong-tai's mind was made up. Ah-Fong was less hostile, but he, too, took a while to get used to the idea.

'You must give us face,' said Ah-Fong.

Polly explained that she was a grown girl and could date anyone she liked.

For the rest of the week after the fateful announcement was first made, she was testy and restless. Maina visited her at her flat to console her every evening. At that time she was so angry she declared she didn't care if she and her mother never saw each other again.

'And Ah-Mah say she don't want to see you either,' she informed him. 'She said "don't bring that *hak gwei* here!"'

Maina laughed in spite of himself.

'Is not funny, Maina! Not nice she call you things like that! Is too bad, can't you see?'

'Don't fight with your family because of me, Polly. There's no need for you to protect me, sweetheart.'

'So, what you're saying? You want to walk away because ... because of this? Because Ah-Mah discriminate you?'

'No, don't be silly. Just give her time.'

To amuse her and reduce the tension, Maina took to referring to himself as her *hak gwei*.

He would call her on the phone and say, 'This is your loving black ghost!'

At first she couldn't stand it.

'How you accept this kind of treatment? *Chisin!*' Crazy.

'Hey, Polly, what can I do? I see it everywhere. Do you know people on the train sometimes get up when I sit next to them? Do you know I sometimes have a whole seat to myself on the bus because nobody wants to sit next to a "black ghost"? I'm not going to fight with your mum, Polly. Forget it.'

As she listened to his laments, Polly felt the pain as though she herself were the victim. The thought of people walking away from her as though she had the plague filled her with horror. She wished there was something she could do. But her mind drew a blank.

'Ok, I'll be your loving yellow ghost,' she offered.

'How nice. But it's impossible. To your people, you're either a person or a ghost, right? And if you want to qualify as a ghost, you have to become something else, like white or black. So what is it going to be?'

She began to lighten up and in the subsequent weeks her anger towards her mother abated.

One day Maina got a phone call from his sister in Nairobi. When he heard her voice his face darkened with alarm. It was too expensive to phone. He immediately knew it was an emergency. Her husband, Macharia, had been car-jacked in the middle of the city as he drove to work. Shocked to see a revolver staring him in the face, he had been slow to get out of the car and the hooded assailant shot him in the head. There were two of them. They threw his limp body out on the street and drove off, firing a few shots in the air. A crowd quickly gathered. Someone called the ambulance.

The injured man lay in a pool of blood in the middle of the road. Passers-by were shocked to see that he wasn't dead. The traffic ground to a halt. The police eventually arrived and cordoned off a section of one lane. The crowd melted away. It was no one they recognised. Just another shooting in the city. There would be more car-jackings and fatalities by the end of the day. A few more lives laid to waste in the City in the Sun.

Macharia lay in a coma in the intensive care unit at Kenyatta National Hospital. The family held a fundraiser to send him abroad for specialised treatment. They called all their friends and family abroad. They held prayer meetings, comforted each other, and begged God for his intervention. But they couldn't raise enough money, so they sent him to a private hospital in Nairobi that demanded a hundred thousand shillings before they would even see him.

Maina sent what he could, which wasn't much. He begged them to understand. His family said everything came from God and whatever little he could spare would be blessed. But he knew they did not fully understand. Many thought of him as a rich trader who shipped container-loads of goods around the world. They refused to believe him when he complained about the low profit margin after all the expenses and loans had been paid off, and the losses when customers failed to pay. The worst offenders were in fact relatives and close friends, who insisted that debts should occasionally be forgiven.

'It's our way, you know,' a cousin had once informed him 'It's our way of doing business. Don't you know that? You've lived abroad too long.'

'But this is business! I'm trying to make a living here.'

'I know, but it's also a way to help us. Have you any idea how tough things are in Kenya nowadays? We're suffering, and it's all the fault of this criminal government.'

'You've twice had a chance to vote them out. I guess it's your way, eh?'

'I know. The future generations will never forgive us.'

Macharia was in a coma in a public hospital for a few weeks before he died. Maina suffered alone, separated from his loved ones by a twelve-hour flight he could not afford, after the funds he had sent his sister.

The hospital and burial expenses nearly ruined the entire family. Phone calls and e-mail messages kept coming. They begged him to send more money. His brother told him about the things some people were whispering about him: that he had gone abroad and abandoned his people. He had become a Chinese citizen. They said he had renounced his Kenyan citizenship and was going to change his name to something unpronounceable.

The day of that e-mail from his brother, he was so distressed that at one point he had to stop on the street and lean against a wall. People rushed past him, oblivious of the torment in his heart. No doubt fighting their own battles too. Just another busy day in Hong Kong. People rushing off somewhere, to some appointment, to shop, to clinch a business deal, to make some money. Chatting loudly on their phones. Life went on.

Polly stood by him during the crisis. Although she wasn't a Christian, she prayed with him and did whatever she could to comfort him. She told her mother about it one evening. There was still some tension between the two of them. Her mother remained silent for a long time. She seemed to be having some difficulty making sense of it all, or so it seemed to Polly. But Polly was wrong.

Fong-tai understood alright. She was simply trying to get used to the idea that a world that seemed so alien could suddenly and without warning intrude into her protected existence. An existence that was supposed to be a safe haven from earlier troubles across the border. Hong Kong had been a refuge for many, ever since shedding its identity as a sleepy pristine fishing community.

'It seems like such a dangerous country,' said Fong-tai, with bated breath. 'They just shoot you and take your car. Just like that.'

'Maina says it happens all the time. So many guns come in from neighbouring countries where they have wars, it seems. I'm so afraid to go there.'

'I don't want to hear you talking of going there, you hear me?' At last, confirmation, if any were needed, of her worst fears about the folly of her daughter's romantic interest.

Polly said nothing. No need to fight again. She needn't have worried. The last thing on Fong-tai's mind was a fight. As she reflected on the tragedy in Maina's family, she became more and more morose.

'They shot him and threw him out of the car,' said Polly for the umpteenth time. 'It sounds like a scene from an action movie.'

'It seems there's so much suffering in Fei Jau.' Africa. 'Starvation, wars. People killing each other. Or is the TV exaggerating?' Fong-tai was visibly shaken. She fixed her gaze on the television but was oblivious to the game show. Bright lights and musical jingles ignited the audience's anticipation. Someone was just about to win a lot of money. He was getting a lot of questions right. The audience cheered and clapped their hands, faces beaming with pleasure. Sharing in advance the joy of the imminent win.

Fong-tai tried to imagine what life was like in Africa. Gangsters running amok with guns, robbing and shooting people on the streets. She recalled with terror the suffering her family endured during the Cultural Revolution. Her father, a college instructor, a 'decadent intellectual', was taken away for 're-education', as they called it. They came for him in the middle of the night. Liu Shauje, Miss Liu, as she then was, managed to escape to Hong Kong with her mother. She never saw her father again. They heard he died of starvation and exhaustion working in the fields. An auntie lost her mind. Miss Liu was so traumatised it took her years before she could muster the courage to visit her motherland again.

'Are you alright, Ah-Mah?' Polly saw the wrinkles on her mother's face deepen.

Fong-tai was dabbing at her eyes with a tissue. She turned to face her daughter.

'You cannot understand.'

'Understand what, Ah-Mah?'

Fong-tai merely shook her head. They had never discussed her troubled past. It was a taboo topic. Polly knew so little of her parents' past. Fong-tai thought it was better to protect her that way. Where would I begin? she thought. The young people today have seen nothing. Nothing like what we went through. The more she reflected on what Polly had said about Fei Jau, the more deeply she felt the pain of her family's dis-integration.

'I thought we left all this behind. It's strange how the world goes round and round, isn't it?'

Polly nodded, her eyebrows raised. Sometimes Ah-Mah could be so enigmatic.

'The world of Ah-Maina.'

Polly looked up with surprise. Ah-Maina. Mister Maina. Ah-who? Normally it was 'that boyfriend of yours', or 'your *hak gwei* friend'.

'See how his world comes knocking on our door. Reminding us of things we thought we forgot. And Fei Jau is so far away.'

Polly gave up trying to understand Fong-tai.

Maina racked his mind long into the night trying to find a way out of his financial woes. He had had to borrow money from friends to send to his sister. The rumours about him having abandoned his people had stung deeply. With every new debt he dug himself deeper and deeper into a dark abyss from which he had no idea how he would ever emerge.

When he realised he wasn't going to get any sleep, he crawled out of bed and went to the kitchen. He cracked a can of San Miguel and sat on the sofa. The next thing he knew, Polly was shaking him by the shoulders.

'Haiah! What's up, *lougong*?' moaned Polly, worry etched all over her face. 'Why you always come to sleep here, *la*?'

'I can't sleep, so I come here to think. And then I fall asleep.' He shrugged his shoulders.

'Oh, too bad. *Neih hou maafan-ah*.' You're too troublesome.

'What's the time, Polly?'

'*Chat dim gung*.' Seven thirty. She looked with scorn at the empty cans. 'You say you come to think, but you come to drink! Think and drink same meaning to you? Maybe drink too much, then have problem to think.'

Exasperated, she collapsed on the sofa beside him, clutching her slightly distended belly.

'It's not like that, honey,' he coaxed her.

'I'm worry about you, *la*. We have serious money problem?'

He shook his head. 'No, not too serious.'

'So is okay?'

Maina turned to look at her. Deep down he wondered whether she really understood the mess he was in. He had tried to protect her by telling her as little about his business dealings as possible. But in the last few months, as the pressure piled on, he had begun to open up a little.

He did not tell her about the threatening letters he received at the small office in the mall at Fanling, the unpaid bills, and the dwindling bank balance. Little did he know it worried her so much that she was afraid she would have a miscarriage.

'Yeah, it will be okay, Polly.' He put a reassuring arm around her. 'But we have to find a way out. I'll go to the bank again today.'

She smiled sweetly as she ran a hand through his hairy chest. A calmness swept over him as she held him and kissed his neck, breathing seductively into his ear. Her touch could be so refreshing, and so relaxing; it made him forget his worries, at least temporarily.

'Will you have dinner with your parents tonight?'

'No, I'll come home,' she replied.

Maina remembered their last visit together to her parents' flat in Quarry Bay the previous month. Visits to her parents were still strained, although Fong-tai had almost completely changed her attitude towards him. She even took to fussing over him, constantly urging him to eat more. She asked after his family, and engaged him in conversations in Putonghua about life in Fei Jau. It never ceased to amaze her how it resembled the life she once knew as a girl living in China.

The last visit took place sometime after Polly announced her pregnancy. Polly and her mother had had a row following the announcement, but during that visit neither parent was saying much. The meal passed without incident. Until it was time to go.

Maina noted with surprise that Fong-tai remained quiet. Perhaps her husband had cautioned her to act civilly after that row with her daughter. She flared up when Polly accidentally dropped a bowl in the kitchen while helping to clear up. It was an inexpensive bowl, nothing to get worked up about. But it triggered off the anger that Fong-tai had kept bottled up all along. With his limited Cantonese, Maina could only pick up fragments of the row. Ah-Fong himself remained quiet. He resigned himself to watching his favourite Chinese drama while he picked his teeth and sipped Chinese wine.

Maina was boiling inside. He couldn't stand the scolding that Polly was enduring. But there was nothing he could do about it. Polly had told him on numerous occasions about Fong-tai's temper. Now he had a chance to witness it first-hand. Polly was trying hard not to talk back to her mother and, from what Maina could see, she was doing a pretty good job of it. Eventually, reduced to tears, she scampered from the kitchen and ran into her old room. Fong-tai went on scolding her while she did the dishes.

Ah-Fong was reclining on his rocking chair. While they waited for the storm to blow over, he offered Maina a cigarette. Maina accepted graciously, thinking of it as some sort of olive branch.

Later as they headed back to Tai Wo by minibus, Polly recounted the details of the row. Maina hadn't been too keen to find out because he feared it was all about him. Fong-tai had complained bitterly about the family losing face on account of Polly's out-of-wedlock pregnancy and dubious relationship. And she was an only child! She had also reminded Polly that if they ever got married, they would have to prepare about HK$50,000 for her bride price, otherwise her family would lose face even more.

'I don't understand Ah-Mah,' said Maina, when they got back home.

Polly relaxed her hold on him and turned to peer into his face.

'Don't understand what?'

'First she doesn't want us to get married. Then she says, oh, by the way, if you do get married, this is how much you should pay. What's going on here?'

'*Mjih wo.*' I don't know. 'I know for you it's difficult to understand Chinese customs sometimes. The money is not for her; it's to buy me things – you know, jewellery and stuff.'

'Oh, I understand bride price alright. We have that in Fei Jau. Anyway, we don't have money for a wedding. So what are we going to do? I have to give them face, right?'

'Maina?'

'What is it now, honey?'

'I talked to my uncle.'

Maina's heart missed a beat. He lit a cigarette and inhaled deeply. Polly rested her head on his shoulder, blowing the smoke away.

'You want to know what we discuss?'

'I don't want to hear about your uncle!'

'You too proud, *lougong.* My uncle's really nice, *la!*'

Polly's uncle ran karaoke bars in some of the seedier districts of Hong Kong, like Sham Shui Po and Mongkok. He also had links with other amusement establishments, of which Polly spoke disparagingly. But she vehemently denied he had Triad connections, or anything unsavoury like that. For Maina, the uncle's business dealings remained shrouded in mystery. When he heard how the uncle was miraculously released from police custody in Shenzhen after a business dispute, Maina feared the worst. The saga included an alleged kidnapping, arson at a nightclub in the wee hours of morning, and police officers being investigated for alleged corruption.

'I'm not accepting any money from that man, all right?'

Polly got up languidly, and without a word, fetched her handbag. She produced a white envelope, which she calmly placed on the coffee table.

'We don't have choice, honey,' she said, as she headed to the bathroom.

Maina stared at the envelope as though waiting to see it explode like a time bomb. Right here in front of him was part of the solution to his problems. But how could he accept a gift from someone like the infamous uncle? Was this a trick to lure him into shady dealings? Would this be the first drag that turned him into an addict?

He stared long and hard at the envelope. But with his mind in turmoil, he could hardly focus. Instead he saw imaginary words screaming at him in bold, uncompromising Chinese characters. The words seemed to mock him, daring him to reach out and touch them. He thought he heard Polly singing in the bathroom. But the sound quickly changed to the harsh raucous laughter from the bar in Shenzhen where the fateful deal was sealed. Thinking he was finally going mad, Maina jumped to his feet and slapped his temple, as though trying to emerge from a trance. He then reached out for the envelope but his hand froze in mid-air as the phone rang.

'Why you don't answer it?' Polly called out.

Maina stood still, as though transfixed to the spot. Then he heard Polly answer the phone. She screamed some expletives in Putonghua and then slammed the phone down so hard it must have damaged the caller's eardrum.

Finally recovering his composure, Maina called out: 'Polly, I can't accept this man's money. Take it back, please.'

Polly emerged from the bedroom, still doing her make-up. 'You think my uncle a bad guy, but you think he worse than those crooks you trade with? Anyway I know you too proud to accept charity. So this is loan. Is cheque.'

Maina shook his head as Polly reached for the door.

Is cheque. She made it sound like the checks he was more familiar with. The random ones.

'You want breakfast? I wait you at *chahlou* downstairs. Oh, by the way, that money not my idea.'

'Whose idea was it?'

'Ah-Mah.'

AND STILL HOPE SURVIVES

By Glaydah Namukasa

Jonathan first held me when I hit a bump and stumbled into him. 'I am sorry, sir,' I said. I pulled away and searched the muddy ground under me for my shoe.

'Lost something?' he asked. The gentleness in his thick voice reassured my fluttering heart.

'A shoe,' I said. 'Do you have a torch?'

'No, madam, but I can help you. I live just here, up in this flat. I can get you light.'

No sir, I wanted to say, but the darkness was overwhelming. The starless sky was weighed down by the total eclipse of the moon. This, along with the electricity supply cut, turned the night into solid blinding darkness. I needed the light.

And so I met my future husband. Ours was an unforgettable marriage. It comprised of a battle between Jonathan and his family. A battle sparked off by Jonathan's decision to marry me, a 'half-caste.' This was a marriage that separated us from the world around us. My family was thousands of miles away. Miles I had never travelled. What little I knew about myself was not enough to give me a clue of where my home was. I only knew that I was born to a Kenyan mother and a *mzungu* father, whom my mother had last seen the night I was conceived, that I had grown up with my mother in Kenya, that she was dead, and that I had migrated to Uganda.

Jonathan's family regarded him as dead. His father had disowned him in my presence.

'I am burying you today, Jonathan,' Jonathan's father said, when Jonathan broke the news of our marriage to him. 'To me you are dead. To bring a half-caste into our family is a total disgrace. I cannot be disgraced. I would rather be without a son. Therefore, I have no son. I have seven daughters; my only son is dead. I am burying you, Jonathan, today!'

Jonathan's mother remembered the labour pains she went through when giving birth to him.

She said, 'You are still my son, Jonathan. But that woman will never be my daughter. And the children born by her will never be my grandchildren.'

Jonathan was a rare kind of man: he wasn't dumb, but he certainly kept dumb. We walked away from his parents' home.

184

We were married. Other than me and Jonathan, there was the District Commissioner, who joined our hands in matrimony, and one of Jonathan's friends – the one who remained true even after learning that Jonathan was to marry a 'half-caste'. I became my husband's family, and he became the family that I could see, touch and care for.

Botanical Beach had always been my favourite outing. Botanical Beach is where we spent our honeymoon evenings. I was not a swimmer, but I liked water. And this was a beautiful stretch. I had liked it as a photographer, before we were married, when I would take pictures of Jonathan as he swam. I enjoyed watching his charcoal-black skin gleam in the water. I liked watching as the waves surged and hit the shore, washing over my feet as if to give me a taste of what I was missing.

But on the second day of our honeymoon, as I watched Jonathan swim, I realised the waters were but a burst balloon in a child's hands. My heart grieved over the fact that Jonathan's parents had disowned him because of me. I needed something to erase the grief, but the water had no solution. All it did was stream to the shore, touching my feet with a warm kiss that barely reached my heart.

Jonathan's wet arms around me brought me back to myself.

He said, 'Gina, my dear wife. I've a suggestion.'

I turned to face him, hoping the suggestion would be a solution to the problem.

'We have to make our own family as soon as circumstances warrant.'

I didn't know what to say to him. He was right, but I could not tell him that. I tried to focus on the water but the more I looked at it, the more I hated it. It could not smash the rock in our marriage. The water lapping against the shore was only a continual reminder that water takes a lifetime to wear down rock.

'Jonathan …' I sighed out his name.

'I know my parents, Gina,' he said. Jonathan had the power to read my eyes. 'I've known them for the past twenty-five years. I am a man of thirty now. A married man. I can have my own family.'

He was right, and I told him.

We needed a child. We needed children. We needed a family! Each day that broke I waited to give Jonathan good news. But there was no good news. Months drifted along. A year elapsed. No pregnancy. My worries became a part of me, and I became Jonathan's worry. We went to see a doctor.

'Give it time,' the doctor said. 'There is nothing wrong with either of you. It seems as if you wait for a baby each day that passes. You need to relax. Ease the tension. The baby will come.'

The baby did not come in the next six months. Relaxation became a mystery to me. How could I relax when I saw my periods each month? When the day to break good news to Jonathan never came to pass? I sat back and looked at myself: a rootless foreigner who couldn't have children.

The break of another year multiplied my sorrows. Three years. Four years. Still, relaxation was unheard of in my life. I wished I could cultivate a fraction of Jonathan's hope. Instead, one question weighed on my heart: Where was the family I wanted to have?

One rainy evening brought Jonathan's mother. Jonathan was away when she arrived. I welcomed her but the welcome smile stuck to my lips.

'I've not come to see you,' she said. 'If my son is not home, I will wait for him right here on this sofa.'

She reminded me that I wasn't her daughter. She told me her son was not married yet, that I could be no wife. That I was just a 'half-caste'.

The nine years since I had last seen her had not changed even a hair on her head. Her flabby body swallowed the sixty-five years, and her tongue was as venomous as ever.

Jonathan returned. He found me in bed, crying.

'Not again, Gina,' Jonathan said. 'Or, has my mother …?'

'She's done nothing,' I said.

'Then what? Well, let me dry those tears.' He wiped my tears with his shirt, and then held my hand as we moved to the sitting-room.

That was Jonathan – his compassionate feelings ever steadfast, even towards his parents after what they had done to him. He still referred to his mother as 'my mother'.

'I am their blood, and the truth will remain the truth,' he always said.

In the sitting-room, Jonathan's mother sat impassive. Jonathan and I sat on the sofa opposite her. I did my best to avert my eyes from her vindictive stare but I had nowhere to focus. I hated looking at the walls because my eyes only met the pictures I saw every day. Pictures of Jonathan and me on our wedding day, Jonathan's portrait: head and shoulders – the one I had painted with my own hands – and the various art pieces I had made. I longed to paint a picture of Jonathan holding his baby in his arms! My eyes roamed the room. The room was just as neat as always. I wished I had a child to disorganise it so I could arrange everything again.

Jonathan's words stirred me from my daily daydream. He was saying, 'You've really thought of us, mother.'

'Jonathan, my son,' she said. 'I will get straight to the matter.' She sat forward and stared at Jonathan. 'You have everything. Look at your house. Look at your investment. Look at your money. But you don't have a child! You don't have a child because you don't have a wife.'

She paused, as if she wanted to get a reaction from either of us. She got none.

She continued, 'That woman seated by your side is not a wife. She can never be. Maybe to someone else but not to my son. She's just a half-caste! A curse! She can't be a wife. That's why you have no child. She's barren!'

The words were a scoop of pepper thrown right into my eyes. A machete slicing my heart into two. That one word, 'barren', was a killing blow. I got up to leave the room, but Jonathan grabbed my hand. He whispered to me that I was his wife. That he loved me. I sat back and cupped my face in an effort to stifle the threatening tears.

'You need a wife, Jonathan,' her implacable voice cut into me. 'That demon gluing you to a barren half-caste will be handled.'

'Enough, mother!' Jonathan jumped up. 'She's called Gina. She's my wife. Mrs Mutyaba Gina. Now, just get out, mother ...'

I had never seen Jonathan lose his temper. Anger was always an emotion that was under his control, but not today. Yet, not even the anger overshadowed his dignified voice.

He extended some notes to his mother saying, 'This is for your transport, mother. Have a safe journey.'

She took the money and stood up. She turned and glared at me. Those eyes: Vindictive. Cursing. I stared back, ready to face more of her stinging words.

She turned to Jonathan and said, 'The next time I come back here, I will bring you a wife.'

More pepper thrown into my eyes. Another crack in my heart. The world around me whirled. I went to the bedroom. Jonathan foll-owed me.

'Please drive your mother to the station, my dear Jonathan,' I said.

Jonathan didn't listen. Instead, he went and closed the door when she stepped out. He returned and sat beside me on the bed.

'She is right, Jonathan,' I said to him later. 'You need a child ...' Thorny words: they pierced my throat, but Jonathan needed a child. He was too good to be childless.

'Gina, if you can't give me a child, then I'll have no child.'

Two more years elapsed. Jonathan's love and devotion to our marriage remained unshaken. The more I encouraged him to get a child, the more he reminded me of his love. Another year passed. Each year added to my age. Each addition drained away more of the little hope I had left. Despair became another part of me. I gave up my visits to doctors. I had so far consulted more than twenty doctors.

'The baby will come,' is all they said but the baby never came.

One month came and went with the absence of my period. Another month; no periods. Still a mystery. Was I going to give Jonathan a child? Was it time to break the good news? I went to the doctor. Tests and examinations confirmed my pregnancy. Unbelievable: the first pregnancy at thirty-six years of age! I told Jonathan. Happiness threatened to weigh down our hearts. I cried. Jonathan cried. We cried. We became closer. We planned for our long-awaited family. It seemed like we had been living in the dark. Darkness that no light could break. But my pregnancy was a candle that lit up even the darkest of corners.

The candlelight didn't last long. One day I was pregnant, the next day I was bleeding profusely; the pain in my lower abdomen was intense. Jonathan froze. The doctor told us it was a 'tubal pregnancy.' That the fertilised ovum had not travelled to the uterus; that it had embedded in the fallopian tube; that the tube was too small for the growing embryo so it had ruptured, and the only solution was an operation. The tube was cut and tied.

Darkness struck again and overshadowed our marriage – darkness so heavy that we became part of it. With two tubes, I had taken a decade to conceive. Only God knew how long I would take to conceive with one tube. I wished for death because then, Jonathan would marry again and have children. Yet I didn't want to die. Jonathan needed me, I needed to be with him, and we needed a family.

After the lapse of two years, another candle was ignited. I missed my period. I was pregnant. No mystery. No crying. No joy. No hope. No planning. One month. Three months. Seven. Nine months! The labour pains begun. Jonathan was my right hand till our son was born.

'Samuel Jonathan Mutyaba,' Jonathan said – his first words after my eight hours of labour. 'Samuel was a baby born to Hannah,' he continued. 'Hannah was a woman whom everyone knew to be barren.'

I had never seen Jonathan read the Bible. Neither had it ever occurred to me that he believed a word of it. Jonathan believed in me, in himself, and in the family he hoped to make. But today, Samuel seemed to have changed everything.

Samuel faced the world on a Monday morning. He was the early-morning dew washing off the night's filth. He compensated for all the lost years. Hopelessness, despair and impatience became components of dust. I had given Jonathan a boy to carry on his name. We were a family. What can I say? That we were happy? Everything around us blossomed. Plants, trees, grass. The skies opened. The heavens smiled down at us.

Samuel grew up. One month. Three months. A year. At first I thought he would connect the two ends in Jonathan's family. Jonathan didn't think so. And he was right. Samuel was a half-caste who could never be a grandchild. Instead, he widened the gap. But Samuel had completed our family. He had created a new life in our family. Samuel two years. Three. Four. Samuel four years …

Samuel never made it to five. Death robbed us of Samuel in broad daylight. One radiant morning had him cycle away from his playground, and led him to death's open arms when his father's reversing car hit him. Our son's death transformed us into two logs that could not even be used for firewood.

As I watched the undertakers lower his little casket into the grave, I realised that it did not only contain Samuel's body; it contained our hope, joy, happiness and life. We buried Samuel: an angel who would always be with us.

Jonathan broke down. He lost his senses. I had heard the last word from him three minutes before Samuel's death.

'This man,' he had said helping Samuel on the bicycle, 'will be a great cyclist. Give him a year. After that, he will outdo the cycling champion.' He watched as Samuel cycled down to his playground, and then he went to the garage ...

Jonathan was admitted to hospital ten minutes after Samuel's burial. I was by his side. His condition deteriorated with each passing second. He became unconscious of himself and everything around him. He lay on the hospital bed, the sightless eyes staring at the ceiling above him. The doctor's diagnosis was tentative. It ranged from 'psychological breakdown' to 'nervous depression' – nothing precise. No one seemed to know what exactly had happened to my husband. And I blamed no one. All I knew was that Jonathan blamed himself for our son's death. My innocent Jonathan.

'Fate, Jonathan,' I whispered to him several times, but he was deaf to my every word.

I tethered my sorrow to a pole and nursed my husband. I loved him. I supported him. Jonathan became the baby I could have. A baby I mothered with all my heart. Changing his nappies, bathing him, feeding him through a 'nasal gastric tube'. My Jonathan: Deaf. Dumb. Blind. I watched each day drift by. I waited for what each moment would bring. I thanked every second that passed because it never went with Jonathan's life. My mind centred on Jonathan. I never cried. If tears could change anything, they would have brought back Samuel. I never slept. I was sleeping awake.

Jonathan's recovery was another process of growing up. One good month taught him how to look and see me. Another taught him how to touch and feel me. The third taught him how to hear me. The fourth taught him how to taste. I waited for his speech. I tried to make him talk. The task was heavier than when I used to teach Samuel. Samuel could try a word after me but Jonathan just kept staring at me. The next month came with a stammer in his speech, then a jabber bringing a smile to my sorrow-puckered face.

On a Sunday, the early-morning sun was breaking through when Jonathan uttered his first word in six months. One word, a messenger from the daylight robber. A word that drained him of his breath. A word that tilted his head upwards:

'SAMUEL!'

The word that killed him.

I floated away to an immeasurable distance. I sank into bottomless depths. The whole world closed in on me. The present was strange. The past a mystery. As for the future, my mind could not form the faintest conjecture. I was a fire burning. A fire consuming nothing. I looked down at Jonathan. Nothing of him had changed. He was still my charcoal-black Jonathan, his gleaming forehead sparking a light in my eyes, the thick devouring lips curving to smile at me, and the sightless eyes generously staring at me. Even in their dead state, they seemed to be exploring my face. Loving me. Encouraging me. Telling me that we could make a family.

'Jonathan,' I said. 'You may be dead. But you are a leaf that will never turn brown. You speak to me, yet you say nothing. Your loud silence is all I hear. Tell me, Jonathan, who am I without you? Where am I without you?'

I held Jonathan's hands. They were cold.

When the doctor entered the room, he took Jonathan's hand away from me. I watched him cover Jonathan's face with a white sheet. I didn't cry. Tears had not brought back Samuel. Tears could not bring back Jonathan. I felt ready to rise above the obstacles that fate had planted in my way. Death had robbed me of the family I had. Death had robbed me of the family I could have. I turned to the doctor. He lowered his eyes. I stood up and moved closer to him. He looked back at me.

'Doctor,' I said. 'Does death always win?'

He took my hand. 'Death wins at times, Gina. But still, hope survives.'

FAITH

By Ruzvidzo Mupfudza

People said Faith was a couple of scriptures short of the Holy Bible. He was part of the township's familiar landmarks. He had been around for as long as anyone could remember. There were those who said that he had gone mad because he had killed a person earlier in his life in order to enhance his success in business. Whatever businesses he had once had were now matters of legend and myth. There were others who said that Faith had gone mad from reading too many books, for he had been a great scholar once. His family simply smiled and shrugged, pointing a finger to their heads, saying that Faith was touched in the head.

But Faith was an eloquent madman, if he was a madman. When I first moved into that township he paid me a courtesy visit. I was quite taken aback by his appearance. His head was clean-shaven and a gorgeous white beard flowed down to his chest. He wore a flaming red gown and he carried a long, hooked, smooth serpentine staff. His eyes were a clear, piercing black and seemed to see through all the ways of man.

'I heard that you are a teacher?' he said in a booming voice. It was such a rich and deep voice that if it spoke to you in the dark without you seeing or knowing its source, you would be forgiven for thinking that it was the voice of God.

'Eh, yes,' I said, looking at him suspiciously, but curiously at the same time.

'Good, then we have something in common, you and I, for I, too, am something of a teacher.'

'Oh, is that so?'

'Indeed, it is so,' he said, nodding sagely. 'I, too, am cursed to walk this Earth delivering life-saving lessons that no one will listen to or take seriously – something I'm sure you go through on a daily basis with your young wards.'

His speech was precise. His bearing was imposing. He was a very impressive man. I nodded, for the teaching profession had lost its lustre; the children one taught always managed to seem to be interested in other things, which they quite clearly thought more important than acquiring a formal education. I invited him into the house, to the consternation of my wife, who, being a housewife, had already heard about Faith.

192

'Can I offer you some tea?'

'Yes, please.'

He was a man who loved his tea. It was while we were imbibing what he called 'the ultimate drink of angels' that I gleaned bits and pieces of insight into him. He had come to me in an attempt to persuade me to join his 'church,' seeing that we both had been called to the sacred role of teaching.

'We are both fishers of man, you and I,' he said after he had taken a long healthy swig of tea, head to one side as if listening to the taste, before sighing and nodding in contentment. Quite clearly, I had passed some secret test of his.

'The quality of a man's house, and ultimately his heart, can be judged by the quality of the tea brewed in the confines of his kitchen,' he said. 'Anyway, as I was saying, we are in the business of saving souls from the damnation of ignorance.'

He had been a member of the Apostolic Faith once, but he grew disenchanted with them when they refused to accept his visions and prophesies. The seers and healers in his church tried to pray for him and give him holy water in an attempt to chase away the demons and evil spirits that they said were afflicting his soul and driving his mind to madness, but to no avail. Accusing them of envy, Faith had decided to break away and form his own sect, called *Chita Chengoro Yemoto* (The Chariots of Fire).

You see, according to Faith's vision, philosophy and testament, the aliens we knew as God had descended to Earth in spaceships whose jet-propulsion systems had emitted fire and thunderous noise. Our early pre-scientific forebears had called these 'chariots of fire'. Our ancestors, having been familiar only with draught-powered chariots were awed by the fire-driven chariots of the aliens.

'You see,' he explained to me, his eyes flaming with passion, 'Adamah, the father of mankind, was the first genetic experiment that was carried out by the visitors from outer space. Indeed, Eve was the first result of the first-ever act of cloning carried out on Earth. When the holy book speaks of Adamah going into a deep sleep, it is, of course, a way of telling simple pre-scientific minds about the anaesthetic-induced sleep that he underwent so that the cloning operation would take place.'

I sat there mesmerised. I did not know whether to take him seriously or not. My wife made her sentiments known by the amount of noise she generated in the kitchen, but Faith seemed oblivious to it all.

That first visit was not the last. In fact, he made a point of visiting me every Monday, Wednesday, and Friday, just before sunset, to expound his philosophies. Apart from the excellent cup of tea that my wife brewed, he genuinely seemed to like me. Everyone wondered what a teacher and a madman had in common. But his views fascinated me, no matter how wayward they sounded. Quite obviously he had read a lot, and probably still did, and this made me even more fascinated by him.

According to one of his grandchildren who was a pupil of mine, Faith had been a professor in the USA for a long time. He had gone there in exile during the war of liberation. There he met a beautiful white woman with whom he fell in love. To the horror and shock of her family, they had married. But the couple were never really accepted. Faith had finally snapped when his wife was raped and killed by men in white hoods before they castrated him, and left him for dead. The hooded men had left a cross burning in his yard.

'That's probably why he speaks of chariots of fire so much,' the grandchild had said.

But then, that was just another fragment woven into the tapestry of the legend that was Faith.

'So you see,' expounded Faith over a cup of his favourite brew, the drink of angels, 'these chariots of fire that we encounter so often in the Bible are spaceships. It was a spaceship that made the Earth tremble at Sinai, and it was a laser beam that engraved the commandments onto the stone tablets.'

'I see, but it sounds a bit far-fetched to me, if you don't mind my saying so.'

'No, I do not mind. I have heard it often enough. Truth, though, always sounds far-fetched the first time it is encountered. Elijah went up in a chariot of fire, and Jesus was beamed up in what we know as Ascension.'

'Are you suggesting that what we call miracles are nothing more than scientific sleight-of-hand tricks?'

'They only appear to be miracles to simple souls, but once the technology that makes them possible becomes commonplace, we begin to take them for granted.'

'Forgive me, *madzibaba* Faith, I sense major contradictions in your thesis and your faith. You seem to debunk the very fundamentals that hold together the religion you purport to serve.'

He sipped his tea and smiled.

'Do I? I only seek to clarify, for I do not believe that ignorance is bliss. The truth of what we call sacred miracles is sometimes revealed in what we perceive as advances, great leaps in science and technology – as well as in *Star Trek* and other so-called science-fiction tracts.'

'*Star Trek*?'

'You sound incredulous. Yes, *Star Trek*. The machine that produces food for them as they explore space is called a replicator, and it is the same thing that Jesus used to turn water into wine, to feed thousands with only twelve loaves and fish. If God did not intend to cleanse the world soon, such technology would become commonplace and cease to occupy the realm of fiction and miracles.'

'The world is coming to an end, is it?'

'The end of time is nigh, my brother. It is as it was described in Genesis 6:11: "Now the Earth was corrupt in God's sight and was full of violence." Even you can see that that's the case in these terrible times we are living in.'

'But hasn't each epoch seemed like the end of time to each generation, whenever existence has been filled with uncertainties?'

'Perhaps, but we stand on the threshold of a new millennium, a time for renewal and new beginnings. Chariots of fire shall descend on the Earth again, and the clean and the righteous shall ascend to the heavens, whilst a great fire shall cleanse the Earth. This fire shall be nothing but the result of nuclear blasts, which shall make the Earth inhabitable for another millennium before a new Earth is put in place. This, I have seen in my visions; this, has God shown me in a prophecy.'

And thus our conversations went, while the fire of conviction burnt brightly in his penetrating black eyes. People began to whisper that I was probably as mad as he was.

There was a night when my youngest son's body began to burn up. My wife was frantic. We needed to rush our precious child to hospital, but we did not have a car. Even though I had been in the teaching profession for more than a decade, I still could not afford one. There was a car at one of the houses at the end of our street.

'Go, rush to them, and beg for a lift to hospital,' my wife implored.

I nodded and began to make my way out of the door. It was at precisely that time that there was pounding on the door. We exchanged startled glances. Who could it be at that time of the night? I opened the door pensively.

'Where is he?'

I was taken aback by both his question and his unexpected presence. I swear, even up to this day, that his penetrating eyes were burning like live coals.

'Come, come, man. Where is the boy who is sick?'

Faith simply sidestepped past me into the house to face my wife who was clutching our trembling son protectively.

'But how ...?' I stammered.

'There's no time for that now.' This, in a tone I had not heard Faith use before. Yet, he spoke to my wife, 'Don't be afraid,' with a caress.

I turned back; she was staring at Faith in fear.

'Go and get the car, and take your friend with you,' she hissed, as the shock on my face suddenly refocused her awareness.

'Go and get the car so that her mind can rest. But I will remain here to pray, for there are evil spirits trying to steal your child's soul.'

I hesitated.

'For heaven's sake, go!' she screamed.

As I dashed out, I heard Faith incant, '*Mwari* God of Abraham, whose spirit spoke through Nehanda and Chaminuka, and was seen in the glory of a burning bush, *erekeri*, heaven seek, *chokwadi*, *bhurebhure* ...'

Apparently the Holy Spirit was upon him and he had begun to speak in tongues.

The man with the car was very understanding. We drove up to our house and I rushed to get my wife and child. I burst into the living room and stopped dead in my tracks. My son looked up at me from behind his favourite mug and smiled sweetly. My wife and Faith sat at the coffee table, drinking tea together. I looked back and forth at the scene, trying to absorb it, unable to understand how it was possible. The heat that had been consuming my son, and the shadow of death that had lain across him, were gone.

'Come, my friend, join us, and let us imbibe this ultimate drink of the angels.' I was stunned by the sight. The face of the man I had woken was a mixture of annoyance and puzzlement.

'*Madzibaba* Faith has chased away the demons and evil spirits, and look, our son is restored to us.'

My son ran to me from his mother, giggling, to grab my legs. But that was not the reason I was unable to move.

I lay in bed, trying to comprehend the events of that strange night. According to my wife, soon after I left the house, our son's breathing had become even more laboured, until the boy had gone limp in her arms.

Frightened, she had called out to Faith, who was caught up in the rapture of his prayers and the agony of battling with dark forces, to save him. And Faith had heeded her call. He beckoned to her to lay the boy on the floor. She said she was agitated when he pressed his own body on top of that of our son's, and she was ready to push him off. But then he pushed himself back onto his knees and laid his rod on our son, keeping his head bowed and his eyes fixed on my boy's face. Three times, he repeated this, she said, until our boy coughed and spluttered back to life. Faith seemed to struggle all over the house with some invisible foe. Finally, spent and exhausted, he collapsed onto the floor where he remained for some time before he sat up and said:

'How about a cup of that special tea of yours?'

'It was a miracle,' breathed my wife, eyes wide with wonder and new-found faith in Faith. 'The man is truly a messenger of God.'

'I thought you said and you always say that he is nothing but a learned township nut?'

'That was before I saw him, with my own eyes, conquer demons and the forces of darkness. Look at our son now, and compare him with the way he was before you left. Surely you have to agree that it's a miracle.'

'Perhaps we panicked and it was nothing more than a passing fever.'

'It was no fever; it was witchcraft, and *madzibaba* Faith saw it in his visions, that's why he rushed here to save our son.'

And thus my wife, who all along had dismissed Faith as nothing more than a raving lunatic, became a fervent follower of *Chita Chengoro Wemoto*.

If I had been the subject of mockery and gossip because of my association with this eccentric man, my wife's new-found devotion and beliefs became the subject of intense ridicule. But she paid no heed to it all.

'The path of all true believers is filled with such thorns,' she would shrug.

She attended prayer meetings with Faith diligently, but could not persuade me to do likewise; the Monday, Wednesday and Friday conversations, over the ultimate drink of the angels, with Faith were more than enough for me. My two eldest children agreed with me, but not our youngest – he, like his mother, firmly believed that Faith, through the power of the Holy Spirit, had saved his life.

'I saw an angel of God, baba,' the boy would say, 'and the tips of its wings brushed my body six times.'

And so it was that it was my wife who cooked Faith's last supper.

'In Judges 13:20, my dear brethren, we are told,' Faith said, his black penetrating eyes filled with a warm soft glow that I had never seen before, 'that "As the flame blazed up from the altar toward heaven, the angel of the Lord ascended in the flame," and so it shall be tonight, on this last day of the world as we know it.'

I was afraid that he was going to convince my wife to kill us all and then commit suicide so that we could be taken into the palms of God.

'The Lord has said to me, "Go ye up to the highest point in the presence of the Lord, for the Lord is about to pass by." And I shall comply.'

'And where is this highest point, *madzibaba*?' my wife asked in awe.

'It has to be the tower-light close to my house, for that shall be my mountain top. I shall go up, and intercede on your behalf, and I am sure there shall be room for us all in the chariot of fire, when it comes.'

As night fell, storm clouds began to gather. There had been no rain for weeks, and we were in the throes of yet another drought. Faith had gone about in the township for days, pleading with people to repent before it was too late.

'Look up,' he said pointing to the darkening skies, 'and see the signs. The signs are there for all to see. Go to the nearest tavern and see how corrupt we have become. Teenage girls fornicate with men old enough to be their grandfathers, while young boys stone their fathers to death for the sake of silver and gold. You have all seen this and lamented but you have not repented or taken the Lord your God into your hearts. Repent, repent, before it's too late, for the end of time is nigh.'

'*Mupostori uyu anoputa mbanje chete*,' laughed a group of men hunched over a 'scud' of *masese*.

Yet again, no one paid him any heed, except for my wife and child, of course. They burst into tears, weeping for the cold-hearted and stubborn nature of people.

I stood with them at the foot of the tower-light and watched Faith climb up, somehow managing the feat with one hand holding a plate of *sadza* and his sacred staff. A group of people also stood there with us, laughing their hearts out at the latest crazy antic from Faith.

'Perhaps we should call the police and fire brigade,' they said.

'Yes, we should, the madman might fall to his death from there.'

'Why doesn't the teacher, his friend, try to talk him down?'

'The teacher will probably follow up there.'

'Either him, or his wife and youngest child. They are Faith's disciples you know.'

'They are just mad, the whole lot of them!'

Faith was no more than a dot, sitting high up in the sky, when the tower-light came on. The sky was pitch-black. There was a blinding flash of lightning and a deafening roar of thunder. The women and children screamed. The men shook their heads and chuckled but they could not hide the fear in their eyes. When it happened again, the women and children scurried away to the safety of their homes. The men pretended to be unconcerned, until there was another flash and roar.

'*Kunze kuye kwashata*,' they said, and began to troop away. 'I am sure that lunatic will come down as soon as the rain starts pouring down.'

It took me a while to convince my wife that it was wiser for us to be indoors, given the state of the weather.

'How can you ask me to abandon *madzibaba*, at this crucial moment?'

'You will not be abandoning him. Did he not himself tell us that he shall proceed to intercede on our behalf before coming back for us? He didn't say anything about us standing in the wind and the rain while he did that, did he?'

So, reluctantly, she allowed me to lead her away. I looked up at the tower-light and I think I saw Faith wave at me with his staff.

The weather became worse as the night matured. Indeed, a strong wind began to blow, threatening to rip off the roofs of our houses. Many trees were uprooted.

'It's a whirlwind,' my wife said in hushed tones. 'God's anger walks the Earth tonight.'

At midnight there was more thunder and lightning, and a crashing sound as the lightning struck the tower-light. We all heard the explosions and felt the earth shake as the lights blew out. But no one dared to go out. Looking out of the window, all one saw was the lightning streak tearing into the tower-lights, and the flames of electrical fire leaping out in all directions. I sighed sadly, and hoped that Faith had had the sense to climb down before the weather had grown worse. I had gone back there with some members of his family and tried to talk him down, but to no avail. The police had said they would come as soon as they found transport, while the fire brigade told us they were attending to a more pressing emergency at a warehouse that had been gutted by a ferocious fire.

The storm and the whirlwind raged all night long and only subsided with the first light of the first day of the new millennium. The world was, not surprisingly, still intact. My wife smiled sheepishly.

'We have to find out if *madzibaba* Faith is still alive,' she said in a subdued voice.

'He is well, but we shall not find him.'

We turned around, startled by our youngest son's self-assured voice. But he did not say anything else. He looked so angelic and mysterious in the morning light. We went to the tower-light, or perhaps I should say the place where it had once stood, as now it lay twisted and charred on the ground. Its mangled remains looked as though they had been cast into a fiery furnace. There was no sign of Faith anywhere.

'Oh, my God!'

It was the first time my wife had blasphemed since the night Faith had 'healed' our son. I turned to look at the cause and was horror-stricken when I saw my little boy, who had taken off his shoes, walk towards the mangled tower-light.

'The wires! The wires! They'll kill you!' I shouted, running after him.

He turned around and smiled at me.

'Do not be afraid, father. Please take off your sandals, for the place you are standing on is holy ground.'

He headed towards the tower-light and picked up something from the ground. He walked back to us, holding Faith's staff in one hand and his flaming red gown draped over his other arm. Both items were clean and unburnt. The people who had gathered to look at what the storm had wrought gasped.

'Behold, like Elijah, the chariot of fire has come and has borne away the prophet Faith, and he has left his rod of power in my hands,' my son's voice commanded in a deep, mellow tone, almost as if the voice of God was speaking through him.

And so it was that news of the strange happenings spread far and wide. Many made a pilgrimage to see the wonder boy who spoke of holy visions and had a healing touch. His head was clean shaven, and he always wore flaming red apparel with an emblem of a chariot of fire on his chest.

What can I say? Faith was never seen again. My son, 'the new prophet', claims that Faith rode the whirlwind and was taken into the bosom of God in a chariot of fire. There are many, not just my wife, who believe him, and needless to say *Chita Chengoro Wemoto* has experienced phenomenal growth ever since. The police said that there were no charred remains at the foot of the tower-light, so it is hardly likely that Faith was struck by lightning or electrocuted and burnt to death. There are those who contend that when he saw that the world had not ended, Faith cast away his rod and gown in frustration, disappointment and despair and walked into the wind and rain. But no one ever reported seeing him. His 'church', under the guidance of my son, continues to grow and grow.

Well, now I've told you the story as I recall it, so please excuse me: my driver's here, and we must go and take delivery of our new jet … for the new prophet, you see … he is still young and is almost crushed by crowds … even in a limousine.

THE MONTH OF SEPTEMBER

By Gitta Sumner

You: darker than blue
rumpled sheets
lift and gather around
glistening skin

Me: soft slow breaths
a warm feeling
spreading across
damp dimpled brown flesh

Us: happily exhausted

'September,' he calls me. 'September, do you love me?'

I look outside the window past his shoulder. Here, the leaves are turning brown, maroon, golden; they're falling off the trees. Spiralling, swinging from one point to another. Where I was born, the dry season has just started. Intense heat blazing out of a flat blue ceiling. Sometimes, the clouds will glide across the sky. Slowly, very, very lazily.

'What's the rush?' they say. 'We're in no hurry. Why are you?'

I smile, and keep on walking.

My birth month is my name. I'll be 27 soon. I am a child of heat and hibernation, that's why my forehead is now buried between his neck and shoulder. Inside the little groove where the skin dips into the collarbone. Just there, where it's warm, like clear water in a rock pool.

At the beach. It's a warm day; a little girl pokes the small dark-blue fish with a stick as they dart in and out of her reach. Teasing her, as the sun warms her bare brown back.

My parents died when I was six. We were living in London at the time. We moved to England when I was one-and-a-half ... maybe, two. I first remember seeing my grandfather at my godmother's house. His plane was delayed. By the time he arrived the funeral service was over and they'd buried my parents; we were waiting for him to pick me up. It was the end of January; it rained – typical.

He was tall and skinny; his fingers were long. Hardly spoke to me actually. He stayed for ten days so that we could sort out my parents' things. Then he took me back home with him. The plane ride lasted six hours. He grunted if I asked any questions.

The first things I remember when I came out of the plane were the palm trees and the sea. It was February and the sea was so blue. The waves played with the sun's rays. I wanted to jump in right there and then.

Mama was at the airport to meet us. She hugged me so tightly. She smelled of salty plantains, sweet *akara* and hot oil. She made me hungry. I fell in love with her the minute I saw her. She was so warm. My grandfather was like … he was like an avocado pear seed: hard and smooth, that was him.

We took the ferry to reach our side of town. They wouldn't let me hang over the railings. I stuck my head between the bars and watched the foam rise away from the boat. The air was cool against my face.

They lived in a two-storey house painted blue like a robin's egg. And, like the minute brown speckles on the fragile shell, the brown stains dotted here and there dispassionately revealed the age of the house. In the middle of the yard, I'd lie back and look at the house standing against the sky. The clouds drifting by seemed to sneak out from behind the roof. I'd wave goodbye – they never returned the gesture.

The inside of the house was cool. The walls of my room were a pale yellow. I had a single bed with a sliding drawer underneath, a wardrobe, a chair and desk. All wood. All made by my grandfather. Mama stitched the blood-orange cushion for my chair; I slept with it instead. A fuel lamp stood on top of the desk.

I had only one suitcase. He'd given my winter things to Oxfam; said I wouldn't need them where I was going. I sat on the bed; I leaned back. The ceiling was a creamy colour. There was a line of small black ants crawling into a small crack above my head. Not too big, not too small. I thought of ants falling on my face as I fell asleep, their tiny legs making their way past the hairs rising from my skin, over the pores dotting its surface. Their teeny steps would tickle me, gently, to sleep.

It was six o'clock when Mama woke me up; I'd slept for five hours. She came into the room; I could smell chicken stew, rice steamed with scotch-bonnet peppers.

'September, wake! Come and eat.'

I watched her; I was half-awake. She laid her head down next to mine. We watched each other. She had a smooth face. I touched her cheek; she didn't blink. My grandfather's first wife died when my mom was only five. Mama, her cousin, was employed to nurse her during her illness. When my grandmother died my grandfather decided that he needed someone to look after his daughter. Mama was already twenty-four; he was five years older. They married.

'Come here,' she said. She lifted me up onto her chest and I slipped my arms under her shoulders.

'They're really gone,' I said.

'Yes, darling, but I'm here. Anything you need you ask. Got me?'

'Yes ... darling.'

She chuckled. 'How did a little girl like you get such a deep voice?'

'My dad.'

'Ah yes, your dad ... Well, if you ask me, it's a pretty voice.'

I squeezed her. She squeezed me back.

'Okay, off this bed. Time to eat. Your grandfather's already had his dinner, so it'll be you and me in the kitchen.'

We ate; we washed up, then she took me next door to meet her friends.

My first night in their house I stood behind my door watching Mama bring light to the darkened corridors. I saw how she lifted each lamp; she pushed something and the glass case rose, exposing the dark belly inside. I crept back into my room and lifted my unlit lamp. I shook it, and heard the liquid sloshing around inside. I looked at it closely. I ran my fingers over the lamp, over the letters rising on the silver base, over the surface of the metal wires criss-crossing the glass – protecting it from me. The metal was slick with oil. But this oil was different; it smelled horrible to my six-year-old nose. A small piece of metal protruded from the side. I hesitated, listening for footsteps outside my door. Nothing. I looked at this thing and ... pushed it. My heart beat hard against my chest. Crack! The rising glass splintered as it pushed against the roof of the lamp. The moonlight shone on small slivers of glass resting on the stretched skin between my thumb and finger. My hands shook as I replaced the lamp on the table.

'Big woman!' a voice boomed from the doorway. 'What have you done now?'

Spinning, I saw Mama standing in the doorway. The lamp she held aloft lighted her warm brown face. The skin around her grey eyes crinkled as she tried unsuccessfully to glare at me.

'Give me that!' she commanded.

Shaking my head, I slowly stepped away from the table. She advanced into the room and set her lamp on the table. She sucked her teeth and looked at me from the corner of her eyes. 'Go get the broom under the ironing table.'

I dashed out of the room into the corridor. In an alcove built into the wall stood a wooden table used for ironing. Underneath, I found a bundle of long, thin, wooden stems tied together with a piece of red cloth. Back inside my room, I handed this to her. Again, she sucked her teeth. Without another word, Mama carefully cleaned up the broken pieces of glass on the table and the floor. She left the room with the broken lamp, leaving me in darkness. The moonlight created shadows on the tiled floor; I stared at these until light once more returned to my room.

'Come here,' she said. 'I'll show you how.'

That night, I learnt how to pour kerosene into the silver base; how to lift the roof of the lamp before pushing the lever that would help raise the glass casing; how to light the kerosene-soaked wick, and how to adjust the tiny flame inside. The country had frequent electricity black-outs. I learned to adapt.

I didn't see or speak to my grandfather until the next day, when we had breakfast together. He sat on one side of the round table and I sat on the other; Mama sat between us. She prayed before we ate; he waited for her to finish. We ate in silence and after that he asked me what I planned to do with my day.

I said, 'I don't know.'

He told me to find something.

Later, I found out that Mama went to the United Methodist Church near the centre of town. She'd wear a white dress to church with a white head-tie wrapped around her head. I wasn't allowed to go. Grandfather didn't think too highly of Christianity. He didn't want my head filled up with all that 'rubbish'. Mama ignored him and went anyway.

I'd miss her company, but she always made up for it when she came home by preparing extra special treats, like small chunks of pawpaw seasoned with salt, cayenne pepper and lime juice; or green mangoes, thickly sliced and lightly dipped in salt. If her service lasted longer than usual she'd placate me by making my favourite: pap. I would sit in front of her parted legs as she rolled the mixture of rice flour and water against the uneven walls of a calabash until there were hundreds and hundreds of small white balls sitting in its base. These would then be poured into a pot filled with boiling water. Finally, she would add sugar and the tangy brown juices of marinated tamarind fruit. I would savour the aromatic steam rising from the full cup that she would place in front of me. She made this for me.

Once school started, my grandfather would ask me what I'd learned. He would check my homework. Any mistakes made meant that I had to rub out my answers and redo the whole exercise.

'Practice makes perfect, madam,' he'd scowl at me. 'Don't make mistakes now and you won't have to pay for them later,' he'd add.

He didn't have to tell me again. I checked and re-checked everything before I showed it to him.

I missed my parents, but I didn't have to tell Mama that. I'd slip my arms under her breasts and clasp my hands, tightly, behind her back; she'd sit still until I was calm. She wouldn't let anyone else cornrow my hair after washing it because she knew that I needed a tender hand to get all the knots out. At times like this, she talked to me about my mother's childhood. I loved her singing and the way she carried the smell of the food she cooked. One day she was Lamb Stew; the next she was Cassava Leaf. If it rained, she found things for me to do and told me stories. She told me stories only when the weather was bad. When the sun shone she'd chase me out of the house. I could sit in the yard and daydream, or I could run up and down the street screaming with all the other children.

'Children should be outside with their friends in the sunlight,' she'd say.

She'd also take me out with her. Once, she said hello to a woman who was carrying a basket filled with sweet potato leaves on her head. She sucked her teeth at Mama. A loooong one. I was surprised, but Mama just laughed. The sky was heavy with grey clouds. We had to walk quickly before the rain came, but still she just laughed. The woman once liked my grandfather. His first wife was alive then.

'The woman teased him and touched his face when she thought no one was looking.' She was like the rash I got from touching stinging nettles in London; she needed a little witch hazel to control her itch. 'Your grandmother paid her a visit one hot day.' Mama's tongue skipped over her words. 'She stopped her teasing.' Mama's laughter rang loud and hard as we walked.

My table, chair, bed-frame and shelves were all made from teak. By him. Brown wood, sometimes streaked a darker shade. Like brown zebras. In time my animals lined the windowsill and the shelves; they lived on top of my cupboard – whole families of grandparents, and parents, and brothers and sisters, and cousins and aunties and uncles. I had a blood-red lion, made from camwood. He sat upright, his head surrounded by a thick mane, held alert as if listening for invisible footsteps. Waiting. Just waiting. An ebony panther dipped its head to an imaginary lake, its ear also cocked for … . The *odum* antelope – eight of them – stood in mid-flight on my windowsill. Their brown heads were slightly turned, as if sensing someone behind. My animals lived in perpetual expectation.

When I turned twelve, my grandfather gave me a box made from rosewood. He carved it himself. There was no ceremony involved; he called me to his concrete shed in the yard and, through the open window, he pushed it into my hands. Then, turning his back to me he proceeded to re-arrange the tools on his work table. That was that. In my room, my fingers traced his creation. On the lid he had carved the outline of the cotton tree. The tree that stood at the centre of town. Mama said it was the 'mother of all trees'. The tree that reached its hands all the way up. Up, up and far into the sky. My grandfather would have considered it sacrilegious for anyone to cut it down. I lifted the lid and inside was a small piece of bark. I knew where it came from. Beside it lay rosewood carvings of a miniature chisel, hammer, jig and mallet. I dipped my nose in the box and breathed the sent of old leather and dried roses and varnish … and him.

Mama died before I turned sixteen. Cerebral malaria, they said. She was only sixty-four. I missed her smell. She brought my history to life with her words. Grandfather talked to his wood … and corrected my homework. Her love was warm and thick like the caramel-coated, fiery-red palm nuts that she gave me to suck. His love was embedded in the wooden animals he created for me, made smooth by his calloused hands.

I watched my grandfather carve. In his silence, I learned how to bring wood to life. How to encase motion in space.

I started taking an art course at a university in London a few weeks after my eighteenth birthday. Grandfather died after I graduated. We had his funeral two weeks after my twenty-first.

I missed watching his hands.

Our mattress sinks in the middle, but we don't mind. We roll towards each other when we sleep. Sometimes, late at night I'll wake and find Rahim's nose kissing mine. Our duvet is thick and soft. It's too small for two people, but we keep each other warm. It's going to be a windy day. It's a September Saturday morning. We'll lie in and watch the sky change colour through the windows; they rise from the ground and open out onto a small veranda that faces a street with a single oak tree. The old oak outside the veranda, that's why we took this flat.

Outside, the wind and tree are fighting each other: one pushes, but the other is too stubborn to fall.

'Do you love me, September?' he asks again. He whispers my name.

He moves and cold air zips down my spine. I move my head from his shoulder to the middle of his chest. I smile to myself.

We had met three years ago at a friend's house. He was helping her install her computer. I was there to collect some books I'd loaned her. She introduced us when I arrived. All I remember was a slow, sweet smile. I thought, 'This could belong to me.'

He later told me that my hand was warm and damp when he shook it. I can believe that. I remember I couldn't stop grinning. I felt like a fool, but I didn't care. I wanted him for myself. Raikiatu finished setting up the computer by herself. We talked and talked about his work, my work, everything and anything. We left together.

Do you know what it feels like when you meet someone and you just know? It's like ... what is it like? Like the first time I tasted brandy. I was sixteen. The heat travelled all over. It spread out from the middle of my chest and crossed my breasts like thousands of fine threads of red-hot magma snaking under my skin. Then it jumped into my stomach and warmed me. Tears rolled out of my eyes, but I liked it.

Abdul-Rahim made my insides burn when I touched him. I liked it. I felt as if my skin was going to slide right off my flesh. I wanted him to see everything that I was, and love it.

He walked me home the first time we met. It was autumn – mid-October. We didn't talk much. We simply walked and enjoyed each other's company. We said goodbye at my door, but I didn't want him to leave. I watched him walk away. Finally, I opened the door to my flat and walked in. Whatever I touched felt odd. I couldn't feel texture. I entered the kitchen and took out an ice tray. I couldn't feel the ice cube I held in my fingers, but I could see my skin stick to a cold smooth surface.

He moves again. 'Does September love Rahim?' I raise my head to look at him, and smile wickedly. He grabs me and rolls over so that I am under him. The duvet slips a little over the edge, but we ignore it.

Raikiatu finally gave me his number. I asked him to go see *The Scent of Green Papaya* with me at a cinema in town. He'd already seen it, but came anyway. In the dark, under the sound system, I could hear him breathe. I wanted to put my hands over his mouth, his whole face. I kept them folded tightly in my lap. When it ended, we walked to a small coffee shop. The waiter brought our orders – hot chocolate for him, milky coffee for me. I sat back and looked at him – really looked at him – as I mixed sugar into my coffee. I could hear the teaspoon hit the side of the cup ... but that's all I heard. He looked back at me. We drank each other up.

He placed his cup down between us, took my mug out of my hand, and set it on the table. He leaned forward. My hand slid over his. The skin on his knuckles felt smooth against my calluses. I could smell his aftershave from where I sat. It reminded me of limes. He turned his hand over so that our palms touched. I smiled at him. We talked with our hands.

He's leaning over me; I feel his weight on my hips. I shift over to ease the strain. He refuses to budge. His face is an inch away from mine. Up close, his pupils are larger. His hands are on either side of my head.

'Move, Rahim,' I say.

He lifts himself an inch or so above me and I slide over so that I can face the windows. He slips his hand under my arm and wraps it across my chest.

'Angry?' he asks.

I squeeze his hand.

A few days after our fourth week together, I found out about his child. I was talking to Raikiatu on the phone.

'You had a good time tonight,' she said.

'Pretty good. Very nice, actually.' I smiled when I thought about our last date.

'He's a nice guy. Very sweet ... intelligent,' she said.

'Handsome, too,' I added.

She laughed. 'Yes, that too.'

There was a lull. I wrapped the phone cord around my fingers. I felt tired but happy. The silence continued. I looked at the TV screen. There was a deer standing in front of an oncoming car; its eyes were luminous marbles.

'Why so silent?'

She didn't respond.

'Look, it's nearly eleven. I'm tired.'

She breathed in deeply. 'You seem serious about each other ...' Her voice petered out.

I remained silent. 'Has he ... has he said anything about his family?' she asked.

'Yeah, his parents ...'

'No, not them,' she interrupted impatiently.

'Who then?' I asked puzzled.

'Did he tell you about Bennie?' she asked.

I didn't answer.

'Didn't think so. Ask him.'

'I will,' I said.

She said goodnight; we hung up.

Mama hardly ever talked about herself. My grandfather hardly ever spoke to her. She'd set me between her legs and help me undo my cornrows while she spoke about my grandmother. Her fingers left behind thick strands of hair waving in the air. I knew more about a dead grandmother than the woman whose fingers regularly massaged my scalp.

My workroom is next to my bedroom. I carve stories out of wood. I look at the raw material and see every single piece I've ever made: faces rising out of wooden blocks; walking sticks with tops shaped like ankhs; genealogy lines carved into the outlines of trees. I make anything that means something to someone – anything my hands will allow. Wood is ... my element, my life. I look at a piece and I can see its past and its future. I can smell the roots of where it began, and the faint scent of its oil lingers long after it has been released to a new home. The feel of the different grain patterns under my fingers become a memory relived daily, weekly … . That's where I sat – in my workroom. Looking at pieces of wood. It didn't help; I couldn't take my mind off him. I could see him.

Rahim: Eyes, hazel

Skin, wet ebony wood

Hair, coal-black, tight curls, short

I grabbed my coat. It was windy outside. I didn't notice. I was in front of his place in twenty minutes. Didn't talk to anyone, didn't see anyone. He opened his door and just stood there, looking at me.

September: Eyes, brown

Skin, brown walnut

Hair, black, short

I walked in. His place reminded me of him. Long and tall, sometimes scruffy, but ordered. He knew where everything was. Books everywhere. He taught history. He hugged me; we stood there swaying in the middle of his living room. I felt too tired to hold myself up. I didn't ask any questions.

The next morning after he'd made me breakfast, he told me everything I wanted to know. He showed me his daughter's picture first.

'She lived with her mother. I had her every other weekend, a week in the Christmas holiday and Easter ... and during the summer.' Rahim smiled when he showed me her photograph. He told me she was three at the time. Her smile was wide – a bright gap-toothed smile. 'That's why I couldn't meet you last Sunday: it was her birthday.' A November child. A sun and snow child.

He took the photo and placed it back into his wallet and continued. 'I took her to the zoo on her third birthday. It was her first time. The baby tigers were her favourite. She wanted to stroke them. She cried when we left.'

He looked outside his window. The sky was cloudy.

'Move over.' He slipped back into the bed.

I tried wrapping my legs around him, but that didn't work. We lay looking at each other.

'We didn't love each other anymore. Anyway, that's what Nanette, Bennie's Mum, told me. She wanted the divorce; I didn't – initially. Bennie was only two at the time.'

His arm tightened around my waist. He was looking at me, but he couldn't see me. I moved closer to him.

'We married way too soon – four months after we'd met. I was 21; Nanette was nearly 23. We thought we were the exception: our marriage would last because we really loved each other.' He laughed then, and rolled over onto his back.

I didn't speak. His left hand was over his eyes. He needed to shave. He reached out his right hand and I took it in mine.

'Once the divorce came through I realised that Nannette was right. As much as I loved Bennie, I found I liked ... not being married to her mother. We made our new lives work together. For her sake.' His hand tightened its grip. 'I remember, I'd hold her in my arms when she slept. She breathed through her mouth while she slept.'

Like you, I wanted to say.

'A year after our divorce I met someone. Aminata. I took it slow; I wanted to be sure about her. We dated for four, five weeks before I introduced her to Bennie. She was four by then. She liked Aminata. I remember the first time I introduced them,' he laughed. 'Bennie wrapped her arms around her legs and she couldn't move.' He stopped speaking.

I wanted to hold him. But I thought I couldn't. He was so tense; his fist was clenched.

I remember when we buried Mama. My grandfather was just the same. I was 16 and wanted comfort. He was 69 and didn't want anyone to come near him, let alone touch him. He had outlived his wives. My parents were dead. I had no one else but him. The day was pleasant, for July. No rain. My tears fell. My grandfather was rigid. Inflexible to the core. As always, I thought.

I reached out and stroked Rahim's stomach. It seemed to help. He breathed in and out deeply. He took his hand away from his eyes; it looked as though he'd been crying all night. He turned to me. I stroked his cheek. It felt like coarse sandpaper.

'Bennie was supposed to stay with me in the second week of December. But Aminata got tickets for an Erykah Badu concert on the Wednesday I was supposed to pick her up. I switched nights with Nanette, and she offered to bring her up on Thursday night instead. I talked to Bennie on the phone on the Tuesday evening. She sounded so upset I promised I'd take her to the aquarium so she could see the underwater animals. She laughed; she was so excited. I remember that, she laughed.' He breathed in, then out.

'The Thursday after the concert, Nanette was on her way with Bennie. It was December. It was dark outside. The road was slippery. Another car crashed into them. They were both ... dead before the ambulance got to the hospital. It's been three years.'

'I'm here, if you want me to stay.' Pitiful, but it was the best I could do. He took my right hand and kissed the palm. He smiled.

'I'm not sorry I didn't tell you before.'

That made me smile. Don't ask, I don't know why.

'I come with a lot of baggage, I know. I wanted to be sure about us.'

I looked at his shoulder.

'Are you?' I asked.

I had pebbles sitting on my tongue. He placed my hand on his cheek.

'Are you?' He asked back.

212

I looked into his eyes.

Mama had no children of her own. She took on a man with a young child. She loved my mother; she loved her ... us completely – I knew that.

Was I strong enough? Was I strong enough to lose him? Could I love a man carrying all ... this? Bennie with Rahim's face. She had his gap-tooth. His tight black curls. Her three-year-old smile resembled her father's at the same age. She was a beautiful child. She was a beautiful ghost child. She would always be Rahim and Nanette's child. Nanette would always be her mother. There the two of them would stand. Forever in the past. Forever in the present.

I came to love and respect the images of the women that Mama weaved together with her words as she talked about my grandmother and mother. She showed me who and where I came from. But ... I loved Mama. She was real. I knew what it meant to be held by her. I could close my eyes and know what it felt like to touch the nutmeg-coloured woman with laughing grey eyes. I stroked her hair and held my cheek against hers. She was real to me. She loved me. I became hers. And she became mine.

And my grandfather? He passed on to me what he could not give to his child. In the depths of his silence, I knew I was loved. In the little time we had together, we grew. We bonded. And the ghosts lived through us. In peace.

I took Rahim's hand and kissed the back of it. I could see the small black hairs below his knuckles. The pebbles fell down my throat.

'Are you sure?' I asked.

He smiled, and pulled me closer.

'I try to be,' he said.

We saw each other nearly every week after that night. Called every night we didn't see each other. I felt it deep inside. My happiness made my bones hurt. I kept thinking of my grandparents. I thought about their marriage. I called Raikiatu.

'Do you think it's a good idea?'

'Mmhmm,' Raikiatu said.

'Raiki?'

'September?'

'Say something.'

'Talk to Rahim.' She hung up.

It was a Friday night. It was raining when Rahim came by. December rain. The drops on his hair looked like clear opals dancing with the light.

He kissed me before he said anything. Long kiss. His lips felt smooth. I smiled and he kissed my teeth. I felt better.

We sat in my living room watching TV with the sound off. We were on the ground and I sat between his legs. My head rested against his shoulder; he played with my hand. He talked about his work, his students.

'Tell me what's wrong,' he finally said. The rain was whipping the trees outside my window. I got up and went to my workroom. He didn't try to stop me. I sat at my desk. It sloped upwards so that I could draw without having to strain my back. Above the desk was a long shelf that circled the room to the doorway. It carried every single animal my grandfather had ever carved for me.

'I remember coming in to say goodbye to him.' I took the teak giraffe off the shelf. One of his first. Its neck was cool. 'It was ... near the end of August; end of my holiday – unfortunately. It was my last year at university, so I was ...' I looked at the animals on my shelf, '... about 21. My grandfather was standing next to one of the windows in the living room. I can see him right now. He was ... he was wearing his cotton pyjamas; they were blue.

'I don't think he could even see anything. These big, fat tears were running down his face. His tears gagged me. I could never speak properly around him. I just held him. He felt so thin in my arms. We cried together.' I stroked the giraffe's neck.

'He died before I came home. We never even spoke about Mama. I'd just sit and watch him carve. Or he'd show me how to create watchful eyes, or later on how to carve a lion's paw as it grips its prey. We hardly ever spoke. The skin on his hands was smooth, but tough.' I wanted to finish so badly that I needed to take a deep breath to steady myself.

'I haven't been back home since the funeral.' I wanted to look at him, but couldn't.

'I could tell you about my family, but ... that isn't enough. I want you to see everything that I came from. They lived together for 40 years, hardly ever spoke, but somehow they understood each other. I want that for us.' My heart was fighting a losing battle with my ribcage.

'Don't we already have it?' He was behind me now.

'Not yet.' I could hear him breathe behind me. 'Will you come back with me? To my grandparents' home, I mean?'

His breathing sounded like air travelling through a clogged pipe. 'Three weeks in July?' he asked.

'That should be enough ... for now.'

214

He nipped my lip when we kissed.

He kisses the side of my neck. Makes me smile ... every time. I lie on my back and pull the duvet to cover my side. He lies partially on top of me. His arm is still across my chest. I can feel his breath in my ear.

'Stop that, Rahim!'

He laughs and softly nuzzles me.

I turn towards him. In seven months, we'll have a spring child, with the harmattan winds at her feet.

Tomorrow I'll hang the wood carving I made of Bennie's face above the mantlepiece in the living room. Soon to be joined by the face of an April child.

'Does Rahim love September?' I ask softly.

He grins. 'Always.'

I laugh and wrap my legs around my baby's father.

BACK HOME

By *Monica Arac de Nyeko*

The night has been calm, perhaps too calm for your liking. Day is peeling herself away from dark, shifting the minutes forward. You are worn out with the fear of return. It's been a long time. Nothing has changed. You have not seen your relations for many years. You are not sure who is dead and who still lives. You stopped taking count. The numbers were too high. Bad news never stopped coming. Sometimes you tried to think of the good memories. They were few. They could not make you laugh anymore.

You have gotten yourself the seat by the bus window. You want to see the green and plant it into your mind. Those will be memories of the road you will never use again. You have been saving money for over two years from your pay at Britannia, the Indian biscuit factory. You knew that one day you would have to make this decision, to travel up north. Your bag is under the bus boot, and is filled with everything you could get your hands on. There is salt. There is soap. With the war, they have become impossible to get. There is the much-loved dried tilapia. The most needed clothes are also stuffed into your travelling bag. There is something for everybody. They are expecting you. You sent word two weeks ago that you were coming back home to them.

This night as you packed your bags to return to the place from which you once fled, you should have been eaten-up with excitement. You have missed home. The laughter with the other village girls as you flirted with the dry season. The baths in the river when she let her banks burst. The cold nights when the moon was high and you trapped *ngwen*. The sunflower stems in the weeded fields searching for a smile in the sun's face. The lustful nights at the *aguma* dances. Reverend Janani's Sunday worship drumbeat the next day, summoning the brethren to the word.

You still remember a little how it used to be. Perhaps ten years back. The road from Pugak all the way to Agoro carried great legends and folktales of once upon a time. There was no pain in belonging. No pity in people's eyes when you said you come from the Acoli tribe. Your relations, uncles and aunts, grandparents and great grandparents called you *nyarwa* – our daughter – and their eyes lit up at the sight of the brand-new Bata sandals pulled out from the paper bags. The second-hand clothes delighted their eyes. Those were all fruits of your monthly labour at Wii Gweng P 7 School where you were a teacher. It all seems like a tale of yore now. Those things that seemed natural only a while ago. Those thoughts that made you smile and stare into the morning with a steady, unruffled gaze. Those moments, which nutured your longings and hatched your hopes.

The morning gains pace. The bus park is a bust of life every passing minute. Everyone you see outside has their head held high. They have so much life in them. They never dread the cry of the owl that brings terrible news. They live according to undeclared codes: 'everyone for themselves – and 'God for us all'. This is Kampala. Welcome to the city of seven hills. Like these bus drivers, who for a day's wage and a few more shillings, honk, call and encourage passengers to enter their vehicles till their voices go hoarse and their ears deafen from the sound of their own tunes.

'Come to my bus. Oh, look how beautiful it is. Express. Express service, via Masindi. I take you direct, no breakdown, for only 10,000 shillings! Hey, hey, hey, beautiful, enter. Don't go there …'

You wonder why the drivers choose to work on this route. Delivering passengers to those places whose music harps with refrains off smoking barrels. Places where foliage stinks of deserted reason. Most of them are so young and full of life. They probably have children who are barely two years old. Why should they risk all that? But they are just like you. Making decisions with questions unanswered. Living life as it ought to be lived. Taking two steps back, one forward, two back, and then hearing the sound of breaking … *pooom*, and the other cringing sound of trying to cling to things collapsing under the weight of the current.

Yes, current. As it commands you on and slouches upon you its weight, you sense mirth at the end of this day. You will see Akena at last. He never forgave you for leaving Mucwini like a bullet darting from a gun. You coiled into his arms that night after choir practice. You asked him to walk you home even when the moon was high and you would have been okay by yourself. You let his warmth into you as you held him so close and called his name. When you left, you turned him into a promise of loneliness, like his name, Akena – 'Alone'. You wrapped him into a wish, surrendering to solitude. His eyes were fixed on the road. Just as it had taken you away from him, he trusted it to bring you back. That bus to the city of seven hills too. The one that spat gravel into his eyes and disappeared behind a cloud of dust chanting, two steps back, one forward, two back … *pooom pooom pooom* …

The days came and went thereafter with no assurance of your return. That feeling, which Akena had the day that you left, grew bigger and bigger. He began to think that perhaps he should have held you tighter, and given you an embrace so warm, like a promise that actually becomes fulfilled. Perhaps he should have seen that moment as only a memory of *yaa*-dark – the colour of your face.

The freedom fighters – men with guns under their arms – came from the forests in the weeks, months, maybe years following that day at the bus park and that *yaa* memory. They got Akena seated by the roadside. His hair was matted into locks, which mimicked the knotting thoughts in his head. He was seated by that same road, which beckons travellers to Kampala with its meandering charm, as if the only reason it was paved was to seduce and steal warmth from the embrace of youth and lovers. It was a hot day and the sun refused to beat down softer, as if it had quarrelled with its mother. That was also the day that the song in Akena's head brought the lure of surrender with it – too tempting to resist. As steadily as the night descends upon day, the desire to speak the truth possessed him.

'*Ai maa doo*. Allah! Allah! Allah! Allah!'

The sun's gaze weakened upon the day. He told the men what only someone who wanted a bloodstained shroud over his eyes could possibly provoke. That they were a bunch of lousy arse-holes who had given the tribe a savage face. That they were not fighting for anything but their lousy penises, which wanted to fuck people's wives and daughters in the name of liberation and freedom. That they had made the otherwise fucked-up government look good. That they should all go and fuck their mothers, whose wombs had borne curses upon the Acoli people.

One-two-two-one-one-two ... *pooom* ... .

As his forefathers and those before them beckoned him, as the rat-tat-tat of the barrel sounded a solemn cry into his head, he carried into his final surrender the colour of yaa, and your voice, which had whispered to him that night, saying:

'I have to leave. Come with me. We shall be okay in Kampala, where the day never ends and the future is void of tinted pasts.'

'Lamunu, I can't, this is home,' he said.

'Akena, please!'

'The war will end one day ... and when it does, someone has to be here to pick up the pieces.'

'Yes, someone; it does not have to be you. Look, everyone is leaving. Some have even gone as far as Kenya and Tanzania. We are only going to Kampala,' you said to him, almost shouting.

You hated the way his voice sounded. Like it was his duty to clean up the floor after the whole of Mucwini had shitted upon it.

'Yes, but I ...' he started and stopped. He had lost his words.

Both of you sat in a silence as painful as a wound throbbing with pus. The burning upon your chest started as if someone was fanning a fire. He did not have to say it. You sensed it. Your harvest was gone and your *kraal* was breaking. But you managed to speak to him again with a voice that hid the dryness in your throat.

You said, 'Akena, I am sorry! I am not going to sit here and wait to die ...'

There was silence again as he let your voice sink deeper into his silence. When he tried again to call your name, his words were long gone; they were headed for the enchanted Karuma waterfalls where only those voices whose fates are sealed go to dance to the songs of bewildered spirits.

The bus is filling up fast. It will be on its way soon. Even if your husband, whom you met in Kampala, comes home and discovers your absence, you will be miles away. The turn boys are packing things on top and calling out for more passengers. Sometimes they want to pack the bus, till people are on top of one another like potato sacks headed for a busy market day. Everyone seems to be engrossed in their own thoughts. You are also trying to capture your demons and think of the good and joy that your return will bring. Amidst your eagerness, there is still doubt in your mind. You are still not very sure that it was the right decision to make, to return, and if that decision was any good for your two sons seated quietly beside you. Your hands are shaking. Isaac, your five-year-old and eldest son, asks you what is wrong.

'Gin mo peke' you say in Acoli and quickly ask him if he wants you to buy him the toffee sweets the eager vender is displaying at the bus window.

He says no and gets back to playing with his plastic toy.

The bus finally fills up. The journey is going to be long – at least seven hours. Some people are standing. Some are on the bus floor with hardly any space to move a hand. None of that hassles you. You came in early and got the three seats at the end of the bus where no one would bother you much. The bus starts to drive out of the park, very slowly through

219

the parked city traffic. The noise of hooting vehicles and drivers cursing goes on for a while. It starts to gradually lessen as the bus leaves the most crowded areas. Your eyes shift from scene to scene and person to person. There are the perfect houses, smartly dressed women, and cars that look like they have just landed from Dubai. This is a part of town in which you have not lived. Those you left at home probably think you have been living like the people you are seeing on the streets now. Taking huge strides to air-conditioned offices. Eating lunch from fast-food restaurants, celebrating first-kiss anniversaries and getting entangled in this world of dreams that you only see when you imagine yourself living their perfect lives.

If only you could seduce yourself to sleep, your knee joints would not complain so hard, you imagine. As always, sleep is proud. Your headache wants to start again. The bus gains great speed when it has made its way completely out of the city. You can feel its wheels bumping at your buttocks over every pothole. The further you draw away from the city, the less cosy it looks. The scene rolls past the outskirts of Kampala. Tin-made and half-collapsed mud houses. You feel you know the people living there. You have met them, dined with them and flown with the same current. Low-paying jobs at Indian factories. Zero medicines and death at Mulago hospital. Owino market with her cheap curry-powder and voodoo merchandise to cure syphilis, AIDS, ditched lovers and those deprived of fortune ...

Your sons stare into your eyes from time to time. They are not speaking as much as they usually do. They probably sniff fear in your breath. They have never been to Mucwini. They have only heard of home, and of Uncle Sabitti. They were born here in Kampala, where everyone comes to seek refuge from poverty, boredom and their own shadows.

This Kampala. It sounds so different when you hear of it from afar. Before you came, many people said it was huge and you could be anything. You could become a breeze or a beautiful *jinni* like the ones from the Tanzanian coast, meet a wealthy expatriate at Just Kicking Pub, marry him, have half-caste kids called Katrina or Foster. People said Kampala was also dangerous. The clock never stops ticking and you could disappear like a sesame pod in grass. They said you had to mind your own business like everyone else or get a broken nose on account of staring at the ladies of the night behind Speak Hotel.

When you came, the city was huge, and life was as tough as those frozen cowhides that are stored in the industrial warehouse near

Britannia. Kampala had landlords who did not understand the lingo of 'Please, Sebo, next month.' There were Indian bosses at Britannia who paid you 80 shillings for packing a whole box of biscuits after burning your hands on those hotplates till they looked like soot. Oh, and the doctors who called your headaches and nightmares, 'post traumatic blah blah blah' and said you should get 'psychosocial' something and that will cost 15 US dollars after a discount.

'Excuse me, did you say um … dollars?'

'Yes, madam, owing to the depreciation of the Ugandan shilling …'

You told Kyazze, your husband about it. You begged him to get you some miracle dollars to cure your ailment. He laughed; his nose grew bigger and he simply said, '*Maa ato!*'

Kyazze-bolingo-yasolo. Even if it sounds more Congolese Lingala than Ugandan, he says that is what his name is. Everyone calls him Kyazze in short. You used to mind when he shouted at you and called you a good-for-nothing bitch who should get out of his house because he was bored stiff with your missionary style. That was when your desire for him burnt hot like your Ma's charcoal stove. That was also about the time he found you at the street corner when you just arrived in Kampala. He told you that you did not belong there. He did not come from your tribe. You knew people back home would not approve. But who would bother about what tribe the man was from, that you coiled up to every night, when you had a roof over your head?

Kyazze got you a job in Britannia, where he worked, when no school would take you as a teacher. Those squint-eyed bosses at Britannia were cruel, aye! They cut your pay for resting for a minute from the biscuit-packing stand. Everyone said Indians were like that. That if you had come to Britannia expecting anything less, then you must have a loose nut in your head or something. You reconciled what your fate had chosen and tried to make the best out of it. Besides, it was worth it. You hid stolen biscuits from the night shift under your skirt and in your knickers and sold them in the market. Kyazze learnt about this and asked you to give him all those shillings.

'That is not going to happen,' you said.

He realised after ten minutes of threats and coaxing that you were firm on this stance. When he didn't have his way with you he interpreted it as a deliberate insult to his shortness. He held your head between his two hands and banged it one, two, three times on the floor. The taste of fresh blood – scarlet, like the memories in your head – filled your mouth and nose as your head rested upon the floor when he finally left you for unconscious. You were not unconscious, but you could not move for a while. You had been unconscious only once. That had been the first time and that was many years ago. You cried loudly and the neighbours rushed in, threatening to break down the door if he did not let them in. These days they barely notice.

'Why do you stay unless you like it?' everyone asks you, as if deciding to leave is something as easy as picking which bunch of oranges to buy.

Later, with barely enough strength to shift your legs, you sat yourself up. You hugged your sons that night. They cried with you as you rocked them to and fro. They too had tasted scarlet in their mouths a time too many. They knew how it felt like to have your head on that concrete floor.

'Very soon, very soon, we are going home to Mucwini,' you said.

Kyazze works the night shift at Britannia. He does not return till eight o'clock in the morning. By the time he would come back you would be long gone.

All through this journey the bus has been quiet. Your boys have been asleep. Myron, the youngest, has his head on your lap. As the bus sails away on the tarmac road, you pat his hair and hum the lullaby you sang to him when he was born.

Mama yela
Mama yela
Mama disturbs me
Mama disturbs me

He was born at the time you heard rumours of peace. Everyone danced and partied. The labour pains started as soon as the Radio Uganda announcer finished the sentence. You thought of home. The good memories and what everything would be like. Young boys and girls would dance to *aguma* and *larakaraka* in the night again. There would be cows in the *dwols*. Ai Ma!

Mama yela
Mama yela

The nurse placed your little baby boy into your waiting arms. You stared into his face. There he was, staring back at you. He waved his little arms in the air, as if knowing his birth coincided with a time of ripening hope.

You bit your lips and held him to your chest. The name you had first heard from a missionary woman came to your mind. She had come to Mucwini to visit the congregation there. In one of her sermons, she said that 'Myron' means 'sweet-scented oil', something like sunflower oil that has been smiled upon by abundant sun. You had been in the sunflower fields yourself before the harvest came and, as the preacher spoke, you recalled that there was always the lingering concern of low yields with sunflowers. Good seeds were hard to come by, and without good seed the prospect of sweet-scented oil did not mean much. The Greek preacher carried on with her sermon. To her, this was a sermon about goodness and how it was very much like sunflower oil. To you, it was a name you would give your son one day. When Isaac was born, times were tough. Sunflower yields were low and fields were almost void of sunflower stems. The sun was dull. No one tilled the land. With Myron, there was sweetness in every scent. There was plenty of good sunflower seed. The sun promised to shine abundantly, allowing the stems a blossoming elegance. And yet, with sunflowers, you could never tell, even with the best seed. Similarly, the hope that surrounded Myron's birth did not last, like a water bubble.

Mama yela
Mama yela

After hours of travel, you have arrived in Gulu town. Gulu declares the nearing end of your journey. In less than two-and-half hours, you will be home. The town, whose charm is wearing out, tilts towards an uncertain edge on the compass, searching for past glory. The streets are filled with people crossing destinies around verandas of buildings riddled with bullet holes. You went to school here a long time ago when it was not so grey and hushed. That time, the day did not weep upon people here with petals as crimson as henna. Buses did not need armed convoys to escort them to the next destination.

A few people had been speaking to each other, but as the bus hits the road to Kitgum District where home – Mucwini – is, there is silence. It is a muteness that only those who have been close enough to the periphery can recognise. The bumps on the road make the bus seem like it won't make the next mile. But it gains speed. This is the most dangerous part to cross. It's also the place where the sight of burnt houses and overgrown compounds starts to make concrete acquaintance with the eye. You become aware of the unusually disruptive squeal of this bus. It is strangely loud, and attracts unnecessary attention. The driver is focused on his wheels. One mother holds her baby close. A nun's head is cast down in prayer. Her fingers pluck at the rosary beads as they disappear inside her palms. You are thinking of Akena. Thinking of him made Kampala bearable. It should make this part of the journey all right then. It doesn't. You hold your boys tight and close your eyes. When you look out again, the dull sun promises a bright smile at the end of this day. Maybe. The bus carries on with its monotonous chant of two steps back, one forward, two back, *poooom pooom* ...

Then it stops. A window opens. The driver shouts to someone outside. His tone is gay. It tempts courage, and a few faces turn towards the outside.

'*Gudune anyim tye nining,*' he asks the lone figure at the side of the road. It's a form of necessary courtesy for those who dare travel this route.

The man does not speak. He wears an old baseball shirt and a pair of faded khaki shorts. His hands are in his pockets. He is at ease in this area where there has been no sign of life for the past fifty miles. To the driver's question, he nods and waves, signalling that the route ahead is okay, almost with a complete lack of interest. The driver thanks him and tosses him a few shillings. The man regards the reward for a while and, like an afterthought, he thanks the driver and looks away.

The bus hits the road again. You are relieved, but your mind is not at ease. Who was the lone man at the roadside? What was he doing in a place where no sign of human habitation has been sighted?

You are gone barely 20 minutes when you feel the falling glass on your skin from the window before you hear the shattering and pounding of ammunition that follows you down, as you duck under the seat, grabbing Myron and Isaac with you. The chant of 'Jesus save us' comes from under one seat. The bus is still moving. Your knees are grinding like a stone has been laid between those joints. Your feet have grown weak; they would not lift you up if you tried.

Myron wakes from his sleep. Your grip is not firm enough on him. He slips and stands up.

'Are those balloons, mummy?' He asks.

You grab him back down so hard that you hit his head on the steel bus seat. He lets out a small cry and goes quiet. No one gets up till the bus stops moving altogether. Even then you are not sure what will happen next.

It's a while before people are sure that it's safe to get out from under their seats. The bus has stopped in the city centre where it's safe. The city dwellers are rushing toward it and shouting. You cannot hear what they are saying. You lift out Isaac from under the seat. You make a go for Myron. He still sleeps. You try to lift him again. There is blood.

'Myron, Myron!' you call out.

He does not wake up. You lift his head up and quickly grab him to your chest. You shake him hard and press him to your chest again and rock.

'Myron, Myron, coo,' you beseech him.

He is stuck to your chest. His hands and feet are limp. He is cold too. The people shouting from outside the bus gain momentum, while the people inside the bus are hurrying to get out. You squeeze through along with them, making for the door to the outside of the bus, crowded with eager people looking for particular faces. Your eyes cloud and, shivering repeatedly, he engulfs and then lets go of you. You want to get Myron fresh air. You want to shake him till he wakes up from his sleep. You miss a step leading out of the bus. You crash down with him.

'*Maa Do!*' you cry.

People are talking about this unfortunate incident, which is the first ambush in several months. You try to lift Myron. You start to crawl between feet that have formed a fortress. A woman from the crowd bends over to you. She asks you to give her the boy. Other people are working quickly inside the bus to get the injured out. You do not pay the woman any attention. You resume your crawl, but this time you can't even crawl. Myron is getting too heavy for you. The woman repeats her plea.

'He is asleep. All he needs,' you say, 'is cold water on his face. It always gets him out of his sleep.'

You press Myron to your chest again. A women steps forward. She persuades you to hand over Myron. You don't hand him over, but you are too weak to protest.

'I have to get home. I have to go home. The water there is cold enough to wake Myron,' you cry.

People are coming from all over town to where the bus is. They want to know if their relatives are inside. A discovery is met by their deafening wails.

'Why did you return to us like this. Why? Why?'

Uncle Sabitti has been waiting for you each day since you sent that letter. He has been coming to town and waiting for the bus every evening. As soon as he arrives at the scene, he walks around searching for you. Isaac is seated beside you. His hands hold yours, urging you to reassure him. The crowd has made a clearing where you are seated. Uncle Sabitti notices you. He comes towards you and kneels beside you. He takes your hands into his; then slowly wraps you in an embrace.

'I want to go home. Take me home,' you say.

You start to cry, like those years back when the girls at school called you names and he held you in his arms and told you that you should never worry what those children said to you because they were not good enough to even hold your bag. Now he is whispering to you, almost in the same voice. He is saying he has been waiting for you. Later, maybe he will find the words to let you know the men from the forest with guns under their arms came again and there is no one else at home but him because when they came he had travelled to the city to buy some quinine for his wife.

He rubs your sore back. He senses something has gone terribly wrong with this trip. Isaac holds your hand. He has been crying too. He has your shyness and voice, Uncle Sabitti thinks, with water in his eyes. You are thinking of the last time when your two sons looked so at peace seated quietly besides you. At that time, there had almost been an assurance of sweetness in every scent and some sunflower oil at the end of the day.

THE WINE GUITAR

By Segun Afolabi

He took the stairs, two at a time, to meet the woman he had paid for. His muscles strained as he moved. Once he thought he might fall, but he held onto the rail. He glimpsed a flash of canary yellow on the landing and the skin beneath the cloth and lost his focus and tripped on the final step.

'Blimey!' the woman in yellow called to her colleague. 'Damaged goods coming yer way.' Her laugh was throaty and wild, but it was not malicious.

The old man rubbed his shin where he had fallen. He brushed away dust from the front of the black suit that had carried him through weddings and funerals and the times when he had sung in front of audiences of hundreds. He no longer sang now; he played the palm wine guitar because his voice was thin and cracked. Sometimes he sang quietly to himself in his room as he practised the instrument.

The canary tittered once more as he made his way towards the room, but he ignored her. Up close, under the weak landing light, the skin around her eyes was puffy. A greasy sheen on her face made her seem unwell or tired. He was glad he had chosen already. He came to the door, but before he entered, she reached out to his shoulder.

'It's Mary, love,' she said, even as he was drawing away. 'For next time. Don't keep ignoring me for Agnes.' She gave a brittle smile and it seemed to him that he had misjudged her.

He saw Agnes sitting on the edge of the bed, reading a letter, her raven hair falling onto the page. Her mouth moved as she focused on the paper, but she did not make a sound. He took in the room – the thick crimson carpet, the dusty net curtains, the armchair with the coat slung across it, the double bed that sighed and squeaked. She looked up at him suddenly as if she could not imagine what he was doing there. He realised she had been completely absorbed in what she'd been reading. He thought he saw tears in her eyes.

'It's you again,' she smiled and dabbed her face with the palm of her hand.

She folded the letter four times, and tucked it into one of the coat pockets. She patted the bed, inviting him to sit next to her. When they were side by side she noticed he was panting from his journey up the stairs.

'Don't listen to Mary,' she said. 'She talks too much. She doesn't mean anything by it.' She didn't seem to hear her own words as she spoke them. Her eyes kept straying to the coat.

He wondered what she was thinking, what news the letter contained, whether Mary was still standing by the door, listening. Giggling.

'Is it all right today, for this?' he asked. He touched the edge of the bed between them, squeezed gently.

'For what? Oh, for that,' she said. 'I'm sorry, I wasn't thinking.' She rose and removed her slip and stood unabashed before him.

His eyes travelled from the bare feet, across the soft flesh to the young face and the eyes that were almost oriental. He did not know where she was from, only that she was young and he was old. They seldom spoke. As his eyes danced over her body, his mind wandered back to how he had spent the day. The struggle. It was evening now, the time when he came alive, but for him the day was a dry well he could not fill. He thought about the next day, where he would go, what he might do, how he could stretch a task so the time would not seem so infinite. He was grateful that the woman did not fidget as he gazed at her. She was used to him now. She could drift into her own reveries. He liked her face, the contemplative eyes, because she did not seem bored by him. He could never guess what she was thinking.

After a while she reached for the slip and pulled it over her head in one movement.

'It's time,' she said. She smiled so he would not be too disappointed. Sometimes she allowed him another few minutes because he was gentle and he never made demands, but today she had seen the letter and now she wanted to be alone.

In the corridor Mary smoked a cigarette as she leant against the wall. When he emerged she glanced at him, but she did not speak. He only nodded to her as he passed. He held the rail as he descended, taking one slow step at a time. At the last moment she stubbed out her cigarette and went to the edge of the landing to watch him.

'Mind the stairs, love,' she cooed. 'You don't want to fall.' She laughed quietly, but the old man did not hear.

There was a restaurant in Tooting he frequented nearly every day – Mama Yinka – where he ate his dinner or had the food sealed in plastic containers to eat later. The lighting was poor, the tables wobbled, the taped music scratched monotonously. He sat at his usual table to be away from the traffic of other customers and the constant to and fro of the kitchen. It was often noisy – he did not eat there at weekends – and it was some distance from where he lived. But he found himself drawn there despite the shabbiness, despite Mama Yinka's squawking and the irritating tapes. He found he could not help himself; the foods he had learned to love no longer gave him pleasure. He who had once tasted every single dish on the menu in an Indian restaurant. He had had a long affair with Mexican food, and had loved Italian and Thai; he remembered his family's obsession with *dim sum*. The hunger now was for the food of his youth, all sophistication and learned habits washed away. He could eat only *akara* and bitter leaf stew, *eba* and *egusi*, the *okro* soup his mother had made. Mama Yinka would fetch him a copy of the *Vanguard* or the *Tribune* to read while he waited for his meal. He could not focus on the tiny print under the dim lights, but he scanned the headlines and gazed at the pictures and found it satisfying.

In the evening, he went to the club where they played music as the young ones danced. Sometimes it was Latin American, sometimes Congolese or hi-life – the music he had loved as a young man. Every night he stood at the back of the hall in Covent Garden with his old friend, Salbatore, as they watched people trickle into the room. Around one o'clock the place would be packed with revellers. He stayed at the back with his guitar close to hand; they would call him and Salbatore to join them sometimes – the old man with his palm wine guitar, Salbatore with his honeyed voice. Usually he was not needed, but he was content to remain there, sipping pineapple juice, listening to the music.

'Why do they play like this?' Salbatore shouted in the old man's ear. 'Who can dance to this music when it's so damn fast?' His face was a rind of lemon forgotten in the afternoon sun. Desiccated. Wrinkled. Sour. He touched his palm to his forehead for a moment and shrieked, 'It's too loud. Why must they play the music so damn loud? It will make us all deaf!'

'I am deaf already!' the old man shouted back.

Salbatore shrugged and looked at the dancers, at the musicians on stage. He adjusted his tie and reached out to hold his saxophone, for luck, and then released it. He was certain they would play tonight.

A woman from behind the bar approached them with two drinks: a pineapple juice and a Red Snapper, and a bowl of pistachio nuts.

'Compliments.' She turned and pointed with her chin towards a man behind the bar.

'You are very kind,' the old man said. He raised his glass to the barman, who was smiling at them.

229

'The other one, he never gives us anything,' Salbatore said to the woman. 'I dread it when I arrive and see the miser's face. I know I'm in for a dry night then. You tell this one, "Salbatore says salud". We'll play you a tune if they allow us on stage.'

The woman laughed and returned to the bar as the two men sipped their drinks. It was a good night, a good omen. The old man thought he might play his guitar after all.

He remembered his courting days, he and his wife, the first time he had taken her to a dance. He held her close so he could smell her scent and when the pace of the music changed, he flung and twisted her, but he would not let go. He remembered her words at one point: 'A man who cannot dance!' and then her giggle. 'What am I going to do with you?'

But she had been delirious in her happiness – they both had – and they did not notice each other's faults then; they saw them only as endearments.

One of the musicians approached the edge of the stage and chanted, '*Olha que belo!, Olha que belo!*' again and again.

The crowd provided the echo until they became one voice and it seemed they were all related in some way; the backing singer was the sister of the man in the plaid shirt who was moving with such vigour in the centre of the dance hall; the sweat-soaked drummer was the father of the rowdy students at the front. The old man wondered about his own children, whether this was a place they might come to relax. He thought not. They were too serious, too determined for this kind of revelry. He could not imagine them, not one of them, able to let go.

When she turned, he could see her plainly. Agnes. The oriental eyes had widened with make-up and the long hair was coiled like a Danish pastry at the crown of her head. He could feel the vitality of the evening draining away from him. His heartbeat quickened. He wanted to be away from there, or for her to be away so he could play the guitar in peace. He was sure they would call him tonight and he did not want to miss the opportunity.

Agnes danced with a man who looked no older than thirty, and when she turned he held her hips from behind as she quivered and waved her arms in the air. She turned again and pouted, making a serious face, before breaking into laughter. She held the man against her, tight, and they moved gently for a while until the music changed. The old man watched with fascination. He could not reconcile this wild creature with the placid woman in the brothel, the letter in her hand, the tears. He shelled a pistachio and threw it into his mouth.

'You're an old dog, Kayode,' Salbatore jeered. 'Push your eyes back into your ancient head. She's too young for the likes of me and you. She's lovely all right, I'll say that.'

'It's getting late.' The old man glanced at his watch, irritated. 'If they don't break soon, there's no way we have a chance tonight. We may as well pack up and go home.'

'What!' his friend shouted. 'On such a night, with the drinks flowing free and this atmosphere? Go home and do what – face my wife? We're not going anywhere.' He had forgotten his complaint about the decibels. The alcohol affected him easily and he swayed his old body and tapped his white plimsoles together in his merriness.

'I'm thirsty again,' the old man said.

They both looked towards the bar which was surrounded by a mass of bodies.

'They've forgotten us already,' Salbatore complained. 'You speak some words of thanks and kindness and they think you're soft. We shouldn't have said anything. We should have told her to refresh our glasses every half hour. Now we've lost our chance.'

'Every hour,' the old man said.

'Eh? Yes, every hour,' Salbatore agreed. 'I must think of my wife.'

The two men left their instruments in the roped-off area and shuffled towards the bar, hoping to catch the eye of the barman or the woman who had brought their drinks earlier. When they reached the counter another staff member served them. The others were too busy to attend to them.

'It's on the house, ask your manager,' Salbatore argued, but it was too hectic for the barman to make sense of what was being said, and he only held out his palm and repeated the price.

'We'll ask tomorrow,' the old man said. 'We'll get here early and pull his ear so he won't forget us again.'

'Yes, you're right,' Salbatore said. 'Too many people, too much noise now.'

They both knew they would not ask tomorrow or the day after that or the next year. They were afraid, secretly, of what others thought of them – two old men – the bar staff, the musicians, the young ones who drifted through the door. Sometimes they heard laughter at their retreating forms. Often it was easier to make false plans than to concede defeat.

The old man paid for the drinks and turned and there she was. Agnes. For a moment he could not hear the music or the sound of his friend's relentless chatter. Her face moved from glee to puzzlement, to recognition and a polite smile.

'It's you,' she said. 'Hello.' She touched her hair and dried her forehead with a handkerchief. She held her dancing partner by the elbow. She seemed no more than a girl.

The old man did not speak. Salbatore looked from the woman to his friend and back again, and for once, he too was quiet.

'Graham, this is Graham,' the woman said. 'I'm sorry, I don't know your name?'

'Pleased to meet you.' Her partner proffered a hand, which was shaken, but still no words issued from the old man.

There was a moment when no one said anything. Even the merengue seemed subdued.

'Kayode,' Salbatore said. 'That's his name. He forgets to speak sometimes. I am Salbatore. Salbatore Gutierrez. Musician, singer, entre-preneur.' He retrieved a tattered business card from his shirt pocket.

The old man slapped his friend's hand. 'Kayode,' he echoed. He reached out to greet the couple.

'Palm wine guitarist,' Salbatore added. 'You didn't give your full title.'

The old man gave his friend a look and said, 'We are to play some music very soon. You must excuse us while we prepare.'

'No? You up there on the stage? Really?' the woman shrilled. 'This is our first time here. I can't wait to hear you.'

The old man held his chest and grimaced.

'Triffic,' Graham said. 'Musicians. Can I get you a drink or ...?'

The old man indicated their full glasses and then began to edge away.

'We'll be watching!' the woman called after them.

It seemed here, under the lights with the music throbbing, a sea of youth everywhere, that she was very young, this Agnes. The old man could not get the childish shrieking out of his head.

'She's nice, your friend,' Salbatore said. 'Both of them. She didn't give her name, though.'

The old man grunted and stopped, and looked back at the couple as they waited to be served at the bar.

'What is her name?' Salbatore persisted. 'You know, you're in a funny mood tonight.'

'I don't know ... Agnes ... Something like that,' the old man replied. He could hear the sudden silence of the stage as the band paused for the intermission. He had a great fear of performing now, and he wanted only to leave.

'Hey, hey – they might call us any minute,' Salbatore said. He took a sip of the Red Snapper and placed it on the floor next to his saxophone.

They braced themselves as the hall manager moved in their direction, but they did not look at him for fear of seeming too eager.

'Kayo, Sal – you're ready to go on? No sax tonight. Short set. Fifteen, twenty minutes, eh?'

'Of course, Mike,' Salbatore said, as he reached again for his drink.

The old man faced straight ahead, his eyes barely taking in the commotion.

'Actually ... Actually, it's not possible,' he started. 'The arthritis – it's troubling me again.'

'Arthritis! What arthritis?' Salbatore asked.

'It's not possible tonight, Mike. I'm sorry.'

'No problem, guys,' the manager said. 'I'll get Robbie to mix a few tracks.'

'What arthritis?' Salbatore repeated. He wanted to call Mike back, to explain that they had changed their minds, but Mike was already moving off into the thick of the crowd.

The old man shrugged and held out his hands, which did not shake. They seemed supple enough to his friend. Salbatore looked from the hands to his friend's face, to the welling in his eyes, and he was more confused than ever.

'Well ... who needs to play tonight anyway? There's always another time,' Salbatore said. He was quiet for a while as he thought of what he could say. 'Mike will probably ask us to play tomorrow. That's right. I'm sure he'll ask us tomorrow.'

They both knew they were old and they were rarely asked, but he said it, regardless. He placed a hand on his friend's shoulder, but the old man did not seem to notice.

Kayode's wife had returned to the place where they had both been born; he had not followed her even though she had asked him. He felt he had been too long now in another man's country; he had forgotten so much about himself, about the past. He was too stubborn and sometimes it seemed to him he had tried at life and failed, or had been carried along a road whose destination was not his own.

'You know, Sal,' he said. 'It's time for this old dog to go to bed.'

Salbatore looked at him. It was scarcely midnight, still early for them, but he did not put up an argument.

'My wife will be suspicious, me coming back so soon,' Salbatore said, but really he looked forward to being with her, as he always did. 'She'll be like this with the questions – *tat, tat, tat.*' He fired an imaginary machine-gun.

The old man snorted and picked up his guitar. Salbatore drained the contents of his glass and hurried after his friend. Usually they talked as they made their way to the bus stop, but Salbatore's efforts to engage his friend were futile and he gave up after a while. They wrapped their scarves tight around themselves, and noticed the cold more because they were silent. All around them the young ones chatted and drank from cans and bottles and occasionally peered at the old men, but they were used to that.

When his bus approached Salbatore asked, 'That girl, tonight – was it the girl?'

The old man shrugged and finally smiled. 'Salbatore, you will live long, my friend. The bus will leave you behind if you don't hurry. Go on now.'

As he waited for his own bus, more people arrived, most of them young and boisterous and, it seemed to him, very happy. He thought of his children who no longer visited him – they only spoke to their mother in the other country. He had provided well for them and now their lives had moved beyond his expectations: an architect, a physician, a solicitor. But they did not love him, the girl and her two brothers. He had been remiss, stern, too often antagonistic towards their mother, and now they had chosen sides. Everything, he felt, was gradually being taken away from him: his family, his voice, his years.

He watched Salbatore struggle to find a place as the bus moved away; the young ones were reluctant to give up their seats. He had let his old friend down. It seemed to be his speciality: his wife, the children, those who had once relied on him. He stamped his feet against the pavement, against the cold.

When it was crowded at Mama Yinka's he was forced to share his table with another diner, and he would eat quickly and depart. Usually he liked to linger, listening to the sounds of conversation, the language and laughter, the occasional drama. He was able to forget his discontent. It was not so easy to be alone and old, to look back at one's life and taste disappointment.

He rested the guitar at the end of his bed and moved to the kitchen which was part of the same room. He placed the *iyan* and the *egusi* in the microwave for five minutes and watched the food rotate until it was warm.

The pounded yam resembled the steam buns they had loved in Chinese restaurants, he and his children. The aroma of the soup filled the little room. He closed his eyes and savoured it and felt he was home. He thought of his wife and his sons and his daughter. He thought he would write or phone or visit one of the children. Probably a letter. He would try to make a connection. He sat on the edge of the bed with the photograph of his wife beside him, and then he began to eat.

NATIVE SUN

By Akin Adesokan

> The sun was behind them, beating them ever harder on their backs, but
> they paid no attention to it; they knew it well. The sun was a native.
>
> Ousmane Sembène, *God's Bits of Wood*

'Zephaniah! Zephaniah! Zephaniaaahhhh!'

From a region of the compound, another voice filtered through faintly, borne by pain or irritation.

'Father, I hear.'

Two minutes later footsteps, as hard shoes shuffling on concrete came closer, then died out as hands struggled with the doorknob. The door finally opened, ushering in a surge of heavy air that made the curtains tremble, followed by a small man whose hand, raised above his head, seemed tied to the knob.

'Father, I here.'

Zephaniah was a very small man, an inch below the doorknob. Although he was wearing a black, hand-woven skullcap that was raised higher on his head by a clump of hair left from a teenage hair style, he could barely measure up to the knob. He looked unstable in the blue-black clogs fitted to his feet, and tilted back and forth until the door finally pulled shut, pushing him forward with the forceful impact of its tensile brace. Zephaniah's feet made a clattering noise on the carpet, and he regained his balance, grinning at the figure leaning on the desk.

'Nothing yet from the capital?' Reverend John Jatau asked, reaching for a straw fan.

'Not'ing, Father.'

'Secretary went with them?'

'He go to prayer.'

'Ah, yes.'

Reverend Jatau glanced at the clock. Ten minutes past one. Looking away, he rested a fleeting eye on the official portraits of the military head of state and the state governor – both hanging above the clock – and turned away, irritated. For the past three weeks he had trained himself to ignore these two portraits, particularly the governor's, with whom he had been engaged in a battle since his first day as the executive chairman of this council. He did not hate the man, he just did not like him – and there was a difference here, as he liked to tell Leto, his sister. It had nothing to do with the fact that the governor was a soldier; so, after all, was the head of state, whom he really liked and respected and to whom he once made a present of a biography of his only hero, the Reverend Martin Luther, patron saint of the Lutheran Church. It was a question of the way the governor carried on about things. From the first day; in fact, right at the moment of his inauguration as council chairman, Reverend Jatau seemed destined to clash with the colonel.

'I can't respect a person who doesn't respect even himself, not to talk of his profession; much less other people, or someone like me.'

Leto had sighed: 'You're just very difficult. He's your superior, and to do your job you have to submit to his authority.'

'I don't blame you,' Reverend Jatau grunted. 'You've spent all your life as a civil servant.'

'Just as you're doing now.'

'Nonsense!'

'Trouble is what you find if you go looking for faults with soldiers. In the end, you are not able to do your job.'

'Because of my oath as a reverend and an elected leader of the people, I will not lie. If he and his cronies, like that district head, think that's a problem, I am not sorry. I am a servant of God and a servant of the people. God help me.'

That was at the beginning, when Leto still thought of herself as a kind of co-chair of the council. Reverend Jatau sat down at the edge of the broad desk, fanning himself slowly and staring at Zephaniah.

'Look, Zepha. Tell Secretary to see me after his prayers.'

'After prayer Secretary eat.'

'All right then. After lunch.'

'After food he sleep.'

'Today is Thursday, Zepha. Secretary can't have siesta on a working day!'

'Everyday he do.'

Reverend Jatau sighed. 'Look, Zepha, just tell him I want to see him. Before close of work. Today. You can go.'

He watched the man turn away, still sitting, weaving his fingers and touching each tip with the thumb. As Zephaniah rose, leaping on the floor, Reverend Jatau walked closer to him.

'I've told you several times, Zepha. You're a Christian; you should stop that pagan habit. Counting your fingers and muttering to yourself puts you in the camp of the Devil.'

Zephaniah seemed to grin: 'Father I remember herbalist woman.'

'No, Zepha, you don't. You shouldn't.'

'Father, I sleep seven days. I never sleep seven hours.'

'But God has since delivered you.'

'Until Sunday, Father,' Zephaniah said respectfully and turned, walking crablike to the door, his clogs making music as he went.

'The poor must pour out, the rich must reach out.'

Reverend Jatau smiled, nodding, satisfied at the sound of his coinage. He would try that at church on Sunday. The congregation would love it. The poor must pour out, the rich must reach out. How apt. But which comes first? If the rich do not reach out first, what will the poor pour out for? That would mean money looking for takers. Hardly possible. Never mind. Just keep thinking about it. Surely the people would love it. The poor must pour out, the rich must reach out. But how would it sound when translated?

He was standing on the verandah of the Council Secretariat, still holding his fan and looking out to the road to Yola. The sun was impartial. An hour now since he dismissed Zephaniah, and he felt hot in spite of the straw fan and the comfort of the shade. Out of an office down the corridor came the usual secretarial noise from an ageing Olympia. Inside the school compound to the left of the street, the last pupil walked the grounds, probably looking for a lost object. From time to time a wind rose into a whirling brown cone and then was quashed by the force of the waves of heat so strong that Reverend Jatau could see the air frying in the distance. Whenever the breeze succeeded in gliding past the heat waves, it sailed all the way down to him on the verandah, resting on the wall to caress the torn publicity posters of the immunisation programme. By three-thirty, he expected those who went to the capital to be back. Then he could relax or get worked up again, depending on their report. It would have been nice to send a radio message to Yola, but there was never electricity during the day. He had campaigned to resolve this problem, promising to ensure that Fufore and its environs got connected to the national grid before the end of his first term. But then this irritant of a governor had stepped in his way from day one, and he had had nothing to contend with but petty, small-minded squabbles. Now, hardly six months in office, it seemed certain that he would be thrown out.

At five feet nine inches, Reverend John Jatau stood tall, his stature reinforced by a career, in his youth, as an amateur boxer prior to his training as a priest in Ian Smith's Rhodesia. A habit of long walks – considered aimless wandering in these parts where herdsmen were known for roaming the plains – kept his physique trim. He biked after work every evening on the pretext of visiting the construction sites: markets or carparks in progress; the irrigation farms of the Lower Benue River Basin Authority; and the home economics centre where old women taught the young darning and weaving, and where the young, in turn, taught them in adult education classes. He stood for hours on his feet, reading the newspapers, which came in a heavy bunch at the end of every week because papers were transported by road to the capital, then to Fufore. His aggressive disposition gave his movement a fidgety edge, so that he always seemed to be in a hurry, and he made the most polite remarks with a hint of anxiety. At 38, his hair had been quick to grey, an onslaught checked by his fortnightly ritual of haircuts. His skin, dark and glowing, was tolerant of his habit of dressing up even for the most informal outing, and not even the sweltering days of March in this small town set in the plains at the edge of the desert could get him to dress light. He didn't sweat so much as he felt hot; Leto always chided him that his anger, coming from within, heated up his body and deceived him by hiding the sweats.

The noise of the typewriter ceased; he turned to look, and saw the typist standing at the door, throwing water accross the corridor. She saw him: 'Ftnoon, sah.'

'Bad habit! What if someone was walking past the door, eh?'

'Sah?'

'What is "sah"? I said you did wrong.'

'Sorry, sah.' And she bent respectfully, withdrawing.

He called out: 'Where's Zepha?'

'Eating.' The woman looked out again.

'Okay, you call the Secretary for me.'

He was returning to his office when he heard the sound of a vehicle. He stopped, stepped back, and saw the gleaming rear of a 504 Peugeot bearing the official number-plate of the state attorney-general. Next to it, was the old Range Rover that had taken his vice-chairman to Yola early that morning. Three men, led by his protocol officer, approached Reverend Jatau. Before he could speak, one of them stretched out his hand, at the end of which a paper stuck out like a gun trained at the reverend's chest.

'For your information. My name's Bello. From Justice Ministry.'

Before taking the paper Reverend Jatau turned to his protocol officer and asked: 'Where is Vice-Chair?'

'She's still in Yola.'

Without hiding his suspicion, he grabbed the paper and ran his eyes over it. It was like a court summons, except that it came directly from the office of the attorney-general, countersigned by the director of the State Security Service.

'I don't understand this,' Reverend Jatau said as he made for his chair, eager to possess control of the situation. 'You,' he said to the protocol officer, 'get the secretary here.'

'We have to be back in Yola before closing time. The governor is waiting,' said Bello

'I don't understand this,' he repeated. 'I sent my deputy to Yola with the report of the investigation panel, a panel appointed by the government itself. Is she detained because the government doesn't like the report, or what? Now they want me, and you won't let me inform my secretary.'

'Well, I don't know. I have orders, and I don't have all day.'

After tossing a few effects into a bag, Reverend Jatau walked to the door, signalling his readiness. Although he had not really sought it, he was being invited to the governor's office for the second time in six months, and he did not look forward to the trip.

A week after New Year's Day, while Reverend Jatau stood leaning on the wall of his office reading a newspaper, trouble paid him a visit in the guise of two herdsmen. They looked tired, dirty and worried, and it took them a while to muster enough breath to be coherent. They seemed to have a grouse, but although he spoke Fulfulde, their language – which his own grandfather had learnt the way Cameroonians learn French – Reverend Jatau had problems following the story. The talking man had begun with prayers and praises; then he interrupted himself to catch his breath or to look to his companion for corroboration or to glance over his shoulder. The chairman was irritated, but he knew these people well enough to endure the situation. They were never frivolous, and even though he was agitated, the man spoke directly enough. Sensing that the man might not get to the story in the next hour, Reverend Jatau invited them into his sitting-room.

The men settled uneasily into the austere chairs, occasionally glancing at the glazed photos of select icons of the Lutheran Church, from Martin Luther down. In a moment, the story had unfolded. The district head of

Fufore and surrounding settlements took tributes twice in a year. Usually he got two head of cattle, which the herdsmen gave with elaborate ceremony. But last year, two weeks before Christmas, they received his orders for upward review. Four head from now on, and three times in a year. He must replenish his own herd, which the scourge of rinderpest had severely depleted. All the herdsmen met and agreed to resist. But men acting on the orders of the district head harassed them, stopping the grazing cattle before the herdsmen set out in the morning. Once, during such a raid, a fight broke out. Two intruders were wounded, and several herdsmen were hunted down, arrested and detained.

Reverend Jatau became impatient, angry, as though he wanted to go after the district head right away. Instead, he called his private secretary to take notes from the men. But the men were ready. When the narrator was done, he reached into a bag and brought out a folded paper. It was a petition, written in Fulfulde and signed by about 175 people. Reading it only increased his fury. Dismissing the men, he promised to investigate the matter.

The following Monday, the petition, in English and Hausa versions, was forwarded to the district head with a covering letter asking for his response.

For a whole week nothing came, except unconfirmed reports that many more herdsmen were being harassed. Again, the chairman sent a reminder and a warning, copies of which were sent to the divisional police officer and the commissioner of justice, who supervised local council affairs. Such actions only produced more herdsmen victims. Then one evening, Reverend Jatau visited the grazing fields in person. Not only was he staggered by the disarray in which he found the usually orderly and peaceable herds, he witnessed a raid: as he and his two officials stood observing the scene of desolation and destruction at a grazing site, thugs of the district head came, shot and killed a cow, and took it away.

That night, he ordered the arrest of the district head.

The following morning, after the church service, the majority of his congregation criticised his action. They supported neither the district head nor the cattle-rearers. They recalled the herdsmen's history of antagonism with the farmers in the area, who were mostly Christians and members of the Lutheran Church. As a rule, the herdsmen felt no qualms about running their cattle through people's farms and destroying crops. When challenged, they usually turned angry, spoiling for a fight. Most people thought that they deserved what they got from the district head who, after all, was one of them and had a divine right to ask for tributes.

Rachel rounded on him after the crowd had disappeared: 'Reverend, you can't stop this thing. It's none of our business.'

'Our business? Who are we? I am the chairman of this council, and whatever happens is my business. I've told you I'm not representing the Jatau family, and I'm not here for the benefit of Christians alone.'

'And I've told you, times without number. Dealing with those people is not the same thing as dealing with God.'

'You mustn't blaspheme, Rachel.'

'You're too good to be doing politics. But since you're doing it, you should do it right.'

'That's what I'm doing.'

'When it becomes a problem, only family and Christians will rally round you.'

'I draw my support from the whole town.'

Reverend Jatau was so disappointed by these reactions that the following week he read one of his ceremonial sermons, a written testimony entitled, 'The Colour of Water, The Faith of Plants, The Loyalty of the Firmament'. His point was clear: although he had a duty to his congregation he would not withhold his passion for politics, and would not discriminate in his duties.

Before the close of work on Monday, the district head was a free man, borne alternately on the back of a horse and on the back of another man in a jubilant procession from the police station to his palace, with a deliberate itinerary that passed through the courtyard of the Council Secretariat, behind the wall of the chairman's office. Reverend Jatau listened to the freedom songs: they both insulted him and praised the military governor.

That same week, the council's congress elected a panel to investigate the matter. Its report, ready in two weeks, recommended the suspension of the district head. Although now free, the district head could not act. The herdsmen began a lawsuit, asking for damages for the terrorism and cattle-stealing.

The state government commenced its own investigations; the governor ordered the reinstatement of the district head within 21 days.

Reverend Jatau went to bed, woke up, and called a press conference: he would not obey the order. He was an elected servant of the people.

The plains. Stretches of cushy yellow grasses, clumps of stunted undergrowths with supplicant leaves raised like hands to the heavens from which comes water, any measure of moisture; hungry fields of gold dotted with the hard, useless droppings of cattle, while the cattle form leisurely groups, chewing the cuds to the envy of elegant egrets dodging the occasional whiplash of gentle tails. Here, a conclave of herdsmen, bent around a dying fire, one propped up on his sandar, the long rod used to drive the cattle, drinking *chai* in a hurry. There, an irritable cow getting out of line, pestered by a randy bull. Sitting in the back of an air-conditioned car and gazing at the field, Reverend Jatau was pleased with the result of his action. A few weeks back no herdsman had the peace of mind to make the customary tea, much less drink it, even in haste. But he put a stop to all of that. God willing, he might even succeed in ending the medieval practice of a district head exacting tolls from poor herdsmen. Although he understood why his congregation could be bitter toward the herdsmen, he had little sympathy for this indignation, believing that the quarrels between cattle-rearers and farmers were fed by ancient suspicion. A fair-minded man of God could resolve the animosity. He would.

'If you're fair,' he muttered to himself, 'you don't have to fear.'

He glanced with self-satisfaction at the desolate electricity poles as the car drove past.

Once this pettiness is over, he was thinking, we should work on connecting to the national grid.

He had always believed that with electricity linking Fufore to other parts of the country, his people would feel a sense of belonging as Nigerians, rather than feeling like outcasts on the margins of northern Cameroon. They did not have to go away from here, hard as things were.

Reverend Jatau hardly ever visited the capital. He once worked there many years ago, at the LCCN headquarters, just after his return from southern Africa. His ultimate ambition was to live in the countryside, among the poor and the needy, where there was much work to be done. He suspected modern government to be partial toward cities – a belief deepened by the experience of living in Harare when it was still Salisbury – and he would be part of government only if it would break with that notion. While the transition plan unfolded, and it was announced that local councils would be run by freely-elected officials, he saw the opportunity to test his ideas about independent candidacy. His primary support came from the Christians, who were a sizeable number, and to spread beyond such parochial base, he had taken to the grazing fields: a nomad among nomads, his campaign team setting up soap boxes next to the tents of the cattle herdsmen. They partook of communal meals of *fra da nono*, the thirst-slaking mix of sorghum and pasteurised milk, and their week-long presence jolted the economy of the plains with campaign money raised by the pennies. After his victory he started making overtures to the herdsmen who had long been hostile to the farmers in the area. It seemed that this gesture struck the Fulani herders as genuine, and so they did not hesitate to run to him once their trouble with the district head began.

He had been sitting in the governor's waiting-room for over two hours; it was almost six o'clock in the evening, and the governor had arrived long ago. He knew this because soon after he was shown into the waiting room, he observed some agitated movements along the corridor, and saw the brisk salutes of the air-force officers who formed the core of the governor's personal staff. Then he saw nothing for a while. The residence, like most of the government offices, sat in the Government Reservation Area, hidden behind a fence of huge baobab and acacia trees, on the left bank of the Benue. The trees were withered now, save the last of their rotting fruits and the nests of weaverbirds in their branches. The acacia had few leaves left, and once in a while, a popping sound came down to him above the hum of the air-conditioner as the acacia beans clattered on the corrugated roofs.

Alert as he hoped to be, and even with the intermittent explosions of the dry fruits, Reverend Jatau could not resist the overpowering urge to nap in the comfort of the air-conditioned room. Stepping in, he had been struck by the sharp contrast with Fufore, a place only an hour's drive away, where electricity during the daytime remained a dream of luxury. He simply dozed off.

It was getting dark when he woke up. He had a brief but powerful feeling that he had either been forgotten or he was already in detention. He stood up and walked round the room, wondering whether he should turn on the lights. Then he realised that his glasses were missing, and out of habit felt in his pockets. There were faint drones as mosquitoes flew past his ears. He remembered that he had put the case in his bag as he was trying to nap. He was reaching for the bag when the door was thrown open, and a light from outside illuminated the room. The figure coughed, and ran his hands along the wall, and the lights came on after some rapid blinks.

He was a dumpy, greying man in air-force uniform, and he seemed somewhat embarrassed to find Reverend Jatau on his feet. Still holding onto the door, he regarded the council chairman up and down, his face now inscrutable.

'*Ya-a?*' It was a question and a form of greeting.

'*Lafia,*' replied Reverend Jatau simply, still standing, and proffering a smile.

'What are you doing here?' The fellow had come into the room and now he sat on the desk.

'I'm awaiting the governor.' He was careful not to say 'waiting for' because that might mean that the governor needed to hurry up, but he also used the word 'governor' deliberately, knowing he would be expected to say 'His Excellency'.

The man stared at him for some time and when he spoke, it was in Hausa: '*Min ya faru?*'

Reverend Jatau stuck to his English: 'I have orders to see him. I came from Fufore. Honourable Chairman of Fufore Local Government.'

'I said, what's the problem?'

The reverend hesitated, wondering who this man was. He tried measuring his rank from the lapels on his uniform. Unfamiliar with air-force ranking, he gave up. He sensed about the man, however, a confidence born out of closeness to power.

'Ministry of Justice says Governor wants to see me,' he said finally, without interest.

The man nodded, swinging his legs: 'But mosquitoes plenty for here, o!'

Reverend Jatau wondered whether that was a declaration or a warning; the man swiftly clapped his palms in space, and examined them under the light.

'I'm the ADC,' he said at last.

The reverend nodded.

'His Excellency is travelling to Lagos tomorrow.'

This statement struck Reverend Jatau like a blow. He looked at the man with a mixture of wonder and helplessness, wishing for clarification, any piece of information. But the *aide-de-camp* was more interested in the mosquitoes. Suddenly, raucous noises burst out at once, from somewhere around him, louder than the claps and the unrelenting hum of the air-conditioner. He struggled up, and removed a walkie-talkie from his hip. He spoke into it as he walked out of the room.

Reverend Jatau sat back in his chair. He had been standing since the ADC introduced himself. He could still hear his voice faintly on the 'parrot', although he could not make out what he was saying. If he was mad at anyone, it was not the governor, and certainly not the ADC, but the Bello fellow, the man from the Ministry of Justice, who took him away from Fufore, only to dump him here and disappear, without a word, without a clue. He had come to terms with the frustrating ways of bureaucracy, and knew from experience how long it took supplicants to get any audience with people on a lower rung of power. But he was not a supplicant. Besides, this was a military governor, a custodian of orders 'with immediate effect', who didn't stand on ceremony.

He rummaged in his bag for the packet of dates, which he had begun eating for lunch after dismissing Zephaniah.

A woman came for him at 8:45 in the morning. He had passed the night in the governor's waiting-room, stretched out on a sofa amid a colony of mosquitoes, hallucinating about a trip on foot through the grazing fields to canvass the herdsmen's support against his impending impeachment. He had slept badly in his reverend's cassock with shoes and socks on, his tongue heavy with the after-taste of dry dates, his face pimpled with the bites of bugs and mosquitoes, his eyes bloodshot from too much worrying. He would like to have a wash but he smirked at the thought. He knew there was no chance of that.

The first sight he encountered on entering Bello's office threw him: sitting on a lone chair and undisturbed by the intrusion was his sister.

'Rachel, what are you doing here?'

'I came for you. I heard that you were arrested.'

'Nonsense. Can't you see I'm free?'

'I can see you're not free. You face is unwashed. You slept in your clothes.'

Years after returning to Fufore following a stint at the LCCN headquarters, Reverend Jatau was still unaccustomed to the way Leto related to him. Just as if she were his mother, or even his wife, her instincts for protection were acutely sharp. Ever since he decided to run for council chairmanship, she had become totally devoted to him, virtually replacing his wife who had packed off to Zimbabwe. This was just nine o'clock, and she had driven from her base to sniff him out of imaginary trouble. Leto lost her husband during the Maitatsine riots six years previously. Since then, she had become unwaveringly focused on relations between her 'people' and the Fulani. In her simple scheme of things, anyone occupying the governor's office at any time was a Fulani, as long as he was not a Christian or did not come from the South. She had been right in her judgments on a few occasions but often, Reverend Jatau thought, she just liked to shoot from the hip.

'This is not a family matter, Rachel. Please respect my wishes and leave. Go back to your farm.'

He said this with deliberate irritation, and Leto was taken aback. She sat there staring at him, apparently unmoved.

The reverend turned to the woman who had brought him: 'Where's the commissioner?'

Just then, the door creaked open, and Bello walked in. Acknowledging no one, he made a beeline for his seat, gathering files, tossing papers in trays, making a deliberate effort to avoid Reverend Jatau's eyes.

'We're going to see the commissioner in a moment,' he said.

There was silence; Reverend Jatau shifted in his seat, somewhat relieved to see Leto still standing. He had been on fire the moment Bello sauntered in; now he boiled over.

'You have some nerve, don't you? You kidnapped me without a satisfactory explanation, drove me to an obscure place and dumped me there like a piece of trash. You ordered me down here, and without apologies and no explanations, you're asking me to come see a commissioner. What sort of indignity is this?!'

'I'm a civil servant.'

'That's nonsense!'

'I work with instructions.'

'Indeed. In fact, I should see the commissioner to ask him a few questions. If he knows about all of this.'

Walking out the room, they came up against an unusual sight. Outside the row of office blocks, on a strip of lawn just before the parking lot, a mass of people had gathered. They stood in a crush, with hands locked into a fence that shape-shifted with the appearance of the reverend, staring straight ahead toward the office of the commissioner. Reverend Jatau thought that they were herdsmen; so persistent was his nightmare, heightened by the conviction that he was fighting for the cause of the cattle-rearers. As he struggled with the faces, he saw Leto slide into the crowd, mixing with people he could now recognise as members of his congregation. They carried no placards, chanted no songs, but there was a resoluteness to their appearance, an unambiguous sign that they were determined, focused. A riot squad on cue.

The golden hue of the morning sun beamed down onto the gathering. The stir had brought out the commissioner himself. A wiry man with a searing gaze, he stood speechless and disdainful, counting his rosary out of habit. Reverend Jatau recalled seeing him once; but now, he thought the man looked too much like one of the two herdsmen who visited him way back. Was he just hallucinating, or was this proof of what an old Lutheran father used to say, that bad faith existed regardless of colour or creed?

'You are trying to cause a riot on the Holy Day of Allah?'

This was all that the commissioner said, and he addressed himself to the reverend.

'I don't know what's happening,' Reverend Jatau said, beside himself.

'You are trying to incite people against the government?'

'Look,' the reverend said, desperate and impatient. 'Your man has kept me miserable all night. I have no idea what's happening. Where's my deputy? I sent her here yesterday. I didn't get any feedback from you. Now you are accusing me of incitement!'

'I hope you realise the consequences of this.'

But the crowd took up the challenge: 'Let him go!' came a loud ripple from the sea of faces.

The commissioner was startled: 'You shall be held responsible for whatever happens,' he said to Reverend Jatau, trembling. 'I have the right to call the police to disperse this band of rioters.'

'We're not rioters,' Leto shouted.

Reverend Jatau descended the steps toward the crowd, speaking as he went: 'Apollonius, Bitrus, Rachel, Matthias, Wycliff. Everybody. Please, go home now or return to your work. The matter will be resolved by the grace of God.'

'We don't trust them!'

'I'm begging you, Matthias, don't try anything stupid. I will speak with Reverend Hong today, whatever happens. Let everyone return home.'

Zephaniah sat under the shade of an acacia tree at the back of the council building. His tranquil disposition belied the sense of anxiety the lack of news from the capital had generated among the middle cadre in the Council Secretariat. For him, the fact that there was no one to scream his name was enough to inspire gratitude. As he recovered from the shock of an exploding acacia shell, he wove his fingers in and out, touching tip with tip, touching each tip with his left thumb, muttering as if in a trance.

Living in a village to the far south of Yola, Zephaniah once had a dream in which he was lost in a forest. After hours of roaming the bush and not finding his way, he sat under a tree to rest. Then he dozed off, and dreamt of seeing a woman who took him to a farm with various plants. The woman, whose face Zephaniah could not see because he walked behind her, taught him the names and uses of the plants on the farm. Nature, she told him, created an ailment in a human being and left its cure inside a plant or in the bile of a crocodile. The antidote to a poison from unripe mangoes lay in lukewarm honey. The yolk of a serpent's egg held the secret to vaginal haemorrhage. The moment she disappeared, he found himself at the spot where he had gotten lost. He stayed in the forest for seven days – living on wild fruits, leaves and barks – and when he turned to go home, he woke up.

He had acquired the gift of healing. When he tried to practise, motivated by nothing but the sheer enthusiasm of his inclination, his parents became worried. To have a dwarf for a son was distressing enough; to have this child take on the craft of alchemy and boast about it in public was dreadful. His mother remembered a distant relative who worked as a priest in Yola. This priest had been known to transform strange children into useful adults who found things to do in the wide domain called the service of God. Zephaniah was taken to live with the priest, actually a reverend, known as Jatau.

The moment Reverend Jatau dismissed the crowd and made to leave for the office of his liaison officer, he was accosted by three soldiers.

'Follow me,' said one of them, flanked by two others who promptly hedged the reverend with their guns.

Reverend Jatau raised his hand to protest.

'No need to argue,' the soldier said. 'Just follow us.'

They walked toward the mango trees near the carpark. The soldiers seemed anxious, glancing over their shoulders and whispering among themselves. Reverend Jatau had gone beyond worry. He had only one thing left, though: his breath. As they walked past the trees, nearing the gates of the government house, the soldier in front stopped, brought out a paper from his pocket, turned to Reverend Jatau and bellowed, reading:

'You shall return to base right away. You shall not try to go into town at all. Any attempt to demonstrate or protest shall be met with severe discipline. And you shall be duly punished for any eventualities!'

At that moment, it dawned on Reverend Jatau that he had been sacked from his job.

While Reverend Jatau was talking to the crowd, the council secretary was meeting with the governor. Later in the afternoon, he was driven to Fufore in an official car from the governor's fleet. Once he arrived at the Council Secretariat he installed himself in the chairman's office as the acting chairman. The man, a self-effacing, miserly-with-words fellow trained in the tradition of second-tier civil service, sent out a circular announcing his assumption of duty as the acting chairman.

Leto was a farmer. She lived in Mayo-Lamido, a small village closer to Yola than Furore but on the same road. She cultivated sorghum, millet, maize, cowpeas and groundnuts – crops that distinguished her from the other farmers in the area. For many years she had been an extension officer with the agricultural project of the Lower Benue Basin Authority, learning the habit of 'modern farming'. Her crops were as diverse as they were unseasonal: while other farmers retired from the fields after the year's harvest in October, then waited for the rain in late March, Leto farmed the whole year.

The irrigation projects never fully took off in of the Lower Benue. But files multiplied in 'keep-in-view' trays. New cars and filing cabinets were imported from the UK and Germany to service the burgeoning staff of the Authority – one of several that were spawned by the outrage following the famine and drought that devastated whole stretches of the savannah regions of sub-Saharan Africa in the mid-1980s. Leto purchased some of the irrigation implements that were considered to be outmoded in light of bigger budgets, in spite of the steady fall in oil earnings. She dug a well near her acquired acres, and routed the pipes through the various plots, employing manual sprinklers. This way, she maintained a constant supply of fresh maize and peanuts in the driest seasons, and the Authority used her farm as proof of the success of their initiatives.

After the protest was dispersed, Leto and other demonstrators returned to the LCCN headquarters in town to monitor events. She believed that her brother's ordeal was caused by religious prejudice: the predominantly Muslim elite in the Fulani heartland of Yola-Fufore-Ganye would never tolerate a Christian council chairman – one who was a Kilba to boot. The district council's action was primed to foster this intolerance; not even Reverend Jatau's enthusiastic support of the beleaguered herdsmen would convince the conservatives. She had no trouble convincing her friends about this.

But Reverend Jatau was not permitted to return to the city, where the church offices were situated – he was whisked back to Fufore, hours after the three soldiers had led him out of the Secretariat. Only later in the evening was a news bulletin aired on the radio announcing the appointment of the council secretary as acting chairman. And there was still no news or the vice-chairman. The broadcast added that policemen were in the streets from Friday afternoon, and had orders to shoot protesters on sight.

Leto returned to Mayo-Lamido early on Saturday to supervise the second weeding of her groundnut plots. She had been on the farm a little over an hour when she noticed a small figure picking his way through the groundnut beds. She thought it was one of the kids, attracted by the fun of a premature harvest of nuts. She walked away from the bantering workmen to drive him off. The figure stumbled from mound to mound, his steps slowed by the mud from the dawn watering of the fields.

'What do you want?' Leto screamed from afar, a clump of weeds dangling from her left hand. A sheaf of papers, or a broad envelope, fluttered in the wind above the figure's head. She moved close.

'Who are you?'

The stumbling figure finally emerged: Zephaniah.

'Oh, Zepha. Why didn't you just go to the house, instead of coming here?'

'Mor'ing,' he said, bowing and extending the envelope toward the woman. 'Letter from Yola.'

Leto wiped her hands on her apron and, still staring at Zephaniah, took the envelope.

'My brother sent you?'

She quickly unfolded the letter and, as she read it, moved under a makeshift shed. It was a circular that contained an account of the incident involving the reverend, and was addressed to leading members of the Lutheran Christian Church of Nigeria. It hinted at the possibility of a legal battle down the line. Every recipient of the circular was expected in Yola for a meeting in three days. Leto left with Zephaniah to meet the men who had brought him in a car.

One of the workmen came running onto the verandah where Leto sat in conversation with the men. He was sweating and panting, and he took a while to identify Leto in the group. Once he had, he stretched across a chair to whisper something to her.

'Ha!' She leapt up.

Everyone was staggered.

'The cattle people have invaded my farm!'

Without another word she made for the road, the workman in tow. The barking of a dog could be heard in the distance.

Cattle graze in a herd, leisurely, given to straying or delaying wherever the grass is green. They spread out, sit to chew the cud, shit, and graze more until the herdsmen decide it is time to move on and strike out with rods to fashion an obedient battalion.

Disorder reigned when Leto appeared on her farm. Several of the workmen's dogs charged at the cows, which were shielded by the sandar-wielding herdsmen, themselves assailed by the workmen with a string of expletives and shouts as cacophonous as the howling of the hounds. Badly aimed stumps and rods flew through the air. Meanwhile the cows continued to trample the farm, protected from the dogs by the aggression of their minders.

Leto aimed straight for the eye of the storm, where a workman's arm raised a hoe as a shield against a herdsman's rod that was trained at a dog that had bitten one of the cows. She stopped just before she got to them, startled by the spectacle of despoilation that had been inflicted on the farm. The peanut leaves were pruned, mounds had been overturned by a stampede of feet. In the cornfield to the right of the battle scene, where rows of knee-high plants had created an impression of a well-tended flower garden, a handful of cows were clipping the lush leaves and swinging their tails with relish, undeterred by the struggle waged on their behalf.

Fired by this sight, Leto set after a herdsman. But she was intercepted by another. A brief struggle began. She pushed the man to the ground, but was not quick enough to dodge a swift blow. A flash in the sun revealed a jackknife, forcing her to stagger back as she suddenly realised that she was unarmed. From another region of the farm the insistent barking of a dog ceased with a whine, as if in response to the commanding boom of a gunshot. Leto swung around, just in time to see sparks burst out of a gun that was trained on a workman. The accompanying sound brought the mêlée to a stop. The freed body of the shot labourer blundered from bed to bed, transfixing all by the sheer force of its agitation. Rod in a limp hand, Leto regarded the sight of the dead dog, the stumbling man finding eternal rest in a pile of twigs near the workmen's shack, the scared flight of some of the herdsmen driving their disordered herd off her farm, the company of helpless onlookers, the bitten cow still reeling in pain, attended by no one. A weevil in green chaff, Zephaniah trudged toward the cow that was wracked by pain.

The Mayo-Lamido parish church of the LCCN stood alone in a patch cleared out of the grassland at the end of a dirt road that was one mile out of the village on the way to Yola. A modest, austere building erected in the 1950s and refurbished every Christmas with a varnished emulsion the colour of milk gone bad, it was further run down by the relentless assault of sun and rain. From the road, the singing voices registered a threnodic note, captive to distance and uncertainty. Reverend Jatau contemplated the sound for a while, wondering if it would become clearer once the noise of the truck that had brought him had died out. It did not; as he proceeded, accompanied by a man from the church headquarters, the singing lost intensity. The closer they moved to it the quieter it became, until he was struck with nothing more than the urgency of a conference in hushed tones.

He stepped into the church, startling the voices that were weary of singing. The excited sighs united in a single voice that burst anew into a hymn in Hausa, rising and rising as he moved through the pews to the lectern. Despite the assurance of his presence and the confidence with which he beamed, an air of terror overwhelmed the congregation. With a detached view, he perceived the effusion of praises as a song of desperation.

'I had planned this sermon for my inauguration,' he said, smiling as the singing subsided. 'But it doesn't even make a valedictory.'

Nobody laughed.

'Yesterday, before the tragedy here, I was writing and thinking of saying something about the forces that threw me out of office. Now, I can't do that. Rachel, my sister and a leader in this church, is in detention. We have two dead men in the mortuary. We will be lucky if it ends there. I have a sermon written out. I don't think I can read it now. I came to assure you of my support, and to get assurance of your support for the legal battle ahead. I am here not to preach peace or foment trouble. I come to say words that must be said: the poor must pour out, the rich must reach out.'

He was silent, unsure of how to proceed, of what meaning to draw from the blank faces staring at him in this solemn building in the midst of the grassland. A few hands waved fans in the room; some swung scarves or head-ties. The mood was grim, the day hot. The sun had found its feet on the solid earth of its homeland.

Reverend Jatau moved a white handkerchief across his sweat-beaded forehead. 'The poor must pour out, the rich must reach out.'

He went quiet again, staring at his wet palms.

'Prosperity has no relatives,' he resumed, banging the lectern.

This last act stirred the congregation. Someone tried to applaud, and was joined by a tentative few. But the spark did not ignite a fire.

'The earth does not discriminate. The servant of the Lord in my care, Zephaniah, most of you know him. In the midst of the tragedy of yesterday, with dead bodies and police all over the place, Zepha did only one thing. He treated a cow that had been bitten by a rabid dog. I've always been suspicious of his magical acts. I remain dubious of them. But I can't be intolerant again.'

His voice trailing off on this rediscovered path, Reverend Jatau held the congregation captive, unaware of the army trucks outside the church. The lectern stood at the centre of the room, with a view of the entrance door. Armed men in battle fatigues and civilian clothing strolled in. Their unified steps were determined, their gaze unwavering. They headed for the man at the lectern, causing the congregation to rise in a song that blundered past its rhythm in search of a stone to hurl at the intruders. More men and women rose as the intruders marched toward the reverend, who was mopping his brow with a sodden piece of cloth. He had finally found his voice, which tumbled out eager to record the moment before the advancing men got close enough to stop him.

THE BROWNS' SAFARI HONEYMOON
By Tony Mochama

All the world shoots the tube and on the way to Burningham flat suburb in London where he 'hankered down', as Jayne was fond of saying (as in 'it's goan rain, darling, let's hanker down'), Joe Brown had time to buy a paper and surreptitiously peer over its edge at the occupants of his carriage, like a pokey neighbour spying over the top of his hedge.

Here were Indians, or Pakistanis (Joe could never tell from which side of the Kashmiri fence these apples fell); silent as temple mice but filling the carriage, anyway, with their sweet, sharp incense.

There were black faces, hanging down like poison-ivy over the red-brick wall of a Cambridge Campus, economic or actual refugees from Gambia and Senegal and ironically named places like Liberia – looking for a new life of peace, at least, if not prosperity, here in Burningham, Great Hearted Britain. Not to wake up to the sound of screams and gunfire, drawing ever nearer (although the men with machetes did visit sometimes – even here in the UK in the middle of the night, and folk would wake up, beads of sweat mixed with blood-red memories, wetting their beds).

Joe felt a lash of love shoot like a bullet from his heart and encase everyone protectively, like an envelope – then he met the hard gaze (dark) of a punk kid (white) with an arm covered in tattoos, his hair cut in the shape of a crown. Perhaps he was a royalty of some unknown Kingdom ('The Third Reich of the King of Darkness') Joe thought. Studs that looked like nails were pinned into his face – Jesus, crucified by short-sighted Romans. A ring hung from his navel, and (Joe had no illusions) another must be attached to his left nipple. Jesus died on a wooden cross, with tent nails anchoring his holy Jewish balls.

The Punk gave him the finger, so Joe retreated quickly beneath the fence, where he read that Chelsea had badly mauled Arsenal's arse and were set to retain the Premier League Cup for the year.

Joe walked down the corridor of the Burningham Building where he lived, and said a cheerful 'halloo' to one of a duo of quite polite Moslem boys who lived in the flat directly opposite his 'hanker down'. Not knowing their names, Jayne, with her wicked sense of humour, had dubbed them 'Machnouk' and 'Makhmoud'. The aristocratically named

Fairhurst Burningham Building, like the tube, was loved by all the world (low rents, low basement rates, the occasional rat). It was an un-segregated, multiracial housing complex, because the skint cannot afford anti-Semitism – prejudice being a privilege of the really rich, or trashy stupid whites. The Browns' privacy was frequently interrupted by other tenants like the black Briton next door always playing his loud Caribbean prejudice music and singing (shouting, screeching) along in a 'Jamaican' accent, or playing his guitar or horn, or crashing his football on paper-thin walls and screaming 'Goal!' because his secret ambitions were to be the next Sean Paul, or Pele of Jamaica ('Where muh real roots are, man!') Compared to him, Machnouk and Mahmoud were quiet and well behaved. Occasionally, when going to the bathroom at four or five in the morning, Joe would hear the faint musical sound of M and M chanting their morning prayers, but that was it – not like Mr Jamaica next door with his cacophonic ways.

Jayne had once pointed out, 'We too keep him awake, darling.'

Joe had turned red with colour, because Jayne was a noisy lover, and it made him uncomfortable that Mr Jamaica next door must have heard them 'at it' on many occasions.

Actually, Mr Jamaica had once inquired pleasantly, 'Had a lovely night, Mr Brown?' at the same time pumping the air horizontally with a folded fist.

Joe had been tempted to wring his neck and end his great musical/soccer ambition. Wring it like Beckham!

No sooner was Joe fumbling for his keys than Jayne swung the front door of their flat open. Abracadabra. There she was. Because, they seemed connected by a telepathic link, Joe often pictured love wires, or maybe love radiation emanating from both their heads and connecting somewhere in the sky.

She was a plain if not-at-all ooglie girl, his Jayne, with straight, brown ordinary hair that fell to her shoulders, frank, brown eyes and a slightly high voice whose 'Englishness' tended to arrow upwards with ex-clamatory remarks, and which Joe found extraordinarily beautiful.

'So,' she asked, brown eyes shining with excitement, her voice lined with anxiety as she led him backwards to a sofa that still embarrassed Joe because of the stains on its surface from one long night of keeping Mr Jamaica awake.

'So, nothing!' Joe said, shoulders stumping. 'The BALLS AGENCY (British American Land-Locked Security) will still not lift their travel ban to Kenya. "Suspected terrorist activities along the Coastline" – that sort of thing!'

'The bastards!' Jayne exclaimed, fire now circling her irises. 'The last terrorist attack in Kenya was yonks ago, and the BALLS have still kept their travel ban slapped on that poor, lovely, little country. How outrageous! Bl-uu-dy bastards!'

'It is a shame,' Joe repeated, mildly.

'Shame,' Jayne emphasised, 'bloody shame! But let me tell you something, Mr Brown. There is no letting some official yobos, who are just a bunch of bloody paranoiacs, get between us and our African honeymoon. No bloody way. I'm not spending my honeymoon in stinking England and don't even start on "alternative holiday destinations", darling dear. It's Kenya, or nowhere – and nowhere is not an option!'

Joe regarded his soon-to-be wife with exasperated affection. When she got like this, there was no changing her mind. The last three months they'd spent together 'living in sin' (although, oddly, Joe was convinced that it was bad luck to see your bride-to-be in her wedding gown the day before you get married, but not bad luck to cohabit for years before the actual event) had been a revelation. Ordinarily calm, she could get passionate about many things (animals rights, holidays in Africa, the war in Iraq).

While looking for one of the Kenyan brochures promoting everything about the country, from game drives in the Serengeti, to the pristine warm and golden beaches to mountain-climbing to the extraordinarily friendly folk (except, of course, for the fierce Masai), Joe had found ten tickets to a strip-tease club somewhere in Lower London – a joint he thought of occasionally but had never ever actually planned on visiting, booked for the day before their Big Day.

Jayne Brown nee Smith, sweet lassie that she was and knowing, 'FHM' men felt about their 'stag parties' had actually organised one for him and nine of his best friends, presuming, of course, that she didn't want to come along to entrap him in some mischief-with-chicks. One could never tell, and what could be nattier than that, on the day before a man's wedding?

On that day, Joe's qualms about marriage, at least to Jayne, vanished like ghosts into the Burningham morning mist, or usquebaugh down a thirsty Scot's throat. She was cool. Now the only problem was where to find stags to go for Jayne's 'surprise bachelors' bash' – people to go cavorting, gambolling and gallivanting with. For Joe's friends, as he himself often admitted, could be counted on the fingertips of one hand. Charlie, Fred, Leslie, Kenneth – that's it.

'Tis not how many maties you can count, Joe-dear,' Jayne had once told him, to his immense relief, 'it's how many you can COUNT on.'

'The stag party' at the straightforwardly-named 'Sunset Strip Tease Show Club' on a Friday in early June, was ho-hum – that is, the pole-dancers did their best to be sexy, gyrating up-and-down like uneasy snakes, but failing to fit into that turn-on bracket because it is hard to be sexy when you're trying to strip to swift songs like, No Doubt's 'I'm Just a Girl', and camp idiot classics like, 'YMCA' which the deejay insisted on playing. Joe, fortified by several pints, got as far as the deejay's cage to demand that he 'change his shit' – but one look from the man and he chickened out. Dude looked like the kind of fish that kept a blade in his boots. And wouldn't hesitate to use it.

Joe got married with a hangover the size of China. Jayne had given him the obligatory snog when the nuptials were concluded, with Joe wondering why folk always clapped after The Big Kiss. Kisses, unlike scoring football goals, are not the sorts of actions that should elicit applause, he believed. She whispered. 'Your mouth reeks of Scotch, darling.'

For some reason, this cracked Joe up – beers and hangovers making some shit funnier than it really is, and straight after The Big Kiss, he erupted into unstoppable giggles. Because it was his Big Day, folk joined him in the obligatory laughter – a very ha, ha, ha wedding party. One of Jane's younger brothers, Darren, a wiseacre from Wesexley, whispered to his mother, 'Told you he was a pothead, Mama,' to which Mrs Smith uttered an alarmed 'shush', half wondering whether this could be true.

Whatever the case, songs were sung, and Leslie – the best man – bombed out of his skull from last night and this afternoon – made a stupid toast to the effect of 'I guess my man Joe's pole-dancing days are behind him.' And for the benefit of anybody who had missed the unspeakable pun, he emphasised, 'Behind him! Get it?'

Then confetti was thrown and Jayne threw her bouquet up in the air. The squealing English lassies missed it but a dog, that was literally on the beat caught it between her teeth and promptly took off with it.

The 'Just Married' London taxi that the lucky couple had hired came to the rescue just after 9 p.m. at Burningham's best hotel – named 'The Burningham Best Hotel' by its Indian proprietor, who had totally failed to appreciate the English preference for subtlety, despite having lived twenty years in the UK. He took the Browns to Heathrow Airport where the 23:05 Airbus to Entebbe, was waiting for them – and for everyone else waiting to check in.

Lined up in Economy Class, Joe Brown free of luggage, the new Mrs Jayne Brown thrilled beyond words as she held his hand, silent – but with shining eyes speaking a thousand languages – the couple shuffled forward behind other travellers.

A small sign caught Joe's eye: 'DO NOT USE THIS AIRPORT AS A TRANSITION POINT FOR DRUGS.'

Beneath it, someone had scrawled: 'Really? Which a–port do a–use to transfa ma coca to Lagos?'

Another sign, below that one: 'There is a travel advisory against the East African nation of Kenya. Suspected Al-Qaeda activists on the loose. British Airways will only fly you to Uganda. It is up to you to make your way to Kenya! By Order of BALLS (British American Land Locked Security).' Joe cursed under his breath, and followed his bride past security, where BALLS agents with metal rods were copping a feel from passengers.

The BA Airbus floated above it all, like steam rising above a coffee-cup, and Joe surrendered to a post-marital, pre-honeymoon reverie, in which everything is perfect and everyday irritations are forgotten. Jayne and he would have perfect kids, with posh, upper-class accents and polite manners: a sweet little girl who would read *Harry Potter* as her brother pottered about in the garage, practising to be the next British Austin Morris (or whoever invented that car). Hell, he would probably be hooking on to some cyber porn site on the Information Super-highway, but why screw up honeymoon bliss with cynicism?

For Joe Brown did love his new wife much, with a slight ache in his heart that is the sign of True Love, and he knew he would be a good husband to her. So what if he was just an average Joe? He was a nice chap. Not sooo nice, mark you, as to be marked as a dull bloke. He liked his pint on Friday night, heckled the players on the occasional live football game on Sato-afternoons, and had once been booked for driving way too fast. Also, he'd joined a kung-fu club in Burningham and had actually fought – even if it was for all of 11 seconds before the newly-migrated Chinese bloke almost broke his neck with a roundhouse kick. Joe hit the canvas, got up, and hit the road at a speed that would have gotten him the bronze for the 100 metres sprint … Cruising on this now amusing memory, Joe drifted off.

The BA pilot's voice sliced into his life with, 'Please fasten your seat belt. We will be landing in Entebbe in 20 minutes.'

Joe realised he'd slept the entire eight-hour trans-Mediterranean flight away thanks to last night's stag activities, in which he'd hardly touched a tanned bum but had battled to keep Leslie in control for hours, and so had gotten no shut-eye.

Also, here was Jayne – his love – coming in beauty, wearing dawn like a cloak, her mouth tasting of aeroplane Colgate, as she kissed him 'good morning'.

At Entebbe Airport, shivering in the cold of the African dawn, the newlyweds were hustled to a small Air Kenya aeroplane on a small, side runway piloted by a big, black, bluff pilot in sunglasses who spoke little, but smiled a lot. His teeth were large squares and were unbelievably white.

As they sat in the six-seater craft, conveniently arranged for just the two of them by Air Kenya as if they were VIP visitors instead of just two lower-middle-class newlyweds from the small hubbub of Burningham, Jayne whispered, 'Do you think he's drunk?'

'Why?' Joe asked

'He's in sunglasses, Joe!'

'I wouldn't worry about that, darling. I think Africans just like gear – like the way they used to wear colobus monkey skins and so on. Those shades, dear, they're just gear. Ornamental.'

Two hours later, the clouds of Entebbe, Uganda had given way to the 8:15 a.m. sunshine of Mombasa, Kenya.

Looking down from the aeroplane, Jayne couldn't help but squeal in sheer delight. Spread below them, like a picnic, was Kenya's white and gold coastline, palm trees like daiquiris and the Indian Ocean, a vast canopy of brilliant, sparkling blue. After two hours of Kenya from the air, the mountains and valleys of the Rift Valley giving way to thick, green forests of Central Province, to the game plains of the Mara and Amboseli – where, flying low over the air, the Browns saw vast herds of zebra, antelope, buffalo and other game migrating south, the aeroplane startling at least one herd into a stampede. And now, this sea-view, this sheer beauty.

'Could eat this country,' Jayne sighed, pressing against her hubby's side, pressing her nose against the plane window, her breath steaming it up.

Then they were coasting down onto a deserted Mombasa Airport, with its one exit into the seaside city, where a sleepy-eyed assistant took the Browns' luggage to a waiting white four-wheel-drive Toyota, which was part of their honeymoon package – courtesy of Gyro-Travels and a lovely lass, called Caroline, at the desk.

Once they were safely ensconced in the back of the large car – air-con on to blow away the morning humidity of Mombasa city – Jayne asked the driver, a friendly looking chap who, like their pilot, had a constant smile, 'Why is the airport so deserted?'

Smile faltering, in fluent but slow Swahili-accented English, Salim explained, 'No foreign visitors are coming to Kenya, especially here, Mombasa. British and American agencies say Al-Qaeda is operating along our coast, but Al-Qaeda is everywhere! We do not know why Bush and Blair – here we call them the 'Axis of Bullies' – have picked on our country. You are the first visitors here in more than a week, yet nothing ever happens in Mombasa. Taxi people are stuck at the airport, suffering for lack of visitors. Their children a-ve been chased from school. No school fees. People who used to depend on tourist-industry, like me, we're quietly starving, quietly driving.'

Abruptly, Salim stopped speaking. 'Sorry, visitors. Just that I'm suu angry. U-xis of bullies,' he muttered, resorting to his odd accent in his annoyance.

Jayne touched his shoulder, 'We're sorry, Salim. We know that "terrorist threat" stuff is all nonsense.'

'BALLS don't have the balls to issue such advisory statements against other nations that are significant trading partners of Britain or the States, like Saudi Arabia and the Philippines, yet there are more terrorists there,' Salim burst out.

He became quiet, smiled weakly, shrugged and switched on the radio. The Beatles, 'I Wannna Hold your Hand' occupied the silence.

The Toyota roared through Mombasa City, the capital of Africa. Sea-resorts, historical sites and discotheques were juxtaposed with turquoise shops; where New Wimpy restaurants melted into Old Town, with its narrow streets still smelling of the 16th century and the slavesweat as Arab supervisors and Portuguese human-merchants hustled them in shackles to their banana destinations or watery graves.

Then they were up at the highway leading out of, the North Coast, with its whispering palms and majestic view of the measureless expanse of the Indian Ocean that touched both exotic Africa and spicy India.

They passed Mtwapa Bridge, with its megalopolitan feel and unhired speedboats rusting under its awns for lack of water enthusiasts to hire them. Then Kilifi Bridge, which nestled in the middle of Kilifi Creek like a kitten in a basket. Further to the North, lay Malindi, known as 'Little Sicily' to many of the Italians who'd settled there. Malindi was also known as *Watamu* (the Sweet Ones) to its locals, after the child-sex that went on there. Other than the paedophiliac pimps, most other 'natives' ran hotels, worked in the casinos, or sold sweets (both confectionary and cunnilingary) to Italian tourists. The serenity of Kilifi, and not the sin city of Malindi, was what the Browns had signed on for. Salim slowly spun the big white Toyota into Kilifi Town. Up and down, the news of the Brown Holiday spread, like measles – only this was good news – and a powerful ripple of excitement ran through Kilifi, grabbing everyone in its enthusiastic embrace.

***

For weeks, Juma Mwanangu hadn't sold many samosas outside on the roadside that led into the Mnarani Club, which is where the Browns had booked their honeymoon. The samosas were now turning black in the humid heat of Kilifi, the hot sun burning Juma Mwanangu's bald pate a solar halo, as passersby who used to say 'hello' to Juma in better days – before the BALLS travel advisories, when tourists still came to Kenya and to Kilifi – now trudged by him. They kept their eyes carefully averted from his samosas and Fanta, which only fuelled their hunger and thirst and which, now that the tourist industry they relied on had been effectively murdered, they couldn't afford anyway. Juma, it can be said and, indeed, has been said, wasn't having a very good life.

His wife would painstakingly make those samosas in their little, grass-thatched hut on the wrong side of town (the right side being the seaside, unofficially reserved for whites), stinking up the place for Juma and their six brown kids with the smells of high-cholesterol, cheap cooking-fat and minced meat rising into midnight.

Juma would take those samosas, along with the sodas, to his hut stall outside Mnamari every morning, sell near nothing the whole day, and then trudge home to Mrs Mwanangu and their six children, who would hungrily gobble down the stock and wash it down with Coca-Colas. The Mwanangus, it can be said, were literally eating their business – not just eating into profits and belching out net losses.

Juma worried about how much longer he could keep asking his brother, a civil servant (ironically in the Ministry of Tourism and Information in Nairobi, Kenya's capital city), for soft loans to buy stock if this tourist famine continued.

That morning the white Toyota spun into town. A driver, whom Juma recognised as Salim but whom he hadn't seen for a long time, stopped outside his stand. Tinted black windows were 'buttoned' down.

A white woman with a pink face, brown hair, brown eyes, a button nose and pale red lips smiled down at Juma. In a crisp English accent, and offering a crisper 1000 Kenya Shillings note, said, 'Could I have a soft drink and any edibles you're selling please?'

She left him 900 shillings richer. In Africa, tips are a lifeline, and some *mzungus* give them generous-like.

That evening, in the Mwanangu household, there was much rejoicing and drinking of *mnazi* wine. With the optimism that only the wa-Swahili people have, the Mwanangus believed that, finally, the terrible luck of the past few months was behind them, the *jinnis* (sea gods) of that misfortune having been dispelled by the coming of the white Toyota.

***

The white Toyota turned onto the gravel path of the Mnarami Seaside Lodge and came to a halt outside a curio shop. The Browns got out of the vehicle; Salim held the door open and Joe helped his wife down, even as he wondered why on Earth folk carried their brides over the threshold, when honeymoon reality consisted of this: the chauffeur, a hand extended, a white shoe stepping down on foreign soil. Perhaps only on movie sets, where thresholds were always deserted, men big, women puny (hence, carriable hand luggage) where nuptial bliss awaited in deserted, white satin sheets.

Jayne wanted to take a look at the curio shop. It was shut. Through large glass windows the couple could see dozens of sculptures – in ebony, in soapstone – of wild animals, of Masai, of hunters and paintings, most of them of the sea views of Kilifi. They were so well done that Joe had a feeling of knowing this was exactly what the Indian Ocean would be like when he finally got there – a distinct feeling of *prèjá vu*.

'What time does this shop open?' he asked Salim, having been warned *a priori* by their Dholuo pilot from Entebbe of the slovenly work habits of the coastal peoples.

'It doesn't,' Salim said. 'Since the tourists do not come, the proprietor – who is also the main artist – kind of retired. Can't afford the rent, you see?'

'To read these advisories, one would think the sea-hotels were swarming with Somali, Afghan and Iraqi terrorist parties on apocalyptical vacations,' said Joe.

'Bull, bollocks and bullshit!' Salim said.

Joe thought of Mujaheedins moonlighting in Mombasa; and smiled.

'Goodness,' Jayne exclaimed, 'Who is this sculptor?'

Salim told her his name was Wanjuki. He was young, just 30. He had been to university. He was a genius with his hands. He'd saved every penny, starved, to hire the space for his curio shop, all the while doing hundreds of sculptures and paintings – some days a sculpture in the morning, a painting in the afternoon, but always *mnazi* wine drinking in the evening. After those painstaking years, patience paid off. Wanjuki got his shop. Then Lady Luck turned and spat on it. Within six months, BALLS issued its 'anti-terrorist travel advisory' (If you don't go there, mates, they cannot kill yer!) and the shop shut.

Where was Wanjuki?

'Please tell him to open up ASAP,' Joe said quickly, hoping to alleviate his wife's obvious distress. 'Tell him the boys – or rather, the boy and girl – are back in town?'

Salim said, semi-sardonically, 'The two *mzungus* who will save Kilifi's condemned economy?' but as he led them to the front office of the Mnarani Seaside Lodge, Jayne spied a little smile on his face.

The front office had all the accessories one associated with African tourist lodges, whether smack bang in the middle of the jungle or out here at the sea-front. There was rough-bark wooden front desk, with a smooth walnut top, which ought to have been polished but which instead had a thin patina of dust – although how dust got blown in from the ocean was anyone's guess. A lion's head snarled from the top of the receptionist's head, making Joe shudder.

'This lion must have been mighty close to the hunter when he shot it,' Joe said out loud, staring at it with his 'I'm gonna devour you' expression. He spoke in a merry, Yankee accent to camouflage the fact that he was dead serious.

The receptionist, a pretty, light-skinned girl (it turned out, later, that her *jina* was Amina) looked at him with olive eyes,

'He speared it,' she replied mildly, 'It was bouncing ("Pouncing, she means," Jayne thought) on a Masai *moran* (warrior) when he killed it with a spear.'

'Goodness gracious,' Jayne shuddered, 'and whatever happened to the poor man?'

Amina shrugged non-comitally, but Salim said, anyway, 'We doo noot nu, manum, but we noo whoot happened to the lion, do we noot?'

Joe suddenly decided he did not like the way this Swahili man's o's inevitably turned into soft double o's that sounded like u's. It was eerily owlish.

Amina stood up. She was shorter than her reception demeanor suggested. But she picked up their heavy luggage in her two brown, plump hands – despite Joe's manly objections and protestations – and briskly walked down a corridor that was decorated with Swahili paintings depicting coastal scenes and people outside Swahili cottages.

Jayne, in what she thought was a whisper, to Joe, marvelled at the ease with which Amina travelled, despite her luggage handicap.

Amina, short and pretty, sighed over her shoulder, 'Spent my childhood carrying pots of water on my head, firewood in my arms and my little sister strapped on my back – back and forth to the Chama Roche. That's a river. So your Louis Vuitton bags are nothing. Also, had to listen out for crocodiles. They are silent, and they slither. They also like little girls and boys – like we were.'

Jayne shuddered again, while Joe was transported in time, to his school-days and the Lewis Carroll poem 'You are Old, Father William, but your jaws are exceptionally strong', while an old song occurred to Jayne – something to do with crocodiles in the Nile with golden smiles, that liked dancing with Egyptians. Amina delivered them outside hotel-room VIII, and curtsied after Joe had given her a tip. Then she left.

Jayne swung door VIII open to reveal a small room with a frayed blue carpet and a small TV and mini fridge (which Joe later discovered was empty). A large double bed squatted in the middle of the room, a huge white mosquito net curling up from its centre towards the ceiling like a tornado.

When Jayne, giggling, threw back the thick blankets, she sneezed because of the fine layer of dust that immediately mussed up, and everything got even more messed as Joe discovered a fan that churned up the dust into airy dust, ready to be breathed in and sneezed out.

'I don't believe this,' Joe yelled, even as Jayne rushed to the room's large blue curtains and pulled them open.

It was as if, all their lives, the Browns had lived in a box and then, suddenly, boundless horizons had been opened up for them. Before their eyes, just beyond the windows, were the whitest sands the honeymooners from Britain had ever beheld. Crystalline sands that ran on into a calm, sky-blue Indian Ocean that rippled out, like a sheet, into the very edges of the sky. An American 'wow' moment that left the two British holiday-makers open-mouthed in childlike wonder.

Joe and Jayne Brown could have been alone in the entire world at that perfect, content moment, except for a flight of seagulls that thundered diagonally down for fish. As they watched, one lucky bird grabbed one unlucky fish in its beak. There was a moment of silvery flaying about, then the fish was gone and Joe suddenly thought that even in this paradise on Earth, predators still stalked the slow. He thought, again, of the BALLS travel advisories and the way he and Jayne were all alone in this 'Eden'. He did not know whether to be glad or sad about that but, definitely, his moment was gone.

Far out in the ocean, he could spot the silhouette of a boat sliding along. Probably a fisherman out to catch one for his family. The bigger fishing vessels that used to come out here to get fish for the fishing factories farther south were gone. Joe knew these boats explored the outer reaches of this ocean, where the waters were deeper and where they wouldn't be metallic eyesores for white eyes on paradise's shores.

And Joe saw in his mind's eye a fisherman yawning in boredom on his idling, bopping boat as his daughter – miles away – yawned in the humid heat of a *makuti* hut in hunger and in frustration, as she tried to do arithmetic on an empty stomach.

Joe, in the two hours or so that he'd actually been on Kenyan soil, appreciated his position, alright. Back home in Britain, he may be pretty much a nobody but he, and his fellow men and women citizens, have the right to 'get away from it all' and come to cavort here on the idyllic seashores of Mombasa without some Big Brother Security Agency taking advantage of their ignorance to tell them to stay away from such shores, just to show the Axis of Bullies that it was actually doing something. Real people, like Wanjuki, Salim, Amina, the imagined fisherman, and the mathematical, undernourished daughter, couldn't 'get away from it all'. They were trapped here, props in a paradise they couldn't afford to live in.

Meanwhile, Jayne was sweeping a swath in white sheets no one had slept in or changed for months, for them to make love on. And because it was his honeymoon, and because he needed to escape from his guilty thoughts and into the mindlessness of meaningful, exotique, sex, Joe stripped down to his boxer shorts and turned his back on the Indian Ocean as he propelled himself into the arms of his wife who, as a child, had been wonder-stuck by this wonderful world of wild Africa, had wanted to pick it up and carry it off with her and sit in it during cold winter nights in Burningham, had carried it in her head all her life and vowed to return to it someday. And 'someday' for Jane Brown – sitting cross-legged, naked, with arms stretched out, like a pale Hindu goddess awaiting sacrifice – was today.

Afterwards, glistening smooth, not just from sex sweat but also because the air really was sweltering, the Browns laughingly hit the showers – sweet, sweet post-coital honeymooners – in love, laughing happily in a way they never could laugh again.

Kilifi, for them, in the years to come, would assume that dreamlike essence of places where we've once been, briefly, and were very happy. Like a magical trip when one was eleven, or losing one's virginity in a beautiful way, to a beautiful person, when one is sixteen – or just a morning when one gets up to a magically pink day and thinks, 'This is it. From today, nothing will ever go wrong again!' and even when you know it must, in that moment you believe completely.

Dressed in imperial bathrobes with royal logos of different colours – white for Jayne and pink for Joe – content in the cocoon of sated silence that filled their hearts with gratitude – for Africa, for each other, for white bath tubs with tiny, dark African spiders – the Browns retraced their steps. They were led this time by a smiling, dark man, called Mbuthia, who solicitously led them to the Mnarami pub, tucked in a back room where the barman got the sea view and the visitors got to hear the waves crashing behind their backs.

There were two waitresses, one light and stout, the other dark and beautiful with a gap between her upper teeth.

'Jambo. Karibu Kenya,' they said in unison, like two choir girls reading out the same script – one in alto, the other in sweet soprano.

Jayne said 'Jambo' pleasantly enough but, in their smile-glazed eyes, Joe read worry and anxiety. Would there be any other visitors coming after the Browns to Kilifi, enough to save the fledging, fallen tourist industry? The brooms sat on the bar counter, behind which brown bottles loomed large: expectant liquid mothers waiting for pink lips to suckle glass nipples. But no babies suckled here.

Joe ordered the famous Kenyan Tusker beer to quench his after-sex, Kilifi-heat thirst, as Jayne asked for a bottle of wine to be uncorked, chiding Joe for his 'unbecoming working-class behaviour'.

'Asking for a pint, instead of something classy even when on honeymoon, huh dear?'

'Classy?' Joe teased his wife, poking a finger lightly at her broad forehead, watching her frank brown eyes. 'This Kenyan beer is like a draught of heaven, honey.'

And it was, with the exception that it was a warm heaven, Kenyans being one of the few people on earth who actually enjoy their booze warm.

The barman, a creepy guy whom the Browns later found out was called Baba Babu, had worked in a bar in Nairobi called 'The Event Horizon' until a crazy young arsonist called Manu burned it down a year back. Baba Babu helped himself to a Pilsner and sat back behind the counter, appearing to listen to the waitresses' dialogue but feeling a billion miles away.

'Hey!' a loud voice cried behind the Browns, 'Hey, hey, hey.'

The delighted boom-box voice, it turned out, belonged to a black American tourist called Paul Amistad, who had defied the ban 'to come square up to the terrorists, having missed the action in Iraq, because 45 is over the God-damned hill'. Instead, Amistad – a psychoanalyst back in 'de Big A-pple' had ended up on this godforsaken, lonely and idyllic holiday in this exotic far-off, isolated sea-spot of Kilifi, in Africa. 'So how bout 'nother beer as we get to better *juana*? That's Swahili for getting to know each other.'

Jayne managed to work her way through her bottle of wine, and Joe and Paul the better part of a crate of 24 Tuskers and Castle beers, with Paul Amistad ranting all the time against BALLS, and the 'white Anglo-sexed down perception of Ma Africa. I mean whazzup wid dem, man?'

'The wankers vaccinate you like you're a puppy full of rabies against all sorts of imaginary diseases before you come here. They impose a travel ban on free citizens, saying the joint is crawling with thugs and terrorists – and you check down here and it's funky paradise. Dig that diesel?'

He looked at the Browns, guffawed and leered, 'For you two, honeymooners, I bet it is.'

Jayne, in her white pyjamas, turned red, suddenly unnecessarily reminded of the Jamaican 'footballer' in the flat next door, back home in Burmingham. Which reminded her she should call home just to assure her mother that the place didn't really radiate with 'malarial Mediterranean mozzies'.

So to the lobby Jayne went, where the phone – exchange, really, a relic from the Second World War, complete with huge switchboard – was manned by the smiling Jackson Mbuthia, who couldn't and wouldn't stop calling her 'madam', as in 'How are you, madam?' 'Can I help you, madam?' 'What does madam want?'

When she returned, Jayne settled for the enjoyment of the sea breeze caressing her back, as Amistad held court to his captive quartet of Joe, Babu, and the two waitresses who had forgotten all about the TV and were debating whether the big, bearded black American was worth a flirt – after he'd finished his exposition, of course. These girls were polite, and wouldn't dream of interrupting a drunk – even a noisy one – midstream. Especially not one from America, even if he was black. Especially if he was black.

'I wish my grandfather and mother had been taken as slaves to the States,' one girl sighed, 'I'd now be an American.'

'Yours were left behind because they were unhealthy,' the other girl said, smiling felinely. 'Me, I'm going to the States on a green card lottery'. She sighed, 'After I win it, of course.'

'You will,' the other girl said, holding her hand. 'Then you can go be a waitress in MacDonalds.'

And the two girls posed, for a second, seeing themselves in their minds' eyes in the Big Mac's distinctive uniforms.

***

Wanjuki, the artist, lay desolately on the blue sheets of a bed in a cottage that also led to the ocean, not giving a damn that his muddy boots were erecting a puddle of mud at the bottom. After all, as his hotelier pal who had lent him the luxurious cottage for a night put it, there would be no tourists coming down to these uselessly splendid seaside cottages for a long, long time.

Tonight, Wanjuki didn't even try to punch a hole through the wall of detachment he felt from himself and from the world at large. His ears picked up the sound of the Indian Ocean crashing gently against the shore, outside. Rather than soothing him, the sound reminded him of an eccentric British tourist he'd encountered once, who had been obsessed with some poet, and kept saying shit like 'The river is a strong brown god!' No shit – as if those whiteys had ever acknowledged brown gods! Jewish, yes, with long, matted, rock-star hair, and George Bernard Shaw beards, but black goyim gods? Never. Forget it.

'The sea is a charcoal-black demon by night. Discuss.'

To Wanjuki, it was as clear as the sky over Mombasa that, one way or the other, his life no longer mattered. The end-game was here, but like a soccer final played to an empty stadium, it had that terrible feeling of anti-climax. All the anti-climaxes of the world put together: The terribly disappointing wedding, the 'bash of the year' that happens in low key, the erection lost at the moment of penetration. Death was just another let-down in a life full of LDSes. If love is LSD, life is LDS: Let DownS – galore.

Wanjuki's stab at immortality, worked through the magic of his fingers, were the sculptures and crafts now lying idle in his closed crafts shop, like decrepit World War I airplanes in a forgotten hanger. Wanjuki had no doubt that no sooner was he in the ground, than everyone would forget him forever.

Which is why, he decided, he wasn't going anywhere underground. In death, he'd simply disappear, like the prophet Moses from the mountain, or Elijah (or was it Elisha who got the taxi-ride to heaven, with God picking up the cab tab?). Anyway, one final act of defiance to wrap up a life full of let downs!

The sea is an even stronger blue god, containing a cargo of drowned sailors, chickens and negroes.

Wanjuki, superb sculptor and noble bankrupt, stood at the edge of the ocean, and at the brink of a rugged, now ruined existence; his left hand that had shaped countless stone images of lions, African masks, gargoyles and copulating Masais, now holding a bottle of cheap *changa'aa*, from which he bitterly sipped as he stared out at the ocean where the sea met India. His cigarette-slim figure trembled, not from fear but because the breeze that blew in from the sea was cold – last gasps of icy breath from a dying Siberian. It was night now. A full moon lit up the sea and turned the sand white with its stadia-like light. Wanjuki distractedly watched crabs criss-cross the beach on scissoring legs, as the occasional dead starfish was swept up onto shore and was unceremoniously dumped there.

'All my life,' Wanjuki thought, 'I have been a starfish. It's about time I found out what it is to be a crab, crawling at the bottom of the sea!'

He thought of how long and how hard he'd toiled tirelessly in Nairobi to come and make a life here by the coast, to smell this clean ocean air every day. He was confident that his talent could feed and clothe him, yet he remained a starfish, and it had all come to naught.

He thought of a petty officer somewhere in the ranks of BALLS handing in a whiny report that pronounced: 'Kenya is an Unsafe Tourist

Destination!' A cheap, burger-eating, Jeep-Cherokee-driving, nice-house-owning American vulgar bugger not aware of the damage he was inflicting on Kenyan lives, and if he or she was aware, s/he really didn't care!

'Tough titty, pretty kitty. Sometimes the milk is sour! Those Africans (savages) will always manage to survive through thick or thin. Survival is deep in their skins.'

Wanjuki decided, definitely, that if he couldn't thrive, there was no need to survive. It would be life with a metaphorical feeding-drip injected inside his head, and Wanjuki couldn't bear the thought of that.

Wanjuki raised his free head and looked out at the ocean. The tide was already in. He walked out into the Indian Ocean, feeling the water swirl comfortingly against his ankles, then his waist, then his chest. Finally, a wave knocked him over, and salt water filled his mouth. The ocean tasted of an over-spiced India.

He remembered reading somewhere that death by drowning was the most painful of deaths, and his resolve to die wavered. Then a big wave knocked him beneath the surface, and Wanjuki decided that that was a sign from God, or the brown gods, that he must not waver from his rendezvous with water. So he stayed under the water, opened his mouth wide and over spiced India, again, swirled in his mouth.

A terrible choking forced Wanjuki to come up for air, and it was then that he heard the shout coming in from shore front.

'Seaward, or leeward, seaward or leeward?' a voice, heavy with geography and poetry insisted.

Then he was under the water again, India all around him, death and poetry inside him. When I'm old I'll wear the bottoms of my trousers rolled! And stride along the beach where the nymphomaniacs call to each other, but do not call to me. I'll commit suicide by crawling along the ocean bed, pretending that I was born a crab. (Actually, I have been crab-walking all my life, on the sidewalks of life, until a mermaid's voice calls out to me and I awake – and do not dream any more!)

Wanjuki, before his attempted suicide, had stopped believing in two things:

1. That the tourists would ever return to Kilifi Creek, Kenya.
2. God (and other related paraphernalia, e.g. Jesus, and props, e.g. Heaven).

He'd resolved to die in the middle of the year, this June 30th.

And what better place to die than inside the restless Indian Ocean, which dumped starfish, Coca-Cola cans and dead Africans on shores all over the place – Malindi, Tanzania, the Reunion Islands, even India – democratically, egalitarian-like, without discriminating or distinguishing between the Coke can and the African?

Wanjuki pitied the sad and pathetic folk who chose to commit suicide in shitty surroundings: in lousy flats; in crappy backyards; swinging from trees; bleeding into bathtabs; gassing themselves in second-hand Japanese cars, like Nissans. Zero imagination; but messy as well, for those who 'discovered' you, the suicide. The sea was tidy, smooth and efficient. No vomit to clean up, or ropes to cut down, or blood to drain, or tubs to Harpic-clean; no heavy, limp bodies to move, or flies or shit.

Wanjuki wanted a death as smooth as the sculptures he'd lovingly given his life for, but which nobody wanted ... but it wasn't Wanjuki's night.

The Browns, drunk as fish from Amistad's booze, had chosen this very moment of Wanjuki's '*Wakati* wake' – as the Swahili called one's date with death – to chase each other, completely in the nude, across the midnight reaches of Kilifi, now white in the moonlight. It was Jayne's drunkenness and high shrieks that translated back to Wanjuki, at sea, as 'seaward or leeward?'

Confident in their isolation (Amistad had disappeared back to his room with one of the Macdonald barmaids for a night of bliss) here on this lovely but lonely Kenyan beach, the Browns had sprinted out, Joe finally tackling Jayne who crashed down on the sand. Joe had immediately stuck his telephone pole – tall, thin and pale – into his wife's exchange, and she had begun screaming in delight at the moonlight as all her bells got a-ringing, and Joe dialed harder, dying to make the connection.

In the end, it was because Jayne liked her sex loud that Wanjuki's life was saved. The 'seaward or leeward?' was in original sound : 'Yes, Lord, ohh love it' being the yell that came from Jayne.

Joe, pumping the exchange as Jayne's long brown hair swept Kilifi's white, moonlit sands, was utterly amazed, absolutely frightened and generally astounded to see a slim, dark silhouette emerge from the Indian Ocean. Terrifyingly, this naked sea-god – eyes wide and wild, mouth twisted in an obscene grin, arms waving like a quadri-armed Vishnu in a vile dance – came charging towards them.

'Leeward, leeward, leeward!' the mad, dark sea-god screamed in a loud voice – tears streaming down its face, long, limp, black penis slapping against a thigh (right) – as it charged at them.

Then it was upon Jayne, the black, naked sea-demon diving on top of the very pink and red English woman, gripping her voluptuous, plump naked form in long Vishnu-like arms, kissing her face in puppy-like licks and slurps, and shouting as he cried, 'Asante, mermaid, asante!'

****

Fifteen days later, in the middle of July, a white London-style taxi drove the Browns down the road towards their Burningham flat in the Fairhurst House. What would Mr Jamaica say when they told him how Jayne's loud lovemaking had saved the life of some mad, genius African sculptor, who was now back in business and a 'born-again Christian' to boot? The Browns absolutely had to tell someone about that honeymoon incident, and Jayne had decided that the only person on Earth that they could tell without dying of embarrassment was Mr Jamaica, who already knew how loud Jayne could be.

'Born-again, is he now?' Mr Jamaica would have said, 'Well, Missus Brown, we heard of dem whiteys preaching gospel to con-vert dem natives to Christin'ty, right. But preaching sex to save dem man's soul, dats damn original missionary work, Missus Brown!'

The Browns were now turning into Patina Street, at the end of which their building stood. They were still laughing hysterically in the back of the taxi as Joe recalled to his wife how he'd thought Wanjuki a *jinni* when the man first emerged from the sea, and then how, when he'd dived on Jayne and had begun slurping her face in gratitude, Joe had been that sure the *jinni* would simply lift her up and go back into the sea with her. Never to be seen, or heard of again.

'Asante, mermaid, asante sana?' Joe panted in accented Swahili, beginning to maniacally kiss Jayne's face, which, this morning was crimson with mirth. The cab-driver decided that it was definitely Kenyan bhang. Pot-heads, post-honeymoon.

When Joe, emerging from the folds of Jayne's ample bosom, next looked up, it was to see the entire Fairhurst building, not too far up the road on the right, shake, undulate and then explode as a fireball roared out from within it.

'That's our floor!' Jayne screamed.

Then refrigerators, doors, door-handles, furniture, hearts and heads, whole bodies, bottles of British booze, and other stuff associated with the living came flying out of the Building of Death, including dead

Jamaicans and footballs burnt black. Patina Street collapsed into total panic, with people – July whites sweltering in the Burningham heat, blacks, Pakistanis, Chinese, dodgy Americans and The Department of General Humanity – fled up and away from the blast, as fast as their legs or wheels could carry them.

'O Lord!' Jayne screamed as the cab-driver, quick-thinking, screeched the car, not to a halt but into a neck-wringing U-turn, horn blaring as he thundered, Hollywood style, down the wrong side of the street. 'Oh my bloody lord!'

Joe, meanwhile, just sat up, stiff as a cadaver, eyes wide open in horror, until their cabby hit another car just a short way down Patina street and came to a sudden stop – leaving the cab driver slumped and bloodied over the steering wheel … and Mr and Mrs Brown unscathed!

BALLS, efficient as ever, quickly decided that it had been M and M, the two Moslem lads who had lived across from the Browns' flat, who were behind the attack.

They had had 'strong links to an Al-Qaeda sleeper cell', said one BALLS spokesman, 'that had tragically woken up in the heart of Burningham, with catastrophic results.'

The Browns were lucky! A Ford Mondeo collided with a Mini – and the Mini woman and her two small children were killed in the crash … right beside the Browns.

123 people were blasted to death in the worst ever terrorist attack on British soil, bringing the number of dead to 126.

The Browns had their 15 minutes of fame on international TV; they were seen everywhere from CNN to SKY News. Jayne Brown tearfully told how traumatic it had been to return from a lovely honeymoon in Kenya only to watch one's home disintegrate before one's eyes. Joe spoke of how polite the two terrorists had been, how 'devout at their 4 and 5 and 6 a.m. prayers.'

'Perfect neighbours!' he said, 'It just goes to show, you never can tell!'

Down at No. 10 Downing Street, Tony Blair – with a determined looking George Bush at his side – encouraged people from 'all over the world, 24-7-365' to 'visit the United Kingdom!'

'Don't shy away,' cried a passionate Tony, with his mad 100-yard stare meant to convey courage, determination or some other indeterminate virtue. 'Let it not be said that in Britain's darkest hour, our friends deserted our island; that they gave victory to the terrorists by shying away from England. We fear not the bombs of these terrible and cowardly people. The only thing to fear is backing down in the face of terror, so come to Great Britain and show solidarity with our great nation, the very cradle of modern democracy.'

President Bush, by contrast, was much shorter in his sentiments, and not quite as eloquent. After a peremptory and perfunctory muttered 'condolences' to the 'deceased, and their affected families' he pursed his craggy face into his now-familiar cunning expression – the smug Cheshire cat about to get the canary. Then he said, staccato: 'We will not be intimated by terrorists. We will catch, and punish, the evil people who committed this awful act, whether they are hiding in Asia or in Africa. For every attack they do on the US or here, in the UK, we will do worse. God bless America and, of course, the Queen.'

THE INTERVIEW

By Helon Habila

The key broke in the lock. It was one of those unexpected catastrophes whose real significance takes some time to sink in, and I must have stood there for over five minutes, just staring at the key stub in my hand before I slowly began to assess my situation.

It was 11 a.m., I was dressed only in pyjamas and slippers; my cousin, Rashid, who owned the flat, had gone out at 6 a.m., and now the key to the front door was broken in the lock. Rashid's flat was somewhere in the middle of a rowdy Ikeja neighbourhood. It was part of a twin arrangement, and yesterday when I arrived a party had been raging on in the other flat; the party had lasted till the wee hours and now the door of the flat was locked. This was my first time in Lagos and I had no one to call to come to my rescue – apart from Rashid, of course, but right now I couldn't call him because my phone was in his room. Even if I could, he wouldn't be able to come because he had travelled out of town and wouldn't be back till the day after tomorrow. I had come for a job interview and would be returning to Jos tomorrow after the interview; I had already said goodbye to Rashid. I was going to leave his key under the doormat.

I sat down on the verandah step, trying to figure out what to do. I was clutching a bottle of Coke and a loaf of bread – which I had gone out to buy 30 minutes ago after I woke up and discovered that there wasn't any food in the house. Yesterday, Rashid had taken me out to a nice restaurant for dinner after picking me up at the airport. Throughout dinner I could only answer Rashid's questions in monosyllables, I felt torpid, totally enervated by the heat.

'Interview, what interview?' my father had shouted, two days ago when I had broken the news of my impending trip. 'This is the first time I am hearing about any interview in Lagos.'

I had just graduated from university and I was tired of being treated like a child, of having my life planned for me. Already my father had set up two job interviews for me in Abuja, where I'd be close enough to be monitored by my parents.

'I'll be gone only two days.'

'But where will you stay? Who do you know in Lagos?' my mother asked gently.

'I am staying in a hotel.'

'A hotel? No daughter of mine is staying in a hotel in Lagos. Don't you read the news? They'll rob you, or kill you for ritual purposes ...'

I turned to my mum and said calmly, 'This is very important to me. I have to do this. If you don't let me go, then ... then ... I am 22! Stop treating me like a baby!'

I had never spoken to them like this before.

'Well,' my mother said, recovering quickly, 'If you want to go then you must go. But you are not staying in a hotel. You'll stay with your cousin, Rashid. He's a nice boy. I'll call him tonight.'

Now, here I was, two days later, with the stub to Rashid's house key in my pocket, dressed in pyjamas, and not feeling very grown-up.

I remained seated on the verandah steps, staring at the half-open iron gate, which seemed to be an integral part of every house I had seen in Lagos. High walls and iron gates; and often the high walls were topped by barbed wire or broken bottles.

As the sun rose higher, so did the humidity. I opened the can of Coke, which had already turned lukewarm, and took a sip. I could go to the next flat and knock on the door and explain my plight; the occupants might know how to contact the landlord who'd get the door open. But it was doubtful they'd be awake by now after last night's party.

I went round and pulled at the back-door handle, but it didn't even turn. I went to the windows and tried each in turn – the bedroom, the living-room, the bathroom – but all were locked. It must be past noon now and a feeling of frustration was beginning to replace the mild perplexity that had been my first reaction to the broken key in the lock. I sat on the square soakaway slab behind the kitchen, my legs buried in the knee-high grass, my elbows on my knees, my head bowed.

Much later, when I raised my head I caught a movement in the next flat. I was facing the tiny kitchen window directly. I wasn't mistaken, there was the movement again. A white blur. They were awake. I ran to the window, climbed onto the soakaway slab and peered through the square window pane into the kitchen. A cooker, a fridge, a sink, a dish rack, but no people.

'Hello!' I shouted, putting my mouth against the pane. 'Is anyone in there?'

No answer.

I went round to the front where a tiny verandah similar to Rashid's led to the front door. It was littered with empty beer bottles and cigarette packs; dry patches of spilled beer made the verandah smell strongly of alcohol. I stepped over the bottles and pressed the doorbell. The bell sounded somewhere in the house, hollow and distant. No answer. I pressed again, and again, and again. I was sure I had seen someone in the kitchen; could they have also seen me and mistaken me for a marauder, a thief reconnoitring? They had to come out sooner or later. A red Mazda was parked right in front of the house, which proved they were still inside. I sat on the verandah and shifted with the shadow as the sun shifted in the sky, and in my mind I rehearsed what to tell them as soon as they came out. I'd express my anger at their indifference. What if it was some emergency, a fire ... or ... a murder ...?

Hours later, I decided to seek help elsewhere. A narrow tarred road ran in front of the house and bordering it on both sides were big residential buildings with dark doorways and provisions stores on their ground floors. I walked down the road, careful not to get knocked down by the recklessly speeding *okada* motorcycles and the ubiquitous yellow *danfo* buses that kept pulling to the kerb to pick up and drop passengers, the bus-conductors precariously hanging from the open doors and calling out destination names.

It was late afternoon and soon it'd be night. I had to have help soon or else I'd be spending the night in the streets. I had exactly 40 naira, the change from my breakfast shopping. I wasn't sure how much it'd cost to make a call from one of the internet and phone cafés that lined the street on both sides, their loud signs advertising cheap calls, both local and international. I stopped in front of one with a rather promising name: God Is Kind Internet Shop. Inside, a huge rectangular table occupied the centre of the room, and on both sides of the table the internet users sat with eyes glued to the screens before them. To one side was a table with a fat woman behind it, a laptop in front of her. But she wasn't looking at the laptop; her tiny eyes were sweeping the room like searchlights, monitoring the browsers. She was obviously the manager. She turned her searchlights on me as I stepped towards her, appraising me from top to bottom.

'You wan browse?' she asked in a bored voice.

'I want to make a call, to Jos.'

'Mobile?'

'What?'

'You wan call mobile?' she explained impatiently.

'Yes.'

'50 naira.'

My heart sank. 'I have 40 naira here, but I can pay the rest later. I had a little accident with a key, and …'

Without a word, she lifted a finger and pointed to a sign pinned to the board behind her: NO CREDIT TODAY, COME BACK TOMORROW.

'No, no, you don't understand …' I began.

'Wetin I no understand? Na you no understand simple English. No credit. Finish. Go.'

Her voice had risen high enough to draw the attention of the nearest browsers, and she was opening her mouth to shout some more. Without another word, I scurried out of the café into the heat and noise and dust of Ikeja. I felt tears running down my cheeks, but I brushed them away impatiently. As I walked the crazy street, instinctively dodging fellow pedestrians and bikers and buses and garbage heaps, my stomach rumbled with hunger. Next to Rashid's house gate was a woman selling *akara*.

She was seated next to the gutter, frying her *akara* over a brazier. I gave her ten naira and in exchange she handed me a handful of *akara* wrapped in brown paper. I went in and sat on Rashid's verandah and ate the hot *akara* hungrily. The red car was still there in front of the next house, and the front door was still shut. I went over as soon as I had finished my *akara* and resumed banging on the door. It was already dark and I was beginning to feel desperate. I couldn't spend the night out on Rashid's verandah; I'd be bitten to death by the mosquitoes. I banged harder on the door, and it was only a while later that I realised I was also shouting as I knocked:

'Please, help me. I just want to use your phone. Please help me, please!'

But like before, the door remained shut, unimpressed. I sat on the verandah steps, exhausted.

Much later, I stood up, telling myself that out there somewhere, there must be someone kind enough to let me use their phone for a minute. Once more I walked out of the iron gate into the street. In the night the street was like a flotilla; the lights from lanterns on the roadside food tables seemed to weave and shake above the dark asphalt. I forced my mind to other thoughts, away from hot food.

Earlier, I had noticed a hotel not far from the internet café; I decided to go there, I might be lucky enough to meet someone whose phone I could use to call my father. Daddy would definitely have friends in Lagos who'd come to get me. In the empty bar I sat in a corner and pretended to be enjoying the loud music coming from a speaker in the ceiling. I sat and waited. I had no plans whatsoever – I was simply shaking the tree, hoping for something to fall out.

Hours later, when I got tired of avoiding the barman's unblinking eyes, I got up and left. I didn't know how many hours I walked the streets, taking random turns, looking into faces hoping to see someone familiar from university, or just a glint of kindness in someone's eyes. Then finally I noticed that the shops had started closing. It was quite late. I'd return to Rashid's verandah and curl up in a corner to wait for the sun to come up. Most of the roadside food sellers had folded up and stolen away into the dark doorways and alley-ways. Even the obnoxious yellow *danfo* buses were few and far between, their conductors wailing out destinations, sounding lonely, like night spirits. My legs involuntarily walked faster.

When I got to Rashid's gate I found the gate secured with a chain and padlock. Only the neighbours could have done this. Suddenly all the day's rejections and disappointments rose up inside me, bitter as bile, threatening to choke me. I held the gate with both hands and began to shake it with all my might. The chains rattled against the gate, the noise sounding loud and harsh in the silent night, and as I shook the gate, I shouted, 'Please. Don't leave me out here. Please open up. Please.'

I shook, and rested, and shook again, and rested. I couldn't see or hear; the sweat poured down my back. Minutes or hours later, I realised that someone was standing behind me, talking to me. I turned, leaning against the gate. He was dressed in a black trench coat that reached to below his knees, and on his head was a tall hat whose brim cast a shadow over his face.

'Sister, sister.' His voice was soft, almost diffident, 'Sister, I can help.'

'No ... thanks,' I said, moving away.

He smelled horribly, as if his pocket was full of rotten eggs, all of them broken. Suddenly my mind was filled with images of ritual killers who plunder the bodies of their victims for vital organs to sell to crooked doctors abroad. A shrill scream waited on my tongue, ready to spring out and tear the night to shreds. Slowly his hand came out of his pocket and he handed me a piece of paper.

'God bless you,' he said, and turned and walked away, disappearing into an alley.

It was a Christian tract, the sort members of the Christian Students' Union used to slip under our doors on campus. I didn't know whether to laugh or to cry. He might be a Christian proselytising, or just a clever criminal who might even now be lurking in some alleyway, watching me, waiting to pounce. I had to get away. But where could I go? There must be a police station somewhere nearby. But from what I had heard, the police were even worse than the criminals.

Then suddenly, from afar, I heard the lonely call of the *danfo* bus conductor: 'Bar Beach. Bar Beach straight, enter with your 30 naira change!'

I ran towards the approaching lights, waving madly. I jumped into the bus's dark interior as soon as it had stopped, panting; my body still shaking. The beach was like a huge party scene with wooden shacks standing shoulder to shoulder, serving as bar rooms and restaurants; people moved from one drinking shack to another, and in an open space before each shack dancers jumped and pranced and overflowed into the next shack, holding bottles of beer by the neck, swigging as they went. I found an empty table in one of the less crowded shacks and sat down. A few drunks came over to make drunken overtures at me, but none of them had a cell phone, so I simply ignored them and they staggered away to the next girl. I noticed a girl seated across the dance floor; she had been staring at me for a while now. She was seated in a group with other girls, all of them smoking steadily, looking bored. They were apparently prostitutes, waiting for custom. I saw her leave the group and start towards me.

'Hello,' she said, pulling a chair and sitting next to me.

Here comes trouble, I thought. 'Hello.'

'I been de watch you from that side since. You be new here?' she asked, blowing smoke in my direction.

I wasn't sure what to answer because I wasn't sure what the question was.

'You de wait for customer?'

'No,' I replied slowly, speaking in my best English, 'I am not waiting for a customer. I am just enjoying the music.'

The posh English worked. I saw the hostility disappear from her face. Her eyes grew uncertain. She stubbed out her cigarette and stood up to go.

'Don't go, please.'

She turned. 'Wetin?'

She must have been over 30, and her face, covered in a thick layer of rouge and lipstick and powder and eye shadow, had the world-weary, distrustful expression that went with the profession.

'I … I … need help … I am in a bit of trouble … Will you help me?'
Something in my voice, or in my face, or in her heart, made her sit down
again.

'Wetin?'

Before I knew it the words began to pour out of me like water, and
several times I had to stop to force back the tears. She made sympathetic
noises, shaking her head, patting my hand. She said her name was
Linda. But she didn't have a mobile phone.

Then, after thinking for a while, she stood up and said, 'Come. Let's
go find Julie. She get mobile.'

She took me to her group of friends who all turned their painted faces
and stared at me curiously.

'Anybody see Julie today?' she asked.

Some of them hissed when they heard the name – apparently Julie
wasn't popular with them. One of them said she had seen Julie earlier in
the afternoon in one of the shacks, called Wine and Dance.

We found Julie at Wine and Dance. She was seated at a table with two
men; all of them were drunk. She was a very large woman, and on her
head was a red wig that was all askew, and which she kept adjusting,
like a man adjusting a recalcitrant hat.

'Wetin you want?' she shouted, as soon as Linda asked to have a
word with her.

Linda looked at me and sighed, 'It is my sister here who has a little
problem, she wan use your phone call her papa.'

One of the men glanced at me slyly. 'Are you sure it is your father you
want to call? It is two in the morning.'

'It's a long story …' I began.

'Well then, sit down and tell us, pretty girl,' the man said, leering at
me. 'My name is Olu. Have a drink. You too, Linda.'

We sat down. Linda told them all that I had told her. The other man
fell asleep halfway through the story. Julie kept glancing from Linda to
me to Olu, who seemed to be her boyfriend.

'Have a drink, both of you,' Olu said again as soon as Linda had
finished her story.

'No, they no wan drink,' Julie said in her deep voice. She reached into
her bag and brought out a Nokia handset, 'Make your call. One minute.
You lucky say I be kind person.'

'Thank you …' I began, my voice trembling, but before I could take
the phone, Olu reached out and snatched it out of Julie's hand.

'So you no wan my drink, *abi*? Well, then you can't make your call, because na my phone be dis. No me buyam for Julie. *Abi*, I lie?'

With a loud roar Julie threw herself at him and they both went down with a huge crash, upsetting the table and seats. They rolled in the sand, hitting out at each other, arms and legs flailing. The dancers formed a circle around them, cheering and urging them on. Julie was now on top of Olu, pinning his arms to the ground; but then suddenly the other man, who had been knocked out of his chair and was rolling around in the sand, came to life. He approached the fighters, and not until he was right upon them did I see the bottle in his hand. He brought it down on Julie's head with all his might. The crowd gave a collective gasp. I saw blood; I saw broken bottles. Julie staggered to her feet, her hands on her head, and then she slumped down again. Hands pushed me forward, encouraging me to join the fight. They thought I was Julie's friend, one of the girls.

I yanked away and fought my way out of the crowd and began running; I ran and ran, as fast as I could. I didn't know where I was going. I just kept running in the sand till I found myself standing in sea water up to my ankles. I knelt down and let the water run over my legs, my thighs, my body, rocking me back and forth.

After a while I got out of the water and moved up to higher ground. I lay on my back, and for the first time I noticed how bright the moon was. I also noticed that here and there on the beach were couples lying in each other's arms. I closed my eyes and I went to sleep.

I didn't know if it was the sun rising or the hand on my shoulder that woke me up, but when I opened my eyes the weak morning sun was out, and Linda was standing over me, shaking me gently. Without a word she handed me a mobile phone.

'How ...' I began.

But she just shook her head and said, 'Go on, call your papa.'

LAND OF MY BONES

By Mildred Kiconco Barya

The hills stand solitary and erect, as if to say: we are not part of what happened. The valleys remain low, as if to say: we do not know how it happened. The golden sun leaves his seat for the moon. The land looks like no creation has been that side of the world save the thousand hills and valleys. The hills are beautifully terraced in a melancholy shade. They look like a sad woman seated in a full moon. A sad woman who cannot be consoled because her children are no more. The hills contain a silence that echoes across the expanse of land. Did it really happen?

And then it's there, a plea, in their formidable eyes, asking for justice, entreating us to look at what happened before our eyes.

The valleys hold a million tears in their undulating shape. They do not rise to join the hills in sad matrimony; the soil holds them down like gripped anger in their fists; like clamped bitterness in their knotted palms against the gods who did not intervene.

The Genocide Memorial is there. A few metres from our feet. It's tall but not high enough to reach the sky. Still, it stands undaunted. A stature that gives command to our feet. Come to me, it beckons.

I watched it all. It happened inside me.

Here is someone, ready to talk, to tell us what happened.

And so we move into the cathedral, the Holy House of God. The Temple of the Most High.

The skulls are there. The face of cruelty. Bodies shrouded in multi-coloured dyes of yellow, red, blue and green. Muted cries. Matted blood. Dark clots carpeting the floor.

The putrid smell of death emanates from the white-washed walls. It mixes with the burning incense and reminds me of dead frogs in a swamp near home. Rotten fish on the banks of Lake Victoria. Human bodies floating, crossing from one land to another on the free transport of the wave. And colourless waters turning a sickening dark red, forcing the little children of fishermen to return home with empty jerry-cans.

In another corner, the men's department; bones shine as if they have been polished with an ivory additive. Starved bodies in a fallen state, in a slumber from which they will never wake. Near the dark, blood-stained white wall, there's a skinny old man who forgot to close his lips and his eyes, before the tyranny of death knocked him. Yellowed teeth in a sneer. And little boys with tiny hands clinging to their fathers – eyeless, noseless, earless, lipless, skinless.

In the middle of the room are scattered arms. Some short ebony hands stopped from growing, lying next to long, fully grown chocolate hands. Chopped limbs of short, medium and long heights spread like scattered seeds. Severed heads with crimson stains. Vacant faces whose eyes were gouged out. The eerie archetype of heartless existence.

In the women's domain, there's a corpulent woman who did not remember to gather her legs together before the machete dislodged her head from her heavy body. Another one on her knees, her large melon eyes looking up to heaven. There's a pregnant mother whose womb was untimely hacked open, spilling a pair of formed foetuses.

Take your eyes off the people, something within me says.

I shift my gaze to the walls. There's a picture of Jesus with a large crown of thorns on his head. Pain etched in the lines across his forehead. Wounds so deep that they look like gorges through which large drops of blood, like icicles, leave the body and stain the background. Next to Jesus are wall hangings of saints whose hands clasp rosaries in prayer.

A loud voice finally breaks the sinister silence. 'We are together in suffering.' Hollow laughter follows closely. The atmosphere turns hysterical. Shrieks split the environment. A threat to sanity.

This place is evil! I want to shout. My tongue cleaves to the roof of my mouth.

A part of me slips away. I clasp my stomach as if that's where I should find strength. My voice is totally gone.

Gatsinzi.

It's useless to attempt to speak. My companion does not hear me. The bones in the church turn into long worms that wriggle towards me. Jesus save me!

Sorry, we are together in suffering.

I struggle to free myself from the screaming banshees coming toward me, the long worms stretching themselves to touch me, to infect me with death. Their screams impregnate me with a fearful dread and I start screaming too. I scream as if a thousand hot needles are pricking my skin. Heels of balance give way. I become light, light as a dry fallen leaf. Collapsing comes softly, falling always hurts.

***

I am in another place. Everything is white and blue. The nurses. The doctors. The sheets. I am surrounded by sickness. Sick people.

'What happened?' I ask Desirée my sister when I get back my voice.

'You were brought here from Rwanda in a critical condition.'

'Where is Gats?'

'He's around.'

My mind painfully retrieves it all. Hurt by hurt. Pain with no other name but pain.

'So it wasn't, isn't, my imagination,' I say.

'What are you talking about?' Desirée leans close to my ear to catch the words which are lost in a spell of fleeting sickness.

'I thought I had been imagining,' I say out loudly.

'Imagining?'

'Yes.'

'Was it like a dream?'

'Nightmare,' I correct her.

'And now whatever it was, is, does it appear real?'

'It's real.'

'Has it got a name?'

'Yes, collapsing.'

'Collapsing?'

'Country of my bones. They talked to me.'

'Bones?'

'Skulls.'

'Skulls?'

'Blood.'

'Doctor!' She yells.

He comes. He feels my pulse. My pulse has nothing to do with what happened, I say. He puts his stethoscope on my chest and listens to my heart.

'My breathing does not know what happened, doctor,' I tell him.

He lets his hand rest on my left breast for some time. I close my eyes and shut out his white garment.

'She's not well, at all,' I hear him tell my sister.

'My wellness has everything to do with what happened!' I yell and with sudden strength jump off the hospital bed and walk resolutely towards the door.

Strong arms carry me back to the bed.

***

I spend seven days in hospital before I regain my sanity. I do not remember most of what happened before the seventh day. When I open my eyes, I am propped between four small pillows, and rows of ropes bind me to the bed. It's hard to turn in my sleep. Relatives I've not seen in a long time are gathered round my bed. I recognise their faces. Their names. And Gatsinzi, my companion, is seated at the edge of my bed. Looking withdrawn and downcast, like sorrow walking through miry clay.

The doctor looks into my eyes and smiles. 'You are doing well,' he says. He has a young demeanour. He's 26 perhaps. My age. He's got one dimple on of his left cheek. I begin to get ideas, but then let my head hit the pillow.

'Someone with a Bible around?' I inquire loudly, intruding on the thoughts of those who have seen the look in the doctor's eye.

Desirée brings one from the nurse's room.

'Go to the Valley of Dry Bones in Ezekiel and read for me,' I command.

She finds chapter 37;

'... the spirit of the Lord set me down in the midst of the valley which was full of bones, and caused me to pass by them round about: and behold, there were very many in the open valley; and, lo, they were very dry. And he said unto me, Son of Man, can these bones live? ... these bones are the whole house of Israel: Behold, they say, our bones are dried, and our hope is lost: we are cut off for our parts ... I will lay sinews upon you, and will bring up flesh upon you, and cover you with skin, and put breath in you, and ye shall leave; and ye shall know that I am the Lord ...'

And so like the bones I rise. The ropes are cut off me. I am free. God's breath moves around my skin. A warm sensation raises my hair on end. I feel a weightlessness that comes with being free. Released. Alive.

'It's a miracle!' Desirée says with delight.

'I thought we were losing you,' one relative says, her voice punctuated with concern.

'I am a remnant. There will always be remnants.'

'To inherit a country of dry bones?' she teases.

'No, land of my bones.'

***

287

Days pass so quickly. I am into my editing work like a phoenix re-bouncing to life.

'Bring the stories, do not stifle the muse,' I tell my friends who claim love for writing.

'I have been writing but somehow, the stories remain incomplete,' they confess.

My only worry is Gatsinzi. I have no idea where he is. An hour in the morning and my 72 pounds are gone. No quarrel. No debate. I am at the computer table, putting final words to my short story for the Common-wealth submission.

'I am gone,' he says.

'See you, I reply,' without taking my eyes off the screen.

'So long,' he responds.

Only I do not think how long. I do not see that he has taken his foremost treasure: the Bible with the blue cover that he has owned since his confirmation class as a small boy of 12. When I open our wardrobe closet, I realise he has taken most of his clothes. His grey tracksuits, his favourite sandals, our much-loved rucksack. Who will tell me what's happened here?

I talk to Desirée over the phone and tell her Gats isn't home, hasn't been home.

'Don't ever worry about a man,' she says in a careless whisper. 'He will come back when he comes back. He's not a lost child.'

I do not protest. I do not ask her in this era of HIV and AIDS, how do you simply welcome back into your life a man when you have no idea where he's gone, where he's been, where he's from, and what's been the world with him?

I swallow my apprehension and carry on with my editing.

A few casual friends drop in for a coffee-tasting spree over the weekend. They know I keep lots of rare coffees that are rich to taste. I throw open the doors and run through the house with the coffee maker. I want the house to smell the richness and freshness of coffee.

'Gats, Gats!' I call out. I take long to remember that he is not in the house. He's not with me anymore.

I run my fingers over the stereo. I listen to the sounds of Cliff Richard. Just like the song, 'It's All in the Game', no one tells me that he won't come back, but then no one says that he will come. The people I talk to mention 'a while'. And so a long while lies between us.

***

288

One sunny morning, a ray of sunlight breaks through my window and drops colours of brightness into my room. I do not have to be anxious about Gatsinzi. Perhaps he will drop in one day. Perhaps he will never return. I begin to familiarise myself with living alone, again.

When I am getting used to being only me again, he comes. Bloodshot eyes, like he has been drinking cheap wine all day long. I fight to prevent my curious mind from asking where he has been.

'Welcome!' I dare him into a warm cuddle.

'Take your filthy fingers off me.'

'Bad mood, hmmm?'

'What right have you, what ownership did you have, to collapse in that cathedral, over a genocide that was not part of you?'

'Holy Grail! What are you talking about?'

'You did not experience that pain. It did not happen to you. It did not even happen to your people. Did you want to show the world that you are more sentimental than all those who have lived it?'

'You are my people! I feel every pain, and every tear that belongs to you belongs to me!' I scream in rage, and try to silence his tirade of words against my frail heart.

'Your reaction was wrong; you did not have to own the genocide. You didn't see your mother in that cathedral; you didn't see your father; you did not smell the blood.'

'Every woman in that building was my mother! Every man a potential father, brother.'

'Who are you?'

'I am the soul of w-o-m-a-n!'

'It doesn't lessen the pain, you know.'

'My purpose is not to lessen the pain but to partake in the suffering.

'Shut up, holy martyr!'

'Sincerely, Gatsinzi.'

'Take your sincerity to hell!'

'Tell me, brother, what hurt you? What is hurting you?' I yell out from my lungs. I do not crouch backwards in fear of a man confronting me for owning a universal sin. I am as unbendable as a tombstone.

'You! You are the pain. You are hurting me,' he says contemptuously.

I do not see how I am hurting him. He is in a rage and I do not understand why my fainting should make him react like I've murdered his mother and danced on her grave. My spine begins to crack and so does my womanness. My hands tremble as my body breaks out in cold fear.

I pick up the percolator and make it sing with water for coffee. Waiting is another painful process; the atmosphere is swollen with anger and bitterness. I let my body drop into the couch. I sit hunched back and my bones begin to rattle because of the new fear that traps me.

Gatsinzi moves towards me. He puts his arms around me. They are cold. His long fingers no longer fascinate me. His long nose does not have the appeal of a song it always rouses in me. His long legs are no longer strong pillars intertwined about mine in rest. His raised forehead is no longer the well-built beam cupped between my breasts at night. His mouth so sweet now releases a lemon sourness. I feel his fingers becoming worms as they touch me.

'Look at me, Nina.'

I look into his red eyes and stare at the image of the grim reaper.

'Shall we consider the matter resolved?' he inquires.

'Which matter?'

'The genocide. Don't ever feel about it. You are Ugandan. I am Rwandan. We are different.'

'What do you mean?'

'Do not own our pain. I hate it when outsiders want to possess what belongs to us.'

'Outsiders! Who are you calling outsiders? You are my people!'

'Honey, spare your memory. Six years of living together do not make you us. They do not entitle you to our pain.' And so we fight over pain as if it's some holy delight.

'Gats, you are my cockroach.'

That latter word severs the last thread holding our lives. He used to love the sound of it whenever I rolled it on my tongue.

'Why should it make you so mad?'

'It was used against us. Our people stood in queues. Cockroaches were separated from the non-cockroaches. It was a cleansing; purifying themselves of us. Are you so dumb?'

'And why are you against me owning a part of your people's pain?'

'When you own it, you become heartless. You portray the others who *should* feel it as though they do not care.'

'You know what? You are a racist!'

'Repeat what you've said.'

'R-a-c-i-s-t! We've been together these six years, and you still let geographical boundaries and political sins come between us.'

Like pus from a festering sore, sweat drips from his face. We exchange harsh words and forget the beauty of being alive. Of living together as loved ones. As friends. My arteries are clogged in sorrow. When the anger melts, a wall of indifference stands between us. A frozen detachment settles between us.

The percolator goes off. Neither of us wants the coffee anymore. We have become two blocks of hardened clay. We do not even feel hungry. We do not feel human anymore. We have become broken cisterns that cannot hold togetherness anymore.

Night comes with her consoling darkness. But sleep does not come to our eyes. She does not visit us. Turning, tossing, and lying awake – the night is long. Perhaps we should talk about separation now that unity fails us.

'Gats, will you be leaving tomorrow?'

'Yes, Ni.'

'And will you be returning after a while?'

'No.'

'Goodnight.'

'Goodnight.'

For the few hours into the break of dawn we manage to feign sleep. In the morning I sit next to him and help him fold the clothes he's dropping into the big rucksack.

'Won't you be needing this?' I lift his long green jumper to his hands.

'Oh yes, thanks.'

'And don't forget your sunglasses, here.'

Our fingers touch lightly. The fire that used to melt us into helpless desire at the mere stroke of our fingers is gone, long before he walks out of our home.

'Here's your *Everyday With Jesus* scriptures to guide you.'

'Oh, my cherished possession.' He drops it into the rucksack.

We look at each other to see who will smile first.

And we laugh.

We drink some coffee. I hand him the black mug.

'You have a long journey ahead of you.'

'Thanks.'

'When you reach where you are going, do send me a postcard.'

'I'll let you know that I am alright. For now I don't know where I will be.' He rises to leave.

'So long.'

'So long.'

A brief touch on the shoulder, and his long fingers disappear through the door. I walk slowly to stand by the window and watch the long strides of a man I have loved.

***

Back to my editing. I carry a big bag of sleeplessness around me. A ballast of sand is lodged in my eyes; I have a tough time reading. For days on end I carry on with sand in my eyes. Hurt is in the silence that poisons the air. I cannot breathe freely. I seek a facelessness, a forgetfulness and a consciousness that does not wear a familiar life. The desire to escape myself hangs over me like a rack swinging from the ceiling.

Sometimes I hold the night in my hands and plead with her to give me sleep. I bid the moon goodnight and day breaks before I know what sleep really is. In the late hours of the day at the office I begin to doze.

When I am home, the air of aimlessness surrounds me. Welcome to my arms, it says. I do not refuse. I scan my bedroom: a stereo; a double bed; a dressing table; a reading chair; a wardrobe; drawers that I open, looking for some clue of what to do. There is nothing to fill up the hollowness in my mind. The dull ache. I consider the mound of books on the table in the corner. I've been through that already.

Worst of all, I cannot write.

I move to the kitchen to make some coffee. I tinkle the coffee spoon whilst waiting for the water to boil. I scoop the sugar from the glass bowl. The clink-clanking sound that my stirring spoon makes as it beats against the ribs of my cup opens my body to warmth. My hands embrace the cup. It's all I have for the lonely nights and cold hours. It is my silent partner steaming within me.

Sometimes vehicles drive past my house when it is darker than midnight. A few restless individuals perhaps, sharing my loneliness without knowing it. When I get tired of being awake in the dark, I switch on the light-bulb and streams of yellow come to listen to the sound of my heart cracking. I pace around the room. Nothingness surrounds my steps. One, two, three, we stride together. The brightness from my bulb is vindictive: it magnifies the loneliness in me. Still, I see no point in switching off the light. Let it be. And so I am wedged in an endless insomnia like a fly suspended in a spider web. I cannot find the company of sleep. I watch the moon. The story of counting sheep is as old as age. It does not help me.

When I am close to losing my sanity, I open up to Roxanne, my Indian colleague in editing. She suggests that I enrol for guitar lessons. I am relieved that she does not mention yoga and exercise.

'When you cannot sleep,' she says, 'the music of the guitar should console you. And you know how to sing.'

Roxanne, on a few occasions, has watched me sing at friends' parties. Believing that guitar lessons might help, I start going to Kampala Music School every evening after work. I get a Korean tutor who tells me that only two things matter when learning the guitar:

'Intirest, and a pazzion to own the skill.'

He cannot be wrong. I get the passion of my poetry and marry it to the learning of guitar. I learn so fast that even I am impressed. On the fifth evening, my music teacher asks why I have not considered a career in music. He says that I am a contralto with exceptional purity of tone, and my fingers are quick at play.

'I don't want to go mad,' I say flatly. My only interest in music is to cure the insomnia I have acquired since Gats left, and to ward off the wave of insanity that knocks at my door on the few nights when I lie in bed and finish all my sleep before dawn. Then my mind is too edgy to be soothed. It's hard to find a neutral state that allows me to stay sane.

Music becomes my preoccupation when restlessness or the state of doing nothing visits my solitary abode. I listen to myself playing. I give up a whole of me I have held back for months. In the inert hours of darkness when the neighbourhood is in deep slumber, I discover truth in the words of Robert Frost: 'Something we were withholding made us weak, until we found it was ourselves.'

I strum the guitar and sing a few songs. At first the songs are impassive, betraying no emotions. Later, they take on an intense, mournful twist. I sing Johnny Cash's, 'Oh, Lonesome Me,' 'I Walk the Line' and 'Folsom Prison Blues.' I get gripped in the Easter hymns of Christ's crucifixion. Then I fill my house with the poignant music of my compositions; lines of orphans crying out in the rain, women becoming pregnant with unwanted children of rebels; a cathedral of dry bones becoming flesh, reclaiming a past inheritance.

The songs work through my body. Every word and note soaks through my skin, consuming me. Filled with new vigour and raw energy, I pluck the guitar with the passion of a spiritual. I make the guitar weep and wail as I dance around the room. The guitar takes me to heights. I forget the night. I forget the world. I sing louder than the most amplified microphone. The house is stuffed with a deafening, crashing tumult of chords. I am possessed. I am immersed in freshness. I am new.

It takes an equally thunderous, defiant knock on my door to realise I have disturbed the neighbourhood.

'Nina!' someone shouts. 'What are you playing that music for? You are awakening the ghosts!'

Abrupt silence.

'Your music is too *disturbing*, my neighbour continues to say. '

'Forgive me for tonight, Richard. Do let me play – this night belongs to me.'

I play the night into morning. I exhaust songs of my past, I sing the moment, and sail into the future. Africa regenerated. My soul is freed. It rises and descends into rapturous rivers of unfathomable depth. The abolition of time and space. Conquering of circumstances. The universe becomes transfigured before my eyes. Individual consciousness is made infinite and alive by a tapestry of memory woven from ages past when the whole race was one man in the blissful Garden of Eden.

When the sun begins to shoot his rays through my window, I stretch on my bed, exhausted but pleased. I have a new definition of happiness. Sorrow brings me new joy. The guitar teacher was right. When I report to the office, it's to resign and embrace my new music career like a bride in the arms of new-found love.

LOVE LONG DISTANCE
By Kadija Sesay

Nothing much had changed, she noted.

She walked bold and erect to the breakfast room of the five-star hotel in Accra, where the staff called her 'Madam' to her face but were concerned that this black madam – who did not have an American accent – was not laden with dollars for tips. She sensed the eyes on her behind, leering eyes. 'Appreciative' some would have called them but those eyes didn't feel as though they were appreciating her behind.

She stepped into the air-conditioned restaurant and looked with a hungry appreciation at the buffet spread. After her long and uncomfortable flight, she was ready for a good solid breakfast. Rice therefore, was a must. *Jollof* rice, chicken, spiced tomato and onion stew, roast turkey (just because it was there), fresh pineapple juice and coffee.

All the time, her backside was being watched. Even after she had slid, hips first, sideways, onto the upholstered chair. Maybe if she ate more yam, more *fufu*, her bum would be rounder, bigger. Maybe they were imagining what was not there. They stared at her when she asked for pepper. Eyes looked her up and down, up and down, as if to ask, 'Who are you? What are you doing here? Where is your arse, fake African woman?'

She looked straight back (insolently, her mother would have called it), as if to say, 'And you, where are your manners?' It was the look that said – as her sister described it on her last, 'I'm-never-going-back-there-again' trip to Mombasa – 'Next time, use the deliveries entrance.'

In front of her, a table of four travelling professionals took breakfast too. One of the men stood up as a woman headed to their table. He stretched out a welcoming, encouraging arm.

'That's nice, is it cool to wear?' He asked his female colleague who was wearing her new traditionally – sewn 'husband and wife' colour co-ordinated outfit.

Her paleness enhanced the rich cotton orangeness of the loose-fitting simple-cut top; her muted brown hair, the end strands of which fell over her shoulders, blended in, matching the long wrap-around skirt that she wore underneath.

She shifted in it, self-consciously. 'Well, sort of.'

Burnt an unevenly soft red, in short sleeves and Crimplene trousers, patterned with snags, the man continued, 'If we have time, we'll take a trip up the Volta Lake – it's very "Heart of Darkness".'

She wanted to vomit up the turkey that she had just so delectably eaten.

Nothing much had really changed.

It was twelve years since she had last been to West Africa, and so being invited to the university to give a guest lecture was an honour as well as an opportunity for her to give herself a few days' break and to re-acquaint herself with her father's homeland. Perhaps, though, it was more about re-acquainting herself with 'self' – that part of her that had somehow become lost. So, was she disappointed or comfortable with the fact that nothing much had changed? Except that it had become more expensive. Much more expensive. The taxi drivers more brazen, perhaps.

'How much is it to Airport Residential?'

'40 cedis.'

'25.'

'No, 40.'

'They told me in the hotel, 25.'

'To there? No, it's 40.'

'30, I'll give you 30.'

'If there is traffic … Get in.'

'So, you had better pray there is plenty of traffic, otherwise it is 25.'

'Well, you know, it's not the traffic, it's the dust.'

That one beats the British Network's Rail standard, 'leaves on the tracks', she had thought.

After downing enough reasonably filtered coffee to get her through the morning, she left the breakfast room. The day ahead could not have a worse start than this. She was trying not to treat the return to her homeland like the reminiscence of an ex-lover, but rather as a new relationship – entering into it with a new freshness – a new approach. But somehow, it wasn't allowing her to. It was going to be more difficult than she had anticipated. But she had only herself to blame. She had left it too long, and despite the fact that 'nothing much had changed', the banter and dialogue that she had expected to come so easily to her with her love of country and continent, did not feel the way she had expected.

Mercy woke up the next morning, ready to tackle the day. Yesterday had been merely introductory: acclimatisation, remaining in bed for most of the day, because menstrual pains allowed her only to eat and sleep plenty, and paying a small fortune to use the internet in the hotel business centre. Even though their generator had come on automatically once the electricity cut out, she had lost her long 'same ol', same ol'' email tirade to her sister. The receptionist unemotionally explained that it was not possible for them to refund even part of the dollars for lost internet access, since it was not their fault that the power had been shut off, but the government's. No credit, either. Today was going to be different, she decided. She wasn't going to put up with the crap that she had put up with the day before. If anyone looked at her like *that* again, said anything in a slightly patronising or provoking manner, she would know what to say. Because despite the fact that she was European raised – she was African, right?

She smiled a bright good morning, this morning, as she walked into the restaurant to take breakfast. She was relieved not to see the 'Heart of Darkness' group. She hoped that they had drowned themselves in the Volta Lake. But was her irritation more with herself than at the situations she was encountering in the country? Wasn't it just a sense of annoyance with herself that she hadn't returned home sooner? Why had she kept away? Something, obviously something, but she couldn't actually feel, or decide, what.

'Madam, you had a call, about ten minutes ago,' the eager voice said that came streaming from the reception desk as she walked back past, heading for her room. She looked at the speaker, brow creased.

'Me?'

'Yes, madam.'

'I don't think so. I've just arrived. I don't know anyone here.'

'Yes, madam, I'm sure it is you.'

She was about to walk straight past but went to the desk as he seemed ready to raise his voice to inform the entire lobby of her personal business, in order to fulfil his duty of giving out information in a timely manner.

'Madam – Room 276?'

'Yes. Who called me?'

'He said he would call back.'

'He?'

'Yes, madam. He said he would call back.'

'He didn't leave his name?'

'No, madam.'

'When did he say he would call back?'

'I told him that you had just gone to breakfast.'

She raised one eyebrow; eyes opened wider.

'I noticed you from yesterday, madam. We try to give personal service. So I expect that he will call back shortly.'

'OK.' She said curtly. She returned to her room.

This mystery man so intrigued her, she found herself sitting still almost, waiting for the call. It was stupid, but she was impatient and curious. After 30 minutes, no phone call. She had just stepped into the shower when the phone rang. She slopped her way out, banging her shin against the edge of the bath, flinging her wet body across the double bed to grab the phone. The dripping wetness on her body was instantly chilled by the air-conditioning.

'Hello.'

Breathless, trying to sound calm.

'Mercy.'

Her bottom lip fell after her very British pronounced 'o'. Only people she had known before she left university called her that. And that voice, that voice had been one that she had encountered at university. Closely encountered. With its deep vibrations, all calmness had gone.

'Mercy.'

Should she put the phone down? Should she speak?

'Mercy.'

So assured, his voice did not even question that she was there, that maybe she did not want to acknowledge him.

'It's good to hear you again. It was so good to hear that you are in town.'

Not even a question mark. Somehow, he knew it was her; knew she was here, but how?

'Hi.'

'Is that all you are going to say?'

'For now, yes.'

'As sharp as ever!' His laugh was a soft rumble. 'What time should I pick you up tomorrow, hon? Lunch or dinner?'

'Dinner, no, lunch.'

'Hon?!' Was that all he had to say! What was she doing!

'Okay. What time?'

'I'll meet you in the foyer at 1 pm.'

'I'll try not to be late. I have a meeting just before, so I'll just call you in your room when I arrive, around one.'

'You asked me what time. I said one. If you can't make it, don't come.'

She paused. 'I don't want to disrupt your day. We'll ...' she said a little more softly.

'No, tomorrow is fine. Not very late. Wait in the foyer then.'

She didn't want him to call her room – no way – he had that way about him. He'd arrive and solicit her room number. The next thing he'd be knocking on her door without any announcement. She didn't want that.

'Yes, I'll wait in the foyer.'

She put down the phone and went back to her shower.

She pulled on her fluorescent green exfoliating gloves. Pulled them on so roughly that she pulled a runner; she hardly noticed. Squeezed mango and lime shower gel into her palm and rubbed it harshly all over her body. She started by rubbing her belly, circular motions, to comfort herself; she moved up, over breasts, shoulders, neck, down her legs, ankles, feet and toes. Around her backside. Scrubbed hard, lifting skin at the same time.

This was unexpected. How did he know she was here? She scrubbed harder. Why had she agreed to have lunch with him? Why had she agreed to even see him? She should have put the phone down immediately. What difference would that have made? He had known she was there – known it was her. He had known. And how? But he had always known how and where to find her. She scrubbed harder. Trying to scrub away the memories of him that had begun to surface.

She should call him back. Tell him not to come. She didn't know his number. She scrubbed harder. She couldn't see him. Maybe the front desk? If he had called – left a number? Maybe they could trace it. Long shot. Harder. She scrubbed, with no shower gel. She didn't notice. The harder she scrubbed, the less effect he had on her.

Steaming water pissing from the shower head would wash it all away – please – wash him away – memories of him – away – cleanse him away. She hoped. Without much hope. And she had thought today couldn't be worse than yesterday.

***

She decided to miss breakfast this morning. Looked at the news on the TV. Four hours. Till 1 p.m. She had planned to read that morning. She had savoured the thought of starting a promising debut novel by a young African woman writer on her trip. And some writing time, too. How the hell was she going to concentrate? Fuck the writing. She would just about be able to read. She hoped. Concentrate on the book. Three hours of Crappy No real News TV later and Channel O music from South Africa zapped itself on to fill up her brain, so that she didn't have to think. She didn't want time to think.

12.30 p.m. She'd hardly read a page. As if she often had time to write let alone to read a book. And he had made her waste it. The feelings of anxiety he created in her were back in their fullness.

She started to hurry to get ready. Damn! Not too much rush otherwise she would become sweaty, despite the air-conditioning. What should she wear, what should she wear? Jeans and T-shirt – casual. She wanted to look like she didn't care – but she wanted to look like she took care of herself – right? An African outfit. Which one? Short skirt? No, she didn't want him to look at her legs. She remembered how he would often murmur in her ear in his low, vibrating rumble that it was her legs that had ensnared him, physically and mentally – and so she didn't want him to look. Something long. But she wanted to look her best, and yes, she admitted to herself, wanted him to realise what he had lost.

She tried on all of the smart and the elegant outfits she had brought, stepping out of each of them and leaving them in a meringue pile on the floor or slinging them pancake style across the bed. She gravitated towards the blue one, her old favourite. The one in which she always felt and knew she looked good. The one in which she felt she would be in control. One last look: head tie, matching, turquoise and silver earrings, light bronze shimmer lipstick – yes – last-minute bangle. In control.

Two minutes past one. She stepped out of her room and walked towards the foyer. He had better be there waiting.

'Mercy!'

What turned first? Her head or her heart? Here was the voice she hadn't expected to hear again. And it jolted her. Mercilessly. She didn't want to feel the same way as she had so many years ago – but how could she stop? How could she stop him?

Tears settled in the corners of her eyes as she faced him. He smiled. Broadly. Eyes wide, grin wider, arms outstretched. And even though she didn't want to – had promised herself that she wouldn't – she smiled back. Warmed by his smile. Warmed by the love she had felt before. And she kept on smiling. As broadly as he did. She didn't move but waited for him to move towards her – to embrace her – to wrap her in his arms.

It's what she really wanted. And she had missed it, missed this, missed his warmth for so long.

She blinked her eyes, to shift the tear position, to see him clearly. A millionth-of-a-second blink – but he was no longer there. Had he been so deeply fixed in her heart that she had formulated him in her head? What was going on? Who was playing tricks on her?

She looked around the lobby to see where and how he had gone, scantily catching other people observances at the same time, wondering if they were watching her strangely – stares, stares – as she expected. She wanted to run back to her room – but what would that achieve? She sat on the curved round seat – sort of like a bass clef – in the middle of the lobby floor. Other waiting people sat on it too; it was designed in such a way, that you could sit next to someone that you didn't know but not sit with them. She perched on the edge; she needed to gather her emotions, her calm and her control.

'Mercy?'

From somewhere, her name again being called. She sat. Staring forward. Back erect.

'Mercy?' Slightly more urgent – it couldn't be him. Mr So Self-Assured. Not him.

She stilled herself not to look.

'I love you Mercy. Do you love me?'

How dare he ask! After all this time. How dare he! A threat – no borders. She couldn't control his impact on her imagination, her emotions or even, she admitted, her life.

He was a permanent threat, wherever she went, no matter if there were borders or not. She had read only yesterday, the Nobel Peace Prize acceptance speech of Mohamed El Baradei:

A recent United Nations High-Level Panel identified five categories of threats that we face:
1. *Poverty, Infectious Disease, and Environmental Degradation;*
2. *Armed Conflict – both within and among states;*
3. *Organized Crime;*
4. *Terrorism; and*
5. *Weapons of Mass Destruction.*

These are all 'threats without borders' – where traditional notions of national security have become obsolete. We cannot respond to these threats by building more walls, developing bigger weapons, or dispatching more troops. Quite to the contrary. By their very nature, these security threats require primarily multinational cooperation.

What about greed? What about hate? What about love? In their concerns for global healing, didn't the UN talk about five paths towards peace? In their identifications of threat was there no healing across borders? Love unconditional?

***

Of course, he hadn't turned up. She sat on the red bass clef seat for an hour at least, then, so as not to seem too conspicuous, she looked at her watch, and then went to the concierge's desk to ask how she could reach the market. Not knowing what she was about to let herself in for, she planned to displace all of her anxiety about this reunion that she had never planned and never expected onto what was to be a frustrating journey; one of the stickiest, longest, most tiring journeys she could ever remember taking, yet one of the most fascinating. She imagined that people probably could do their shopping, including forgotten or special luxury treats before Makola market was even reached.

From the leather-belt salesman who ingeniously carried a hole-puncher (Did customers try the belts on whilst sitting or did they get out at the traffic lights? she wondered. Was this the reason for the traffic hold ups?), tourist maps of Ghana, of Africa, sink scourers, oranges, soap, electrical extension leads, hair extensions (all colours), plaintain chips (light or burnt fried).

Whatever was needed, whatever had been forgotten, could be supplied. Before Makola was even reached.

'Madam! Madam!'

Just a glance was enough to encourage them to her side. But she wanted to look!

Hmm. A nice little vanity set of nail clippers, nail file, eyebrow pluckers...

'No, I don't want to buy ... not today ...'

'Humanity has a clear choice between nuclear weapons and genocide.'

Her personal choice felt just as desperate. In the world scheme of things, her dilemma did not figure at all – but her personal happiness didn't depend on world dilemmas. Her internal self and hidden un-resolutions, challenged.

Here it is, fine. Her hand was on the door handle, ready to jump out at the sight of EPP Bookstore on her left.

'Wait.'

The taxi driver, knowing she was a native, and looking more gullible than she would accept, took her into the courtyard of the bookstore, travel agent and internet café that always seemed to have a sign stating that the internet refused to work. Up the stairs, not much to offer the casual reader of literature, unless a fan of John Grisham or Danielle Steele. Schools were reading Ama Ata Aidoo, so she was at least able to purchase Aidoo's book of short stories. Some of the other books that she had bought yesterday, she now realised, were not only overly expensive, but were 'photocopied fakes' – badly done stapled versions – which were resold for nearly double the amount that the bookstore charged when the bookstore did not have the books in stock. She had been just another Afropean taken for a ride.

**

On her return to the hotel she sat on the balcony of her room, feet amongst her Makola purchases. She watched the sky grow dark. Tiny birds like flakes of burnt paper magically spotted the sky creating an overcast gloom and premonition of rain.

The cheap red and green satin Christmas bows and banners that were swathed across verandah fronts and walls on the hotel across the way were caught by the breeze. They bloated in unison whilst the smoke birds continued to follow each other in the same direction across the grey – blue sky. Their outspread wings shaped them like hearts – hearts that fluttered, tinged transparent cerise, candy orange and pink. When the lights in the garden switched on automatically, creating a dark orange glow on her and over her unturned page, the birds knew no different and continued to follow each other, undisturbed.

It was the bows and banners that blurred her vision: too much of a reminder.

He had returned to Cape Coast after he graduated, said he'd prepare and start building whilst she finished her degree. They discussed the merits of her going on to do a PhD – just one more year – and they agreed that she would do the first year in England and complete her studies in Ghana: long distance for too long was not a good idea. They would meet regularly in either England or Cape Coast which was his home and her father's. At the first opportunity – the Christmas break, as agreed – she went home. He had disappeared. On her student ticket, she was stuck. On her own for three weeks, in a cheap hotel like the one across the road. No answer from his cellphone; his land-line, dead. Her mind would not keep still. She went from thinking that she must have the wrong dates and he was out of town to thinking that she had gotten confused and he had flown to London to be with her. Perhaps a trip out of town had just taken a few more days than anticipated, she kept thinking … she kept thinking … that something more awful had happened and that she should go to the police. But surely everything was okay?

She went to where she believed their home was being built – not even a shell – what had taken place in the past six months? He hadn't mentioned anything wrong in their regular conversations and e-mails – although he hadn't talked of anything in much detail at all. She had tried the one friend of his that she knew who lived there – an ex-student from London. Hadn't heard from him. Didn't even know that he had retuned to Ghana. He suggested someone else – at first, he hesitated – contact details for a woman, but? She was distraught and stranded and he gave her the contact of the 'old friend' of her fiancé's. But she never called. She did not want to know.

Two equal evils – police or another woman. She chose the former. They just laughed and told her to look for her husband in the arms of another woman. What should she expect when she had allowed him to return, alone?

A call from his mobile in the middle of an afternoon back then had cut off after one ring – a missed call. She rang maniacally, sent frantic text messages. At least he was still alive! But she couldn't understand why he wanted to remain dead to her. He was her love, her life, her future. She had to find him or forget him. It took some time, even more time than she imagined it would when she returned to London, as she submerged herself in her studies, to forget him. The first class degree bestowed upon her – the only one in her class – was hardly compensation; rather, it just underlined the fact that a degree was cold comfort in comparison to her-life-that-should-have-been in much hotter climes.

And now this call, twelve years later, as casually as if it was the day of her Christmas arrival? Who the hell did he think he was? The same stupid little girl?

After all this time – dreams dashed, heart in tiny fragments – he had found her! No explanations. She had not met or married anyone else. At first, waiting for him even though she knew it was a stupid thing to do. And when she heard him on the phone yesterday, it was as if nothing had changed between them.

So she was not surprised when her phone rang announcing his arrival to take her to dinner. Always late, she smiled to herself. Should she see this as six hours late – or twelve years late? She had known he would be but somehow, right now, that didn't matter. All that mattered right now was that he was there. She met him in the foyer, just as they had planned, earlier in the day. Her heart rate jumping, jumping.

'I want to know about you, how you have been doing.'

'And I want to know where you went!'

'Mercy, it was so long ago …'

'We were supposed to be married!'

'I know, I know. And you were not here.'

She bit her tongue. Now was not the time to spit.

'So, you found someone else then?'

'Let's just eat and chat. Like we used to.' Soft seductive voice – always. 'Please?'

He kissed her bunched-up fist, slowly unfolded her fingers and kissed her palm. In that way that he did, as if he had never gone.

No, he was not married. Children? He didn't say – just smiled, took her hand and they went to dinner.

Internally she slumped. He was right. Why bring up hurt memories of so long ago?

They sat, ate and talked for – three hours? At least. Glossy on the surface, everything seemed so bright: symbols of wealth, signs of hope. It smelled so right. He had ordered champagne. Champagne? Underneath, who was kidding who, really? It stunk. As expensive-looking cheap champagne often does. Nothing much had changed, still. She felt as empty as she had done during those waiting years, wondering. As anxious as those times, too, as she had not expected to come here for closure. He had her hand in his; in a smooth gesture, closed both of his around hers as if to say, 'let us keep all of that where it is.'

Her compliance had so far resulted in a simpering evening of his stories. He was sorry. He suddenly realised that he was not ready for marriage (... to her, she added mentally).

She looked at him, carefully, as he spoke. The lips that never seemed to taper off – stretched right off his face, like a never-ending story. His high forehead – surely, there was an old wives' tale about that which she had ignored? Had his eyes always been so red? And for the second time on this trip, she felt ready to vomit. And she loved *jollof* rice, but not with this distaste of whining sauce he was pouring out.

She excused herself to go the ladies' bathroom, washed her hands, rubbed them thoroughly. Splashed water on her face and took one of the soft towelettes, spending time slowly wiping her hands, drying carefully between each finger before dumping it in the wicker basket provided.

She pulled back the swing door with force – to re-awaken the energy he had seemed to drain from her and walked out – ready to deal with him on her terms.

She walked bold and erect out of the restaurant. In a few days, she would be on a plane out of here, without the torment she had left with before. Her father had left 41 years ago, and despite his yearnings, abetted by discussions in social gatherings of how the country should be run, he had never returned. She was her father's daughter. She had a feeling that she would be doing the same.

AUTHOR BIOGRAPHIES

Akin Adesokan was born in Ibadan, Nigeria, where he worked as a journalist for *The Guardian* and the initially clandestine news magazine, *TEMPO*, for which he also wrote a weekly fiction column. His first novel, *Roots in the Sky* (Festac Books, 2004), won the Association of Nigerian Authors' Prize for Fiction, in manuscript form in 1996. He has also won the PEN Freedom-to-Write Award (1998), and the Lillian Hellman-Dashiel Hammett Human Rights Award (1999), following his political detention in Nigeria. He teaches Comparative Literature at Indiana University, Bloomington, Indiana, in the US.

Segun Afolabi was born in Kaduna, Nigeria, and grew up there and in various countries, including Canada, Japan and the United Kingdom, where he now lives. His story collection, *A Life Elsewhere*, is published by Jonathan Cape. His novel, *Goodbye Lucille*, was published in 2007.

Mialy Ravelomanana Andriamananjara started writing when she was eight, mostly because she was a lonely child, despite having three older brothers. She spent a lot of time daydreaming and making up stories, which she would then enact in a game called *kindriandriana*, which little Malagasy girls know well. In this game, girls gather stones and use them much as a western girl would play with dolls. Later, she started playing with words, because she loved books and she knew she liked to tell stories. Now that circumstances and family have taken her away from her beloved homeland, she writes when she is homesick and because her stories keep her closer to her past and her culture. The first story that she wrote, 'The Shred' was published in *SABLE* Litmag in 2005.

Monica Arac de Nyeko won the 2007 Caine Prize for African Writing, and was short-listed for the prize in 2004. Her fiction and poetry has appeared in *Memories of Sun*, *The Nation*, *Word from a Granary*, *Tears of Hope*, *Fountain Junior HIV Series*, *Poetry International*, *New Era* and *Wordrite* among others.

Sefi Atta was born in Lagos, Nigeria. A former chartered accountant, she is a graduate of the creative writing program at Antioch University, Los Angeles. Her works have appeared in journals such as *Los Angeles Review* and *Mississippi Review* and have won prizes from Zoetrope, Red Hen

Press, the BBC and the Commonwealth Broadcasting Association. She is also the winner of PEN International's 2004/2005 David TK Wong Prize. In 2002, the opening section of her debut novel *Everything Good Will Come*, was short-listed for the Macmillan Writers Prize for Africa. The novel has been since published in the United States, England and Nigeria, and was awarded the inaugural Wole Soyinka Prize for Literature in Africa in 2006.

Mildred Kiconco Barya is a writer and poet. She believes that her best writing may never see the sun, hence the number of poems and short stories stashed in her drawers. When she is not procrastinating or getting distracted, she provides human resources consultancy services to clients in various organisations. Barya has written features for newspapers, travel articles and essays, and is currently labouring on a novel, *Soul of Rivers*. Hopefully, it shall be completed and delivered into the hands of a publisher, rather than becoming a victim of her 'stash pile'. Her current writings are concerned with HIV/AIDS issues, religious cults and the psychology of identity and belonging. Her poetry collection, *The Price of Memory after the Tsunami* has been published by Mallory International, 2006.

Jackee Budesta Batanda lives in Kampala, Uganda. She was the Africa Regional Winner of the 2003 Commonwealth Short Story Competition, and was short-listed for the Macmillan Writers Prize for Africa 2004. Her story *Remember Atita* was highly recommended by the judges of the Caine Prize, 2004. She has been Writer-in-Residence at Lancaster University. Her stories have been broadcast on the BBC and around the Commonwealth. She is a member of the Uganda Women Writers Association (FEMRITE).

Lesley Emanuel was born in Johannesburg, South Africa. She is a mother and only writes from midnight, while her daughter sleeps. Emanuel is a member of a writing group that was established by the late Lionel Abrahams and is now facilitated by Jane Fox. Her recent work has included the screenplay for a short film by Jyoti Mistry, *We Remember Differently* (produced by Shadowy Meadows Productions, 2005), and a feature film screenplay (with Kay Brown). Emanuel works at the University of the Witwatersrand, where she is also completing her doctoral degree.

Pumla Dineo Gqola is a writer and academic, a Senior Research Specialist at the Human Sciences Research Council (HSRC) and Extraordinary Associate Professor of Humanities at the University of the Western Cape (UWC), South Africa. Her short stories, poems, academic articles and experimental essays have been published in various journals, collections and magazines, including *Running Towards Us: New Writing from South Africa* (Heinemann, 2000), *Chimurenga, Agenda, Meridians, Postcolonial Text, Tyhume* and *Drum* magazine (UK). She is an editor of *fito* (www.fito.co.za), and a contributing poet to the Art for Humanity Women for Children's Rights 2005 campaign. Her website is www.pumladineo.co.za

Wonder Guchu started his career as a secondary school teacher, and is now Entertainment Editor of *The Herald*, Zimbabwe's leading daily newspaper. His short stories were first published in a Zimbabwean weekly newspaper, *The Sunday Mail*, between 1991 and 1998. Some of his poems were also published in a number of magazines and anthologies. In 2003, his story *243rd Street*, was included in the anthology, *Writing Still: Short Stories from Zimbabwe* and in 2004, Weaver Press Zimbabwe published his short story collection, *Sketches of High Density Life*. The book, won the Best First Book Zimbabwe Publishers Association Literary Award in 2005 and has since been published and distributed by Michigan State University.

Brian James was born in Lagos, Nigeria. He is of Sierra Leonean parentage and has attended schools in Nigeria, Sierra Leone, the United Kingdom, The Gambia and Ghana. James started writing at the age of ten, when he wrote a short story, *The Talking River*. Since then he has had several of his stories published in local publications in The Gambia and Sierra Leone. James is at present living in Freetown, Sierra Leone with his parents and his younger sister. He is currently studying Mass Communication at Fourah Bay College.

Mamle Kabu is half Ghanaian and half German. She was born and raised in Ghana, but moved to the UK in her teenage years. She lived and studied in the UK for a decade. In 1992 she returned to Ghana where she now lives. In addition to writing fiction she does research consultancy in development issues. Her short story, 'Human Mathematics' was published in *Mixed: An Anthology of Short Fiction on the Multi-racial Experience*, edited by Chandra Prasad and published by W.W.

Norton, and 'Story of Faith', a short story in *Women Writing Resistance*, an anthology edited by Jennifer Browdy de Hernandez.

Ken N Kamoche was born and raised in Kenya. After obtaining a BCom at Nairobi University, he took MPhil and DPhil degrees at Oxford on a Rhodes Scholarship to study Management. Kamoche has taught management in Hong Kong and is currently Professor of Human Resource Management at Nottingham Business School in the UK. He has published over thirty journal articles and four books including, *Organizational Improvisation*, and *Managing Human Resources in Africa*. One of his poems appeared in a BBC/Heinemann anthology, *The Fate of Vultures*, following a contest. His short stories have appeared in *Kunapipi*, *Wasafiri*, *New York Stories*, *author-me.com*, and in several anthologies. He is also working on a novel and a screenplay. His collection of short stories, *A Fragile Hope* was published by Salt Publishing in 2007.

Patrick Mangeni wa'Ndeda, holds a PhD in Applied Theatre from Griffith University, Australia, and lectures in Theatre at Makerere University, Uganda. He was a poet-in-residence at Akademie Schloss Solitude, Stuttgart, Germany in 1996, and has been Chairperson of the Uganda Writers' Association and a Guest Poet for the 2003 Queensland Poetry Festival in Australia. His plays, *Operation Mulungusi* and *The Prince* won the 2000 National Book Trust of Uganda (NABOTU) Award and were nominated for the Uganda Literature Prize, 2001. He has also written a children's novel, *The Great Temptation*, and has completed two collections: *A Leopard in My Bed and Other Stories*, published by Mallory Publishing in 2006, and *The Second Coming and Other Poems*.

Biram Mboob is a new writer whose work has appeared in a number of publications, including *Tell Tales Volume 2* short story anthology and *SABLE* Litmag. He was the winner of the 2004 Shorelines National Black First Chapter competition. Mboob's writing style is very much influenced by the Golden Age science-fiction classics that he read growing up. His stories aim to paint traditional sci-fi concepts against an African canvas. Born and raised in Africa, Mboob currently lives in London and is hard at work on his first novel.

Nhamo Mhiripiri is Zimbabwean. His other stories are published in the following anthologies: *No More Plastic Balls* and *A Roof to Repair* (College Press, Harare , 2000) and *Creatures Great and Small* (Mambo Press, Gweru,

2005). He lectures in Media and Society Studies at the Midlands State University in Zimbabwe.

Tony Adam Mochama has a Law degree from the University of Nairobi but chose to go into journalism to give him time to write stories ... and drink vodka. He is currently successfully working for the KTN-Standard Media Group in Kenya, where he edits the literary and art pages of the newspaper and runs a vicious (but hopefully funny) little gossip column about the local celebrity scene. He likes travelling to literary senimars in far off places like Russia.

Ruzvidzo Mupfudza is a 35-year-old male Zimbabwean, born in Guruve. He graduated from the University of Zimbabwe in 1994 with a BA Honours (English) degree, after which he taught English at a local high school for eight years. In 1999 he enrolled for an MA (English) at the University of Zimbabwe. In 2002 he left teaching and joined the Zimbabwe Broadcasting Corporation as a Chief Producer of Social and Cultural Programmes in their Kidznet Business Unit. In 2003 he joined DDB Hash 3, an advertising agency, as a copywriter. He left DDB Hash 3 at the end of 2003 and joined the Zimbabwe Mirror Newspapers Group as an Assistant Editor. In September 2004, he became Deputy Editor in charge of the *Daily Mirror* after which he was moved to the *Sunday Mirror* (a weekly paper) as the Acting Editor.

J Tsitsi Mutiti is a Zimbabwean writer who lecturers at the Chinhoyi University of Technology. She has been published in the anthology, *A Roof to Repair*. She is interested in issues that revolve around powerlessness in its many manifestations.

Glaydah Namukasa is a midwife and a writer, and is currently a committee member of the Uganda Female Writers' Association. She has participated twice in the British Council's Crossing Borders Writers Scheme. Her first novel, *The Deadly Ambition*, was published by Mallory Publishing in 2006. Namukasa has published a short story, 'The Naked Bones', and a poem, 'That Place' (the latter was published in the FEMRITE Wordwrite Journal). Her short story, 'dreams.com', published on author-me. She received the Macmillan Writers' Prize for Africa, Senior Prize, for her novel, *Voice of a Dream*, 2005 which was published in 2006.

Ndiwalana Fredrick was one of the pioneer students on the Crossing Borders British Council Writing project for Young African Writers. His first major work, *Images of Life*, a collection of short stories on life in Africa, is yet to be published. He is currently working on a novel, *Sande* in addition to writing biographies. Ndiwalana is a graduate of Makerere University, with higher degrees in Banking and Development Studies. Ndiwalana lives in Uganda with his wife and two children, where he is employed as a bank Branch Manager.

Osita Obi read English at the University of Nigeria, Nsukka and worked as a journalist after graduation in 1988. His short stories and poems have appeared in various journals within and outside of Nigeria, including *Revue Noire* and *Farafina Online*. Obi is the author of *The Girl Who Loved the Wind and Other Stories* (Snaap Press, Enugu, 2003) and is now resident in Spain.

Gitta (pronounced Jitta) Sumner is a Sierra Leonean who is currently living in London and working on completing a short story collection based on her travels in different countries. She completed her degree in Creative Writing at Minnesata State University, Moorhead. The story in this collection is dedicated to her grandmother, Hajah Jonta Koroma, her late grandfather, S Ibrahim Koroma; her mother, Hawah and her three sisters, Mahota, Konima, and Miehawah, and last but not least, her niece and nephew, Mahalia and David Kamanda-Bongay. With love and memories of living in a pink house on Havelock Street in Freetown.

Binyavanga Wainaina is a Kenyan writer. He is the founding editor of *Kwani?* – one of Africa's leading literary magazines (www.kwani.org). In 2002 he won the Caine prize for African writing. He has received a special commendation from the Kenya Publisher's Association for his work as a writer and publisher. He has been published in *National Geographic*, *Granta* and *Chimurenga*. His first book, *Discovering Home*, will be published by Granta Books in 2008. He is the Visiting Writer at Union College, Schenectady, New York.

EDITOR BIOGRAPHIES

Helon Habila was born in Nigeria, where he worked as a literary editor and as a lecturer. His first novel, *Waiting for an Angel* (Hamish Hamilton 2002) won the 2003 Commonwealth Prize for Best First Novel, Africa Region. He won the Caine Prize in 2001. His second novel, *Measuring Time*, was published in 2007. Habila co-edited the British Council's *New Writing 14* anthology with Lavinia Greenlaw, and was the Chinua Achebe Fellow in Global Africana Studies in 2005/6.

Kadija Sesay is of Sierra Leonean parentage. She is the founder/publisher of *SABLE* Litmag. She has edited the following anthologies: *Six Plays by Black and Asian Women Writers, Write Black, Write British: From Post Colonial to Black British Writing,* and has co-edited *IC3: The Penguin Book of New Black Writing in Britain* and *Dance the Guns to Silence: 100 Poems for Ken Saro-Wiwa.* She is the series editor for the Inscribe imprint for Peepal Tree Press. Sesay has published and broadcast poems and short stories in publications at home and abroad. She is currently the General Secretary of African Writers Abroad (PEN) Centre, a Fellow of the George Bell Institute and a Kennedy Fellow in Arts Management from the Kennedy Center of the Performing Arts in Washington DC. http://www.sablelitmag.org

GLOSSARY

An Affair to Dismember
mwenyewe – himself

The End of Skill
Adweneasa – the name of a particular design of kente cloth. It literally means 'the end of skill', but it tends to be interpreted in several different ways.
Oyokoman – a royal Ashanti clan.
Oyokoman Adweneasa – *Adweneasa* kente woven with the *Oyokoman* warp pattern and colours.

The Promised Land
tour de main – dexterity
rougaille – a dish made of freshly diced tomatoes, onions, crushed peanuts and chilli to accompany rice
Tonga soa – welcome
tamboho – Old walls usually made of red laterite extracted from rice fields. They were crudely erected around richer homes in the 19th century by slaves. Many of them have survived time. Their height can reach 4 to 5 metres.
ébauche – outline
kabosa – a plucked stringed instrument that resembles the guitar, often made of recycled steel, fishing lino. Very popular with young men.

'Regrets'

'Six routes
partent du pied de l'arbre-voyageur:
la première conduit au village-de-l'oubli,
la seconde est un cul-de-sac,
la troisième n'est pas la bonne,
la quatrième a vu passer la chère-aimèe
mais n'a pas garde la trace de ses pas,
la cinquième
est pour celui-que-mord-le-regret,
et la dernière...

je ne sais si praticable.'
de Flavien RANAIVO, *'Mes Chansons de toujours'*, 1955

'Six paths
start from the bottom of the traveller's tree
the first leads to the village of oblivion
the second to a cul de sac
the third is not the right one
the fourth has seen my beloved
but has kept no trace of her footsteps
the fifth is for the one-that-regrets-bite
and the last one ...
I don't know if it's usable.'
from Flavien RANAIVO, *'Mes Chansons de toujours'*, 1955

Remember, Olduvai
enkang – traditional Masai enclosure of homes
maquina – machine (Spanish)
livre – book (French)
nyumba – house (Swahili)
mwana – son (Swahili)
chambre – room (French)
silla – chair (Spanish)
jardain – garden (French)
'immigré' – immigrate (French) – used differently for the purposes of the
    story
favela – slum quarter (Portuguese)
diaro – diary (From the Portuguese term, diario)
festa – celebration (Portuguese)
ville – town (French)
musique – music (French)
ugali – East African staple food, a traditional cornmeal mush
fromage – cheese (French)
umlungu – white person or those who practice magic (Zulu). Also means
    'God' in the Bungu dialect
nyota – star (Swahili)
lit – bed (French)

Spokesman
rombe – a worthless person
gogo – grandmother
mangoromera – A type of fetish for fighting
shura – an omen presaging the death of a loved one
chef – used by Zimbabweans to indicate respect for one's social superiors
n'anga – sorcerer
tsotsi – Dishonest or criminal type

In the Clarity of a Third Class Compartment
braai – barbeque
stompie – cigarette butt
babbelas – hangover
dagga – marijuana
gryp – grab
cherrie – girl, young girl, girlfriend
sommer – for no particular reason; just, merely.
sfebe – slut (highly offensive)
'Ek is nie jou broer nie' – I'm not your brother
broer – brother
skollie – hooligan, lowlife
kwaad – cross, angry
ne? – not so?
klap – hit, slap

Devils at the Door
'Commando' – used as a military rank title by the local militia during the
     civil war in Sierra Leone
kamajor – local militia
Una opin dis gate. If una allow wi for opin am wisef una – all go die. – Open
     this gate! If we have to open it ourselves, you will all die.
Una an ghanaman dem? – Are you Ghanaians?
ECOMOG don kam! – The ECOMOG troops are here!

It Will Never be Yesterday
ngome – a type of home brewed beer
pata-patas – slippers
Mashuramurove – stork birds
Shuramurove – stork bird

Dancing to the Jazz Goblin and His Rhythm
mbanje – marijuana
une – one (A)
punani – a slang term used to describe the female sex organ. Indian in origin. Used commonly in Jamaica

Superstitions about Rats
eina – exclamation of pain
oke – adult male
braai – barbeque

The Legendary Old Crosser
The crosser counts each person and gets to eight and exclaims when he notices that she is *'embarazada'* – pregnant.
Quien es tu hombre? – Which one is your husband?
C'est moi – It's me
Tu? Con ésta?
Qui, si.
Vale (The crosser checks with Osaro, he acknowledges that he is the father of her baby and the crosser is satisfied that there is someone to take care of her)
Avance. Desde ahora es caliese y silencio. – Let's move on. From now on, there must be quiet and silence
Qué pasa? – What's happened? (What's the problem)
Arriba aqui, moreno, muchos morenos – There are many black people who are crossing here, now
Vamos – Let's go
Aqui, Calamacarro, arriba. – Calamacarro, here we come.

On the Last Day
dedededede kalira munamwenge – This is a children's game that is played in the evening at twilight. It involves the child spreading out both hands like a bird about to fly. The child then begins rotating in spinning motion while saying the words *dedede*. The child accelerates the spinning and the utterance of the words until he/she falls down, often out of dizziness.

Random Check
lougong – husband

la – an untranslatable particle to make a statement 'soft'

ugali – maizemeal

chapatti – Indian bread

ndugu – brother

hak gwei – black ghost

chisin – crazy

neih hou maafan-ah – you're too troublesome

Chat dim gung – seven o'clock

mijh wo – don't really know

chahlou – tea house

Faith

madzibaba – deferential term of addressing male members of Zimbabwean apostolic sects.

Mwari – God

baba – father

chokwadi – truth

erekeri – 'nonsensical' incantation done by someone who is supposedly speaking in tongues

bhure bhure – as in the case of 'erekeri', another 'nonsensical' incantation done by someone who is supposedly speaking in tongues

mbanje – marijuana/dagga

Mupostori uyu anoputa mbanje chete – This religious man smokes dagga

sadza – a Zimbabwean staple food

masese – traditional beer or dregs/left overs

kunze kuye kwashata – the weather is now very bad

Back Home

yaa – shea butter (its oil is often dark, used in this case to mean darkness)

ngwen – white ants

aguma – an Acholi dance accompanied by thumb-pianos, nine-string arched harps and other traditional musical instruments, danced by boys and girls in a live performance at night

Nyarwa – our daughter

Gin mo peke – There is nothing

Jinni – Genie

Maa ato! – a cry of lamentation

larakaraka – a ceremonial dance among the Acholi. It is performed during ceremonies like marriage but is mainly a courtship dance

318

Dwo – a place where cattle are kept.
Gudune anyim tye nining? – How is the road ahead?
Maa Do! – a cry of lamentation.

The Wine Guitar
akara – fried bean balls
eba – grated cassava, with added boiled water and stirred to a soft dough
egusi (soup) – melon seed soup
okro/okra (soup) – diced and chopped okra served with pepper soup and
    eba
Olha que belo! Olha que belo! – Hello, beautiful! (Hi gorgeous!)
iyan – pounded yam

Native Sun
chai – a variety of spiced tea

The Brown's Safari Honeymoon
mzungu – what we call dem white folks here
jinnis – sea ghosts, found along the coast
preja vu – the feeling of 'I will be there someday'
a priori – prior to
makuti – grass thatched rooftop
jambo – hello!
karibu – welcome
juana – to know each other
tuli-juana desembari (as in, 'Kadija and I got to know each other in
    December')
chang'aa – moonshine
wakati – at that time
asante – thanks

The Interview
danfo – passenger bus.
okada – motorbike used for conveying passengers
akara – bean cake
abi – variable meaning – 'is that so?' or 'is that not so?'

Love Long Distance
Jollof rice – a spicy West African rice dish, traditionally cooked with
    various meats and vegetables